THE WATER WITCH

Or, The Skimmer of the Seas.

THE WATER WITCH

Or, The Skimmer of the Seas.

JAMES FENIMORE COOPER

"Mais, qui diable alloit-il faire dans cette galère!"

WILDSIDE PRESS

THE WATER WITCH

Published by Wildside Press, LLC.

www.wildsidepress.com

PREFACE.

CHRISTENDOM is gradually extricating itself from the ignorance, ferocity, and crimes of the middle ages. It is no longer subject of boast, that the hand which wields the sword, never held a pen, and men have long since ceased to be ashamed of knowledge. The multiplied means of imparting principles and facts, and a more general diffusion of intelligence, have conduced to establish sounder ethics and juster practices, throughout the whole civilized world. Thus, he who admits the conviction, as hope declines with his years, that man deteriorates, is probably as far from the truth, as the visionary who sees the dawn of a golden age, in the commencement of the nineteenth century. That we have greatly improved on the opinions and practices of our ancestors, is quite as certain as that there will be occasion to meliorate the legacy of morals which we shall transmit to posterity.

When the progress of civilization compelled Europe to correct the violence and injustice which were so openly practised, until the art of printing became known, the other hemisphere made America the scene of those acts, which shame prevented her from exhibiting nearer home. There was little of a lawless, mercenary, violent, and selfish nature, that the self-styled masters of the continent hesitated to commit, when removed from the immediate responsibilities of the society in which they had been educated. The Drakes, Rogers', and Dampiers of that day, though enrolled in the list of naval heroes were no other than pirates, acting under the sanction of commissions; and the scenes that occurred among the marauders of the land, were often of a character to disgrace human nature.

That the colonies which formed the root of this republic escaped the more serious evils of a corruption so gross and so widely spread, can only be ascribed to the characters of those by whom they were peopled.

Perhaps nine-tenths of all the white inhabitants of the Union are the direct descendants of men who quitted Europe in order to worship God according to conviction and conscience. If the Puritans of New-England, the Friends of Jersey, Pennsylvania and Delaware, the Catholics of Maryland, the Presbyterians of the upper counties of Virginia and of the Carolinas, and the Huguenots, brought with them the exaggeration of their peculiar sects, it was an exaggeration that tended to correct most of their ordinary practices. Still the English Provinces were not permitted, altogether, to escape from the moral dependency that seems nearly inseparable from colonial government, or to be entirely exempt from the wide contamination of the times.

The State of New-York, as is well known, was originally a colony of the United Provinces. The settlement was made in the year 1613; and the Dutch East India Company, under whose authority the establishment was made, claimed the whole country between the Connecticut and the mouth of Delaware-bay, a territory which, as it had a corresponding depth, equalled the whole surface of the present kingdom of France. Of this vast region, however, they never occupied but a narrow belt on each side of the Hudson, with, here and there, a settlement on a few of the river flats, more inland.

There is a providence in the destiny of nations, that sets at nought the most profound of human calculations. Had the dominion of the Dutch continued a century longer, there would have existed in the very heart of the Union a people opposed to its establishment, by their language, origin, and habits. The conquest of the English in 1663, though unjust and iniquitous in itself, removed the danger, by opening the way for the introduction of that great community of character which now so happily prevails.

Though the English, the French, the Swedes, the Dutch, the Danes, the Spaniards, and the Norwegians, all had colonies within the country which now composes the United States, the people of the latter are more homogeneous in character, language, and opinions, than those of any other great nation that is familiarly known. This identity of character is owing to the early predominance of the English, and to the circumstance that New-England and Virginia, the two great sources of internal emigration, were entirely of English origin. Still, New-York retains, to the present hour, a variety of usages that were obtained from Holland. Her edifices of painted bricks, her streets lined with trees, her inconvenient and awkward stoops and a large proportion of her names, are equally derived from the Dutch. Until the commencement of this century, even the language of Holland prevailed in the streets of the capital, and though a nation of singular boldness and originality in all that relates to navigation, the greatest sea-port of the country betrays many evidences of a taste which must be referred to the same origin.

The reader will find in these facts a sufficient explanation of most of the peculiar customs, and of some of the peculiar practices, that are exhibited in the course of the following tale. Slavery, a divided language, and a distinct people, are no longer to be found, within the fair regions of New-York; and, without pretending to any peculiar exemption from the weaknesses of humanity, it may be permitted us to hope, that these are not the only features of the narrative, which a better policy, and a more equitable administration of power, have made purely historical.

Early released from the fetters of the middle ages, fetters that bound the mind equally with the person, America has preceded rather than followed Europe, in that march of improvement which is rendering the present era so remarkable. Under a system, broad, liberal, and just as hers, though she may have to contend with rivalries that are sustained by a more concentrated competition, and which are as absurd by their pretension of liberality as they are offensive by their monopolies, there is nothing to fear, in the end. Her political motto should be Justice, and her first and greatest care to see it administered to her own citizens.

The reader is left to make the application.

CHAPTER 1.

"What, shall this speech be spoke for our excuse?
Or shall we on without apology."

Romeo and Juliet.

THE fine estuary which penetrates the American coast, between the fortieth and forty-first degrees of latitude, is formed by the confluence of the Hudson, the Hackensack, the Passaic, the Raritan, and a multitude of smaller streams; all of which pour their tribute into the ocean, within the space named. The islands of Nassau and Staten are happily placed to exclude the tempests of the open sea, while the deep and broad arms of the latter offer every desirable facility for foreign trade and internal intercourse. To this fortunate disposition of land and water, with a temperate climate, a central position, and an immense interior, that is now penetrated, in every direction, either by artificial or by natural streams, the city of New-York is indebted for its extraordinary prosperity. Though not wanting in beauty, there are many bays that surpass this in the charms of scenery; but it may be questioned if the world possesses another site that unites so many natural advantages for the growth and support of a widely extended commerce. As if never wearied with her kindness, Nature has placed the island of Manhattan at the precise point that is most desirable for the position of a town. Millions might inhabit the spot, and yet a ship should load near every door; and while the surface of the land just possesses the inequalities that are required for health and cleanliness, its bosom is filled with the material most needed in construction.

The consequences of so unusual a concurrence of favorable circumstances, are well known. A vigorous, healthful, and continued growth, that has no parallel even in the history of this extraordinary and fortunate country, has already raised the insignificant provincial town of the last century to the level of the second-rate cities of the other hemisphere. The New-Amsterdam of this continent already rivals its parent of the other; and, so far as human powers may pretend to predict, a few fleeting years will place her on a level with the proudest capitals of Europe.

It would seem that, as Nature has given its periods to the stages of animal life, it has also set limits to all moral and political ascendency. While the city of the Medici is receding from its crumbling walls, like the human form shrinking into "the lean and slipper'd pantaloon," the Queen of the Adriatic sleeping on her muddy isles, and Rome itself is only to be traced by fallen temples and buried columns, the youthful vigor of America is fast covering the wilds of the West with the happiest fruits of human industry.

By the Manhattanese, who is familiar with the forest of masts, the miles of wharves, the countless villas, the hundred churches, the castles, the smoking and busy vessels that crowd his bay, the daily increase and the general movement of his native town, the picture we are about to sketch will scarcely be recognized. He who shall come a generation later will probably smile, that subject of admiration should have been found in the existing condition of the city: and yet we shall attempt to carry the recollections of the reader but a century back, in the brief history of his country.

As the sun rose on the morning of the 3d of June 171-, the report of a cannon was heard rolling along the waters of the Hudson. Smoke issued from an embrasure of a small fortress, that stood on the point of land where the river and the bay mingle their waters. The explosion was followed by the appearance of a flag, which, as it rose to the summit of its staff and unfolded itself heavily in the light current of air, showed the blue field and red cross of the English ensign. At the distance of several miles, the dark masts of a ship were to be seen, faintly relieved by the verlant back-ground of the heights of Staten Island. A little cloud floated over this object, and then an answering signal came dull and rumbling to the town. The flag that the cruiser set was not visible in the distance.

At the precise moment that the noise of the first gun was heard, the door of one of the principal dwellings of the town opened, and a man, who might have been its master, appeared on its stoop, as the ill-arranged entrances of the buildings of the place are still termed. He was seemingly prepared for some expedition that was likely to consume the day. A black of middle age followed the burgher to the threshold; and another negro, who had not yet reached the stature of manhood, bore under his arm a small bundle, that probably contained articles of the first necessity to the comfort of his master.

"Thrift, Mr. Euclid, thrift is your true philosopher's stone;" commenced, or rather continued in a rich full-mouthed Dutch, the proprietor of the dwelling, who had evidently been giving a leave-taking charge to his principal slave, before quitting the house — "Thrift hath made many a man rich, but it never yet brought any one to want. It is thrift which has built up the credit of my house, and, though it is said by myself, a broader back and firmer base belongs to no mer-chant in the colonies You are but the reflection of your master's prosperity, you rogue, and so much the greater need that you took to his interests. If the substance is wasted, what will become of the shadow? When I get delicate, you will sicken:

when I am a-hungered, you will be famished; when I die, you may be — ahem — Euclid. I leave thee in charge with goods and chattels, house and stable, with my character in the neighborhood. I am going to the Lust in Rust, for a mouthful of better air. Plague and fevers! I believe the people will continue to come into this crowded town, until it gets to be as pestilent as Rotterdam in the dog-days. You have now come to years when a man obtains his reflection, boy, and I expect suitable care and discretion about the premises, while my back is turned. Now, harkee, sirrah: I am not entirely pleased with the character of thy company. It is not altogether as respectable as becomes the confidential servant of a man of a certain station in the world. There are thy two cousins, Brom and Kobus, who are no better than a couple of blackguards; and as for the English negro, Diomede — he is a devil's imp! Thou hast the other locks at disposal, and," drawing with visible reluctance the instrument from his pocket, "here is the key of the stable. Not a hoof is to quit it, but to go to the pump — and see that each animal has its food to a minute. The devil's roysterers! a Manhattan negro takes a Flemish gelding for a gaunt hound that is never out of breath, and away he goes, at night, scampering along the highways like a Yankee witch switching through the air on a broomstick — but mark me, master Euclid, I have eyes in my head, as thou knowest by bitter experience! D'ye remember, ragamuffin, the time when I saw thee, from the Hague, riding the beasts, as if the devil spurred them, along the dykes of Leyden, without remorse as without leave?"

"I alway b'rieve some make-mischief tell Masser dat time;" returned the negro sulkily, though not without doubt.

"His own eyes were the tell-tales. If masters had no eyes, a pretty world would the negroes make of it! I have got the measure of every black heel, on the island, registered in the big book, you see me so often looking into, especially on Sundays; and, if either of the tire-legs I have named dares to enter my grounds, let him expect to pay a visit to the city Provost. What do the wild-cats mean? Do they think that the geldings were bought in Holland, with charges for breaking in, shipment, insurance, freight, and risk of diseases, to have their flesh melted from their ribs like a cook's candle?"

"Ere no'tin' done in all 'e island, but a color' man do him! He do a mischief, and he do all a work, too! I won'er what color Masser t'ink war' Captain Kidd?"

"Black or white, he was a rank rogue; and you see the end he came to. I warrant you, now, that water-thief began his iniquities by riding the neighbors' horses, at night. His fate should be a warning to every negro in the colony. The imps of darkness! The English have no such scarcity of rogues at home, that they could not spare us the pirate to hang up on one of the islands, as a scarecrow to the blacks of Manhattan."

"Well, I t'ink 'e sight do a white man some good, too;" returned Euclid, who had all the pertinacity of a spoiled Dutch negro, singularly blended with affection for him in whose service he had been born. "I hear ebbery body say, 'er' e war' but two color man in he ship, and 'em bot' war' Guinea-born."

"A modest tongue, thou midnight scamperer! look to my geldings — Here — here are two Dutch florins, three stivers, and a Spanish pistareen for thee; one of the florins is for thy old mother, and with the others thou canst lighten thy heart in the Paus merrymakings — if I hear that either of thy rascally cousins, or the English Diomede, has put a leg across beast of mine, it will be the worse for all Africa! Famine and skeletons! here have I been seven years trying to fatten the nags, and they still look more like weasels than a pair of solid geldings."

The close of this speech was rather muttered in the distance, and by way of soliloquy, than actually administered to the namesake of the great mathematician. The air of the negro had been a little equivocal, during the parting admonition. There was an evident struggle, in his mind, between an innate love of disobedience, and a secret dread of his master's means of information. So long as the latter continued in sight, the black watched his form in doubt; and when it had turned a corner, he stood at gaze, for a moment, with a negro on a neighboring stoop; then both shook their heads significantly, laughed aloud, and retired. That night, the confidential servant attended to the interests of his absent master, with a fidelity and care which proved he felt his own existence identified with that of a man who claimed so close a right in his person; and just as the clock struck ten, he and the negro last mentioned mounted the sluggish and over-fattened horses, and galloped, as hard as foot could be laid to the earth, several miles deeper into the island, to attend a frolic at one of the usual haunts of the people of their color and condition.

Had Alderman Myndert Van Beverout suspected the calamity which was so soon to succeed his absence, it is probable that his mien would have been less composed, as he pursued his way from his own door, on the occasion named. That he had confidence in the virtue of his menaces, however, may be inferred from the tranquillity which immediately took possession of features that were never disturbed, without wearing an appearance of unnatural effort. The substantial burgher was a little turned of fifty: and an English wag, who had imported from the mother country a love for the humor of his nation, had once, in a conflict of wits before the city council, described him to be a man of alliterations. When called upon to explain away this breach of parliamentary decorum, the punster had gotten rid of the matter, by describing his opponent to be "short, solid and sturdy, in stature; full, flushed and funny, in face; and proud, ponderous and pragmatical, in propensities." But, as is usual, in all sayings of effort there was more smartness than truth in this description; though, after making a trifling allowance for the coloring of political rivalry, the reader may receive its physical portion as sufficiently descriptive to answer all the necessary purposes of this tale. If we add, that he was a trader of great wealth and shrewdness, and a bachelor, we need say no more in this stage of the narrative.

Notwithstanding the early hour at which this industrious and flourishing merchant quitted his abode, his movement along the narrow streets of his native town was measured and dignified. More than once, he stopped to speak to some favorite family-servant, invariably terminating his inquiries after the health of the master, by some facetious observation adapted to the habits and capacity of the slave. From this, it would seem, that, while he had so exaggerated notions of domestic discipline, the worthy burgher was far from being one who indulged, by inclination, in the menaces he has been heard to utter. He had just dismissed one of these loitering negroes, when, on turning a corner, a man of his own color, for the first time that morning, suddenly stood before him. The startled citizen made an involuntary movement to avoid the unexpected interview, and then, perceiving the difficulty of such a step, he submitted, with as good a grace as if it had been one of his own seeking.

"The orb of day — the morning gun — and Mr Alderman Van Beverout!" exclaimed the individual encountered. "Such is the order of events, at this early hour, on each successive revolution of our earth."

The countenance of the Alderman had barely time to recover its composure, ere he was required to answer to this free and somewhat facetious salutation. Uncovering his head, he bowed so ceremoniously as to leave the other no reason to exult in his pleasantry, as he answered —

"The colony has reason to regret the services of a governor who can quit his bed so soon. That we of business habits stir betimes, is quite in reason; but there are those in this town, who would scarce believe their eyes did they enjoy my present happiness."

"Sir, there are many in this colony who have great reason to distrust their senses, though none can be mistaken in believing they see Alderman Van Beverout in a well-employed man. He that dealeth in the produce of the beaver must have the animal's perseverance and forethought! Now, were I a king-at-arms, there should be a concession made in thy favor, Myndert, of a shield bearing the animal mordant, a mantle of fur, with two Mohawk hunters for supporters, and the motto, 'Industry.'"

"Or what think you, my Lord," returned the other, who did not more than half relish the pleasantry of his companion, "of a spotless shield for a clear conscience, with an open hand for a crest, and the motto, 'Frugality and Justice?'"

"I like the open hand, though the conceit is pretending. I see you would intimate that the Van Beverouts have not need, at this late day, to search a herald's office for honors. I remember, now I bethink me, on some occasion to have seen their bearings; a windmill, courant; dyke, coulant; field, vert, sprinkled with black cattle — No! then, memory is treacherous; the morning air is pregnant with food for the imagination!"

"Which is not a coin to satisfy a creditor, my Lord," said the caustic Myndert.

"Therein has truth been, pithily, spoken. This is an ill-judged step, Alderman Van Beverout, that lets a gentleman out by night, like the ghost in Hamlet, to flee into the narrow house with the crowing of the cock. The ear of my royal cousin hath been poisoned, worse than was the ear of 'murdered Denmark,' or the partisans of this Mister Hunter would have little cause to triumph."

"Is it not possible to give such pledges to those who have turned the key, as will enable your lordship to apply the antidote."

The question stuck a chord that changed the whole manner of the other. His air, which had borne the character of a genteel trifler, became more grave and dignified; and notwithstanding there was the evidence of a reckless disposition in his features, dress and carriage, his tall and not ungraceful form, as he walked slowly onward, by the side of the compact Alderman, was not without much of that insinuating ease and blandishment, which long familiarity with good company can give even to the lowest moral worth.

"Your question, worthy Sir, manifests great goodness of heart, and corroborates that reputation for generosity, the world so freely gives. It is true that the Queen has been persuaded to sign the mandate of my recall, and it is certain that Mr. Hunter has the government of the colony; but these are facts that might be reversed, were I once in a position to approach my kinswoman. I do not disclaim certain indiscretions, Sir; it would ill become me to deny them, in presence of one whose virtue is as severe as that of Alderman Van Beverout. I have my failings; perhaps, as you have just been pleased to intimate, it would have been better had my motto been frugality; but the open hand, dear Sir, is a part of the design you will not deny me, either. If I have weaknesses, my enemies cannot refuse to say that I never yet deserted a friend."

"Not having had occasion to tax your friendship, I shall not be the first to make the charge.

"Your impartiality has come to be a proverb! 'As honest as Alderman Van Beverout;' 'as generous as Alderman Van Beverout,' are terms in each man's mouth; some say 'as rich;' (the small blue eye of the burgher twinkled.) But honesty, and riches, and generosity, are of little value, without influence. Men should have their natural consideration in society. Now is this colony rather Dutch than English, and yet, you see, how few names are found in the list of the Council, that have been known in the province half a century! Here are your Alexanders and Heathcotes, your Morris's and Kennedies, de Lanceys and Livingstons, filling the Council and the legislative halls; but we find few of the Van Rensselaers, Van Courtlandts, Van Schuylers, Stuyvesants, Van Beekmans, and Van Beverouts, in their natural stations. All nations and religions have precedency, in the royal favor, over the children of the Patriarchs. The Bohemian Felipses; the Huguenot de Lanceys, and Bayards, and Jays; the King-hating Morrises and Ludlows — in short, all have greater estimation in the eyes of government, than the most ancient Patroon!"

"This has long and truly been the case. I cannot remember when it was otherwise!"

"It may not be denied. But it would little become political discretion to affect precipitancy in the judgment of character. If my own administration can be stigmatized with the same apparent prejudice, it proves the clearer how strong is misrepresentation at home. Time was wanting to enlighten my mind and that time has been refused me. In another year, my worthy Sir, the Council should have been filled with Van's!"

"In such a case, my Lord, the unhappy condition in which you are now placed might indeed have been avoided."

"Is it too late to arrest the evil? It is time Anne had been undeceived, and her mind regained. There wanteth nothing to such a consummation of justice, Sir, but opportunity. It touches me to the heart, to think that this disgrace should befall one so near the royal blood! 'Tis a spot on the escutcheon of the crown, that all loyal subjects must feel desirous to efface, and so small an effort would effect the object, too, with certain — Mr. Alderman Myndert Van Beverout —?"

"My Lord, late Governor," returned the other, observing that his companion hesitated.

"What think you of this Hanoverian settlement? — Shall a German wear the crown of a Plantagenet?"

"It hath been worn by a Hollander."

"Aptly answered! Worn, and worn worthily! There is affinity between the people, and there is reason in that reply. How have I failed in wisdom, in not seeking earlier the aid of thy advice, excellent Sir! Ah, Myndert, there is a blessing on the enterprises of all who come of the Low Countries!"

"They are industrious to earn, and slow to squander."

"That expenditure is the ruin of many a worthy subject! And yet accident — chance — fortune — or whatever you may choose to call it, interferes nefariously, at times, with a gentleman's prosperity. I am an adorer of constancy in friendship, Sir, and hold the principle that men should aid each other through this dark vale of life — Mr. Alderman Van Beverout —?"

"My Lord Cornbury?"

"I was about to say, that should I quit the Province, without expressing part of the regret I feel, at not having sooner ascertained the merits of its original owners, and your own in particular, I should do injustice to sensibilities, that are only too acute for the peace of him who endures them."

"Is there then hope that your lordship's creditors will relent, or has the Earl furnished means to open the prison-door?"

"You use the pleasantest terms, Sir! — but I love directness of language, above all other qualities. No doubt the prison-door, as you have so clearly expressed it, might be opened, and lucky would be the man who should turn the key. I am pained when I think of the displeasure of the Queen, which, sooner or later, will surely visit my luckless persecutors. On the other hand, I find relief in thinking of the favor she will extend to those who have proved my friends, in such a strait. They that wear crowns love not to see disgrace befall the meanest of their blood, for something of the taint may sully even the ermine of Majesty. Mr. Alderman — !"

"My Lord?"

" — How fare the Flemish geldings?"

"Bravely, and many thanks, my Lord; the rogues are fat as butter! There is hope of a little rest for the innocents, since business calls me to the Lust in Rust. There should be a law, Lord Governor, to gibbet the black that rides a beast at night."

"I bethought of some condign punishment for so heartless a crime, but there is little hope for it under the administration of this Mr. Hunter. Yes, Sir; were I once more in the presence of my royal cousin, there would quickly be an end to this delusion, and the colony should be once more restored to a healthful state. The men of a generation should cease to lord it over the men of a century. But we must be wary of letting our design, my dear Sir, get wind: it is a truly Dutch idea, and the profits, both pecuniary and political, should belong to the gentlemen of that descent — My dear Van Beverout — ?"

"My good Lord?"

"Is the blooming Alida obedient? Trust me, there has no family event occurred, during my residence in the colony, in which I have taken a nearer interest, than in that desirable connexion. The wooing of the young Patroon of Kinderhook is an affair of concern to the province. It is a meritorious youth!"

"With an excellent estate, my Lord!"

"And a gravity beyond his years."

"I would give a guarantee, at a risk, that two-thirds of his income goes to increase the capital, at the beginning of each season!"

"He seems a man to live on air!"

"My old friend, the last Patroon, left noble assets," continued the Alderman, rubbing his hands; "besides the manor."

"Which is no paddock!"

"It reaches from the Hudson to the line of Massachusetts. A hundred thousand acres of hill and bottom, and well peopled by frugal Hollanders."

"Respectable in possession, and a mine of gold in reversion! Such men, Sir, should be cherished. We owe it to his station to admit him to a share of this, our project to undeceive the Queen. How superior are the claims of such a gentleman to the empty pretensions of your Captain Ludlow!"

"He has truly a very good and an improving estate!"

"These Ludlows, Sir, people that fled the realm for plotting against the crown, are offensive to a loyal subject. Indeed, too much of this objection may be imputed to many in the province, that come of English blood. I am sorry to say, that they are fomenters of discord, disturbers of the public mind, and captious disputants about prerogatives and vested rights. But there is a repose in the Dutch character which lends it dignity! The descendants of the Hollanders are men to be counted on; where we leave them today, we see them tomorrow. As we say in politics, Sir, we know where to find them. Does it not seem to you particularly offensive that this Captain Ludlow should command the only royal cruiser on the station?"

"I should like it better, my Lord, were he to serve in Europe," returned the Alderman, glancing a look behind him, and lowering his voice. "There was lately a rumor that his ship was in truth to be sent among the islands."

"Matters are getting very wrong, most worthy Sir; and the greater the necessity there should be one at court to undeceive the Queen. Innovators should be made to give way to men whose names are historical, in the colony."

"'Twould be no worse for Her Majesty's credit."

"'Twould be another jewel in her crown! Should this Captain Ludlow actually marry your niece, the family would altogether change its character — I have the worst memory — thy mother, Myndert, was a — a —"

"The pious woman was a Van Busser."

"The union of thy sister with the Huguenot then reduces the fair Alida to the quality of a half-blood. The Ludlow connexion would destroy the leaven of the race! I think the man is penniless!"

"I cannot say that, my Lord, for I would not willingly injure the credit of my worst enemy; but, though wealthy, he is far from having the estate of the young Patroon of Kinderhook."

"He should indeed be sent into the Indies — Myndert — ?"

"My Lord?"

"It would be unjust to my sentiments in favor of Mr. Oloff Van Staats, were we to exclude him from the advantages of our project. This much shall I exact from your friendship, in his favor; the necessary sum may be divided, in moieties, between you; a common bond shall render the affair compact; and then, as we shall be masters of our own secret, there can be little doubt of the prudence of our measures. The amount is written in this bit of paper."

"Two thousand pounds, my Lord!"

"Pardon me, dear Sir; not a penny more than one for each of you. Justice to Van Staats requires that you let him into the affair. Were it not for the suit with your niece, I should take the young gentleman with me, to push his fortunes at court."

"Truly, my Lord, this greatly exceeds my means. The high prices of furs the past season, and delays in returns have placed a seal upon our silver — "

"The premium would be high."

"Coin is getting so scarce, daily, that the face of a Carolus is almost as great a stranger, as the face of a debtor —"

"The returns certain."

"While one's creditors meet him, at every corner —"

"The concern would be altogether Dutch."

"And last advices from Holland tell us to reserve our gold, for some extraordinary movements in the commercial world."

"Mr. Alderman Myndert Van Beverout!"

"My Lord Viscount Cornbury —"

"Plutus preserve thee, Sir — but have a care! though I scent the morning air, and must return, it is not forbid to tell the secrets of my prison-house. There is one, in yonder cage, who whispers that the 'Skimmer of the Seas' is on the coast! Be wary, worthy burgher, or the second part of the tragedy of Kidd may yet be enacted in these seas."

"I leave such transactions to my superiors," retorted the Alderman, with another stiff and ceremonious bow. "Enterprises that are said to have occupied the Earl of Bellamont, Governor Fletcher, and my Lord Cornbury, are above the ambition of an humble merchant."

"Adieu, tenacious Sir; quiet thine impatience for the extraordinary Dutch movements!" said Cornbury, affecting to laugh, though he secretly felt the sting the other had applied, since common report implicated not only him, but his two official predecessors, in several of the lawless proceedings of the American Bucca-neers: "Be vigilant, or la demoiselle Barbérie will give another cross to the purity of the stagnant pool!"

The bows that were exchanged were strictly in character. The Alderman was unmoved, rigid, and formal, while his companion could not forget his ease of manner, even at a moment of so much vexation. Foiled in an effort, that nothing but his desperate condition, and nearly desperate character, could have induced him to attempt, the degenerate descendant of the virtuous Clarendon walked towards his place of confinement, with the step of one who assumed a superiority over his fellows, and yet with a mind so indurated by habitual depravity, as to have left it scarcely the trace of a dignified or virtuous quality.

CHAPTER II.

"His words are bonds, his oaths are oracles;
His love sincere, his thoughts immaculate —"
                                        Two Gentlemen of Verona.

THE philosophy of Alderman Van Beverout was not easily disturbed. Still there was a play of the nether muscles of the face, which might be construed into self-complacency at his victory, while a certain contraction of those which controlled the expression of the forehead seemed to betray a full consciousness of the imminent risk he had run. The left hand was thrust into a pocket, where it diligently fingered the provision of Spanish coin without which the merchant never left his abode; while the other struck the cane it held on the pavement, with the force of a resolute and decided man. In this manner he proceeded in his walk, for several minutes longer, shortly quitting the lower streets, to enter one that ran along the ridge, which crowned the land, in that quarter of the island. Here he soon stopped before the door of a house which, in that provincial town, had altogether the air of a patrician dwelling.

Two false gables, each of which was surmounted by an iron weathercock, intersected the roof of this building, and the high and narrow stoop was built of the red free-stone of the country. The material of the edifice itself was, as usual, the small, hard brick of Holland, painted a delicate cream-color.

A single blow of the massive glittering knocker brought a servant to the door. The promptitude with which this summons was answered showed that, notwithstanding the early hour, the Alderman was an expected guest. The countenance of him who acted as porter betrayed no surprise when he saw the person who applied for admission, and every movement of the black denoted preparation and readiness for his reception. Declining his invitation to enter, however, the Alderman placed his back against the iron railing of the stoop, and opened a discourse with the negro. The latter was aged, with a head that was grizzled, a nose that was levelled nearly to the plane of his face, features that were wrinkled and confused, and with a form which, though still solid, was bending with its load of years.

"Brave cheer to thee, old Cupid!" commenced the burgher, in the hearty and cordial manner with which the masters of that period were wont to address their indulged slaves. "A clear conscience is a good night-cap, and you look bright as the morning sun! I hope my friend the young Patroon has slept sound as yourself, and that he has shown his face already, to prove it."

The negro answered with the slow clipping manner that characterized his condition and years.

"He'm werry wakeful, Masser Al'erman. I t'ink he no sleep half he time, lately. All he a'tiverty and wiwacerty gone, an' he do no single t'ing but smoke. A gentle'um who smoke alway, Masser Al'erman, get to be a melercholy man, at last. I do t'ink 'ere be one young lady in York who be he deat', some time!"

"We'll find the means to get the pipe out of his mouth," said the other, looking askance at the black, as if to express more than he uttered. "Romance and pretty girls play the deuce with our philosophy, in youth, as thou knowest by experience, old Cupid."

"I no good for any t'ing, dat-a-way, now, not'ing," calmly returned the black. "I see a one time, when few color' man in York hab more respect among a fair sec', but dat a great while gone by. Now, de modder of your Euclid, Masser Al'erman, war' a pretty woman, do' she hab but poor conduc'. Den a war' young heself, and I use to visit at de Al'erman's fadder's; afore a English come, and when ole Patroon war' a young man. Golly! I great affection for Euclid, do' a young dog nebber come a near me!"

"He's a blackguard! My back is no sooner turned, than the rascal's atop of one of his master's geldings.'

"He'm werry young, master My'nert: no one get a wis'om fore a gray hair."

"He's forty every minute, and the rogue gets impudence with his years. Age is a reverend and respectable condition, when it brings gravity and thought; but, if a young fool be tiresome, an old fool is contemptible. I'll warrant me, you never were so thoughtless, or so heartless, Cupid, as to ride an overworked beast, at night!"

"Well, I get pretty ole, Masser Myn'ert an' I forget all he do when a young man. But here be'e Patroon, who know how to tell'e Al'erman such t'ing better than a poor color' slave."

"A fair rising and a lucky day to you, Patroon!" cried the Alderman, saluting a large, slow-moving, gentlemanly-looking young man of five-and-twenty, who advanced, with the gravity of one of twice that number of years, from the interior of the house, towards its outer door "The winds are bespoken, and here is as fine a day as ever shone out of a clear sky, whether it came from the pure atmosphere of Holland, or of old England itself. Colonies and patronage! If the people on the other side of the ocean had more faith in mother Nature, and less opinion of themselves, they would find it very tolerable breathing in the plantations. But the conceited rogues are like the man who blew the bellows, and fancied he made the music; and there is never a hobbling imp of them all, but he believes he is straighter and sounder, than the best in the colonies. Here is our bay, now, as smooth as if it were shut in with twenty dykes, and the voyage will be as safe as if it were made on a canal."

"Dat werry well, if a do it," grumbled Cupid, who busied himself affectionately about the person of his master. "I think it alway better to travel on 'e land, when a gentle'um own so much as Masser Oloff Der war' 'e time a ferry-boat go down, wid crowd of people; and nobody ebber come up again to say how he feel."

"Here is some mistake!" interrupted the Alderman, throwing an uneasy glance at his young friend. "I count four-and-fifty years, and remember no such calamity."

"He'm werry sing'lar how a young folk do forget! 'Ere war' drown six people in dat werry-boat. A two Yankee, a Canada Frenchman, and a poor woman from a Jarseys. Ebbery body war werry sorry for a poor woman from a Jarseys!"

"Thy tally is false, Master Cupid," promptly rejoined the Alderman, who was rather expert at figures. "Two Yankees, a Frenchman, and your Jersey woman, make but four."

"Well, den I s'pose 'ere war' one Yankee; but I, know all war' drown, for 'e Gubbenor lose he fine coach-horses in dat werry-boat."

"The old fellow is right, sure enough; for I remember the calamity of the horses, as if it were but yesterday. But Death is monarch of the earth, and none of us may hope to escape his scythe, when the appointed hour shall come! Here are no nags to lose, today; and we may commence our voyage, Patroon, with cheerful faces and light hearts. Shall we proceed?"

Oloff Van Staats, or the Patroon of Kinderhook, as, by the courtesy of the colony, he was commonly termed, did not want for personal firmness. On the contrary, like most of those who were descended from the Hollanders, he was rather distinguished for steadiness in danger, and obstinacy in resistance. The little skirmish which had just taken place, between his friend and his slave, had proceeded from the several apprehensions; the one feeling a sort of parental interest in his safety, and the other having particular reasons for wishing him to persevere in his intention to embark, instead of any justifiable cause in the character of the young proprietor himself. A sign to the boy who bore a portmanteau, settled the controversy; and then Mr. Van Staats intimated his readiness to move.

Cupid lingered on the stoop, until his master had turned a corner; then, shaking his head with all the misgivings of an ignorant and superstitious mind, he drove the young fry of blacks, who thronged the door, into the house, closing all after him with singular and scrupulous care. How far the presentiment of the black was warranted by the event, will be seen in the course of the narrative.

The wide avenue, in which Oloff Van Staats dwelt, was but a few hundred yards in length. It terminated, at one end, with the fortress; and at the other, it was crossed by a high stockade, which bore the name of the city walls; a defence that was provided against any sudden irruption of the Indians, who then hunted, and even dwelt in some numbers, in the lower counties of the colony.

It requires great familiarity with the growth of the town, to recognize, in this description, the noble street that now runs for a league through the centre of the island. From this avenue, which was then, as it is still, called the Broadway, our adventurers descended into a lower quarter of the town, holding free converse by the way.

"That Cupid is a negro to keep the roof on a house, in its master's absence, Patroon," observed the Alderman, soon after they had left the stoop. "He looks like a padlock, and one might sleep, without a dream, with such a guardian near his dwelling. I wish I had brought the honest fellow the key of my stable!"

"I have heard my father say, that the keys of his own were always better near his own pillow," coolly returned the proprietor of a hundred thousand acres.

"Ah, the curse of Cain! It is needless to look for the fur of a marten on the back of a cat. But, Mr. Van Staats, while walking to your door this morning, it was my fortune to meet the late governor, who is permitted by his creditors to take the air, at an hour when he thinks the eyes of the impertinent will be shut. I believe, Patroon, you were so lucky as to get back your moneys, before the royal displeasure visited the man?"

"I was so lucky as never to trust him."

"That was better still, for it would have been a barren investment — great jeopardy to principal, and no return. But we had discourse of various interests, and, among others, something was hazarded concerning your amatory pretensions to my niece."

"Neither the wishes of Oloff Van Staats, nor the inclinations of la belle Barbérie, are a subject for the Governor in Council," said the Patroon of Kinderhook, stiffly.

"Nor was it thus treated. The Viscount spoke me fair, and, had he not pushed the matter beyond discretion, we might have come to happier conclusions."

"I am glad that there was some restraint in the discourse."

"The man certainly exceeded reason, for he led the conference into personalities that no prudent man could relish. Still he said it was possible that the Coquette might yet be ordered for service among the islands!"

It has been said, that Oloff Van Staats was a fair personable young man of vast stature, and with much of the air of a gentleman of his country; for, though a British subject, he was rather a Hollander in feelings, habits, and opinions. He colored at the allusion to the presence of his known rival, though his companion was at a loss to discover whether pride or vexation was at the bottom of his emotion.

"If Captain Ludlow prefer a cruise in the Indies, to duty on this coast, I hope he may obtain his wish," was the cautious answer.

"Your liberal man enjoys a sounding name, and an empty coffer," observed the Alderman, drily. "To me it seems that a petition to the admiral to send so meritorious an officer on service where he may distinguish himself, should deserve his thanks. The freebooters are playing the devil's game with the sugar trade, and even the French are getting troublesome, further south."

"He has certainly the reputation of an active cruiser."

"Blixum and philosophy! If you wish to succeed with Alida, Patroon, you must put more briskness into the adventure. The girl has a cross of the Frenchman in her temper, and none of your deliberations and taciturnities will gain the day. This visit to the Lust in Rust is Cupid's own handywork, and I hope to see you both return to town as amicable as the Stadtholder and the States General after a sharp struggle for the year's subsidy has been settled by a compromise."

"The success of this suit is the affair nearest my —" The young man paused as if surprised at his own communicativeness; and, taking advantage of the haste in which his toilette had been made, he thrust a hand into his vest, covering with its broad palm a portion of the human frame which poets do not describe as the seat of the passions.

"If you mean stomach, Sir, you will not have reason to be disappointed," retorted the Alderman, a little more severely than was usual with one so callous. "The heiress of Myndert Van Beverout will not be a penniless bride, and Monsieur Barbérie did not close the books of life without taking good care of the balance-sheet — but yonder are those devils of ferrymen quitting the wharf without us! Scamper ahead, Brutus, and tell them to wait the legal minute. The rogues are never exact; sometimes starting before I am ready, and sometimes keeping me waiting in the sun, as if I were no better than a dried dun-fish. Punctuality is the soul of business, and one of my habits does not like to be ahead, nor behind his time."

In this manner the worthy burgher, who would have been glad to regulate the movements of others, on all occasions, a good deal by his own, vented his complaints, while he and his companion hurried on to overtake the slow-moving boat in which they were to embark. A brief description of the scene will not be without interest, to a generation that may be termed modern in reference to the time of which we write.

A deep narrow creek penetrated the island, at this point, for the distance of a quarter of a mile. Each of its banks had a row of buildings, as the houses line a canal in the cities of Holland. As the natural course of the inlet was necessarily respected, the street had taken a curvature not unlike that of a new moon. The houses were ultra-Dutch, being low, angular, fastidiously neat, and all erected with their gables to the street. Each had its ugly and inconvenient entrance, termed a stoop, its vane or weathercock, its dormer-windows, and its graduated battlement-walls. Near the apex of one of the latter, a little iron crane projected into the street. A small boat, of the same metal, swung from its end — a sign that the building to which it was appended was the ferry-house.

An inherent love of artificial and confined navigation had probably induced the burghers to select this spot, as the place whence so many craft departed from the town: since, it is certain, that the two rivers could have furnished divers points more favorable for such an object, inasmuch as they possess the advantage of wide and unobstructed channels.

Fifty blacks were already in the street, dipping their brooms into the creek, and flourishing water over the side-walks, and on the fronts of the low edifices. This light but daily duty was relieved by clamorous collisions of wit, and by shouts of merriment, in which the whole street would join, as with one joyous and reckless movement of the spirit.

The language of this light-hearted and noisy race was Dutch, already corrupted by English idioms, and occasionally by English words — a system of change that has probably given rise to an opinion, among some of the descendants of the earlier colonists, that the latter tongue is merely a patois of the former. This opinion, which so much resembles that certain well-read English scholars entertain of the plagiarisms of the continental writers, when they first begin to dip into their works, is not strictly true; since the language of England has probably bestowed as much on the dialect of which we speak, as it has ever received from the purer sources of the school of Holland. Here and there, a grave burgher, still in his night-cap, might be seen with a head thrust out of an upper window, listening to these barbarisms of speech, and taking note of all the merry jibes, that flew from mouth to mouth with an indomitable gravity, that no levity of those beneath could undermine.

As the movement of the ferry-boat was necessarily slow, the Alderman and his companion were enabled to step into it, before the fasts were thrown aboard. The periagua, as the craft was called, partook of a European and an American character. It possessed the length, narrowness, and clean bow, of the canoe, from which its name was derived, with the flat bottom and lee-boards of a boat constructed for the shallow waters of the Low Countries. Twenty years ago, vessels of this description abounded in our rivers, and even now, their two long and unsupported masts and high narrow-headed sails, are daily seen bending like reeds to the breeze, and dancing lightly over the billows of the bay. There is a variety of the class, of a size and pretension altogether superior to that just mentioned, which deserves a place among the most picturesque and striking boats that float. He who has had occasion to navigate the southern shore of the Sound must have often seen the vessel to which we allude. It is distinguished by its great length, and masts which, naked of cordage, rise from the hull like two tall and faultless trees. When the eye runs over the daring height of canvas, the noble confidence of the rig, and sees the comparatively vast machine handled with ease and grace by the dexterity of two fearless and expert mariners, it excites some such admiration as that which springs from the view of a severe temple of antiquity The nakedness and simplicity of the construction, coupled with the boldness and rapidity of its movements, impart to the craft an air of grandeur, that its ordinary uses would not give reason to expect.

Though, in some respects, of singularly aquatic habits, the original colonists of New-York were far less adventurous, as mariners, than their present descendants. A passage across the bay did not often occur in the tranquil lives of the burghers; and it is still within the memory of man, that a voyage between the two principal towns of the State was an event to excite the solicitude of friends, and the anxiety of the traveller. The perils of the Tappaan Zee, as one of the wider reaches of the Hudson is still termed, was often dealt with by the good wives of the colony, in their relations of marvels; and she who had oftenest encountered them unharmed, was deemed a sort of marine amazon.

CHAPTER III.

" — I have great comfort from this fellow: methinks he hath no
drowning mark upon him; his complexion is perfect gallows."

Tempest.

It has been said that the periagua was in motion, before our two adventurers succeeded in stepping on board. The arrival of the Patroon of Kinderhook and of
Alderman Van Beverout was expected, and the schipper had taken his departure
at the precise moment of the turn in the current, in order to show, with a sort of
pretending independence which has a peculiar charm for men in his situation,
that 'time and tide wait for no man.' Still there were limits to his decision; for,
while he put the boat in motion, especial care was taken that the circumstance
should not subject a customer so important and constant as the Alderman, to any
serious inconvenience. When he and his friend had embarked, the painters were
thrown aboard, and the crew of the ferry-boat began to set their vessel, in earnest,
towards the mouth of the creek. During these movements, a young negro was
seated in the bow of the periagua, with his legs dangling, one on each side of the
cut-water, forming no bad apology for a figure-head. He held a conch to his
mouth, and with his two glossy cheeks inflated like those of Eolus, and his dark
glittering eyes expressing the delight he found in drawing sounds from the shell,
he continued to give forth the signal for departure.

"Put up the conch, thou bawler!" cried the Alderman, giving the younker a
rap on his naked poll, in passing, with the end of his cane, that might have disturbed the harmony of one less bent on clamor. "A thousand windy trumpeters
would be silence itself, compared to such a pair of lungs! How now Master
Schipper, is this your punctuality, to start before your passengers are ready?"

The undisturbed boatman, without removing the pipe from his mouth,
pointed to the bubbles on the water which were already floating outward, a certain evidence that the tide was on the ebb.

"I care nothing for your ins and outs, your ebbs and floods," returned the
Alderman, in heat. "There is no better time-piece than the leg and eye of a punctual man. It is no more pleasant to go before one is ready, than to tarry when all
business is done. Harkee, Master Schipper, you are not the only navigator in this
bay, nor is your craft the swiftest that was ever launched. Have a care; though an
acquiescing man by nature, I know how to encourage an opposition, when the

public good seriously calls for my support."

To the attack on himself, the schipper was stoically indifferent, but to impeach the qualities of the periagua was to attack one who depended solely on his eloquence for vindication. Removing his pipe, therefore, he rejoined on the Alderman, with that sort of freedom, that the sturdy Hollanders never failed to use to all offenders, regardless alike of rank or personal qualities.

"Der wind-gall and Aldermen!" he growled, in the dialect of the country; "I should be glad to see the boat in York-bay that can show the Milk-Maid her stern! The Mayor and council-men had better order the tide to turn when they please; and then as each man will think of his own pleasure, a pretty set of whirl-pools they will give us in the harbor!"

The schipper, having delivered himself of his sentiments, to this effect, resumed his pipe, like a man who felt he deserved the meed of victory, whether he were to receive it, or not.

"It is useless to dispute with an obstinate man," muttered the Alderman making his way through vegetable baskets, butter-tubs, and all the garniture of a market-boat, to the place occupied by his niece, in the stern-sheets. "Good morrow to thee Alida dear; early rising will make a flower-garden of thy cheeks, and the fresh air of the Lust in Rust will give even thy roses a deeper bloom."

The mollified burgher then saluted the cheek whose bloom had been deep-ened by his remark, with a warmth that showed he was not without natural affec-tion; touched his hat, in return for a low bow that he received from an aged white man-servant; in a clean but ancient livery; and nodded to a young negress, whose second-hand finery sufficiently showed she was a personal attendant of the heiress.

A second glance at Alida de Barbérie was scarcely necessary to betray her mixed descent. From her Norman father, a Huguenot of the petite noblesse, she had inherited her raven hair, the large, brilliant coal-black eyes, in which wildness was singularly relieved by sweetness, a classical and faultless profile, and a form which was both taller and more flexible than commonly fell to the lot of the damsels of Holland. From her mother, la belle Barbérie, as the maiden was often playfully termed, had received a skin, fair and spotless as the flower of France, and a bloom which rivalled the rich tints of an evening sky in her native land. Some of the em bon point, for which the sister of the Alderman had been a little remark-able, had descended also to her fairer daughter. In Alida, however, this peculiarity did not exceed the fullness which became her years, rounding her person and softening the outlines of her form, rather than diminishing its ease and grace

These personal advantages were embellished by a neat but modest travelling habit, a little beaver that was shaded by a cluster of drooping feathers, and a mien that, under the embarrassment of her situation preserved the happiest medium between modesty and perfect self-possession.

When Alderman Van Beverout joined this fair creature, in whose future happiness he was fully justified in taking the deep interest which he has betrayed in some of the opening scenes of this volume, he found her engaged in a courteous discourse with the young man, who was generally considered as the one, among the numerous pretenders to her favor, who was most likely to succeed. Had other cause been wanting, this sight alone would have been sufficient to restore his good-humor: and, making a place for himself, by quietly dispossessing François, the domestic of his niece, the persevering burgher endeavored to encourage an intercourse, that he had reason to think must terminate in the result he both meditated and desired.

In the present effort, however, the Alderman failed. There is a feeling which universally pervades landsmen and landswomen, when they first embark on an element to which they are strangers, that ordinarily shuts their mouths and renders them meditative. In the older and more observant travellers, it is observation and comparison; while with the younger and more susceptible, it is very apt to take the character of sentiment. Without stopping to analyze the cause, or the consequences, in the instance of the Patroon and la belle Barbérie, it will be sufficient to state, that in spite of all the efforts of the worthy burgher, who had navigated the sluggish creek too often to be the subject of any new emotions, his youthful companions gradually grew silent and thoughtful. Though a celibite in his own person, Myndert had not now to learn that the infant god as often does his mischief through this quiet agency, as in any other manner. He became, therefore, mute in his turn, watching the slow movement of the periagua with as much assiduity as if he saw his own image on the water.

A quarter of an hour of this characteristic, and it is to be inferred agreeable navigation, brought the boat to the mouth of the inlet. Here a powerful effort forced her into the tide's-way, and she might be said to put forth on her voyage. But while the black crew were trimming the sails, and making the other necessary preparations for departure, a voice was heard hailing them from the shore, with an order rather than a request, that they would stay their movements.

"Hilloa, the periagua!" it cried. "Haul over your head-sheet, and jam the tiller down into the lap of that comfortable-looking old gentleman. Come: bear a hand, my hummers! or your race-horse of a craft will get the bit into its mouth, and run away with you."

This summons produced a pause in the movements of the crew. After regarding each other, in surprise and admiration, the watermen drew the head-sheet over, put the helm a-lee, without however invading the lap of the Alderman, and the boat became stationary, at the distance of a few rods from the shore. While the new passenger was preparing to come off in a yawl, those who awaited his movements had leisure to examine his appearance, and to form their different surmises concerning his character.

It is scarcely necessary to say, that the stranger was a son of the ocean. He was of a firmly knit and active frame, standing exactly six feet in his stockings. The shoulders though square were compact, the chest full and high, the limbs round, neat, and muscular — the whole indicating a form in which strength and activity were apportioned with the greatest accuracy. A small bullet head was set firmly on its broad foundation, and it was thickly covered with a mass of brown hair that was already a little grizzled. The face was that of a man of thirty, and it was worthy of the frame, being manly, bold, decided, and rather handsome; though it expressed little more than high daring, perfect coolness, some obstinacy, and a certain degree of contempt for others, that its owner did not always take the trouble to conceal. The color was a rich, deep, and uniform red, such as much exposure is apt to give to men whose complexions are, by nature, light and florid.

The dress of the stranger was quite as remarkable as his person. He wore a short pea-jacket, cut tight and tastefully; a little, low, and rakish cap, and full bell-mouthed trowsers, all in a spotlessly white duck; a material well adapted to the season and the climate. The first was made without buttons, affording an apology for the use of a rich Indian shawl, that belted his body and kept the garment tight to his frame. Faultlessly clean linen appeared through the opening above, and a collar, of the same material, fell over the gay bandanna, which was thrown, with a single careless turn, around his throat. The latter was a manufacture then little known in Europe, and its use was almost entirely confined to seamen of the long voyage. One of its ends was suffered to blow about in the wind, but the other was brought down with care over the chest, where it was confined, by springing the blade of a small knife with an ivory handle, in a manner to confine the silk to the linen: a sort of breast-pin that is even now much used by mariners. If we add, that light, canvas slippers, with foul-anchors worked in worsted upon their insteps, covered his feet, we shall say all that is necessary of his attire.

The appearance of one, of the air and dress we have just described, excited a strong sensation among the blacks who scrubbed the stoops and pavements. He was closely attended to the place where he hailed the periagua, by four or five loungers, who studied his manner and movements with the admiration that men of their class seldom fail to bestow on those who bear about them the evidence of having passed lives of adventure, and perhaps of hardship and daring. Beckoning to one of these idlers to follow him, the hero of the India-shawl stepped into an empty boat, and casting loose its fast, he sculled the light yawl towards the craft which was awaiting his arrival. There was, in truth, something in the reckless air, the decision, and the manly attitudes of so fine a specimen of a seaman, that might have attracted notice from those who were more practised in the world than the little crowd of admirers he left behind him. With an easy play of wrist and elbow, he caused the yawl to glide ahead like some indolent marine animal swimming through its element, and as he stood, firm as a planted statue, with a foot on each gunwale, there was much of that confidence created by his steadiness, that one acquires by viewing the repeated and successful efforts of a skilful rope-dancer. When the yawl reached the side of the periagua, he dropped a small Spanish coin into the open palm of the negro, and sprang on the side of the latter, with an exertion of muscle that sent the little boat he quitted half-way back towards the shore, leaving the frightened black to steady himself, in his rocking tenement, in the best manner he could.

The tread and posture of the stranger, when he gained the half-deck of the periagua, was finely nautical, and confident to audacity. He seemed to analyze the half-maritime character of the crew and passengers, at a glance, and to feel that sort of superiority over his companions, which men of his profession were then a little too wont to entertain towards those whose ambition could be bounded by terra-firma. His eye turned upward, at the simple rig and modest sails of the periagua, while his upper lip curled with the knowing expression of a critic. Then kicking the fore-sheet clear of its elect, and suffering the sail to fill, he stepped from one butter-tub to another, making a stepping-stone of the lap of a countryman by the way, and alighted in the stern-sheets in the midst of the party of Alderman Van Beverout, with the agility and fearlessness of a feathered Mercury. With a coolness that did infinite credit to his powers for commanding, his next act was to dispossess the amazed schipper of the helm, taking the tiller into his own hands, with as much composure as if he were the every-day occupant of the post. When he saw that the boat was beginning to move through the water, he found leisure to bestow some observation on his fellow-voyagers. The first that met his bold and reckless eye was François, the domestic of Alida.

"If it come to blow in squalls, Commodore," observed the intruder, with a gravity that half deceived the attentive Frenchman, while he pointed to the bag in which the latter wore his hair, "you'll be troubled to carry your broad pennant. But so experienced an officer has not put to sea without having a storm-cue in readiness for foul weather."

The valet did not, or affected not to understand the allusion, maintaining an air of dignified but silent superiority.

"The gentleman is in a foreign service, and does not understand an English mariner! The worst that can come, after all, of too much top-hamper, is to cut away, and let it drift with the scud. May I make bold to ask, judge, if the courts have done any thing, of late, concerning the freebooters among the islands?"

"I have not the honor to bear Her Majesty's commission," coldly returned Van Staats of Kinderhook, to whom this question had been hardily put.

"The best navigator is sometimes puzzled by a hazy observation, and many an old seaman has taken a fog-bank for solid ground. Since you are not in the courts, Sir, I wish you joy; for it is running among shoals to be cruising there, whether as judge or suitor. One is never fairly snug and landlocked, while in company of a lawyer, and yet the devil himself cannot always give the sharks a good offing. A pretty sheet of water, friends, and one as snug as rotten cables and foul winds can render desirable, is this bay of York!"

"You are a mariner of the long voyage," returned the Patroon, unwilling that Alida should not believe him equal to bandying wits with the stranger.

"Long, or short; Calcutta, or Cape Cod; dead reckoning, eye-sight, or star-gazing, all's one to your real dolphin. The shape of the coast between Fundy and Horn, is as familiar to my eye, as an admirer to this pretty young lady; and as to the other shore, I have run it down oftener than the Commodore, here, has ever set his pennant, blow high or blow low. A cruise like this is a Sunday in my navigation; though I dare say, you took leave of the wife, blessed the children, overhauled the will, and sent to ask a good word from the priest, before you came aboard?"

"Had these ceremonies been observed, the danger would not have been increased," said the young Patroon, anxious to steal a glance at la belle Barbérie, though his timidity caused him, in truth, to look the other way. "One is never nearer danger, for being prepared to meet it."

"True; we must all die, when the reckoning is out. Hang or drown — gibbet or bullet clears the world of a great deal of rubbish, or the decks would get to be so littered that the vessel could not be worked. The last cruise is the longest of all; and honest papers, with a clean bill of health, may help a man into port, when he is past keeping the open sea. How now, schipper! what lies are floating about the docks this morning? when did the last Albany-man get his tub down the river, or whose gelding has been ridden to death in chase of a witch."

"The devil's babes!" muttered the Alderman; "there is no want of roisterers to torment such innocents!"

"Have the buccaneers taken to praying, or does their trade thrive in this heel of the war?" continued the mariner of the India-shawl, disregarding the complaint of the burgher. "The times are getting heavy for men of metal, as may be seen by the manner in which yon cruiser wears out her ground-tackle, instead of trying the open sea. May I spring every spar I carry, but I would have the boat out and give her an airing, before tomorrow, if the Queen would condescend to put your humble servant in charge of the craft! The man lies there, at his anchors, as if he had a good freight of real Hollands in his hold, and was waiting for a few bales of beaver-skins to barter for his strong waters."

As the stranger coolly expressed this opinion of Her Majesty's ship Coquette, he rolled his glance over the persons of his companions, suffering it to rest, a moment, with a secret significance, on the steady eye of the burgher.

"Well —" he continued, "the sloop answers for a floating vane to tell which way the tide is running, if she does nothing better; and that must be a great assistance, Schipper, in the navigation of one who keeps as bright a look-out on the manner in which the world whirls round, as a gentleman of your sagacity!"

"If the news in the creek be true," rejoined the unoffended owner of the periagua, "there will be other business for Captain Ludlow and the Coquette, before many days!"

"Ah! having eaten all his meat and bread, the man will be obliged to victual his ship anew! 'Twere a pity so active a gentleman should keep a fast, in a brisk tide's-way. And when his coppers are once more filled, and the dinner is fairly eaten, what dost think will be his next duty?"

"There is a report, among the boatmen of the South Bay, that something was seen, yester'night, off the outer side of Long Island!"

"I'll answer for the truth of that rumor, for having come up with the evening flood, I saw it myself."

"Der duyvel's luck! and what dost take it to be?"

"The Atlantic Ocean; if you doubt my word, I appeal to this well-ballasted old gentleman, who being a schoolmaster, is able to give you latitude and longitude for its truth."

"I am Alderman Van Beverout," muttered the object of this new attack, between his teeth, though apparently but half-disposed to notice one who set so little bounds to his discourse.

"I beg a thousand pardons!" returned the strange seaman, with a grave inclination of his body. "The stolidity of your worship's countenance deceived me. It may be, indeed, unreasonable to expect any Alderman to know the position of the Atlantic Ocean! And yet, gentlemen, on the honor of a man who has seen much salt water in his time, I do assure you the sea, I speak of, is actually there. If there be any thing on it, or in it, that should not in reason be so, this worthy commander of the periagua will let us know the rest."

"A wood-boat from the inlet says, the 'Skimmer of the Seas' was lately seen standing along the coast," returned the ferry-man, in the tone of one who is certain of delivering matter of general interest.

"Your true sea-dog, who runs in and out of inlets, is a man for marvels!" coolly observed the stranger. "They know the color of the sea at night, and are for ever steering in the wind's eye in search of adventures. I wonder, more of them are not kept at making almanacs! There was a mistake, concerning a thunder-storm, in the last I bought, and all for the want of proper science. And pray, friend, who is this 'Skimmer of the Seas,' that is said to be running after his needle, like a tailor who has found a hole in his neighbor's coat?"

"The witches may tell! I only know that such a rover there is, and that he is here today, and there tomorrow. Some say, it is only a craft of mist, that skims the top of the seas, like a sailing water-fowl, and others think it is the sprite of a vessel that was rifled and burnt by Kidd, in the Indian Ocean, looking for its gold and the killed. I saw him once, myself, but the distance was so great, and his manœuvres so unnatural, that I could hardly give a good account of his hull, or rig."

"This is matter that don't get into the log every watch! Whereaway, or in what seas, didst meet the thing?"

"'Twas off the Branch. We were fishing in thick weather, and when the mist lifted, a little, there was a craft seen standing in-shore, running like a race-horse; but while we got our anchor, she had made a league of offing, on the other tack!"

"A certain proof of either her, or your, activity! But what might have been the form and shape of your fly-away?"

"Nothing determined. To one she seemed a full-rigged and booming ship; another took her for a Bermudian scudder, while to me she had the look of twenty periaguas built into a single craft. It is well known, however, that a West-Indiaman went to sea that night, and, though it is now three years, no tidings of her, or her crew, have ever come to any in York. I have never gone upon the banks to fish since that day, in thick weather."

"You have done well," observed the stranger, "I have seen many wonderful sights, myself, on the rolling ocean; and he, whose business it is to lay between wind and water, like you, my friend, should never trust himself within reach of one of those devil's flyers I could tell you a tale of an affair in the calm latitudes, under the burning sun, that would be a lesson to all of over-bold curiosity! Commission and character are not affairs for your in-shore coaster."

"We have time to hear it," observed the Patroon, whose attention had been excited by the discourse, and who read in the dark eye of Alida that she felt an interest in the expected narrative.

But the countenance of the stranger suddenly grew serious. He shook his head, like one who had sufficient reasons for his silence; and, relinquishing the tiller, he quite coolly obliged a gaping countryman, in the centre of the boat, to yield his place, where he laid his own athletic form, at full length, folded his arms on his breast, and shut his eyes. In less than five minutes, all within hearing had audible evidence that this extraordinary son of the ocean was in a sound sleep.

CHAPTER IV.

" — Be patient, for the prize I'll bring thee to,
Shall hoodwink this mischance — ."
Tempest.

THE air, audacity, and language of the unknown mariner, had produced a marked sensation among the passengers of the periagua. It was plain, by the playfulness that lurked about the coal-black eye of la belle Barbérie, that she had been amused by his sarcasms, though the boldness of his manner had caused her to maintain the reserve which she believed necessary to her sex and condition. The Patroon studied the countenance of his mistress, and, though half offended by the freedom of the intruder, he had believed it wisest to tolerate his liberties, as the natural excesses of a spirit that had been lately released from the monotony of a sea-life. The repose which usually reigned in the countenance of the Alderman had been a little troubled; but he succeeded in concealing his discontent from any impertinent observation. When the chief actor in the foregoing scene, therefore, saw fit to withdraw, the usual tranquillity was restored, and his presence appeared to be forgotten.

An ebbing tide and a freshening breeze quickly carried the periagua past the smaller islands of the bay and brought the cruiser called the Coquette more distinctly into view. This vessel, a ship of twenty guns, lay abreast of the hamlet on the shores of Staten Island, which was the destination of the ferry-boat. Here was the usual anchorage of outward-bound ships, which awaited a change of wind; and it was here, that vessels then, as in our times, were subject to those examinations and delays which are imposed for the safety of the inhabitants of the city. The Coquette was alone, however; for the arrival of a trader, from a distant port, was an event of unfrequent occurrence, at the commencement of the eighteenth century.

The course of the periagua brought her within fifty feet of the sloop-of-war. As the former approached, a movement of curiosity and interest occurred among those she contained.

"Take more room for your milk-maid," grumbled the Alderman, observing that the schipper was willing to gratify his passengers, by running as near as possible to the dark sides of the cruiser. "Seas and oceans! is not York-bay wide enough, that you must brush the dust out of the muzzles of the guns of yon lazy ship? If the Queen knew how her money was eaten and drunk, by the idle knaves aboard her, she would send them all to hunt for freebooters among the islands. Look at the land, Alida, child, and you'll think no more of the fright the gaping dunce is giving thee; he only wishes to show his skill in steering."

But the niece manifested none of the terror that the uncle was willing to ascribe to her fears. Instead of turning pale, the color deepened on her cheeks, as the periagua came dancing along, under the lee of the cruiser; and if her respiration became quicker than usual, it was scarcely produced by the agitation of alarm. The near sight of the tall masts, and of the maze of cordage that hung nearly above their heads, however, prevented the change from being noted. A hundred curious eyes were already peeping at them, through the ports, or over the bulwarks of the ship, when suddenly, an officer, who wore the undress of a naval captain of that day, sprang into the main rigging of the cruiser, and saluted the party in the periagua, by waving his hat, hurriedly, like one who was agreeably taken by surprise.

"A fair sky and gentle breezes to each and all!" he cried with the hearty manner of a seaman. "I kiss my hand to the fair Alida; and the Alderman will take a sailor's good wishes; Mr. Van Staats, I salute you."

"Ay," muttered the burgher, "your idlers have nothing better to do, than to make words answer for deeds. A lazy war and a distant enemy make you seamen the lords of the land, Captain Ludlow."

Alida blushed still deeper, hesitated, and then, by a movement that was half involuntary, she waved her handkerchief. The young Patroon arose, and answered the salutation by a courteous bow. By this time the ferry-boat was nearly past the ship, and the scowl was quitting the face of the Alderman, when the mariner of the India-shawl sprang to his feet, and, in a moment, he stood again in the centre of their party.

"A pretty sea-boat, and a neat show aloft!" he said, as his understanding eye scanned the rigging of the royal cruiser, taking the tiller at the same time, with all his former indifference, from the hands of the schipper. "Her Majesty should have good service from such a racer, and no doubt the youth in her rigging is a man to get most out of his craft. We'll take another observation. Draw away your head-sheet, boy."

The stranger had put the helm a-lee, while speaking, and by the time the order he had given was uttered, the quick-working boat was about, and nearly filled on the other tack. In another minute, she was again brushing along the side of the sloop-of-war. A common complaint against this hardy interference with the regular duty of the boat, was about to break out of the lips of the Alderman and the schipper, when he of the India-shawl lifted his cap, and addressed the officer in the rigging, with all the self-possession he had manifested in the intercourse with those nearer his person.

"Has Her Majesty need of a man in her service who has seen, in his time, more blue water than hard ground; or is there no empty berth in so gallant a cruiser, for one who must do a seaman's duty, or starve?"

The descendant of the king-hating Ludlows, as the Lord Cornbury had styled the race of the commander of the Coquette, was quite as much surprised by the appearance of him who put this question, as he was by the coolness with which a mariner of ordinary condition presumed to address an officer who bore so high a commission as his own. He had, however, sufficient time to recollect in whose presence he stood, ere he replied, for the stranger had again placed the helm a-lee, and caused the foresail to be thrown aback — a change that made the periagua stationary.

"The Queen will always receive a bold mariner in her pay, if he come prepared to serve with skill and fidelity," he said; "as a proof of which, let a rope be thrown the periagua; we shall treat more at our ease under Her Majesty's pennant. I shall be proud to entertain Alderman Van Beverout, in the mean time: and a cutter will always be at his command, when he shall have occasion to quit us."

"Your land-loving Aldermen find their way from a Queen's cruiser to the shore, more easily than a seaman of twenty years' experience;" returned the other, without giving the burgher time to express his thanks for the polite offer of the other. "You have gone through the Gibraltar passage, without doubt, noble captain, being a gentleman that has got so fine a boat under his orders?"

"Duty has taken me into the Italian seas, more than once," answered Ludlow, half disposed to resent this familiarity, though too anxious to keep the periagua near, to quarrel with him who so evidently had produced the unexpected pleasure.

"Then you know that, though a lady might fan a ship through the straits eastward, it needs a Levant breeze to bring her out again. Her Majesty's pennants are long, and when they get foul around the limbs of a thoroughly-bred sea-dog, it passes all his art to clear the jam. It is most worthy of remark that the better the seaman, the less his power to cast loose the knot!"

"If the pennant be so long, it may reach farther than you wish! — But a bold volunteer has no occasion to dread a press."

"I fear the berth I wish is filled," returned the other, curling his lip: "let draw the fore-sheet, lad; we will take our departure, leaving the fly of the pennant well under our lee. Adieu, brave Captain; when you have need of a thorough rover, and dream of stern-chases and wet sails, think of him who visited your ship at her lazy moorings."

Ludlow bit his lip, and though his fine face reddened to the temples, he met the arch glance of Alida, and laughed. But he who had so hardily braved the resentment of a man, powerful as the commander of a royal cruiser in a British colony, appeared to understand the hazard of his situation. The periagua whirled round on her heel, and the next minute it was bending to the breeze, and dashing through the little waves towards the shore. Three boats left the cruiser at the same moment. One, which evidently contained her captain, advanced with the usual dignified movement of a barge landing an officer of rank, but the others were urged ahead with all the earnestness of a hot chase.

"Unless disposed to serve the Queen, you have not done well, my friend, to brave one of her commanders at the muzzles of his guns." observed the Patroon, so soon as the state of the case became too evident to doubt of the intentions of the man-of-war's men.

"That Captain Ludlow would gladly take some of us out of this boat, by fair means or by foul, is a fact clear as a bright star in a cloudless night; and, well knowing a seaman's duty to his superiors, I shall leave him to his choice."

"In which case you will shortly eat Her Majesty's bread," pithily returned the Alderman.

"The food is unpalatable, and I reject it — and yet here is a boat, whose' crew seem determined to make one swallow worse fare."

The unknown mariner ceased speaking, for the situation of the periagua, was truly getting to be a little critical. At least so it seemed to the less-instructed landsmen, who were witnesses of this unexpected rencontre. As the ferry-boat had drawn in with the island, the wind hauled more through the pass which communicates with the outer bay, and it became necessary to heave about, twice, in order to fetch to windward of the usual landing-place. The first of these manœuvres had been executed, and as it necessarily changed their course, the passengers saw that the cutter to which the stranger alluded was enabled to get within-shore of them; or nearer to the wharf, where they ought to land, than they were themselves. Instead of suffering himself to be led off by a pursuit, that he knew might easily be rendered useless, the officer who commanded this boat cheered his men, and pulled swiftly to the point of debarkation. On the other hand, a second cutter, which had already reached the line of the periagua's course, lay on its oars, and awaited its approach. The unknown mariner manifested no intention to avoid the interview. He still held the tiller, and as effectually commanded the little vessel as if his authority were of a more regular character. The audacity and decision of his air and conduct, aided by the consummate mariner in which he worked the boat, might alone have achieved this momentary usurpation, had not the general feeling against impressment been so much in his favor.

"The devil's fangs!" grumbled the schipper. "If you should keep the Milk-Maid away, we shall lose a little in distance, though I think the man-of-war's men will be puzzled to catch her, with a flowing sheet!"

"The Queen has sent a message by the gentleman," the mariner rejoined: "it would be unmannerly to refuse to hear it."

"Heave-to, the periagua!" shouted the young officer, in the cutter. "In Her Majesty's name, I command you, obey."

"God bless the royal lady!" returned he of the foul anchors and gay shawl, while the swift ferry-boat continued to dash ahead. "We owe her duty, and are glad to see so proper a gentleman employed in her behalf."

By this time the boats were fifty feet asunder. No sooner was there room, than the periagua once more flew round, and commenced anew its course, dashing in again towards the shore. It was necessary, however, to venture within an oar's-length of the cutter, or to keep away — a loss of ground to which he who controlled her movements showed no disposition to submit. The officer arose, and, as the periagua drew near, it was evident his hand held a pistol, though he seemed reluctant to exhibit the weapon. The mariner stepped aside, in a manner to offer a full view of all in his group, as he sarcastically observed —

"Choose your object, Sir; in such a party, a man of sentiment may have a preference."

The young man colored, as much with shame at, the degrading duty he had been commissioned to perform, as with vexation at his failure. Recovering his self-composure, however, he lifted his hat to la belle Barbérie, and the periagua dashed on, in triumph. Still the leading cutter was near the shore, where it soon arrived, the crew lying on their oars at the end of the wharf, in evident expectation of the arrival of the ferry-boat. At this sight, the schipper shook his head, and looked up in the bold face of his passenger, in a manner to betray how much his mind misgave the result. But the tall mariner maintained his coolness, and began to make merry allusions to the service which he had braved with so much temerity, and from which no one believed he was yet likely to escape. By the former manœuvres, the periagua had gained a position well to windward of the wharf; and she was now steered close upon the wind, directly for the shore. Against the consequences of a perseverance in this course, however, the schipper saw fit to remonstrate.

"Shipwrecks and rocky bottoms!" exclaimed the alarmed waterman. "A Holland galliot would go to pieces, if you should run her in among those stepping-stones, with this breeze! No honest boatman loves to see a man stowed in a cruiser's hold, like a thief caged in his prison; but when it comes to breaking the nose of the Milk-Maid, it is asking too much of her owner, to stand by and look on."

"There shall not be a dimple of her lovely countenance deranged," answered his cool passenger. "Now, lower away your sails, and we'll run along the shore, down to yon wharf. 'Twould be an ungallant act to treat the dairy-girl with so little ceremony, gentlemen, after the lively foot and quick evolutions she has shown in our behalf. The best dancer in the island could not have better played her part, though jigging under the music of a three-stringed fiddle!"

By this time the sails were lowered, and the periagua was gliding down towards the place of landing, running always at the distance of some fifty feet from the shore.

"Every craft has its allotted time, like a mortal," continued the inexplicable mariner of the India-shawl. "If she is to die a sudden death, there is your beam-end and stern-way, which takes her into the grave without funeral service, or parish prayers; your dropsy is being water-logged; gout and rheumatism kill like a broken back and loose joints; indigestion is a shifting cargo, with guns adrift; the gallows is a bottomry-bond, with lawyers' fees; while fire, drowning, death by religious melancholy, and suicide, are a careless gunner, sunken rocks, false lights, and a lubberly captain."

Ere any were apprized of his intention, this singular being then sprang from the boat on the cap of a little rock, over which the waves were washing, whence he bounded, from stone to stone, by vigorous efforts, till he fairly leaped to land. In another minute, he was lost to view, among the dwellings of the hamlet.

The arrival of the periagua, which immediately after reached the wharf, the disappointment of the cutter's crew, and the return of both the boats to their ship, succeeded as matters of course.

CHAPTER V.

Oliv. "Did he write this?"
Clo. "Ay, Madam."
                    What You Will.

IF we say that Alida de Barbérie did not cast a glance behind her, as the party quitted the wharf, in order to see whether the boat that contained the commander of the cruiser followed the example of the others, we shall probably portray the maiden as one that was less subject to the influence of coquetry than the truth would justify. To the great discontent of the Alderman, whatever might have been the feelings of his niece, on the occasion, the barge continued to approach the shore, in a manner which showed that the young seaman betrayed no visible interest in the result of the chase.

The heights of Staten Island, a century ago, were covered, much as they are at present, with a growth of dwarf-trees. Foot-paths led among this meagre vegetation, in divers directions; and as the hamlet at the Quarantine-Ground was the point whence they all diverged, it required a practised guide to thread their mazes, without a loss of both time and distance. It would seem, however, that the worthy burgher was fully equal to the office; for, moving with more than his usual agility, he soon led his companions into the wood, and, by frequently altering his course, so completely confounded their sense of the relative bearings of places, that it is not probable one of them all could very readily have extricated himself from the labyrinth.

"Clouds and shady bowers!" exclaimed Myndert, when he had achieved, to his own satisfaction, this evasion of the pursuit he wished to avoid; "little oaks and green pines are pleasant on a June morning. You shall have mountain air and a sea-breeze Patroon, to quicken the appetite at the Lust in Rust. If Alicia will speak, the girl can say that a mouthful of the elixir is better for a rosy cheek, than all the concoctions and washes that were ever invented to give a man a heart-ache."

"If the place be as much changed as the road that leads to it," returned la belle Barbérie, glancing her dark eye, in vain, in the direction of the bay they had quitted, "I should scarcely venture an opinion on a subject of which I am obliged to confess utter ignorance."

"Ah, woman is nought but vanities! To see and to be seen, is the delight of

41

the sex. Though we are a thousand times more comfortable in this wood than we should be in walking along the water-side, why, the sea-gulls and snipes lose the benefit of our company! The salt water, and all who live on it, are to be avoided by a wise man, Mr. Van Staats, except as they both serve to cheapen freight and to render trade brisk. You'll thank me for this care, niece of mine, when you reach the bluff, cool as a package of furs free from moth, and fresh and beautiful as a Holland tulip, with the dew on it."

"To resemble the latter, one might consent to walk blindfold, dearest uncle; and so we dismiss the subject. François, fais moi le plaisir de porter ce petit livre; malgré la fraîcheur de la fôret, j'ai besoin de m'évanter."

The valet took the book, with an empressement that defeated the more tardy politeness of the Patroon; and when he saw, by the vexed eye and flushed cheek of his young mistress, that she was incommoded rather by an internal than by the external heat, he whispered considerately —

"Que ma chère Mademoiselle Alide ne se fâche pas! Elle ne manquerait jamais d'admirateurs, dans un désert. Ah! si Mam'selle allait voir la patrie de ses ancêtres! —"

"Merci bien, mon cher; gardez les feuilles, fortement fermées. Il y a des papiers dedans."

"Monsieur François," said the Alderman, separating his niece, with little ceremony, from her nearly parental attendant, by the interposition of his own bulky person, and motioning for the others to proceed, "a word with thee in confidence. I have noted, in the course of a busy and I hope a profitable life, that a faithful servant is an honest counsellor. Next to Holland and England, both of which are great commercial nations, and the Indies, which are necessary to these colonies, together with a natural preference for the land in which I was born, I have always been of opinion, that France is a very good sort of a country. I think, Mr. Francis, that dislike to the seas has kept you from returning thither, since the decease of my late brother-in-law?"

"Wid like for Mam'selle Alide, Monsieur, avec votre permission."

"Your affection for my niece, honest François, is not to be doubted. It is as certain as the payment of a good draft, by Crommeline, Van Stopper, and Van Gelt, of Amsterdam. Ah! old valet! she is fresh and blooming as a rose, and a girl of excellent qualities! 'Tis a pity that she is a little opinionated; a defect that she doubtless inherits from her Norman ancestors; since all of my family have ever been remarkable for listening to reason. The Normans were an obstinate race, as witness the siege of Rochelle, by which oversight real estate in that city must have lost much in value!"

"Mille excuses, Monsieur Bevre' — ; more beautiful as de rose, and no opinâtre du tout. Mon Dieu! pour sa qualité, c'est une famille tres ancienne."

"That was a weak point with my brother Barbérie, and, after all, it did not add a cipher to the sum-total of the assets. The best blood, Mr. François, is that which has been best fed. The line of Hugh Capet himself would fail, without the butcher; and the butcher would certainly fail, without customers that can pay. François, thou art a man who understands the value of a sure footing in the world; would it not be a thousand pities, that such a girl as Alida should throw herself away on one whose best foundation is no better than a rolling ship?"

"Certainement, Monsieur; Mam'selle be too good to roll in de ship."

"Obliged to follow a husband, up and down; among freebooters and dishonest traders; in fair weather and foul; hot and cold; wet and dry; bilge-water and salt-water; cramps and nausea; salt-junk and no junk; gales and calms — and all for a hasty judgment formed in sanguine youth."

The face of the valet had responded to the Alderman's enumeration of the evils that would attend so ill-judged a step in his niece, as faithfully as if each muscle had been a mirror, to reflect the contortions of one suffering under the malady of the sea.

"Parbleu, c'est horrible cette mer!" he ejaculated; when the other had done. "It is grand malheur, dere should be watair but for drink, and for la propreté, avec fosse to keep de carp round le château. Mais, Mam'selle be no haste jugement, and she shall have mari on la terre solide."

"'Twould be better, that the estate of my brother-in-law should be kept in sight, judicious François, than to be sent adrift on the high seas."

"Dere vas marin dans la famille de Barbérie nevair."

"Bonds and balances! if the savings of one I could name, frugal François, were added in current coin the sum-total would sink a common ship. You know it is my intention to remember Alida, in settling accounts with the world."

"If Monsieur de Barbérie vas 'live, Monsieur Alderman, he should say des choses convenables; mais, malheureusement, mon chèr, maître est mort; and, sair, I shall be bold to remercier pour lui, et pour toute sa famille."

"Women are perverse, and sometimes they have pleasure in doing the very thing they are desired not to do."

"Ma foi, oui!"

"Prudent men should manage them with soft words and rich gifts; with these, they become orderly as a pair of well-broke geldings."

"Monsieur know," said the old valet, rubbing his hands, and laughing with the subdued voice of a well-bred domestic, though he could not conceal a jocular wink; "pourtant il est garcon! Le cadeau be good for de demoiselles, and bettair as for de dames."

"Wedlock and blinkers! it is we gâssons, as you call us, who ought to know. Your hen-pecked husband has no time to generalize among the sex, in order to understand the real quality of the article. Now, here is Van Staats of Kinderhook, faithful François; what think you of such a youth for a husband for Alida?"

"Pourtant, Mam'selle like de vivacité; Monsieur le Patroon be nevair trop vif."

"The more likely to be sure — Hist, I hear a footstep. We are followed — chased, perhaps, I should say, to speak in the language of these sea-gentry. Now is the time to show this Captain Ludlow, how a Frenchman can wind him round his finger, on terra-firma. Loiter in the rear, and draw our navigator on a wrong course. When he has run into a fog, come yourself, with all speed, to the oak on the bluff. There we shall await you."

Flattered by this confidence, and really persuaded that he was furthering the happiness of her he served, the old valet nodded, in reply to the Alderman's wink and chuckle, and immediately relaxed his speed. The former pushed ahead; and, in a minute, he and those who followed had turned short to the left, and were out of sight.

Though faithfully and even affectionately attached to Alida, her servant had many of the qualifications of an European domestic. Trained in all the ruses of his profession, he was of that school which believes civilization is to be measured by artifice; and success lost some of its value, when it had been effected by the vulgar machinery of truth and common sense. No wonder then the retainer entered into the views of the Alderman, with more than a usual relish for the duty. He heard the cracking of the dried twigs beneath the footstep of him who followed; and in order that there might be no chance of missing the desired interview, the valet began to hum a French air, in so loud a key, as to be certain the sounds would reach any ear that was nigh. The twigs snapped more rapidly, the footsteps seemed nearer, and then the hero of the India-shawl sprang to the side of the expecting François.

The disappointment seemed mutual, and on the part of the domestic it entirely disconcerted all his pre-arranged schemes for misleading the commander of the Coquette. Not so with the bold mariner. So far from his self-possession being disturbed, it would have been no easy matter to restrain his audacity ever in situations far more trying than any in which he has yet been presented to the reader.

"What cheer, in thy woodland cruise, Monsieur Broad-Pennant?" he said, with infinite coolness, the instant his steady glance had ascertained they were alone. "This is safer navigation for an officer of thy draught of water, than running about the bay, in a periagua. What may be the longitude, and where-a-way did you part company from the consorts?"

"Sair, I valk in de vood for de plaisir, and I go on de bay for de — parbleu, non! 'tis to follow ma jeune maîtresse I go on de bay; and, sair, I wish dey who do love de bay and de sea, would not come into de vood, du tout."

"Well spoken, and with ample spirit — what, a student too! one in a wood should glean something from his labors. Is it the art of furling a main cue, that is taught in this pretty volume?"

As the mariner put his question, he very deliberately took the book from François, who, instead of resenting the liberty, rather offered the volume, in exultation.

"No, sair, it is not how to furl la queue, but how to touch de soul; not de art to haul over de calm, but — oui, c'est plein de connoissance et d'esprit! Ah! ha! you know de Cid! le grand homme! l'homme de génie! If you read, Monsieur Marin, you shall see la vraie poésie! Not de big book and no single rhyme — Sair, I do not vish to say vat is penible, mais it is not one book widout rhyme; it was not écrit on de sea. Le diable! que le vrai génie, et les nobles sentiments, se trouvent dans ce livre, la!"

"Ay, I see it is a log-book, for every man to note his mind in. I return you Master Cid, with his fine sentiments, in the bargain. Great as was his genius, it would seem he was not the man to write all that I find between the leaves."

"He not write him all! Yes, sair, he shall write him six time more dan all, if la France a besoin. Que l'envie de ces Anglais se découvre quand on parle des beaux génies de la France!"

"I will only say, if the gentleman wrote the whole that is in the book, and it is as fine as you would make a plain seafaring man believe, he did wrong not to print it."

"Print!" echoed François, opening his eyes, and the volume, by a common impulse, "Imprimé! ha! here is papier of Mam'selle Alide, assurément."

"Take better heed of it then," interrupted the seaman of the shawl. "As for your Cid, to me it is an useless volume, since it teaches neither the latitude of a shoal, nor the shape of a coast."

"Sair, it teach de morale; de rock of de passion et les grands mouvements de l'ame! Oui, Sair; it teach all, un Monsieur vish to know. Tout le monde read him in la France; en province, comme en ville. If sa Majesté, le Grand Louis, be not so mal avisé, as to chasser Messieurs les Huguenots from his royaume, I shall go to Paris, to hear le Cid, moi-même!"

"A good journey to you, Monsieur Cue. We may meet on the road, until which time I take my departure. The day may come, when we shall converse with a rolling sea beneath us. Till then, brave cheer!"

"Adieu, Monsieur," returned François, bowing with a politeness that had become too familiar to be forgotten. "If we do not meet but in de sea, we shall not meet, nevair. Ah, ha, ha! Monsieur le Marin n'aime pas à entendre parler de la gloire de la France! Je voudrais bien savoir lire ce f — e Shak-a-spear, pour voir, combien l'immortel Corneille lui est supérieur. Ma foi, oui; Monsieur Pierre Corneille est vraiment un homme illustre!"

The faithful, self-complacent, and aged valet then pursued his way towards the large oak on the bluff; for as he ceased speaking, the mariner of the gay sash had turned deeper into the woods, and left him alone. Proud of the manner, in which he had met the audacity of the stranger, prouder still of the reputation of the author, whose fame had been known in France long before his own departure from Europe, and not a little consoled with the reflection that he had contributed his mite to support the honor of his distant and well-beloved country, the honest François pressed the volume affectionately beneath his arm, and hastened on after his mistress.

Though the position of Staten Island and its surrounding bays is so familiar to the Manhattanese an explanation of the localities may be agreeable to readers who dwell at a distance from the scene of the tale.

It has already been said, that the principal communication between the bays of Raritan and York, is called the Narrows. At the mouth of this passage, the land on Staten Island rises in a high bluff, which overhangs the water, not unlike the tale-fraught cape of Misenum. From this elevated point, the eye not only commands a view of both estuaries and the city, but it looks far beyond the point of Sandy-Hook, into the open sea. It is here that, in our own days, ships are first noted in the offing, and whence the news of the approach of his vessel is communicated to the expecting merchant by means of the telegraph. In the early part of the last century, arrivals were too rare to support such an establishment. The bluff was therefore little resorted to, except by some occasional admirer of scenery, or by those countrymen whom business, at long intervals, drew to the spot. It had been early cleared of its wood, and the oak already mentioned was the only tree standing in a space of some ten or a dozen acres.

It has been seen that Alderman Van Beverout had appointed this solitary oak, as the place of rendezvous with François. Thither then he took his way on parting from the valet, and to this spot we must now transfer the scene. A rude seat had been placed around the root of the tree, and here the whole party, with the exception of the absent domestic, were soon seated: In a minute, however, they were joined by the exulting François, who immediately related the particulars of his recent interview with the stranger.

"A clear conscience, with cordial friends, and a fair balance-sheet, may keep a man warm in January, even in this climate," said the Alderman, willing to turn the discourse; "but what with rebellious blacks, hot streets, and spoiling furs, it passeth mortal powers to keep cool in yonder overgrown and crowded town. Thou seest, Patroon, the spot of white on the opposite side of the bay. Breezes and fanning! that is the Lust in Rust, where cordial enters the mouth at every breath, and where a man has room to cast up the sum-total of his thoughts, any hour in the twenty-four."

"We seem quite as effectually alone on this hill, with the advantage of having a city in the view," remarked Alida, with an emphasis that showed she meant even more than she expressed.

"We are by ourselves, niece of mine," returned the Alderman, rubbing his hands as if he secretly felicitated himself that the fact were so. "That truth cannot be denied, and good company we are, though the opinion comes from one who is not a cipher in the party. Modesty is a poor man's wealth, but as we grow substantial in the world, Patroon, one can afford to begin to speak truth of himself, as well as of his neighbor."

"In which case, little, but good, will be uttered from the mouth of Alderman Van Beverout," said Ludlow, appearing so suddenly from behind the root of the tree, as effectually to shut the mouth of the burgher. "My desire to offer the services of the ship to your party, has led to this abrupt intrusion, and I hope will obtain its pardon."

"The power to forgive is a prerogative of the Governor, who represents the Queen," drily returned the Alderman. "If Her Majesty has so little employment for her cruisers, that their captains can dispose of them, in behalf of old men and young maidens — why, happy is the age, and commerce should flourish!"

"If the two duties are compatible, the greater the reason why a commander should felicitate himself that he may be of service to so many. You are bound to the Jersey Highlands, Mr. Van Beverout?"

"I am bound to a comfortable and very private abode, called the Lust in Rust, Captain Cornelius Van Cuyler Ludlow."

The young man bit his lip, and his healthful but brown cheek flushed a deeper red than common, though he preserved his composure.

"And I am bound to sea," he soon said. "The wind is getting fresh, and your boat, which I see, at this moment, standing in for the islands, will find it difficult to make way against its force. The Coquette's anchor will be aweigh, in twenty minutes; and I shall find two hours of an ebbing tide, and a top-gallant breeze, but too short a time for the pleasure of entertaining such guests. I am certain that the fears of la Belle will favor my wishes, whichsoever side of the question her inclinations may happen to be."

"And they are with her uncle;" quickly returned Alida. "I am so little of a sailor, that prudence, if not pusillanimity, teaches me to depend on the experience of older heads."

"Older I may not pretend to be," said Ludlow, coloring; "but Mr. Van Beverout will see no pretension in believing myself as good a judge of wind and tide, as even he himself can be."

"You are said to command Her Majesty's sloop with skill, Captain Ludlow, and it is creditable to the colony, that it has produced so good an officer; though I believe your grandfather came into the province, so lately as on the restoration of King Charles the Second?"

"We cannot claim descent from the United Provinces, Alderman Van Beverout, on the paternal side, but whatever may have been the political opinions of my grandfather, those of his descendant have never been questioned. Let me entreat the fair Alida to take counsel of the apprehension I am sure she feels, and to persuade her uncle that the Coquette is safer than his periagua."

"It is said to be easier to enter than to quit your ship," returned the laughing Alida. "By certain symptoms that attended our passage to the island, your Coquette, like others, is fond of conquest. One is not safe beneath so malign an influence."

"This is a reputation given by our enemies. I had hoped for a different answer from la belle Barbérie."

The close of the sentence was uttered with an emphasis that caused the blood to quicken its movement in the veins of the maiden. It was fortunate that neither of their companions was very observant, or else suspicions might have been excited, that a better intelligence existed between the young sailor and the heiress, than would have comported with their wishes and intentions.

"I had hoped for a different answer from la belle Barbérie," repeated Ludlow, in a lower voice, but with even a still more emphatic tone than before.

There was evidently a struggle in the mind of Alida. She overcame it, before her confusion could be noted; and, turning to the valet, she said, with the composure and grace that became a gentlewoman —

"Rends moi le livre, François."

"Le voici — ah! ma chère Mam'selle Alide, que ce Monsieur le marin se fâchait à cause de la gloire, et des beaux vers de notre illustre M. Pierre Corneille!"

"Here is an English sailor, that I am sure will not deny the merit of an admired writer, even though he come of a nation that is commonly thought hostile, François," returned his mistress, smiling "Captain Ludlow, it is now a month since I am your debtor, by promise, for a volume of Corneille, and I here acquit myself of the obligation. When you have perused the contents of this book, with the attention they deserve, I may hope —"

"For a speedy opinion of their merits."

"I was about to say, to receive the volume again, as it is a legacy from my father," steadily rejoined Alida.

"Legacies and foreign tongues!" muttered the Alderman. "One is well enough; but for the other, English and Dutch are all that the wisest man need learn. I never could understand an account of protit and loss in any other tongue, Patroon; and even a favorable balance never appears so great as it is, unless the account be rendered in one or the other of these rational dialects. Captain Ludlow, we thank you for your politeness, but here is one of my fellows to tell us that my own periagua is arrived; and, wishing you a happy and a long cruise, as we say of lives, I bid you, adieu."

The young seaman returned the salutations of the party, with a better grace than his previous solicitude to persuade them to enter his ship, might have given reason to expect. He even saw them descend the hill, towards the water of the outer bay, with entire composure; and it was only after they had entered a thicket which hid them from view, that he permitted his feelings to have sway.

Then indeed he drew the volume from his pocket and opened its leaves with an eagerness he could no longer control. It seemed as if he expected to read more, in the pages, than the author had caused to be placed there; but when his eye caught sight of a sealed billet, the legacy of M. de Barbérie fell at his feet; and the paper was torn asunder, with all the anxiety of one who expected to find in its contents a decree of life or death.

Amazement was clearly the first emotion of the young seaman. He read and re-read; struck his brow with his hand; gazed about him at the land and at the water; re-perused the note; examined the superscription, which was simply to 'Capt. Ludlow, of Her Majesty's ship Coquette:' smiled; muttered between his teeth; seemed vexed, and yet delighted; read the note again, word by word, and finally thrust it into his pocket, with the air of a man who had found reason for both regret and satisfaction in its contents.

CHAPTER VI.

" — What, has this thing appeared again, tonight?"

Hamlet.

"The face of man is the log-book of his thoughts, and Captain Ludlow's seems agreeable," observed a voice, that came from one, who was not far from the commander of the Coquette, while the latter was still enacting the pantomime described in the close of the preceding chapter.

"Who speaks of thoughts and log-books or who dares to pry into my movements?" demanded the young sailor, fiercely.

"One who has trifled with the first and scribbled in the last too often, not to know how to meet a squall, whether it be seen in the clouds or only on the face of man. As for looking into your movements, Captain Ludlow, I have watched too many big ships in my time, to turn aside at each light cruiser that happens to cross my course. I hope, Sir, you have an answer; every hail has its right to a civil reply."

Ludlow could scarce believe his senses, when, on turning to face the intruder, he saw himself confronted by the audacious eye and calm mien of the mariner who had, once before that morning, braved his resentment. Curbing his indignation, however, the young man endeavored to emulate the coolness which, notwithstanding his inferior condition, imparted to the air of the other something that was imposing, if it were not absolutely authoritative. Perhaps the singularity of the adventure aided in effecting an object, that was a little difficult of attainment in one accustomed to receive so much habitual deference from most of those who made the sea their home. Swallowing his resentment, the young commander answered —

"He that knows how to face his enemies with spirit, may be accounted sufficiently bold; but he who braves the anger of his friends, is fool-hardy."

"And he who does neither, is wiser than both," rejoined the reckless hero of the sash. "Captain Ludlow, we meet on equal terms, at present, and the parley may be managed with some freedom."

"Equality is a word that ill applies to men of stations so different."

"Of our stations and duties it is not necessary to speak. I hope that, when the proper time shall come, both may be found ready to be at the first, and equal to discharge the last. But Captain Ludlow, backed by the broadside of the Coquette

51

and the cross-fire of his marines, is not Captain Ludlow alone, on a sea bluff, with a crutch no better than his own arm, and a stout heart. As the first, he is like a spar supported by backstays and forestays, braces and standing rigging; while, as the latter, he is the stick, which keeps its head aloft by the soundness and quality of its timber. You have the appearance of one who can go alone, even though it blew heavier than at present, if one may judge of the force of the breeze, by the manner it presses on the sails of yonder boat in the bay."

"Yonder boat begins to feel the wind, truly!" said Ludlow, suddenly losing all other interest in the appearance of the periagua which held Alida and her friends, and which, at that instant, shot out from beneath the cover of the hill into the broad opening of Raritan bay. "What think you of the time, my friend? a man of your years should speak with knowledge of the weather."

"Women and winds are only understood, when fairly in motion," returned he of the sash; "now, any mortal who consulted comfort and the skies, would have preferred a passage in Her Majesty's ship Coquette, to one in yonder dancing periagua; and yet the fluttering silk we see, in the boat, tells us there is one who has thought otherwise."

"You are a man of singular intelligence," cried Ludlow, again facing the intruder; "as well as one of singular —"

"Effrontery," rejoined the other, observing that the commander hesitated. "Let the commissioned officer of the Queen speak boldly; I am no better than a top-man, or at most a quarter-master."

"I wish to say nothing disagreeable, but I find your knowledge of my offer to convey the lady and her friends to the residence of Alderman Van Beverout, a little surprising."

"And I see nothing to wonder at, in your offer to convey the lady anywhere, though the liberality to her friends is not an act of so clear explanation. When young men speak from the heart, their words are not uttered in whispers."

"Which would imply that you overheard our conversation. I believe it, for here is cover at hand to conceal you. It may be, Sir, that you have eyes, as well as ears."

"I confess to have seen your countenance, changing sides, like a member of parliament turning to a new leaf in his conscience, at the Minister's signal while you overhauled a bit of paper —"

"Whose contents you could not know!"

"Whose contents I took to be some private orders, given by a lady who is too much of a coquette herself, to accept your offer to sail in a vessel of the same name."

"By Heavens, the fellow has reason in his inexplicable impudence!" muttered Ludlow, pacing backward and forward beneath the shadow of the tree. "The language and the acts of the girl are in contradiction; and I am a fool to be trifled with, like a midshipman fresh broken loose from his mother's apron-string. Harkee, Master-a-a — You've a name I suppose, like any other straggler on the ocean."

"Yes. When the hail is loud enough to be heard, I answer to the call of Thomas Tiller."

"Well then, Master Tiller, so clever a seaman should be glad to serve the Queen."

"Were it not for duty to another, whose claim comes first, nothing could be more agreeable than to lend a lady in distress a helping hand."

"And who is he, who may prefer a claim to your services, in competition with the majesty of these realms?" demanded Ludlow, with a little of the pretension that, when speaking of its privileges, is apt to distinguish the manner of one who has been accustomed to regard royalty with reverence.

"Myself. When our affairs call us the same way no one can be readier than I, to keep Her Majesty's company; but —"

"This is presuming too far, on the trifling of a moment," interrupted Ludlow; "you know, sirrah, that I have the right to command your services, without entering into a parley for them; and which, notwithstanding your gay appearance, may, after all, be little worth the trouble."

"There is no need to push matters to extremity, between us, Captain Ludlow," resumed the stranger who had appeared to muse for a moment, "If I have baffled your pursuit once today, it was perhaps to make my merit in entering the ship freely, less undeniable. We are here alone, and your Honor will account it no boasting, if I say that a man, well limbed and active, who stands six feet between plank and earline, is not likely to be led against his will, like a yawl towing at the stern of a four-and-forty. I am a seaman, Sir; and though the ocean is my home, I never venture on it without sufficient footing. Look abroad from this hill, and say whether there is any craft in view, except the cruiser of the Queen, which would be likely to suit the taste of a mariner of the long voyage?"

"By which you would have me understand, you are here in quest of service?"

"Nothing less; and though the opinion of a fore-mast Jack may be of little value, you will not be displeased to hear, that I might look further without finding a prettier sea-boat, or a swifter, than the one which sails under your own orders. A seaman of your station, Captain Ludlow, is not now to learn, that a man speaks differently, while his name is his own, and after he has given it away to the crown; and therefore I hope my present freedom will not be long remembered."

"I have met men of your humor before, my friend, and I have not now to learn, that a thorough man-of-war's man is as impudent on shore, as he is obedient afloat. Is that a sail, in the offing, or is it the wing of a sea-fowl, glittering in the sun?"

"It may be either," observed the audacious mariner, turning his eye leisurely towards the open ocean, "for we have a wide look-out from this windy bluff. Here are gulls sporting above the waves, that turn their feathers towards the light."

"Look more seaward. That spot of shining white should be the canvas of some craft, hovering in the offing!"

"Nothing more probable, in so light a breeze Your coasters are in and out, like water-rats on a wharf, at any hour of the twenty-four — and yet to me it seems the comb of a breaking sea."

"'Tis snow-white duck; such as your swift rover wears on his loftier spars!"

"A duck that is flown," returned the stranger drily, "for it is no longer to be seen. These fly-aways, Captain Ludlow, give us seamen many sleepless nights and idle chases. I was once running down the coast of Italy, between the island of Corsica and the main, when one of these delusions beset the crew, in a manner that hath taught me to put little faith in eyes, unless backed by a clear horizon and a cool head."

"I'll hear the circumstance," said Ludlow, withdrawing his gaze from the distant ocean, like one who was satisfied his senses had been deceived. "What of this marvel of the Italian seas?"

"A marvel truly, as your Honor will confess, when I read you the affair, much in the words I had it logged, for the knowledge of all concerned. It was the last hour of the second dog-watch, on Easter-Sunday, with the wind here at southeast, easterly. A light air filled the upper canvas, and just gave us command of the ship. The mountains of Corsica, with Monte Christo and Elba, had all been sunk some hours, and we were on the yards, keeping a look-out for a land-fall on the Roman coast. A low, thick bank of drifting fog lay along the sea, in-shore of us, which all believed to be the sweat of the land, and thought no more of; though none wished to enter it, for that is a coast where foul airs rise, and through which the gulls and land-birds refuse to fly. Well, here we lay, the mainsail in the brails, the top-sails beating the mast-heads, like a maiden fanning herself when she sees her lover, and nothing full but the upper duck, with the sun fairly below the water in the western board. I was then young, and quick of eye, as of foot, and therefore among the first to see the sight!"

"Which was — ?" said Ludlow, interested in spite of his assumed air of indifference.

"Why, here just above the bank of foul air, that ever rests on that coast, there was seen an object, that looked like ribs of bright light, as if a thousand stars had quitted their usual berths in the heaven, to warn us off the land, by a supernatural beacon. The sight was in itself altogether out of nature and surprising. As the night thickened, it grew brighter and more glowing, as if 'twere meant in earnest to warn us from the coast. But when the word was passed to send the glasses aloft, there was seen a glittering cross on high, and far above the spars on which earthly ships carry their private signals."

"This was indeed extraordinary! and what did you, to come at the character of the heavenly symbol?"

"We wore off shore, and left it a clear berth for bolder mariners. Glad enough was I to see, with the morning sun, the snowy hills of Corsica, again!"

"And the appearance of that object was never explained?"

"Nor ever will be. I have since spoke with the mariners of that sea concerning the sight, but never found any who could pretend to have seen it. There was indeed one bold enough to say, there is a church, far inland, of height and magnitude sufficient to be seen some leagues at sea, and that, favored by our position and the mists that hung above the low grounds, we had seen its upper works, looming above the fogs, and lighted for some brilliant ceremony; but we were all too old in seaman's experience to credit so wild a tale. I know not but a church may loom, as well as a hill or a ship; but he, who pretends to say, that the hands of man can thus pile stones among the clouds, should be certain of believers, ere he pushes the tale too far."

"Your narrative is extraordinary, and the marvel should have been looked into closer. It may truly have been a church, for there stands an edifice at Rome, which towers to treble the height of a cruiser's masts."

"Having rarely troubled churches, I know not why a church should trouble me," said the mariner of the sash, while he turned his back on the ocean, as if indisposed to regard the waste of water longer. "It is now twelve years since that sight was seen, and though a seaman of many voyages, my eyes have not looked upon the Roman coast, from that hour to this. Will your Honor lead the way from the bluff, as becomes your rank?"

"Your tale of the burning cross and looming church, Master Tiller, had almost caused me to forget to watch the movements of yon periagua," returned Ludlow, who still continued to face the bay. "That obstinate old Dutchman — I say, Sir, that Mr. Alderman Van Beverout has greater confidence in this description of craft than I feel myself. I like not the looks of yonder cloud, which is rising from out the mouth of Raritan; and here, seaward, we have a gloomy horizon. By Heaven! there is a sail playing in the offing or my eye hath lost its use and judgment."

"Your Honor sees the wing of the sporting gull, again; it had been nigh to deceive my sight, which would be to cheat the look-out of a man that has the advantage of some ten or fifteen years' more practice in marine appearances. I remember once, when beating in among the islands of the China seas, with the trades here at south-east —"

"Enough of your marvels, friend; the church is as much as I can swallow, in one morning — It may have been a gull! for I confess the object small; yet it had the steadiness and size of a distant sail! There is some reason to expect one on our coast, for whom a bright and seaman's watch must be had."

"This may then leave me a choice of ships," rejoined Tiller. "I thank your Honor for having spoken, before I had given myself away to the Queen; who is a lady that is much more apt to receive gifts of this nature, than to return them."

"If your respect aboard shall bear any proportion to your hardihood on shore, you may be accounted a model of civility! But a mariner of your pretension should have some regard to the character of the vessel in which he takes service."

"That of which your Honor spoke, is then a buccaneer?"

"If not a buccaneer, one but little better. A lawless trader, under the most favorable view; and there are those who think that he, who has gone so far, has not stopt short of the end. But the reputation of the 'Skimmer of the Seas' must be known to one who has navigated the ocean, long as you."

"You will overlook the curiosity of a seafaring man, in a matter of his profession," returned the mariner of the sash, with strong and evident interest in his manner. "I am lately from a distant ocean, and though many tales of the buccaneers of the islands have been narrated, I do not remember to have heard of that rover, before his name came into the discourse between me and the schipper of the boat, that plies between this landing and the city. I am not, altogether, what I seem, Captain Ludlow; and when further acquaintance and hard service shall have brought me more before the eyes of my commander, he may not repent having induced a thorough seaman to enter his ship, by a little condescension and good-nature shown while the man was still his own master. Your Honor will take no offence at my boldness, when I tell you, I should be glad to know more of this unlawful trader."

Ludlow riveted his eyes on the unmoved and manly countenance of his companion. There was a vague and undefined suspicion in the look; but it vanished, as the practised organs drank in the assurance, which so much physical promise afforded, of the aid of a bold and active mariner. Rather amused than offended by the freedom of the request, he turned upon his heel, and as they descended the bluff, on their way towards the place of landing, he continued the dialogue.

"You are truly from a distant ocean," said the young captain of the Coquette, smiling like a man who apologizes to himself for an act of what he thought undue condescension, "if the exploits of a brigantine known by the name of the 'Water-Witch,' and of him who commands her, under the fit appellation of the 'Skimmer of the Seas,' have not yet reached your ears. It is now five summers, since orders have been in the colonies for the cruisers to be on the alert to hunt the picaroon; and it is even said, the daring smuggler has often braved the pennants of the narrow seas. 'Twould be a bigger ship, not knighthood, to the lucky officer who should catch the knave!"

"He must drive a money-gaining trade, to run these risks, and to brave the efforts of so many skilful gentlemen! May I add to a presumption that your Honor already finds too bold, if one may judge by a displeased eye, by asking if report speaks to the face and other particulars of the person of this — free trader, one must call him, though freebooter should be a better word."

"What matters the personal condition of a rogue?" said Captain Ludlow, who perhaps remembered that the freedom of their intercourse had been carried as far as comported with prudence.

"What matter, truly! I asked because the description answers a little to that of a man I once knew, in the seas of farther India, and who has long since disappeared, though no one can say whither he has gone. But this 'Skimmer of the Seas' is some Spaniard of the Main, or perhaps a Dutchman come from the country that is awash, in order to taste of terra-firma?"

"Spaniard of the southern coast never carried so bold a sail in these seas, nor was there ever known a Dutchman with so light a heel. The fellow is said to laugh at the swiftest cruiser out of England! As to his figure, I have heard little good of it. 'Tis said, he is some soured officer of better days, who has quitted the intercourse of honest men, because roguery is so plainly written on his face, that he vainly tries to hide it."

"Mine was a proper man, and one that need not have been ashamed to show his countenance among his fellows," said he of the sash. "This cannot be the same, if indeed there be any on the coast. Is't known, your Honor, that the man is truly here?"

"So goes a rumor; though so many idle tales have led me before to seek the smuggler where he was not, that I give but little faith to the report. The periagua has the wind more at west, and the cloud in the mouth of the Raritan is breaking into scud. The Alderman will have a lucky run of it!"

"And the gulls have gone more seaward — a certain sign of pleasant weather;" returned the other, glancing a quick but keen look over the horizon in the offing. "I believe our rover, with his light duck, has taken flight among them!"

"We will then go in pursuit. My ship is bound to sea; and it is time, Master Tiller, that I know in what berth you are willing to serve the Queen."

"God bless her Majesty! Anne is a royal lady and she had a Lord High Admiral for her husband. As for a berth, Sir, one always wishes to be captain even though he may be compelled to eat his ration in the lee-scuppers. I suppose the first-lieutenancy is filled, to your Honor's liking?"

"Sirrah, this is trifling; one of your years and experience need not be told, that commissions are obtained by service."

"Under favor — I confess the error. Captain Ludlow, you are a man of honor, and will not deceive a sailor who puts trust in your word."

"Sailor, or landsman, he is safe who has the gage."

"Then, Sir, I ask it. Suffer me to enter your ship; to look into my future messmates, and to judge of their characters; to see if the vessel suits my humor; and then to quit her, if I find it convenient."

"Fellow," said Ludlow, "this impudence almost surpasseth patience!"

"The request is reasonable, as can be shown;" gravely returned the unknown mariner. "Now, Captain Ludlow of the Coquette would gladly tie himself, for better for worse, to a fair lady who is lately gone on the water, and yet there are thousands who might be had with less difficulty."

"Still deeper and deeper in thy effrontery — and what if this be true?"

"Sir, a ship is a seaman's mistress — nay, when fairly under a pennant, with a war declared, he may be said to be wedded to her, lawfully or not. He becomes 'bone of her bone, and flesh of her flesh, until death doth them part.' To such a long compact, there should be liberty of choice. Has not your mariner a taste, as well as your lover? The harpings and counter of his ship are the waist and shoulders; the rigging, the ringlets; the cut and fit of the sails, the fashion of the millinery; the guns are always called the teeth, and her paint is the blush and bloom! Here is matter of choice, Sir; and, without leave to make it, I must wish your Honor a happy cruise, and the Queen a better servitor."

"Why, Master Tiller," cried Ludlow, laughing, "you trust too much to these stunted oaks, if you believe it exceeds my power to hunt you out of their cover, at pleasure. But I take you at your word. The Coquette shall receive you on these conditions, and with the confidence that a first-rate city belle would enter a country ball-room."

"I follow in your Honor's wake, without more words," returned he of the sash, for the first time respectfully raising his canvas cap to the young commander. "Though not actually married, consider me a man betrothed."

It is not necessary to pursue the discourse between the two seamen any further. It was maintained, and with sufficient freedom on the part of the inferior, until they reached the shore, and came in full view of the pennant of the Queen; when, with the tact of an old man-of-war's man, he threw into his manner all the respect that was usually required by the difference of rank.

Half an hour later, the Coquette was rolling at a single anchor, as the puffs of wind came off the hills on her three top-sails; and shortly after, she was seen standing through the Narrows, with a fresh southwesterly breeze. In all these movements, there was nothing to attract attention. Notwithstanding the sarcastic allusions of Alderman Van Beverout, the cruiser was far from being idle; and her passage outward was a circumstance of so common occurrence, that it excited no comment among the boatmen of the bay, and the coasters, who alone witnessed her departure.

CHAPTER VII.

" — I am no pilot; yet, wert thou as far
As that vast shore wash'd with the furthest sea,
I would adventure for such merchandise."

Romeo And Juliet.

A happy mixture of land and water, seen by a bright moon, and beneath the sky of the fortieth degree of latitude, cannot fail to make a pleasing picture. Such was the landscape which the reader must now endeavor to present to his mind.

The wide estuary of Raritan is shut in from the winds and billows of the open sea, by a long, low, and narrow cape, or point, which, by a medley of the Dutch and English languages, that is by no means rare in the names of places that lie within the former territories of the United Provinces of Holland, is known by the name of Sandy-Hook. This tongue of land appears to have been made by the unremitting and opposing actions of the waves, on one side, and of the currents of the different rivers, that empty their waters into the bay, on the other. It is commonly connected with the low coast of New-Jersey, to the south; but there are periods, of many years in succession, during which there exists an inlet from the sea, between what may be termed the inner end of the cape, and the main-land. During these periods, Sandy-Hook, of course, becomes an island. Such was the fact at the time of which it is our business to write.

The outer, or ocean side of this low and narrow bank of sand, is a smooth and regular beach, like that seen on most of the Jersey coast, while the inner is indented, in a manner to form several convenient anchoring-grounds, for ships that seek a shelter from easterly gales. One of the latter is a circular and pretty cove, in which vessels of a light draught are completely embayed, and where they may, in safety, ride secure from any winds that blow. The harbor, or, as it is always called, the Cove, lies at the point where the cape joins the main, and the inlet just named communicates directly with its waters, whenever the passage is open. The Shrewsbury, a river of the fourth or fifth class, or in other words a stream of a few hundred feet in width, and of no great length, comes from the south, running nearly parallel with the coast, and becomes a tributary of the Bay, also, at a point near the Cove. Between the Shrewsbury and the sea, the land resembles that on the cape, being low and sandy, though not entirely without fertility. It is covered with a modest growth of pines and oaks, where it is not either subject to the labors of the husbandman, or in natural meadow. But the western bank of the

60

river is an abrupt and high acclivity, which rises to the elevation of a mountain. It was near the base of the latter that Alderman Van Beverout, for reasons that may be more fully developed as we proceed in our tale, had seen fit to erect his villa, which, agreeably to a usage of Holland, he had called the Lust in Rust; an appellation that the merchant, who had read a few of the classics in his boyhood, was wont to say meant nothing more nor less than 'Otium cum dignitate.'

If a love of retirement and a pure air had its influence in determining the selection of the burgher of Manhattan, he could not have made a better choice. The adjoining lands had been occupied early in the previous century, by a respectable family of the name of Hartshorne, which continues seated at the place, to the present hour. The extent of their possessions served, at that day, to keep others at a distance. If to this fact be added the formation and quality of the ground, which was, at so early a period, of trifling value for agricultural purposes, it will be seen there was as little motive, as there was opportunity, for strangers to intrude. As to the air it was refreshed by the breezes of the ocean, which was scarcely a mile distant; while it had nothing to render it unhealthy, or impure. With this sketch of the general features of the scene where so many of our incidents occurred, we shall proceed to describe the habitation of the Alderman, a little more in detail.

The villa of the Lust in Rust was a low, irregular edifice, in bricks, white-washed to the color of the driven snow, and in a taste that was altogether Dutch. There were many gables and weather-cocks, a dozen small and twisted chimneys, with numberless facilities that were intended for the nests of storks. These airy sites were, however, untenanted, to the great admiration of the honest architect, who, like many others that bring with them into this hemisphere habits and opinions that are better suited to the other, never ceased expressing his surprise on the subject, though all the negroes of the neighborhood united in affirming there was no such bird in America. In front of the house, there was a narrow but an exceedingly neat lawn, encircled by shrubbery; while two old elms, that seemed coeval with the mountain, grew in the rich soil of which the base of the latter was composed. Nor was there a want of shade on any part of the natural terrace, that was occupied by the buildings. It was thickly sprinkled with fruit-trees, and here and there was a pine, or an oak, of the native growth. A declivity that was rather rapid fell away in front, to the level of the mouth of the river. In short, it was an ample but an unpretending country-house, in which no domestic convenience had been forgotten; while it had little to boast of in the way of architecture, except its rusty vanes and twisted chimneys. A few out-houses, for the accommodation of the negroes, were nigh; and nearer to the river, there were barns and stables, of dimensions and materials altogether superior to those that the appearance of the arable land, or the condition of the small farm, would seem to render necessary. The periagua, in which the proprietor had made his passage across the outer bay, lay at a small wooden wharf immediately below.

For the earlier hours of the evening, the flashing of candles, and a general and noisy movement among the blacks, had denoted the presence of the master of the villa. But the activity had gradually subsided: and before the clock struck nine, the manner in which the lights were distributed, and the general silence, showed that the party, most probably fatigued with their journey, had already separated for the night. The clamor of the negroes had ceased, and the quiet of deep sleep was already prevailing among their humble dwellings.

At the northern extremity of the villa, which, it will be remembered, leaned against the mountain, and facing the east, or fronting the river and the sea, there stood a little wing, even more deeply embowered in shrubbery and low trees, than the other parts of the edifice, and which was constructed altogether in a different style. This was a pavilion erected for the particular accommodation, and at the cost, of la belle Barbérie. Here the heiress of the two fortunes was accustomed to keep her own little ménage, during the weeks passed in the country; and here she amused herself, in those pretty and feminine employments that suited her years and tastes. In compliment to the beauty and origin of its inhabitant, the gallant François had christened this particular portion of the villa, la Cour des Fées a name that had gotten into general use, though somewhat corrupted in sound.

On the present occasion, the blinds of the principal apartment of the pavilion were open, and its mistress was still to be seen at one of the windows. Alida was at an age when the sex is most sensible of lively impressions, and she looked abroad on the loveliness of the landscape, and on the soft stillness of the night, with the pleasure that such a mind is wont to receive from objects of natural beauty.

There was a young moon, and a firmament glowing with a myriad of stars. The light was shed softly on the water, though, here and there, the ocean glittered with its rays. A nearly imperceptible, but what seamen call a heavy air came off the sea, bringing with it the refreshing coolness of the hour. The surface of the immense waste was perfectly unruffled, both within and without the barrier of sand that forms the cape; but the body of the element was heaving and setting heavily, in a manner to resemble the sleeping respiration of some being of huge physical frame. The roar of the surf, which rolled up in long and white curls upon the sands, was the only audible sound; but that was heavy and incessant, sometimes swelling on the air, hollow and threatening, and at others dying, in dull and distant murmurs, on the ear. There was a charm in these varieties of sound, and in the solemn stillness of such a night, that drew Alida into her little balcony; and she leaned forward, beyond its shadow of sweet-brier, to gaze at a part of the bay that was not visible, in the front view, from her windows.

La belle Barbérie smiled, when she saw the dim masts and dark hull of a ship, which was anchored near the end of the cape, and within its protection. There was the look of womanly pride in her dark eye, and haply some consciousness of womanly power in the swell of her rich lip, while a taper finger beat the bar of the balcony, rapidly, and without consciousness of its employment.

"The loyal Captain Ludlow has quickly ended his cruise!" said the maiden aloud, for she spoke under the influence of a triumph that was too natural to be suppressed. "I shall become a convert to my uncle's opinions, and think the Queen badly served."

"He who serves one mistress, faithfully, has no light task," returned a voice from among the shrubbery that grew beneath and nearly veiled the window; "but he, who is devoted to two, may well despair of success with both!"

Alida recoiled, and, at the next instant, she saw her place occupied by the commander of the Coquette. Before venturing to cross the low barrier that still separated him from the little parlor, the young man endeavored to read the eye of its occupant; and then, either mistaking its expression, or bold in his years and hopes, he entered the room.

Though certainly unused to have her apartment scaled with so little ceremony, there was neither apprehension, nor wonder, in the countenance of the fair descendant of the Huguenot. The blood mantled more richly on her cheek; and the brightness of an eye, that was never dull, increased, while her fine form became firm and commanding.

"I have heard that Captain Ludlow gained much of his renown by gallantry in boarding," she said, in a voice whose meaning admitted of no misconception; "but I had hoped his ambition was satisfied with laurels so fairly won from the enemies of his country!"

"A thousand pardons, fairest Alida," interrupted the youth; "you know the obstacles that the jealous watchfulness of your uncle opposes to my desire to speak with you."

"They are then opposed in vain, for Alderman Van Beverout has weakly believed the sex and condition of his ward would protect her from these coups-de-main."

"Nay, Alida; this is being more capricious than the winds! You know, too well, how far my suit is unpleasant to your gardian, to torture a slight departure from cold observances into cause of serious complaint. I had hoped — perhaps, I should say, I have presumed on the contents of your letter, for which I return a thousand thanks; but do not thus cruelly destroy expectations that have so lately been raised beyond the point, perhaps, which reason may justify."

The glow, which had begun to subside on the face of la belle Barbérie, again deepened, and for a moment it appeared as if her high self-dependence was a little weakened. After an instant of reflection, however, she answered steadily, though not entirely without emotion.

"Reason, Captain Ludlow, has limited female propriety within narrow limits," she said. "In answering your letter, I have consulted good-nature more than prudence; and I find that you are not slow in causing me to repent the error."

"If I ever cause you to repent confidence in me, sweet Alida, may disgrace in my profession, and the distrust of the whole sex, be my punishment! But, have I not reason to complain of this inconstancy, on your part? Ought I to expect so severe a reprimand — severe, because cold and ironical — for an offence, venial as the wish to proclaim my gratitude?"

"Gratitude!" repeated Alida, and this time her wonder was not feigned. "The word is strong, Sir; and it expresses more than an act of courtesy, so simple as that which may attend the lending a volume of popular poetry, can have any right to claim."

"I have strangely misconceived the meaning of the letter, or this has been a day of folly!" said Ludlow, endeavoring to swallow his discontent. "But, no; I have your own words to refute that averted eye and cold look; and, by the faith of a sailor! Alida, I will believe your deliberate and well-reflected thoughts, before these capricious fancies, which are unworthy of your nature. Here are the very words; I shall not easily part with the flattering hopes they convey!"

La belle Barbérie now regarded the young man in open amazement. Her color changed; for of the indiscretion of writing, she knew she was not guiltless — but of having written in terms to justify the confidence of the other, she felt no consciousness. The customs of the age, the profession of her suitor, and the hour, induced her to look steadily in to his face, to see whether the man stood before her in all the decency of his reason. But Ludlow had the reputation of being exempt from a vice that was then but too common among seamen, and there was nothing in his ingenuous and really handsome features, to cause her to distrust his present discretion. She touched a bell, and signed to her companion to be seated.

"François," said his mistress, when the old valet but half awake, entered the apartment, "fais moi le plaisir de m'apporter de cette eau de la fontaine du bosquet, et du vin — le Capitaine Ludlow a soif; et rapelle-toi, bon François, il ne faut pas déranger mon oncle à cette heure; il doit être bien fatigué de son voyage."

When her respectful and respectable servitor had received his commission and departed, Alida took a seat herself, in the confidence of having deprived the visit of Ludlow of its clandestine character, and at the same time having employed the valet on an errand that would leave her sufficient leisure, to investigate the inexplicable meaning of her companion.

"You have my word, Captain Ludlow, that this unseasonable appearance in the pavilion, is indiscreet, not to call it cruel," she said, so soon as they were again alone; "but that you have it, in any manner, to justify your imprudence, I must continue to doubt until confronted by proof."

"I had thought to have made a very different use of this," returned Ludlow, drawing a letter — we admit it with some reluctance in one so simple and so manly — from his bosom: "and even now, I take shame in producing it, though at your own orders.

"Some magic has wrought a marvel, or the scrawl has no such importance," observed Alida, taking a billet that she now began to repent having ever written. "The language of politeness and female reserve must admit of strange perversions, or all who read are not the best interpreters."

La belle Barbérie ceased speaking, for the instant her eye fell on the paper, an absorbing and intense curiosity got the better of her resentment. We shall give the contents of the letter, precisely in the words which caused so much amazement, and possibly some little uneasiness, to the fair creature who was perusing it.

"The life of a seaman," said the paper, in a delicate and beautiful female hand, "is one of danger and exposure. It inspires confidence in woman, by the frankness to which it gives birth, and it merits indulgence by its privations. She who writes this, is not insensible to the merit of men of this bold calling. Admiration for the sea, and for those who live on it has been her weakness through life; and her visions of the future, like her recollections of the past, are not entirely exempt from a contemplation of its pleasures. The usages of different nations — glory in arms — change of scene — with constancy in the affections, all sweetened by affluence, are temptations too strong for a female imagination, and they should not be without their influence on the judgment of man. Adieu."

This note was read, re-perused, and for the third time conned, ere Alida ventured to raise her eyes to the face of the expectant young man.

"And this indelicate and unfeminine rhapsody, Captain Ludlow has seen proper to ascribe to me!" she said, while her voice trembled between pride and mortification.

"To whom else can I impute it? No other, lovely Alida, could utter language so charming, in words so properly chosen."

The long lashes of the maiden played quickly above their dark organs, and then, conquering feelings that were strangely in contradiction to each other, she said with dignity, turning to a little ebony éscritoire which lay beside her dressing-box —

"My correspondence is neither very important nor very extensive; but such as it is, happily for the reputation of the writer's taste, if not for her sanity, I believe it is in my power to show the trifle I thought it decorous to write, in reply to your own letter. Here is a copy," she added, opening what in fact was a draught, and reading aloud.

"I thank Capt. Ludlow for his attention in affording me an opportunity of reading a narrative of the cruel deeds of the buccaneers. In addition to the ordinary feelings of humanity, one cannot but regret, that men so heartless are to be found in a profession that is commonly thought to be generous and tender of the weak. We will, however, hope, that the very wicked and cowardly, among seamen, exist only as foils to render the qualities of the very bold and manly more conspicuous. No one can be more sensible of this truth than the friends of Captain Ludlow," the voice of Alida fell a little, as she came to this sentence, "who has not now to earn a reputation for mercy. In return, I send the copy of the Cid, which honest François affirms to be superior to all other poems, not even excepting Homer — a book, which I believe he is innocent of calumniating, from ignorance of its contents. Again thanking Capt. Ludlow for this instance of his repeated attentions I beg he will keep the volume, until he shall return from his intended cruise."

"This note is but a copy of the one you have, or ought to have," said the niece of the Alderman, as she raised her glowing face from leaning over the paper, "though it is not signed, like that, with the name of Alida de Barbérie."

When this explanation was over, both parties sat looking at each other, in silent amazement. Still Alida saw, or thought she saw, that, notwithstanding the previous professions of her admirer, the young man rejoiced he had been deceived. Respect for delicacy and reserve in the other sex is so general and so natural among men, that they who succeed the most in destroying its barriers, rarely fail to regret their triumph; and he who truly loves can never long exult in any violation of propriety, in the object of his affections, even though the concession be made in his own favor. Under the influence of this commendable and healthful feeling, Ludlow, while he was in some respects mortified at the turn affairs had taken, felt sensibly relieved from a load of doubt, to which the extraordinary language of the letter, he believed his mistress to have written, had given birth. His companion read the state of his mind, in a countenance that was frank as face of sailor could be; and though secretly pleased to gain her former place in his respect, she was also vexed and wounded that he had ever presumed to distrust her reserve. She still held the inexplicable billet and her eyes naturally sought the lines. A sudden thought seemed to strike her mind, and returning the paper, she said coldly —

"Captain Ludlow should know his correspondent better; I much mistake if this be the first of her communications."

The young man colored to the temples, and hid his face, for a moment, in the hollow of his hands.

"You admit the truth of my suspicions," continued la belle Barbérie, "and cannot be insensible of my justice, when I add, that henceforth —"

"Listen to me, Alida," cried the youth, half breathless in his haste to interrupt a decision that he dreaded; "hear me, and as Heaven is my judge, you shall hear only truth. I confess this is not the first of the letters, written in the same hand — perhaps I should say in the same spirit — but, on the honor of a loyal officer, I affirm, that until circumstances led me to think myself so happy — so — very happy —"

"I understand you, Sir: the work was anonymous, until you saw fit to inscribe my name as its author. Ludlow! Ludlow! how meanly have you thought of the woman you profess to love!"

"That were impossible! I mingle little with those who study the finesse of life; and loving, as I do, my noble profession, Alida, was it so unnatural to believe that another might view it with the same eyes? But since you disavow the letter — nay, your disavowal is unnecessary — I see my vanity has even deceived me in the writing — but since the delusion is over, I confess that I rejoice it is not so."

La belle Barbérie smiled, and her countenance grew brighter. She enjoyed the triumph of knowing that she merited the respect of her suitor, and it was a triumph heightened by recent mortification. Then succeeded a pause of more than a minute. The embarrassment of the silence was happily interrupted by the return of François.

"Mam'selle Alide, voici de l'eau de la fontaine," said the valet; "mais Monsieur votre oncle s'esi couché, et il a mis la cléf de la cave an vin dessous son oreiller. Ma foi, ce n'est pas facile d'avoir du bon vin du tout, en Amerique, mais après que Monsieur le maire s'est couché, c'est toujours impossible; voila!"

"N'importe, mon cher; le capitaine va partir, et il n'a plus soif."

"Dere is assez de jin," continued the valet, who felt for the captain's disappointment, "mais, Monsieur Loodle, have du gout, an' he n'aime pas so strong liqueur."

"He has swallowed already more than was necessary for one occasion," said Alida, smiling on her admirer, in a manner that left him doubtful whether he ought most to repine, or to rejoice. "Thank you, good François; your duty for the night shall end with lighting the captain to the door."

Then saluting the young commander, in a manner that would not admit of denial, la belle Barbérie dismissed her lover and the valet, together.

"You have a pleasant office, Monsieur François," said the former, as he was lighted to the outer door of the pavilion; "it is one that many a gallant gentleman would envy."

"Oui, Sair. It be grand plaisir to serve Mam'selle Alide. Je porte de fan, de book, mais quant an vin, Monsieur le Capitaine, parole d'honneur, c'est toujours impossible après que l'Aldermain s'est couché."

"Ay — the book — I think you had the agreeable duty, today, of carrying the book of la Belle?"

"Vraiment, oui! 'Twas ouvrage de Monsieur Pierre Corneille. On prétend, que Monsieur Shak-a-spear en a emprunté d'assez beaux sentiments!"

"And the paper between the leaves? — you were charged also with that note, good François?"

The valet paused, shrugged his shoulders, and aid one of his long yellow fingers on the plane of an enormous aquiline nose, while he seemed to muse. Then shaking his head perpendicularly, he preceded the captain, as before, muttering, as usual, half in French and half in English —

"For le papier, I know, rien du tout; c'est bien possible, parceque, voyez vous, Monsieur le Capitaine, Mam'selle Alide did say, prenez-y garde; but I no see him, depuis. Je suppose 'twas beaux compliments écrits on de vers of M. Pierre Corneille. Quel génie que celui de cet homme là! — n'est ce pas, Monsieur?"

"It is of no consequence, good François," said Ludlow, slipping a guinea into the hands of the valet. "If you should ever discover what became of that paper, however, you will oblige me by letting me know. Good night; mes devoirs à la

Belle!"

"Bon soir, Monsieur le Capitaine; c'est un brave Monsieur que celui-la, et de très bonne famille! Il n'a pas de si grandes terres, que Monsieur le Patteroon, pourtant, on dit, qu'il doit avoir de jolies maisons et assez de rentes publiques! J'aime à servir un si généreux et loyal maître, mais, malheureusement, il est marin! M. de Barbérie n'avait pas trop d'amitié pour les gens de cette profession là."

CHAPTER VIII.

" — Well, Jessica, go in;
Perhaps, I will return immediately;
Do as I bid you,
Shut doors after you: Fast bind, fast find;
A proverb never stale, in thrifty mind."

Merchant of Venice.

THE decision, with which la demoiselle Barbérie had dismissed her suitor, was owing to some consciousness that she had need of opportunity to reflect on the singular nature of the events which had just happened, no less than to a sense of the impropriety of his visiting her at that hour, and in a manner so equivocal. But, like others who act from feverish impulses, when alone the maiden repented of her precipitation; and she remembered fifty questions which might aid in clearing the affair of its mystery, that she would now gladly put. It was too late, however, for she had heard Ludlow take his leave, and had listened, in breathless silence, to his footstep, as he passed the shrubbery of her little lawn. François reappeared at the door, to repeat his wishes for her rest and happiness, and then she believed she was finally alone for the night, since the ladies of that age and country, were little apt to require the assistance of their attendants, in assuming, or in divesting themselves of, their ordinary attire.

It was still early, and the recent interview had deprived Alida of all inclination for sleep. She placed the lights in a distant corner of the apartment, and approached a window. The moon had so far changed its position, as to cast a different light upon the water. The hollow washing of the surf, the dull but heavy breathing of the air from the sea, and the soft shadows of the trees and mountain, were much the same. The Coquette lay, as before, at her anchor near the cape, and the Shrewsbury glittered towards the south, until its surface was concealed by the projection of a high and nearly perpendicular bluff.

The stillness was profound, for, with the exception of the dwelling of the family who occupied the estate nearest the villa, there was no other habitation within some miles of the place. Still the solitude of the situation was undisturbed by any apprehension of danger, or any tradition of violence from rude and lawless men. The peaceable character of the colonists, who dwelt in the interior country, was proverbial, and their habits simple; while the ocean was never entered by those barbarians, who then rendered some of the seas of the other hemisphere as fearful as they were pleasant.

Notwithstanding this known and customary character of tranquillity, and the lateness of the hour, Alida had not been many moments in her balcony, before she heard the sound of oars. The stroke was measured, and the noise low and distant, but it was too familiar to be mistaken. She wondered at the expedition of Ludlow, who was not accustomed to show such haste in quitting her presence, and leaned over the railing to catch a glimpse of his departing boat. Each moment she expected to see the little bark issue from out of the shadows of the land, into the sheet of brightness which stretched nearly to the cruiser. She gazed long, and in vain, for no barge appeared, and yet the sound had become inaudible. A light still hung at the peak of the Coquette, a sign that the commander was out of his vessel.

The view of a fine ship, seen by the aid of the moon, with its symmetry of spars, and its delicate tracery of cordage, and the heavy and grand movements of the hull as it rolls on the sluggish billows of a calm sea, is ever a pleasing and indeed an imposing spectacle. Alida knew that more, than a hundred human beings slept within the black and silent mass, and her thoughts insensibly wandered to the business of their daring lives, their limited abode, and yet wandering existence, their frank and manly qualities, their devotion to the cause of those who occupied the land, their broken and interrupted connexion with the rest of the human family, and finally to those weakened domestic ties, and to that reputation for inconstancy, which are apparently a natural consequence of all. She sighed, and her eye wandered from the ship to that ocean on which it was constructed to dwell. From the distant, low, and nearly imperceptible shore of the island of Nassau, to the coast of New-Jersey, there was one broad and untenanted waste. Even the sea-fowl rested his tired wing, and slept tranquilly on the water. The broad space appeared like some great and unfrequented desert, or rather like a denser and more material copy of the firmament by which it was canopied.

It has been mentioned that a stunted growth of oaks and pines covered much of the sandy ridge that formed the cape. The same covering furnished a dark setting to the waters of the Cove. Above this outline of wood, which fringed the margin of the sea. Alida now fancied she saw an object in motion. At first, she believed some ragged and naked tree, of which the coast had many, was so placed as to deceive her vision, and had thrown its naked lines upon the back-ground of water, in a manner to assume the shape and tracery of a light-rigged vessel. But when the dark and symmetrical spars were distinctly seen, gliding past objects that were known to be stationary, it was impossible to doubt their character. The maiden wondered, and her surprise was not unmixed with apprehension. It seemed as if the stranger for such the vessel must needs be, was recklessly approaching a surf, that, in its most tranquil moments, was dangerous to such a fabric, and that he steered, unconscious of hazard, directly upon the land. Even the movement was mysterious and unusual. Sails there were none; and yet the light and lofty spars were soon hid behind a thicket that covered a knoll near the margin of the sea. Alida expected, each moment, to hear the cry of mariners in distress, and then, as the minutes passed and no such fearful sound interrupted the stillness of the night, she began to bethink her of those lawless rovers, who were known to abound among the Carribean isles, and who were said sometimes even to enter and to refit, in the smaller and more secret inlets of the American continent. The tales, coupled with the deeds, character, and fate of the notorious Kidd, were then still recent, and although magnified and colored by vulgar exaggerations, as all such tales are known to be, enough was believed, by the better instructed, to make his life and death the subject of many curious and mysterious rumors. At this moment, she would have gladly recalled the young commander of the Coquette, to apprize him of the enemy that was nigh; and then, ashamed of terrors that she was fain to hope savored more of woman's weakness than of truth, she endeavored to believe the whole some ordinary movement of a coaster, who, familiar with his situation, could rot possibly be either in want of aid, or an object of alarm. Just as this natural and consoling conclusion crossed her mind, she very audibly heard a step in her pavilion. It seemed near the door of the room she occupied. Breathless, more with the excitement of her imagination, than with any actual fear created by this new cause of alarm, the maiden quitted the balcony, and stood motionless to listen. The door, in truth, was opened, with singular caution, and, for an instant, Alida saw nothing but a confused area in the centre of which appeared the figure of a menacing and rapacious freebooter.

"Northern lights and moonshine!" growled Alderman Van Beverout, for it was no other than the uncle of the heiress, whose untimely and unexpected visit had caused her so much alarm. "This sky-watching, and turning of night into day, will be the destruction of thy beauty, niece; and then we shall see how plenty Patroons are for husbands! A bright eye and a blooming cheek are thy stock in trade, girl; and she is a spendthrift of both, who is out of her bed when the clock hath struck ten."

"Your discipline would deprive many a beauty of the means of using her power," returned la demoiselle, smiling, as much at the folly of her recent fears, as with affection for her reprover. "They tell me, that ten is the witching time of night, for the necromancy of the dames of Europe."

"Witch me no witches! The name reminds one of the cunning Yankees, a race that would outwit Lucifer himself, if left to set the conditions to their bargain. Here is the Patroon, wishing to let in a family of the knaves among the honest Dutchmen of his manor; and we have just settled a dispute between us, on this subject, by making the lawful trial."

"Which, it may be proper to hope, dearest uncle, was not the trial by battle?"

"Peace and olive-branches, no! The Patroon of Kinderhook is the last man in the Americas, that is likely to suffer by the blows of Myndert Van Beverout. I challenged the boy to hold a fine eel, that the blacks have brought out of the river to help in breaking our morning fasts, that it might be seen if he were fit to deal with the slippery rogues. By the merit of the peaceable St. Nicholas! but the son of old Hendrick Van Staats had a busy time of it! The lad griped the fish, as the ancient tradition has it that thy uncle clenched the Holland florin, when my father put it between my fingers, within the month, in order to see if the true saving grace was likely to abide in the family for another generation. My heart misgave me for a moment; for young Oloff has the fist of a vice, and I thought the goodly names of the Harmans, and Rips, Corneliuses, and Dircks of the manor rent-roll were likely to be contaminated by the company of an Increase or a Peleg; but just as the Patroon thought he had the watery viper by the throat, the fish gave an unexpected twist, and slid through his fingers by the tail. Flaws and loop-holes! but that experiment has as much wisdom as wit in it!"

"And to me, it seemeth better, now that Providence has brought all the colonies under one government, that these prejudices should be forgotten. We are a people, sprung from many nations, and our effort should be to preserve the liberality and intelligence, while we forget the weaknesses, of all."

"Bravely said, for the child of a Huguenot! But I defy the man, who brings prejudice to my door. I like a merry trade, and a quick calculation. Let me see the man in all New-England, that can tell the color of a balance-sheet quicker than one that can be named, and I'll gladly hunt up the satchel and go to school again. I love a man the better for looking to his own interests, I; and, yet common honesty teaches us, that there should be a convention between men, beyond which none of reputation and character ought to go."

"Which convention shall be understood, by every man, to be the limits of his own faculties; by which means the dull may rival the quick of thought. I fear me, uncle, there should be an eel kept on every coast, to which a trader comes!"

"Prejudice and conceit, child, acting on a drowsy head; 'tis time thou seekest thy pillow, and in the morning we shall see if young Oloff of the Manor shall have better success with thy favor, than with the prototype of the Jonathans. Here, put out these flaring candles, and take a modest lamp to light thee to thy bed. Glaring windows, so near midnight give a house an extravagant name, in the neighborhood."

"Our reputation for sobriety may suffer in the opinion of the eels," returned Alida, laughing, "but here are few others, I believe, to call us dissipated."

"One never knows — one never knows —" muttered the Alderman, extinguishing the two large candles of his niece, and substituting his own little handlamp in their place. "This broad light only invites to wakefulness, while the dim taper I leave is good as a sleeping draught. Kiss me, wilful one, and draw thy curtains close, for the negroes will soon rise to load the periagua, that they may go up with the tide to the city. The noise of the chattering black guards may disturb thy slumbers!"

"Truly, it would seem there was little here to invite such active navigation," returned Alida, saluting the cheek of her uncle at his order. "The love of trade must be strong, when it finds the materials of commerce, in a solitude like this."

"Thou hast divined the reason, child. Thy father Monsieur de Barbérie had his peculiar opinions on the subject, and doubtless he did not fail to transmit some of them to his offspring. And yet, when the Huguenot was driven from his château and his clayey Norman lands, the man had no distaste, himself, for an account-current, provided the balance was in his own favor. Nations and characters! I find but little difference, after all, in trade; whether it be driven with a Mohawk for his pack of furs, or with a Seigneur, who has been driven from his lands. Each strives to get the profit on his own side of the account, and the loss on that of his neighbor. So rest thee well, girl; and remember that matrimony is no more than a capital bargain, on whose success depends the sum-total of a woman's comfort — and so once more, good night."

La belle Barbérie attended her uncle, dutifully to the door of her pavilion, which she bolted after him; and then, finding her little apartment gloomy by the light of the small and feeble lamp he had left, she was pleased to bring its flame in contact with the wicks of the two candles he had just extinguished. Placing the three, near each other, on a table, the maiden again drew nigh a window. The unexpected interview with the Alderman had consumed several minutes, and she was curious to know more of the unaccountable movements of the mysterious vessel.

The same deep silence reigned about the villa, and the slumbering ocean was heaving and setting as heavily as before. Alida again looked for the boat of

Ludlow; but her eye ran over the whole distance of the bright and broad streak, between her and the cruiser, in vain. There was the slight ripple of the water in the glittering of the moon's rays, but no speck, like that the barge would make, was visible. The lantern still shone at the cruiser's peak. Once, indeed, she thought the sound of oars was again to be heard, and much nearer than before; and yet no effort of her quick and roving sight could detect the position of the boat. But to all these doubts succeeded an alarm which sprang from a new and very different source.

The existence of the inlet, which united the ocean with the waters of the Cove, was but little known, except to the few whose avocations kept them near the spot. The pass being much more than half the time closed, its varying character, and the little use that could be made of it under any circumstances, prevented the place from being a subject of general interest, with the coasters. Even when open the depth of its water was uncertain, since a week or two of calms, or of westerly winds, would permit the tides to clean its channel, while a single easterly gale was sufficient to choke the entire inlet with sand. No wonder, then, that Alida felt an amazement which was not quite free from superstitious alarm when, at that hour and in such a scene, she saw a vessel gliding, as it were unaided by sails or sweeps, out of the thicket that fringed the ocean side of the Cove, into its very centre.

The strange and mysterious craft was a brigantine of that mixed construction, which is much used, even in the most ancient and classical seas of the other hemisphere, and which is supposed to unite the advantages of both a square and of a fore-and-aft rigged vessel, but which is nowhere seen to display the same beauty of form, and symmetry of equipment, as on the coasts of this Union. The first and smallest of its masts had all the complicated machinery of a ship, with its superior and inferior spars, its wider reaching, though light and manageable yards, and its various sails, shaped and arranged to meet every vicissitude and caprice of the winds; while the latter, or larger of the two, rose like the straight trunk of a pine from the hull, simple in its cordage, and spreading a single sheet of canvas, that, in itself, was sufficient to drive the fabric with vast velocity through the water. The hull was low, graceful in its outlines, dark as the raven's wing, and so modelled as to float on its element like a sea-gull riding the billows. There were many delicate and attenuated lines among its spars, which were intended to spread broader folds of canvas to the light airs, when necessary; but these additions to the tracery of the machine, which added so much to its beauty by day, were now, seen as it was by the dimmer and more treacherous rays of the moon, scarcely visible. In short, as the vessel had entered the Cove floating with the tide, and it was so singularly graceful and fairy-like in form, that Alida, at first, was fain to discredit her senses, and to believe it no more than some illusion of the fancy. Like most others, she was ignorant of the temporary inlet, and, under the circumstances, it was not difficult to lend a momentary credence to so pleasing an idea.

But the delusion was only momentary. The brigantine turned in its course, and, gliding into the part of the Cove where the curvature of the shores offered most protection from the winds and waves, and perhaps from curious eyes, its motion ceased. A heavy plunge in the water was audible even at the villa, and Alida then knew that an anchor had fallen into the bay.

Although the coast of North America offered little to invite lawless depredation, and it was in general believed to be so safe, yet the possibility that cupidity might be invited by the retired situation of her uncle's villa, did not fail to suggest itself to the mind of the young heiress. Both she and her guardian were reputed to be wealthy; and disappointment, on the open sea, might drive desperate men to the commission of crimes that in more prosperous moments would not suggest themselves. The freebooters were said to have formerly visited the coast of the neighboring island, and men were just then commencing those excavations for hidden treasures and secreted booty, which have been, at distant intervals, continued to our own time.

There are situations in which the mind insensibly gives credit to impressions, that the reason in common disapproves. The present was one in which Alide de Barbérie, though of a resolute and even a masculine understanding, felt disposed to believe there might be truth in those tales, that she had hitherto heard, only to deride. Still keeping her eye on the Motionless vessel, she drew back into her window and wrapped the curtain round her form, undecided whether to alarm the family or not, and acting under a vague impression that, though so distant, her person might be seen. She was hardly thus secreted, before the shrubbery was violently agitated, a footstep was heard in the lawn beneath her window, and then one leaped so lightly into the balcony, and from the balcony into the centre of the room, that the passage of the figure seemed like the flitting of some creature of supernatural attributes.

CHAPTER IX.

"Why look you, how you stare!
I would be friends with you, and have your love."
Shylock.

THE first impulse of Alida, at this second invasion of her pavilion, was certainly to flee. But timidity was not her weakness, and as natural firmness gave her time to examine the person of the individual who had so unceremoniously entered, curiosity aided in inducing her to remain. Perhaps a vague, but a very natural, expectation that she was again to dismiss the commander of the Coquette, had its influence on her first decision. In order that the reader may judge how far this boldness was excusable, we shall describe the person of the intruder.

The stranger was one in the very bud of young and active manhood. His years could not have exceeded two-and-twenty, nor would he probably have been thought so old, had not his features been shaded by a rich, brown hue, that in some degree, served as a foil to a natural complexion, which, though never fair, was still clear and blooming. A pair of dark, bushy, and jet-black, silken whiskers, that were in singular contrast to eye-lashes and brows of almost feminine beauty and softness, aided also in giving a decided expression to a face that might otherwise have been wanting in some of that character which is thought essential to comeliness in man. The forehead was smooth and low; the nose, though prominent and bold in outline, of exceeding delicacy in detail; the mouth and lips full, a little inclined to be arch, though the former appeared as if it might at times be pensive; the teeth were even and unsullied; and the chin was small, round, dimpled, and so carefully divested of the distinguishing mark of the sex, that one could fancy nature had contributed all its growth to adorn the neighboring cheeks and temples. If to these features be added a pair of full and brilliant coal-black eyes, that appeared to vary their expression at their master's will, the reader will at once see, that the privacy of Alida had been invaded by one whose personal attractions might, under other circumstances, have been dangerous to the imagination of a female, whose taste was in some degree influenced by a standard created by her own loveliness.

The dress of the stranger was as unique as his personal attractions were extraordinary. The fashion of the garments resembled that of those already described as worn by the man who has announced himself as Master Tiller; but the materials were altogether richer, and, judging only from the exterior, more worthy of the wearer.

The light frock was of a thick purple silk, of an Indian manufacture, cut with exceeding care to fit the fine outlines of a form that was rather round, than square; active, than athletic. The loose trowsers were of a fine white jean, the cap of scarlet velvet, ornamented with gold, and the body was belted with a large cord of scarlet silk, twisted in the form of a ship's cable. At the ends of the latter, little anchors, wrought in bullion, were attached as gay and fitting appendages.

In contrast to an attire so whimsical and uncommon, however, a pair of small and richly-mounted pistols were at the stranger's girdle; and the haft, of a curiously-carved Asiatic dagger was seen projecting, rather ostentatiously, from between the folds of the upper garment.

"What cheer! what cheer!" cried a voice, that was more in harmony with the appearance of the speaker, than with the rough, professional salutation he uttered, so soon as he had fairly landed in the centre of Alida's little saloon. "Come forth, my dealer in the covering of the beaver, for here is one who brings gold to thy coffers. Ha! now that this trio of lights hath done its office, it may be extinguished, lest it pilot others to the forbidden haven!"

"Your pardon, Sir," said the mistress of the pavilion, advancing from behind the curtain, with an air of coolness that her beating heart had nigh betrayed to be counterfeit; "having so unexpected a guest to entertain, the additional candles are necessary."

The start, recoil, and evident alarm of the intruder, lent Alida a little more assurance; for courage is a quality that appears to gain force, in a degree proportioned to the amount in which it is abstracted from the dreaded object. Still, when she saw a hand on a pistol, the maiden was again about to flee; nor was her resolution to remain confirmed, until she met the mild and alluring eye of the intruder, as, quitting his hold of the weapon, he advanced with an air so mild and graceful, as to cause curiosity to take the place of fear.

"Though Alderman Van Beverout be not punctual to his appointment," said the gay young stranger "he has more than atoned for his absence by the substitute he sends. I hope she comes authorized to arrange the whole of our treaty?"

"I claim no right to hear, or to dictate, in matters not my own. My utmost powers extend to expressing a desire, that this pavilion may be exempt from the discussion of affairs, as much beyond my knowledge as they are separated from my interests."

"Then why this signal?" demanded the stranger, pointing, with a serious air, to the lights that still burned near each other in face of an open window "It is awkward to mislead, in transactions that are so delicate!"

"Your allusion, Sir, is not understood. These lights are no more than what are usually seen in my apartment at this hour — with, indeed, the addition of a lamp, left by my uncle, Alderman Van Beverout."

"Your uncle!" exclaimed the other, advancing so near Alida, as to cause her to retire a step, his countenance expressing a deep and newly-awakened interest — "your uncle! — This, then, is one far-famed and justly extolled; la belle Barbérie!" he added, gallantly lifting his cap, as if he had just discovered the condition and the unusual personal attractions of his companion.

It was not in nature for Alida to be displeased. All her fancied causes of terror were forgotten; for, in addition to their improbable and uncertain nature, the stranger had sufficiently given her to understand, that he was expected by her uncle. If we add, that the singular attraction and softness of his face and voice aided in quieting her fears, we shall probably do no violence either to the truth or to a very natural feeling. Profoundly ignorant of the details of commerce, and accustomed to hear its mysteries extolled as exercising the keenest and best faculties of man, she saw nothing extraordinary in those who were actively engaged in the pursuit having reasons for concealing their movements from the jealousy and rivalry of competitors. Like most of her sex, she had great dependence on the characters of those she loved; and, though nature, education, and habit, had created a striking difference between the guardian and his ward, their harmony had never been interrupted by any breach of affection.

"This then is la belle Barbérie!" repeated the young sailor, for such his dress denoted him to be, studying her features with an expression of face, in which pleasure vied with evident and touching melancholy. "Fame hath done no injustice, for here is all that might justify the folly or madness of man!"

"This is familiar dialogue for an utter stranger," returned Alida, blushing, though the quick dark eye that seemed to fathom all her thoughts, saw it was not in anger. "I do not deny that the partiality of friends, coupled with my origin, have obtained the appellation, which is given, however, more in playfulness than in any serious opinion of its being merited — and now, as the hour is getting late, and this visit is at least unusual, you will permit me to seek my uncle."

"Stay!" interrupted the stranger — "it is long — very long, since so soothing, so gentle a pleasure has been mine! This is a life of mysteries, beautiful Alida, though its incidents seem so vulgar, and of every-day occurrence. There is mystery in its beginning and its end; in its impulses; its sympathies and all its discordant passions. No, do not quit me. I am from off the sea, where none but coarse and vulgar-minded men have long been my associates; and thy presence is a balm to a bruised and wounded spirit."

Interested, if possible, more by the touching and melancholy tones of the speaker, than by his extraordinary language, Alida hesitated. Her reason told her that propriety, and even prudence, required she should apprize her uncle of the stranger's presence; but propriety and prudence lose much of their influence, when female curiosity is sustained by a secret and powerful sympathy. Her own eloquent eye met the open and imploring look of organs, that seemed endowed with the fabled power to charm; and while her judgment told her there was so much to alarm her senses pleaded powerfully in behalf of the gentle mariner.

"An expected guest of my uncle will have, leisure to repose, after the privations and hardships of so weary a voyage," she said. "This is a house whose door is never closed against the rites of hospitality."

"If there is aught about my person or attire, to alarm you," returned the stranger, earnestly, "speak, that it may be cast away — These arms — these foolish arms, had better not have been here," he added, casting the pistols and dagger indignantly, through a window, into the shrubbery; "Ah! if you knew how unwillingly I would harm any — and, least of all, a woman — you would not fear me!"

"I fear you not," returned la Belle, firmly. "I dread the misconceptions of the world."

"What world is here to disturb us? Thou livest in thy pavilion, beautiful Alida, remote from towns and envy, like some favored damsel, over whose happy and charmed life presides a benignant genius. See, here are all the pretty materials, with which thy sex seeks innocent and happy amusement. Thou touchest this lute, when melancholy renders thought pleasing; here are colors to mock, or to eclipse, the beauties of the fields and the mountain, the flower, and the tree; and from these pages are culled thoughts, pure and rich in imagery, as thy spirit is spotless, and thy person lovely!"

Alida listened in amazement; for, while he spoke the young mariner touched the different articles he named, with a melancholy interest, which seemed to say how deeply he regretted that fortune had placed him in a profession, in which their use was nearly denied.

"It is not common for those who live on the sea, to feel this interest in the trifles which constitute a woman's pleasure," she said, lingering, spite of her better resolution to depart.

"The spirit of our rude and boisterous trade is then known to you?"

"It were not possible for the relation of a merchant, so extensively known as my uncle, to be ignorant altogether of mariners."

"Ay, here is proof of it," returned the stranger, speaking so quick as again to betray how sensitively his mind was constructed. "The History of the American Buccaneers is a rare book to be found in a lady's library! What pleasure can a mind like that of la belle Barbérie find in these recitals of bloody violence?"

"What pleasure, truly!" returned Alida, half tempted, by the wild and excited eye of her companion, not withstanding all the contradictory evidence which surrounded him, to believe she was addressing one of the very rovers in question. "The book was lent me by a brave seaman, who holds himself in readiness to repress their depredations; and while reading of so much wickedness, I endeavor to recall the devotion of those who risk their lives, in order to protect the weak and innocent — My uncle will be angered, should I longer delay to apprize him of your presence."

"A single moment! It is long — very long, since I have entered a sanctuary like this! Here is music; and there the frame for the gaudy tambour — these windows look on a landscape, soft as thine own nature; and yonder ocean can be admired without dreading its terrific power, or feeling disgust at its coarser scenes. Thou shouldst be happy, here!"

The stranger turned, and perceived that he was alone. Disappointment was strongly painted on his handsome face; but, ere there was time for second thought, another voice was heard grumbling at the door of the saloon.

"Compacts and treaties! What, in the name of good faith, hath brought thee hither? Is this the way to keep a cloak on our movements? or dost suppose that the Queen will knight me, for being known as thy correspondent?"

"Lanterns and false-beacons!" returned the other, mimicking the voice of the disconcerted burgher, and pointing to the lights that still stood where last described. "Can the port be entered without respecting the land-marks and signals?"

"This comes of moonlight and sentiment! When the girl should have been asleep, she is up, gazing at the stars, and disconcerting a burgher's speculations — But fear thee not, Master Seadrift; my niece has discretion, and if we have no better pledge for her silence, there is that of necessity; since there is no one here for a confidant, but her old Norman valet, and the Patroon of Kinderhook, both of whom are dreaming of other matter than a little gainful traffic."

"Fear thee not, Alderman;" returned the other, still maintaining his air of mockery. "We have the pledge of character, if no other; since the uncle cannot part with reputation, without the niece sharing in the loss."

"What sin is there in pushing commerce a step beyond the limits of the law? These English are a nation of monopolists; and they make no scruple of tying us of the colonies, hand and foot, heart and soul, with their acts of Parliament, saying 'with us shalt thou trade, or not at all.' By the character of the best burgomaster of Amsterdam, and they came by the province, too, in no such honesty, that we should lie down and obey!"

"Wherein there is much comfort to a dealer in the contraband. Justly reasoned, my worthy Alderman. Thy logic will, at any time, make a smooth pillow, especially if the adventure be not without its profit. And now, having so commendabiy disposed of the moral of our bargain, let us approach its legitimate, if not its lawful, conclusion. There," he added, drawing a small bag from an inner pocket of his frock, and tossing it carelessly on a table; "there is thy gold. Eighty broad Johannes is no bad return for a few packages of furs; and even avarice itself will own, that six months is no long investment for the usury."

"That boat of thine, most lively Seadrift, is a marine humming-bird!" returned Myndert, with a joyful tremor of the voice, that betrayed his deep and entire satisfaction. "Didst say just eighty? But spare thyself the trouble of looking for the memorandum; I will tell the gold myself, to save thee the trouble. Truly, the adventure hath not been bad! A few kegs of Jamaica, with a little powder and lead, and a blanket or two, with now and then a penny bauble for a chief, are knowingly, ay! and speedily transmuted into the yellow metal, by thy good aid. This affair was managed on the French coast?"

"More northward, where the frost helped the bargain. Thy beavers and martens, honest burgher, will be flaunting in the presence of the Emperor, at the next holidays. What is there in the face of the Braganza, that thou studiest it so hard?"

"The piece peems none of the heaviest — but, luckily, I have scales at hand —"

"Hold!" said the stranger, laying his hand, which according to a fashion of that day, was clad in a delicate and scented glove, lightly on the arm of the other: "No scales between us, Sir! That was taken in return for thy adventure; heavy or light, it must go down. We deal in confidence, and this hesitation offends me. Another such doubt of my integrity, and our connexion is at an end."

"A calamity I should deplore, quite or nearly as much as thyself," returned Myndert, affecting to laugh; though he slipped the suspected doubloon into the bag again, in a manner that at once removed the object of contention from view.

"A little particularity in the balance part of commerce serves to maintain friend-ships. But a trifle shall not cause us to waste the precious time. — Hast brought goods suited to the colonies?"

"In plenty."

"And ingeniously assorted? Colonies and monopoly! — But there is a two-fold satisfaction in this clandestine traffic! I never get the notice of thy arrival, Master Seadrift, but the heart within me leapeth of gladness! There is a double pleasure in circumventing the legislation of your London wiseacres!"

"The chiefest of which is — ?"

"A goodly return for the investment, truly — I desire not to deny the agency of natural causes; but, trust me, there is a sort of professional glory in thus defeating the selfishness of our rulers. What! are we born of woman, to be used as the instruments of their prosperity! Give us equal legislation, a right to decide on the policy of enactments, and then, like a loyal and obedient subject —"

"Thou wouldst still deal in the contraband!"

"Well, well, multiplying idle words is not multiplying gold. The list of the articles introduced can be forthcoming?"

"It is here, and ready to be examined. But there is a fancy come over me, Alderman Van Beverout, which, like others of my caprices, thou knowest must have its way. There should be a witness to our bargain."

"Judges and juries! Thou forgettest, man, that a clumsy galliot could sail through the tightest clause, of these extra-legal compacts. The courts receive the evidence of this sort of traffic, as the grave receives the dead; to swallow all, and be forgotten."

"I care not for the courts, and little desire do I feel to enter them. But the presence of la belle Barbérie may serve to prevent any misconceptions, that might bring our connexion to a premature close. Let her be summoned."

"The girl is altogether ignorant of traffic, and it might unsettle her opinions of her uncle's stability. If a man does not maintain credit within his own doors, how can he expect it in the streets?"

"Many have credit on the highway, who receive none at home. But thou knowest my humor; no niece — no traffic."

"Alida is a dutiful and affectionate child, and I would not willingly disturb her slumbers. Here is the Patroon of Kinderhook, a man who loves English legis-lation as little as myself — he will be less reluctant to see an honest shilling turned into gold. I will awake him: no man was ever yet offended at an offer to share in a profitable adventure."

"Let him sleep on. I deal not with your lords of manors and mortgages. Bring forth the lady, for there will be matter fit for her delicacy."

"Duty and the ten commandments! You never had the charge of a child, Master Seadrift, and cannot know the weight of responsibility —"

"No niece — no traffic!" interrupted the wilful dealer in contraband, returning his invoice to his pocket, and preparing to rise from the table, where he had already seated himself. "The lady knows of my presence; and it were safer for us both, that she entered more deeply into our confidence."

"Thou art as despotic as the English navigation-law! I hear the foot of the child still pacing her chamber, and she shall come. But there need be no explanations, to recall old intercourse. The affair can pass as a bit of accidental speculation — a by-play, in the traffic of life."

"As thou pleasest. I shall deal less in words than in business. Keep thine own secrets, burgher, and they are safe. Still, I would have the lady, for there is a presentiment that our connexion is in danger."

"I like not that word presentiment," grumbled the Alderman, taking a light, and snuffing it with deliberate care; "drop but a single letter, and one dreams of the pains and penalties of the Exchequer. Remember thou art a trafficker, who conceals his appearance on account of the cleverness of his speculations."

"That is my calling, to the letter. Were all others as clever, the trade would certainly cease. Go, bring the lady."

The Alderman, who probably saw the necessity of making some explanation to his niece, and who, it would seem, fully understood the positive character of his companion, no longer hesitated; but, first casting a suspicious glance out of the still open window he left the room.

CHAPTER X.

" — Alack, what heinous sin is it in me
To be ashamed, to be my father's child!
But though I am a daughter to his blood
I am not to his manners."

Merchant of Venice.

THE moment the stranger was again alone, the entire expression of his countenance underwent a change. The reckless and bold expression deserted his eye,
which once more became soft, if not pensive, as it wandered over the different
elegant objects that served to amuse the leisure of la belle Barbérie. He arose, and
touched the strings of a lute, and then, like Fear, started back, as if recoiling at the
sound he had made. All recollection of the object of his visit was evidently forgotten, in a new and livelier interest; and had there been one to watch his movements, the last motive imputed to his presence would probably have been the one
that was true. There was so little of that vulgar and common character, which is
usually seen in men of his pursuit, in the gentle aspect and subdued air of his fine
features, that it might be fancied he was thus singularly endowed by nature, in
order that deception might triumph, if there were moments when a disregard of
opinion was seen in his demeanor, it rather appeared assumed than easy; and even
when most disposed to display lawless indifference to the ordinary regulations of
society, in his interview with the Alderman, it had been blended with a reserve of
manner that was strangely in contrast with his humor.

On the other hand, it were idle to say that Alida de Barbérie had no
unpleasant suspicions concerning the character of her uncle's guest. That baneful
influence, which necessarily exerts itself near an irresponsible power, coupled
with the natural indifference with which the principal regards the dependant, had
caused the English Ministry to fill too many of their posts of honor and profit, in
the colonies, with needy and dissolute men of rank, or of high political connexions at home. The Province of New-York had, in this respect, been particularly unfortunate. The gift of it by Charles to his brother and successor, had left it
without the protection of those charters and other privileges that had been
granted to most of the governments of America. The connexion with the crown
was direct, and, for a long period, the majority of the inhabitants were considered
as of a different race, and of course as of one less to be considered, than that of
their conquerors. Such was the laxity of the times on the subject of injustice to

the people of this hemisphere, that the predatory expeditions of Drake and others against the wealthy occupants of the more southern countries, seem to have left no spots on their escutcheons; and the honors and favors of Queen Elizabeth had been liberally extended to men who would now be deemed freebooters. In short, that system of violence and specious morality, which commenced with the gifts of Ferdinand and Isabella, and the bulls of the Popes, was continued, with more or less of modification, until the descendants of those single-minded and virtuous men who peopled the Union, took the powers of government into their own hands, and proclaimed political ethics that were previously as little practised as understood.

Alida knew that both the Earl of Bellamont and the unprincipled nobleman who has been introduced in the earlier pages of this tale, had not escaped the imputation of conniving at acts on the sea, far more flagrant than any of an unlawful trade; and it will therefore create little surprise, that she saw reason to distrust the legality of some of her uncle's speculations, with less pain than might be felt by one of her sex and opinions at the present hour. Her suspicions, however, fell far short of the truth; for it were scarce possible to have presented a mariner, who bore about him fewer of those signs of his rude calling, than he whom she had so unexpectedly met.

Perhaps, too, the powerful charm, that existed in the voice and countenance of one so singularly gifted by nature, had its influence in persuading Alida to reappear. At all events, she was soon seen to enter the room, with an air, that manifested more of curiosity and wonder, than of displeasure.

"My niece has heard that thou comest from the old countries, Master Seadrift," said the wary Alderman, who preceded Alida, "and the woman is uppermost in her heart. Thou wilt never be forgiven, should the eye of any maiden in Manhattan get sight of thy finery before she has passed judgment on its merit."

"I cannot wish a more impartial or a fairer judge;" returned the other, doffing his cap in the gallant and careless manner of his trade. "Here are silks from the looms of Tuscany, and Lyonnois brocades, that any Lombard, or dame of France, might envy. Ribbons of every hue and dye, and laces that seem to copy the fret-work of the richest cathedral of your Fleming!"

"Thou hast journeyed much, in thy time, Master Seadrift, and speakest of countries and usages with understanding," said the Alderman. "But how stand the prices of these precious goods? Thou knowest the long war, and the moral certainty of its continuance; this German succession to the throne, and the late earthquakes in the country, too, have much unsettled prices, and cause us thoughtful burghers to be wary in our traffic. — Didst inquire the cost of geldings, when last in Holland?"

"The animals go a-begging! — As to the value of my goods, that you know is fixed; for I admit of no parley between friends."

"Thy obstinacy is unreasonable, Master Seadrift. A wise merchant will always look to the state of the market, and one so practised should know that a nimble sixpence multiplies faster than a slow-moving shilling. 'Tis the constant rolling of the ball that causes the snow to cleave! Goods that come light should not go heavy, and quick settlements follow sudden bargains. Thou knowest our York saying, that 'first offers are the best.'"

"He that likes may purchase, and he that prefers his gold to fine laces, rich silks, and stiff brocades, has only to sleep with his money-bags under his pillow. There are others who wait, with impatience, to see the articles; and I have not crossed the Atlantic, with a freight that scarcely ballasts the brigantine, to throw away the valuables on the lowest bidder."

"Nay, uncle," said Alida, in a little trepidation "we cannot judge of the quality of Master Seadrift's articles, by report. I dare to say, he has not landed without a sample of his wares?"

"Custom and friendships!" muttered Myndert; "of what use is an established correspondence, if it is to be broken on account of a little cheapening? But produce thy stores, Mr. Dogmatism; I warrant me the fashions are of some rejected use, or that the color of the goods be impaired by the usual negligence of thy careless mariners. We will, at least pay thee the compliment to look at the effects."

"'Tis as you please," returned the other. "The bales are in the usual place, at the wharf, under the inspection of honest Master Tiller — but if so inferior in quality, they will scarce repay the trouble of the walk."

"I'll go, I'll go," said the Alderman, adjusting his wig and removing his spectacles; "'twould not be treating an old correspondent well, to refuse to look at his samples — thou wilt follow, Master Seadrift, and so I will pay thee the compliment to examine the effects — though the long war, the glut of furs, the overabundance of the last year's harvests, and the perfect quiet in the mining districts, have thrown all commerce flat on its back. I'll go, however; lest thou shouldst say, thy interests were neglected. Thy Master Tiller is an indiscreet agent; he gave me a fright today that exceeds any alarm I have felt since the failure of Van Halt, Balance, and Diddle."

The voice of Myndert became inaudible, for, in his haste not to neglect the interests of his guest, the tenacious trader had already quitted the room, and half of his parting speech was uttered in the antechamber of the pavilion.

"'Twould scarce comport with the propriety of my sex, to mingle with the seamen, and the others who doubtless surround the bales," said Alida, in whose face there was a marked expression of hesitation and curiosity.

"It will not be necessary," returned her companion. "I have, at hand, specimens of all that you would see. But, why this haste? We are yet in the early hours of the night, and the Alderman will be occupied long, ere he comes to the determination to pay the prices my people are sure to ask. I am lately from off the sea, beautiful Alida, and thou canst not know the pleasure I find in breathing even the atmosphere of a woman's presence."

La belle Barbérie retired a step or two, she knew not why; and her hand was placed upon the cord of the bell, before she was aware of the manner in which she betrayed her alarm.

"To me it does not seem that I am a creature so terrific, that thou need'st dread my presence," continued the gay mariner, with a smile that expressed as much of secret irony, as of that pensive character which had again taken possession of his countenance; "but ring, and bring your attendants to relieve fears that are natural to thy sex, and therefore seducing to mine. Shall I pull the cord? — for this pretty hand trembles too much, to do its office."

"I know not that any would answer, for it is past the hour of attendance — it is better that I go to the examination of the bales."

The strange and singularly-attired being, who occasioned so much uneasiness to Alida, regarded her a moment with a kind and melancholy solicitude.

"Thus they are all, till altered by too much intercourse with a cold and corrupt world!" he rather whispered, than uttered aloud. "Would that thus they might all continue! Thou art a singular compound of thy sex's weakness, and of manly resolution, belle Barbérie; but trust me," and he laid his hand on his heart with an earnestness that spoke well for his sincerity; "ere word, or act, to harm or to offend thee, should proceed from any who obey will of mine, nature itself must undergo a change. Start not, for I call one to show the specimens you would see."

He then applied a little silver whistle to his lips, and drew a low signal from the instrument, motioning to Alida to await the result, without alarm. In half a minute, there was a rustling among the leaves of the shrubbery, a moment of attentive pause, and then a dark object entered the window, and rolled heavily to the centre of the floor.

"Here are our commodities, and trust me the price shall not be dwelt on, between us," resumed Master Seadrift, undoing the fastenings of the little bale, that had entered the saloon, seemingly without the aid of hands. "These goods are so many gages of neutrality, between us; so approach, and examine, without fear. You will find some among them to reward the hazard."

The bale was now open, and as its master appeared to be singularly expert in suiting a female fancy, it became impossible for Alida to resist any longer. She gradually lost her reserve, as the examination proceeded; and before the owner of the treasures had got into the third of his packages, the hands of the heiress were as actively employed as his own, in gaining access to their view.

"This is a stuff of the Lombard territories," said the vender of the goods, pleased with the confidence he had succeeded in establishing between his beautiful customer and himself. "Thou seest, it is rich, flowery, and variegated as the land it came from. One might fancy the vines and vegetation of that deep soil were shooting from this labor of the loom — nay, the piece is sufficient for any toilette, however ample; see, it is endless as the plains that reared the little animal who supplies the texture. I have parted of that fabric to many dames of England, who have not disdained to traffic with one that risks much in their behalf."

"I fear there are many who find a pleasure in these stuffs, chiefly because their use is forbidden."

"'Twould not be out of nature! Look; this box contains ornaments of the elephant's tooth, cut by a cunning artificer in the far Eastern lands; they do not disfigure a lady's dressing-table, and have a moral, for they remind her of countries where the sex is less happy than at home. Ah! here is a treasure of Mechlin, wrought in a fashion of my own design."

"'Tis beautifully fancied, and might do credit to one who professed the painter's art."

"My youth was much employed in these conceits," returned the trader, unfolding the rich and delicate lace in a manner to show that he had still pleasure in contemplating its texture and quality. "There was a compact between me and the maker, that enough should be furnished to reach from the high church-tower of his town, to the pavement beneath; and yet, you see how little remains! The London dames found it to their taste, and it was not easy to bring even this trifle into the colonies."

"You chose a remarkable measure for an article that was to visit so many different countries, without the formalities of law!"

"We thought to start in the favor of the church, which rarely frowns on those who respect its privileges. Under the sanction of such authority, I will lay aside all that remains, certain it will be needed for thy use."

"So rare a manufacture should be costly?"

La belle Barbérie spoke hesitatingly, and as she raised her eyes, they met the dark organs of her companion, fixed on her face, in a manner that seemed to express a consciousness of the ascendency he was gaining. Startled, at she knew not what the maiden again added hastily —

"This may be fitter for a court lady, than a girl of the colonies."

"None who have yet worn of it, so well become it — I lay it here, as a make-weight in my bargain with the Alderman. This is satin of Tuscany; a country where nature exhibits its extremes, and one whose merchants were princes. Your Florentine was subtle in his fabrics, and happy in his conceits of forms and colors, for which he stood indebted to the riches of his own climate. Observe — the hue of this glossy surface is scarcely so delicate as I have seen the rosy light, at even, playing on the sides of his Apennines!"

"You have then visited the regions, in whose fabrics you deal?" said Alida, suffering the articles to fall from her hand, in the stronger interest she began to feel in their owner.

"'Tis my habit. Here have we a chain from the city of the Isles. The hand of a Venetian could alone form these delicate and nearly insensible links: I refused a string of spotless pearls for that same golden web."

"It was indiscreet, in one who trades at so much hazard."

"I kept the bauble for my pleasure! — Whim is sometimes stronger than the thirst of gain; and this chain does not quit me, till I bestow it on the lady of my love."

"One so actively employed can scarcely spare time to seek a fitting object for the gift."

"Is merit and loveliness in the sex, so rare? La belle Barbérie speaks in the security of many conquests, or she would not deal thus lightly, in a matter that is so serious with most females."

"Among other countries your vessel hath visited a land of witchcraft, or you would not pretend to a knowledge of things, that, in their very nature, must be hidden from a stranger. Of what value may be those beautiful feathers of the ostrich?"

"They came of swarthy Africa, though so spotless themselves. The bunch was had, by secret traffic, from a Moorish man, in exchange for a few skins of Lachrymyæ Christi, that he swallowed with his eyes shut. I dealt with the fellow, only in pity for his thirst, and do not pride myself on the value of the commodity.

It shall go, too, to quicken love between me and thy uncle."

Alida could not object to this liberality, though she was not without a secret opinion that the gifts were no more than delicate and well-concealed offerings to herself. The effect of this suspicion was two-fold; it caused the maiden to become more reserved in the expression of her tastes, though it in no degree lessened her confidence in, and admiration of, the wayward and remarkable trader.

"My uncle will have cause to commend thy generous spirit," said the heiress, bending her head a little coldly, at this repeated declaration of her companion's intentions, "though it would seem that, in trade, justice is as much to be desired as generosity — this seemeth a curious design, wrought with the needle!"

"It is the labor of many a day, fashioned by the hand of a recluse. I bought it of a nun, in France, who passed years in toil, upon the conceit, which is of more value than the material. The meek daughter of solitude wept when she parted with the fabric, for, in her eyes, it had the tie of association and habit. A companion might be lost to one who lives in the confusion of the world, and it should not cause more real sorrow, than parting from the product of her needle, gave that mild resident of the cloisters!"

"And is it permitted for your sex to visit those places of religious retirement?" asked Alida. "I come of a race that pays little deference to monastic life, for we are refugees from the severity of Louis; but yet I never heard my father charge these females with being so regardless of their vows."

"The fact was so repeated to me; for, surely, my sex are not admitted to traffic, directly, with the modest sisters;" (a smile, that Alida was half-disposed to think bold, played about the handsome mouth of the speaker) "but it was so reported. What is your opinion of the merit of woman, in thus seeking refuge from the cares, and haply from the sins, of the world, in institutions of this order."

"Truly the question exceedeth my knowledge. This is not a country to immure females, and the custom causes us of America little thought."

"The usage hath its abuses," continued the dealer in contraband, speaking thoughtfully; "but it is not without its good. There are many of the weak and vain, that would be happier in the cloisters, than if left to the seductions and follies of life. Ah! here is work of English hands. I scarcely know how the articles found their way into the company of the products of the foreign looms. My bales contain, in general, little that is vulgarly sanctioned by the law. Speak me, frankly, belle Alida, and say if you share in the prejudices against the character of us free-traders?"

"I pretend not to judge of regulations that exceed the knowledge and practices of my sex," returned the maiden, with commendable reserve. "There are some who think the abuse of power a justification of its resistance, while others deem a breach of law to be a breach of morals."

"The latter is the doctrine of your man of invested moneys and established fortune! He has entrenched his gains behind acknowledged barriers, and he preaches their sanctity, because they favor his selfishness. We skimmers of the sea —"

Alida started so suddenly, as to cause her companion to cease speaking.

"Are my words frightful, that you pale at their sound?"

"I hope they were used rather in accident, than with their dreaded meaning. I would not have it said — no! 'tis but a chance that springs from some resemblance in your callings. One, like you, can never be the man whose name has grown into a proverb!"

"One like me, beautiful Alida, is much as fortune wills. Of what man, or of what name wouldst speak?"

"'Tis nothing," returned la belle Barbérie, gazing unconsciously at the polished and graceful features of the stranger, longer than was wont in maiden. "Proceed with your explanation — these are rich velvets!"

"They come of Venice, too; but commerce is like the favor which attends the rich, and the Queen of the Adriatic is already far on the decline. That which causes the increase of the husbandman, occasions the downfall of a city. The lagunes are filling with fat soil, and the keel of the trader is less frequent there than of old. Ages hence, the plow may trace furrows where the Bucentaur has floated! The outer India passage has changed the current of prosperity, which ever rushes in the widest and newest track. Nations might learn a moral, by studying the sleepy canals and instructive magnificence of that fallen town; but pride fattens on its own lazy recollections, to the last! — As I was saying, we rovers deal little in musty maxims, that are made by the great and prosperous at home, and are trumpeted abroad, in order that the weak and unhappy should be the more closely riveted in their fetters."

"Methinks you push the principle further than is necessary, for one whose greatest offence against established usage is a little hazardous commerce. These are opinions, that might unsettle the world."

"Rather settle it, by referring all to the rule of right. When governments shall lay their foundations in natural justice, when their object shall be to remove the temptations to err, instead of creating them, and when bodies of men shall feel and acknowledge the responsibilities of individuals — why, then the Water-

Witch, herself, might become a revenue-cutter, and her owner an officer of the customs!"

The velvet fell from the hands of la belle Barbérie, and she arose from her seat with precipitation.

"Speak plainly," said Alida with all her natural firmness. "With whom am I about to traffic?"

"An outcast of society — a man condemned in the opinions of the world — the outlaw — the flagrant wanderer of the ocean — the lawless 'Skimmer of the Seas!'" cried a voice, at the open window.

In another minute, Ludlow was in the room Alida uttered a shriek, veiled her face in her robe, and rushed from the apartment.

CHAPTER XI.

" — Truth will come to light;
Murder cannot be hid long, a man's son may;
But in the end, truth will out."
                                        Launcelot.

THE officer of the Queen had leaped into the pavilion, with the flushed features and all the hurry of an excited man. The exclamations and retreat of la belle Barbérie, for a single moment, diverted his attention; and then he turned, suddenly, not to say fiercely, towards her companion. It is not necessary to repeat the description of the stranger's person, in order to render the change, which instantly occurred in the countenance of Ludlow, intelligible to the reader. His eye, at first, refused to believe there was no other present; and when it had, again and again, searched the whole apartment, it returned to the face and form of the dealer in contraband, with an expression of incredulity and wonder.

"Here is some mistake!" exclaimed the commander of the Coquette, after time had been given for a thorough examination of the room.

"Your gentle manner of entrance," returned the stranger, across whose face there had passed a glow, that might have come equally of anger or of surprise, "has driven the lady from the room. But as you wear the livery of the Queen, I presume you have authority for invading the dwelling of the subject?"

"I had believed — nay, there was reason to be certain, that one whom all of proper loyalty execrate, was to be found here;" stammered the still-confused Ludlow. "There can scarce be a deception, for I plainly heard the discourse of my captors — and yet here is none!"

"I thank you for the high consideration you bestow on my presence."

The manner, rather than the words, of the speaker, induced Ludlow to rivet another look on his countenance. There was a mixed expression of doubt, admiration, and possibly of uneasiness, if not of actual jealousy, in the eye, which slowly read all his lineaments, though the former seemed the stronger sensation of the three.

"We have never met before!" cried Ludlow, when the organ began to grow dim, with the length and steadiness of its gaze.

"The ocean has many paths, and men may journey on them, long, without crossing each other."

"Thou hast served the Queen, though I see thee in this doubtful situation?"

"Never. I am not one to bind myself to the servitude of any woman that lives," returned the free trader, while a mild smile played about his lip "though she wore a thousand diadems! Anne never had an hour of my time, nor a single wish of my heart."

"This is bold language, Sir, for the ear of her officer. The arrival of an unknown brigantine, certain incidents which have occurred to myself this night, your presence here, that bale of articles forbidden by the law, create suspicions that must be satisfied. Who are you?"

"The flagrant wanderer of the ocean — the outcast of society — the condemned in the opinions of world — the lawless 'Skimmer of the Seas!'"

"This cannot be! The tongues of men speak of the personal deformity of that wanderer, no less than of his bold disregard of the law. You would deceive me."

"If then men err so much in that which is visible and unimportant," returned the other, proudly, "is there not reason to doubt their accuracy in matters of more weight. I am surely what I seem, if I am not what I say."

"I will not credit so improbable a tale — give me some proof that what I hear is true."

"Look at that brigantine, whose delicate spars are almost confounded with the back-ground of trees," said the other, approaching the window, and directing the attention of his companion to the Cove: "'Tis the bark that has so often foiled the efforts of all thy cruisers, and which transports me and my wealth whither I will, without the fetters of arbitrary laws, and the meddling inquiries of venal hirelings. The scud, which floats above the sea, is not freer than that vessel, and scarcely more swift. Well is she named the Water-Witch! for her performances on the wide ocean have been such as seem to exceed all natural means. The froth of the sea does not dance more lightly above the waves, than yonder graceful fabric, when driven by the breeze. She is a thing to be loved, Ludlow; trust me, I never yet set affections on woman, with the warmth I feel for the faithful and beautiful machine!"

"This is little more than any mariner could say, in praise of a vessel that he admired."

"Will you say it, Sir, in favor of yon lumbering sloop of Queen Anne? Your Coquette is none of the fairest, and there was more of pretension than of truth, at her christening."

"By the title of my royal mistress, young beardless, but there is an insolence in this language, that might become him you wish to represent! My ship, heavy or light of foot, as she may be, is fated to bring yonder false trader to the judgment."

"By the craft and qualities of the Water-Witch! but this is language that might become one who was at liberty to act his pleasure," returned the stranger tauntingly imitating the tone, in which his angry companion had spoken. "You would have proof of my identity: listen. There is one who vaunts his power, that forgets he is a dupe of my agent, and that even while his words are so full of boldness, he is a captive!"

The brown cheek of Ludlow reddened, and he turned toward the lighter and far less vigorous frame of his companion, as if about to strike him to the earth, when a door opened, and Alida appeared in the saloon.

The meeting, between the commander of the Coquette and his mistress, was not without embarrassment. The anger of the former and the confusion of the latter, for a moment, kept both silent; but as la belle Barbérie had not returned without an object, she was quick to speak.

"I know not whether to approve, or to condemn, the boldness that has prompted Captain Ludlow to enter my pavilion, at this unseasonable hour, and in so unceremonious a manner," she said, "for I am still ignorant of his motive. When he shall please to let me hear it, I may judge better of the merit of the excuse."

"True, we will hear his explanation before condemnation," added the stranger, offering a seat to Alida, which she coldly declined. "Beyond a doubt the gentleman has a motive."

If looks could have destroyed, the speaker would have been annihilated. But as the lady seemed indifferent to the last remark, Ludlow prepared to enter on his vindication.

"I shall not attempt to conceal that an artifice has been practised," he said, "which is accompanied by consequences that I find awkward. The air and manner of the seaman, whose bold conduct you witnessed in the boat, induced me to confide in him more than was prudent, and I have been rewarded by deception."

"In other words, Captain Ludlow is not as sagacious as he had reason to believe," said an ironical voice, at his elbow.

"In what manner am I to blame, or why is my privacy to be interrupted, because a wandering seaman has deceived the commander of the Coquette?" rejoined Alida. "Not only that audacious mariner, but this — this person," she added, adopting a word that use has appropriated to the multitude, "is a stranger to me. There is no other connexion between us, than that you see."

"It is not necessary to say why I landed," continued Ludlow; "but I was weak enough to allow that unknown mariner to quit my ship, in my company; and when I would return, he found means to disarm my men, and make me a prisoner."

"And yet, art thou, for a captive, tolerably free!" added the ironical voice.

"Of what service is this freedom, without the means of using it? The sea separates me from my ship, and my faithful boat's-crew are in fetters. I have been little watched, myself; but though forbidden to approach certain points, enough has been seen to leave no doubts of the character of those whom Alderman Van Beverout entertains."

"Thou wouldst also say, and his niece, Ludlow?"

"I would say nothing harsh to, or disrespectful of, Alida de Barbérie. I will not deny that a harrowing idea possessed me — but I see my error, and repent having been so hasty."

"We may then resume our commerce," said the trader, cooly seating himself before the open bale, while Ludlow and the maiden stood regarding each other in mute surprise. "It is pleasant to exhibit these forbidden treasures to an officer of the Queen. It may prove the means of gaining the royal patronage. We were last among the velvets, and on the lagunes, of Venice. Here is one of a color and quality to form a bridal dress for the Doge himself, in his nuptials with the sea! We men of the ocean look upon that ceremony as a pledge Hymen will not forget us, though we may wander from his altars. Do I justice to the faith of the craft, Captain Ludlow? — or are you a sworn devotee of Neptune, and content to breathe your sighs to Venus, when afloat? Well, if the damps and salt air of the ocean rust the golden chain, it is the fault of cruel nature! — Ah! here is —"

A shrill whistle sounded among the shrubbery, and the speaker became mute. Throwing his cloths carelessly on the bale, he arose again, and seemed to hesitate. Throughout the interview with Ludlow, the air of the free-trader had been mild, though, at times, it was playful; and not for an instant had he seemed to return the resentment which the other had so plainly manifested. It now became perplexed, and, by the workings of his features, it would seem that he vacillated in his opinions. The sounds of the whistle were heard, again.

"Ay, ay, Master Tom!" muttered the dealer in contraband. "Thy note is audible, but why this haste? Beautiful Alida, this shrill summons is to say, that the moment of parting is arrived!"

"We met with less of preparation," returned la belle Barbérie, who preserved all the distant reserve of her sex, under the jealous eyes of her admirer.

"We met without a warning, but shall our separation be without a memorial? Am I to return with all these valuables to the brigantine, or, in their place, must I take the customary golden tribute?"

"I know not that I dare make a traffic which is not sanctioned by the law, in presence of a servitor of the Queen," returned Alida, smiling. "I will not deny that you have much to excite a woman's envy; but our royal mistress might forget her sex, and show little pity, were she to hear of my weakness."

"No fear of that, lady. 'Tis they who are most stern in creating these harsh regulations, that show most frailty in their breach. By the virtues of honest Leadenhall itself, but I should like to tempt the royal Anne, in her closet, with such a display of goodly laces and heavy brocades!"

"That might be more hazardous than wise!"

"I know not. Though seated on a throne, she is but woman. Disguise nature as thou wilt, she is a universal tyrant, and governs all alike. The head that wears a crown dreams of the conquests of the sex, rather than of the conquests of states; the hand that wields the sceptre is fitted to display its prettiness, with the pencil, or the needle; and though words and ideas may be taught and sounded forth with the pomp of royalty; the tone is still that of woman."

"Without bringing into question the merits of our present royal mistress," said Alida, who was a little apt to assert her sex's rights, "there is the example of the glorious Elizabeth, to refute his charge."

"Ay, we have had our Cleopatras in the sea-fight, and fear was found stronger than love! The sea has monsters, and so may have the land. He, that made the earth gave it laws that 'tis not good to break. We men are jealous of our qualities, and little like to see them usurped; and trust me, lady, she that forgets the means that nature bestows, may mourn in sorrow over the fatal error. But, shall we deal in velvet, or is your taste more leaning to brocade?"

Alida and Ludlow listened in admiration to the capricious and fanciful language of the unaccountable trader, and both were equally at a loss to estimate his character. The equivocal air was in general well maintained, though the commander of the Coquette had detected an earnestness and feeling in his manner, when he more particularly addressed la belle Barbérie, that excited an uneasiness he was ashamed to admit, even to himself. That the maiden herself observed this change, might also be inferred, from a richer glow which diffused itself over her features, though it is scarce probable that she was conscious of its effects. When questioned as to her determination concerning his goods, she again regarded Ludlow, doubtingly, ere she answered.

"That you have not studied woman in vain," she laughingly replied, "I must fain acknowledge. And yet, ere I make a decision, suffer me to consult those who, being more accustomed to deal with the laws, are better judges of the propriety of the purchases."

"If this request were not reasonable in itself, it were due to your beauty and station, lady, to grant it. I leave the bale in your care; and, before tomorrow's sun has set, one will await the answer Captain Ludlow, are we to part in friendship, or does your duty to the Queen proscribe the word."

"If what you seem," said Ludlow, "you are a being inexplicable! If this be some masquerade, as I half suspect, 'tis well maintained, at least, though not worthily assumed."

"You are not the first who has refused credit to his senses, in a manner wherein the Water-Witch and her commander have been concerned. Peace, honest Tom — thy whistle will not hasten Father Time! Friend, or not, Captain Ludlow need not be told he is my prisoner."

"That I have fallen into the power of a miscreant —"

"Hist! — if thou hast love of bodily ease and whole bones. Master Thomas Tiller is a man of rude humor, and he as little likes contumely as another. Besides, the honest mariner did but obey my orders, and his character is protected by a superior responsibility."

"Thy orders!" repeated Ludlow, with an expression of eye and lip that might have offended one more disposed to take offence than him he addressed. "The fellow who so well succeeded in his artifice, is one much more likely to command than to obey. If any here be the 'Skimmer of the Seas,' it is he."

"We are no more than the driving spray, which goes whither the winds list. But in what hath the man offended, that he finds so little favor with the Queen's captain? He has not had the boldness to propose a secret traffic with so loyal a gentleman!"

"'Tis well, Sir; you choose a happy occasion for this pleasantry. I landed to manifest the respect that I feel for this lady, and I care not if the world knows the object of the visit. 'Twas no silly artifice that led me hither."

"Spoken with the frankness of a seaman!" said the inexplicable dealer in contraband, though his color lessened and his voice appeared to hesitate. "I admire this loyalty in man to woman; for, as custom has so strongly fettered them in the expression of their inclinations, it is due from us to leave as little doubt as possible of our intentions. It is difficult to think that la belle Barbérie can do wiser than to reward so much manly admiration!"

The stranger cast a glance, which Alida fancied betrayed solicitude, as he spoke, at the maiden and he appeared to expect she would reply.

"When the time shall come for a decision," returned the half-pleased and yet half-offended subject of his allusion, "it may be necessary to call upon very different counsellors for advice. I hear the step of my uncle. Captain Ludlow, I leave it to your discretion to meet him, or not."

The heavy footstep was approaching through the outer rooms of the pavilion. Ludlow hesitated; cast a reproachful look at his mistress; and then he instantly quitted the apartment, by the place through which he had entered. A noise in the shrubbery sufficiently proved that his return was expected, and that he was closely watched.

"Noah's Ark, and our grandmothers!" exclaimed Myndert, appearing at the door with a face red with his exertions. "You have brought us the cast-off finery of our ancestors, Master Seadrift. Here are stuffs of an age that is past, and they should be bartered for gold that hath been spent."

"What now! what now!" responded the free-trader, whose tone and manner seemed to change, at will, in order to suit the; humor of whomsoever he was brought to speak with. "What now, pertinacious burgher, that thou shouldst cry down wares that are but too good for these distant regions! Many is the English duchess who pines to possess but the tithe of these beautiful stuffs I offer thy niece, and, faith — rare is the English duchess that would become them half so well!"

"The girl is seemly, and thy velvets and brocades are passable, but the heavy articles are not fit to offer to a Mohawk Sachem. There must be a reduction of prices, or the invoice cannot pass."

"The greater the pity. But if sail we must, sail we will! The brigantine knows the channel over the Nantucket sands; and, my life on it! the Yankees will find others than the Mohawks for chapmen."

"Thou art as quick in thy motions, Master Seadrift, as the boat itself. Who said that a compromise might not be made, when discussion was prudently and fairly exhausted? Strike off the odd florins, leave the balance in round thousands, and thy trade is done for the season!"

"Not a stiver. Here, count me back the faces of the Braganza; throw enough of thin ducats into the scales to make up the sum, and let thy slaves push inland with the articles, before the morning light comes to tell the story. Here has been one among us, who may do mischief, if he will; though I know not how far he is master of the main secret."

Alderman Van Beverout stared a little wildly about him, adjusted his wig, like one fully conscious of the value of appearances in this world, and then cautiously drew the curtains before the windows.

"I know of none more than common, my niece excepted;" he said, when all these precautions had been observed. "'Tis true the Patroon of Kinderhook is in the house, but as the man sleeps, he is a witness in our favor. We have the testimony of his presence, while his tongue is silent."

"Well, be it so;" rejoined the free-trader, reading, in the imploring eyes of Alida, a petition that he would say no more. "I knew by instinct there was one unusual, and it was not for me to discover that he sleeps. There are dealers on the coast, who, for the sake of insurance, would charge his presence in their bills."

"Say no more, worthy Master Seadrift, and take the gold. To confess the truth, the goods are in the periagua and fairly out of the river. I knew we should come to conclusions in the matter, and time is precious, as there is a cruiser of the Queen so nigh. The rogues will pass the pennant, like innocent market-people, and I'll risk a Flemish gelding against a Virginia nag, that they inquire if the captain has no need of vegetables for his soup! Ah! ha-ha-ha! That Ludlow is a simpleton, niece of mine, and he is not yet fit to deal with men of mature years. You'll think better of his qualities, one day, and bid him be gone like an unwelcome dun."

"I hope these proceedings may be legally sanctioned, uncle?"

"Sanctioned! Luck sanctions all. It is in trade as in war: success gives character and booty, in both. Your rich dealer is sure to be your honest dealer. Plantations and Orders in Council! What are our rulers doing at home, that they need be so vociferous about a little contraband? The rogues will declaim, by the hour, concerning bribery and corruption, while more than half of them get their seats as clandestinely — ay, and as illegally, as you get these rare Mechlin laces. Should the Queen take offence at our dealings, Master Seadrift, bring me another season, or two, as profitable as the last, and I'll be your passenger to London, go on 'change, buy a seat in Parliament, and answer to the royal displeasure from my place, as they call it. By the responsibility of the States General! but I should expect, in such a case, to return Sir Myndert, and then the Manhattanese might hear of a Lady Van Beverout, in which case, pretty Alida, thy assets would be sadly diminished! — so go to thy bed, child, and dream of fine laces, and rich velvets, and duty to old uncles, and discretion, and all manner of agreeable things — kiss me, jade, and to thy pillow."

Alida obeyed, and was preparing to quit the room, when the free-trader presented himself before her with an air at once so gallant and respectful, that she could scarce take offence at the freedom.

"I should fail in gratitude," he said, "were I to part from so generous a customer, without thanks for her liberality. The hope of meeting again, will hasten my return."

"I know not that you are my debtor for these thanks," returned Alida, though she saw that the Alderman was carefully collecting the contents of the bale, and that he had already placed three or four of the most tempting of its articles on her dressing-table. "We cannot be said to have bargained."

"I have parted with more than is visible to vulgar eyes," returned the stranger, dropping his voice, and speaking with an earnestness that caused his auditor to start. "Whether there will be a return for the gift, or perhaps I had better call it loss — time and my stars must show!"

He then took her hand, and raided it to his lips, by an action so graceful and so gentle, as not to alarm the maiden, until the freedom was done. La belle Barbérie reddened to her forehead, seemed disposed to condemn the liberty, frowned, smiled, and curtsying in confusion, withdrew.

Several minutes passed in profound silence, after Alida had disappeared. The stranger was thoughtful, though his bright eye kindled, as if merry thoughts were uppermost; and he paced the room, entirely heedless of the existence of the Alderman. The latter, however, soon took occasion to remind his companion of his presence.

"No fear of the girl's prating," exclaimed the Alderman, when his task was ended. "She is an excellent and dutiful niece; and here, you see, is a balance on her side of the account, that would shut the mouth of the wife of the First Lord of the Treasury. I disliked the manner in which you would have the child introduced; for, look you, I do not think that either Monsieur Barbérie, or my late sister, would altogether approve of her entering into traffic, so very young — but what is done, is done; and the Norman himself could not deny that I have made a fair set-off, of very excellent commodities, for his daughter's benefit. When dost mean to sail Master Seadrift?"

"With the morning tide. I little like the neighborhood of these meddling guarda-costas."

"Bravely answered! Prudence is a cardinal quality in a private trader; and it is a quality that I esteem in Master Skimmer, next to his punctuality Dates and obligations! I wish half of the firms, of three and four names, without counting the Co.'s, were as much to be depended on. Dost not think it safer to repass the inlet, under favor of the darkness?"

"'Tis impossible. The flood is entering it like water rushing through a raceway, and we have the wind at east. But, fear not; the brigantine carries no vulgar freight, and your commerce has given us a swept hold. The Queen and the Braganza, with Holland ducats, might show their faces even in the Royal Exchequer itself! We have no want of passes, and the Miller's-Maid is just as good a name to hail by, as the 'Water-witch.' We begin to tire of this constant running, and have half a mind to taste the pleasures of your Jersey sports, for a week. There should be shooting on the upper plains?"

"Heaven forbid! Heaven forbid! Master Seadrift. I had all the deer taken for the skins, ten years ago — and as to birds, they deserted us, to a pigeon, when the last tribe of the savages went west of the Delaware. Thou hast discharged thy brigantine to better effect, than thou couldst ever discharge thy fowling-pieces. I hope the hospitality of the Lust in Rust is no problem — but, blushes and curiosity! I could wish to keep a fair countenance, among my neighbors. Art sure the impertinent masts of the brigantine will not be seen above the trees, when the day comes? This Captain Ludlow is no laggard when he thinks his duty actually concerned."

"We shall endeavor to keep him quiet. The cover of the trees, and the berth of the boat, make all snug, as respects his people. I leave worthy Tiller to settle balances between us; and so, I take my leave. Master Alderman — a word at parting Does the Viscount Cornbury still tarry in the Provinces?"

"Like a fixture. There is not a mercantile house in the colony more firmly established."

"There are unsettled affairs between us. A small premium would buy the obligations —"

"Heaven keep thee, Master Seadrift, and pleasant voyages, back and forth! As for the Viscount's responsibility — the Queen may trust him with another Province, but Myndert Van Beverout would not give him credit for the tail of a marten; and so, again, Heaven preserve thee!"

The dealer in contraband appeared to tear himself from the sight of all the little elegancies that adorned the apartment of la belle Barbérie, with reluctance. His adieus to the Alderman were rather cavalier, for he still maintained a cold and abstracted air; but as the other scarcely observed the forms of decorum, in his evident desire to get rid of his guest, the latter was finally obliged to depart. He disappeared by the low balcony, where he had entered.

When Myndert Van Beverout was alone, he shut the windows of the pavilion of his niece, and retired to his own part of the dwelling. Here the thrifty burgher first busied himself in making sundry calculations, with a zeal that proved how much his mind was engrossed by the occupation. After this preliminary step, he gave a short but secret conference to the mariner of the India-shawl, during which there was much clinking of gold pieces. But when the latter retired, the master of the villa first looked to the trifling securities which were then, as now, observed in the fastenings of an American country house; when he walked forth upon the lawn, like one who felt the necessity of breathing the open air He cast more than one inquiring glance at the windows of the room which was occupied by Oloff Van Staats, where all was happily silent; at the equally immovable brigantine in the Cove; and at the more distant and still motionless hull of the cruiser of the crown. All around him was in the quiet of midnight Even the boats, which he knew to be plying between the land and the little vessel at anchor, were invisible; and he re-entered his habitation, with the security one would be apt to feel, under similar circumstances, in a region so little tenanted, and so little watched, as that in which he lived.

CHAPTER XII.

"Come on, Nerissa; I have work in hand,
That you, yet, know not of —"

Merchant of Venice.

NOTWITHSTANDING the active movements which had taken place in and around the buildings of the Lust in Rust, during the night which ended with our last chapter, none but the initiated were in the smallest degree aware of their existence. Oloff Van Staats was early afoot; and when he appeared on the lawn, to scent the morning air, there was nothing visible, to give rise to a suspicion that aught extraordinary had occurred during his slumbers. La Cour des Fées was still closed, but the person of the faithful François was seen, near the abode of his young mistress, busied in some of those pretty little offices, that can easily be imagined would be agreeable to a maiden of her years and station. Van Staats of Kinderhook had as little of romance in his composition, as could well be in a youth of five-and-twenty, who was commonly thought to be enamoured, and who was not altogether ignorant of the conventional sympathies of the passion. The man was mortal, and as the personal attractions of la belle Barbérie were sufficiently obvious, he had not entirely escaped the fate, which seems nearly inseparable from young fancy, when excited by beauty. He drew nigh to the pavilion, and, by a guarded but decisive manœuvre, he managed to come so close to the valet, as to render a verbal communication not only natural, but nearly unavoidable.

"A fair morning and a healthful air, Monsieur François;" commenced the young Patroon, acknowledging the low salute of the domestic, by gravely lifting his own beaver. "This is a comfortable abode for the warm months, and one it might be well to visit oftener."

"When Monsieur le Patteron shall be de lor' of ce manoir, aussi, he shall come when he shall have la volonté," returned François, who knew that a pleasantry of his ought not to be construed into an engagement on the part of her he served, while it could not fail to be agreeable to him who heard it. "Monsieur de Van Staats, est grand propriétaire sur la rivière, and one day, peut-être, he shall be propriétaire sur la mèr!"

"I have thought of imitating the example of the Alderman, honest Francis, and of building a villa on the coast; but there will be time for that, when I shall find myself more established in life! Your young mistress is not yet moving, Francis?"

"Ma foi, non — Mam'selle Alide sleep! — 'tis good symptôme, Monsieur Patteron, pour les jeunes personnes, to tres bien sleep. Monsieur, et toute la famille de Barbérie sleep à merveille! Oui, c'est toujours une famille remarquable, poui le sommeil!"

"Yet one would wish to breathe this fresh and invigorating air, which comes from off the sea, like a balm, in the early hours of the day."

"Sans doute, Monsieur. C'est un miracle, how Mam'selle love de air! Personne do not love air more, as Mam'selle Alide. Bah! — It was grand plaisir to see how Monsieur de Barbérie love de air!"

"Perhaps, Mr. Francis, your young lady is ignorant of the hour. It might be well to knock at the door, or perhaps at the window. I confess, I should much admire to see her bright face, smiling from that window, on this soft morning scene."

It is not probable that the imagination of the Patroon of Kinderhook ever before took so high a flight; and there was reason to suspect, by the wavering and alarmed glance that he cast around him after so unequivocal an expression of weakness, that he already repented his temerity. François, who would not willingly disoblige a man that was known to possess a hundred thousand acres of land, with manorial rights, besides personals of no mean amount, felt embarrassed by the request; but was enabled to recollect in time, that the heiress was known to possess a decision of character that might choose to control her own pleasures.

"Well, I shall be too happy to knock; mais, Monsieur sais, dat sleep est si agréable, pour les jeunes personnes! On n'a jamais knock, dans la famille de Monsieur de Barbérie, et je suis sûr, que Mam'selle Alide, do not love to hear de knock — pourtant, si Monsieur le Patteron le veut, I shall consult ses — Voila! Monsieur Bevre, qui vient sans knock à la fenêtre. J'ai l'honneur de vous laisser avec Monsieur Al'erman."

And so the complaisant but still considerate valet bowed himself out of a dilemma, that he found, as he muttered to himself, while retiring, 'tant soit peu ennuyant.'

The air and manner of the Alderman, as he approached his guest, were, like the character of the man, hale, hearty and a little occupied with his own enjoyments and feelings. He hemmed thrice, ere he was near enough to speak; and each of the strong expirations seemed to invite the admiration of the Patroon, for the strength of his lungs, and for the purity of the atmosphere around a villa which acknowledged him for its owner.

"Zephyrs and Spas! but this is the abode of health, Patroon!" cried the burgher, as soon as these demonstrations of his own bodily condition had been sufficiently repeated. "One sometimes feels in this air equal to holding a discourse, across the Atlantic, with his friends at Scheveling, or the Helder. A broad and deep chest, air like this from the sea, with a clear conscience, and a lucky hit in the way of trade, cause the lungs of a man to play as easily and as imperceptibly as the wings of a humming-bird. Let me see; there are few four-score men in thy stock. The last Patroon closed the books at sixty-six; and his father went but a little beyond seventy. I wonder, there has never been an intermarriage, among you, with the Van Courtlandts; that blood is as good as an insurance to four-score and ten, of itself."

"I find the air of your villa, Mr. Van Beverout, a cordial that one could wish to take often," returned the other, who had far less of the brusque manner of the trader, than his companion. "It is a pity that all who have the choice, do not profit by their opportunities to breathe it."

"You allude to the lazy mariners in yon vessel! Her Majesty's servants are seldom in a hurry; and as for this brigantine in the Cove, the fellow seems to have gotten in by magic! I warrant me, now, the rogue is there for no good, and that the Queen's Exchequer will be none the richer for his visit. Harkee, you Brom," calling to an aged black, who was working at no great distance from the dwelling, and who was deep in his master's confidence, "hast seen any boats plying between yonder roguish-looking brigantine and the land?"

The negro shook his head, like the earthen image of a mandarin, and laughed loud and heartily.

"I b'rieve he do all he mischief among a Yankee, an' he only come here to take he breat'," said the wily slave. "Well, I wish, wid all a heart, dere would come free-trader, some time, along our shore Dat gib a chance to poor black man, to make an honest penny!"

"You see, Patroon, human nature itself rises against monopoly! That was the voice of instinct, speaking with the tongue of Brom; and it is no easy task, for a merchant, to keep his dependants obedient to laws, which, in themselves, create so constant a temptation to break them. Well, well; we will always hope for the best, and endeavor to act like dutiful subjects. The boat is not amiss, as to form and rig, let her come from where she will. Dost think the wind will be off the land this morning?"

"There are signs of a change in the clouds. One could wish that all should be out in the air, to taste this pleasant sea-breeze while it lasts."

"Come, come," cried the Alderman, who had for a moment studied the state of the heavens with a solicitude, that he feared might attract his companion's attention. "We will taste our breakfast. This is the spot to show the use of teeth! The negroes have not been idle during the night, Mr. Van Staats — he-e-em — I say, Sir, they have not been idle — and we shall have a choice among the dainties of the river and bay. That cloud above the mouth of the Raritan appears to rise, and we may yet have a breeze at west!"

"Yonder comes a boat in the direction of the city," observed the other, reluctantly obeying a motion of the Alderman to retire to the apartment where they were accustomed to break their fasts. "To me, it seems to approach with more than ordinary speed."

"There are stout arms at its oars! Can it be a messenger for the cruiser? no — it rather steers more for our own landing. These Jersey-men are often overtaken by the night, between York and their own doors. And now, Patroon, we will to our knives and forks, like men who have taken the best stomachics."

"And are we to refresh ourselves alone?" demanded the young man, who ever and anon cast a sidelong and wistful glance at the closed and immovable shutters of la Cour des Fées.

"Thy mother hath spoilt thee, young Oloff; unless the coffee comes from a pretty female hand, it loses its savor. I take thy meaning, and think none the worse of thee; for the weakness is natural at thy years. Celibacy and independence! A man must get beyond forty, before he is ever sure of being his own master. Come hither, Master Francis. It is time my niece had shaken off this laziness, and shown her bright face to the sun. We wait for her fair services at the table. I see nothing of that lazy hussy, Dinah, any more than of her mistress."

"Assurément non, Monsieur," returned the valet. "Mam'selle Dinah do not love trop d'activité. Mais, Monsieur Al'erman, elles sont jeunes, toutes les deux! Le sommeil est bien salutaire, pour la jeunesse."

"The girl is no longer in her cradle, Francis, and it is time to rattle at the windows. As for the black minx, who should have been up and at her duty this hour, there will be a balance to settle between us. Come, Patroon — the appetite will not await the laziness of a wilful girl; we will to the table. Dost think the wind will stand at west this morning?"

Thus saying, the Alderman led the way into the little parlor, where a neat and comfortable service invited them to break their morning fast. He was followed by Oloff Van Staats, with a lingering step for the young man really longed to see the windows of the pavilion open, and the fair face of Alida smiling amid the other beautiful objects of the scene. François proceeded to take such measures to arouse his mistress, as he believed to comport with his duty to her uncle, and his own ideas of bienséance. After some little delay, the Alderman and his guest took their seats at the table; the former loudly protesting against the necessity of waiting for the idle, and throwing in an occasional moral concerning the particular merit of punctuality in domestic economy, as well as in the affairs of commerce.

"The ancients divided time," said the somewhat pertinacious commentator, "into years, months, weeks, days, hours, minutes, and moments, as they divided numbers into units, tens, hundreds, thousands, and tens of thousands; and both with an object. If we commence at the bottom, and employ well the moments, Mr. Van Staats, we turn the minutes into tens, the hours into hundreds, and the weeks and months into thousands — ay! and when there is a happy state of trade, into tens of thousands! Missing an hour, therefore, is somewhat like dropping an important figure in a complex calculation, and the whole labor may be useless, for want of punctuality in one, as for want of accuracy in the other. Your father, the late Patroon, was what may be called a minute-man. He was as certain to be seen in his pew, at church, at the stroke of the clock, as to pay a bill, when its items had been properly examined. Ah! it was a blessing to hold one of his notes, though they were far scarcer than broad pieces, or bullion. I have heard it said, Patroon, that the manor is backed by plenty of Johannes and Dutch ducats!"

"The descendant has no reason to reproach his ancestors with want of fore-sight."

"Prudently answered — not a word too much, not too little — a principle on which all honest men settle their accounts. By proper management, such a foundation might be made to uphold an estate that should count thousands with the best of Holland or England. Growth and majority! Patroon; but we of the colonies must come to man's estate in time, like our cousins on the dykes of the Low Countries, or our rulers among the smithies of England. Erasmus, look at that cloud over the Raritan, and tell me if it rises."

The negro reported that the vapor was stationary; and, at the same time, by way of episode, he told his master that the boat which had been seen approaching the land had reached the wharf, and that some of its crew were ascending the hill towards the Lust in Rust.

"Let them come of all hospitality," returned the Alderman, heartily; "I warrant me, they are honest farmers from the interior, a-hungered with the toil of the night. Go tell the cook to feed them with the best, and bid them welcome. And harkee, boy — if there be among them any comfortable yeoman, bid the man enter and sit at our table. This is not a country, Patroon, to be nice about the quality of the cloth a man has on his back, or whether he wears a wig or only his own hair. What is the fellow gaping at?"

Erasmus rubbed his eyes, and then showing his teeth to the full extent of a double row, that glittered like pearls, he gave his master to understand, that the negro, introduced to the reader under the name of Euclid, and who was certainly his own brother of the half-blood, or by the mother's side, was entering the villa. The intelligence caused a sudden cessation of the masticating process in the Alderman, who had not, however, time to express his wonder ere two doors simultaneously opened, and François presented himself at the one, while the shining and doubting face of the slave from town darkened the other. The eyes of Myndert rolled first to this side and then to that, a certain misgiving of the heart preventing him from speaking to either; for he saw, in the disturbed features of each, omens that bade him prepare himself for unwelcome tidings. The reader will perceive, by the description we shall give that there was abundant reason for the sagacious burgher's alarm.

The visage of the valet, at all times meagre and long, seemed extended to far more than its usual dimensions, the under jaw appearing fallen and trebly attenuated. The light-blue protruding eyes were open to the utmost, and they expressed a certain confused wildness, that was none the less striking, for the painful expression of mental suffering, with which it was mingled. Both hands were raised, with the palms outward; while the shoulders of the poor fellow were elevated so high, as entirely to destroy the little symmetry that Nature had bestowed on that particular part of his frame.

On the other hand, the look of the negro was guilty, dogged, and cunning. His eye leered askance, seeming to wish to play around the person of his master, as, it will be seen, his language endeavored to play around his understanding. The hands crushed the crown of a woollen hat between their fingers, and one of his feet described semicircles with its toe, by performing nervous evolutions on its heel.

"Well!" ejaculated Myndert, regarding each in turn. "What news from the Canadas? — Is the Queen dead, or has she restored the colony to the United Provinces?"

"Mam'selle Alide!" exclaimed, or rather groaned, François.

"The poor dumb beast! —" muttered Euclid.

The knives and the forks fell from the hands of Myndert and his guest, as it were by a simultaneous paralysis. The latter involuntarily arose; while the former planted his solid person still more firmly in its seat, like one who was preparing to meet some severe and expected shock, with all the physical resolution he could muster.

" — What of my niece! — What of my geldings? — You have called upon Dinah?"

"Sans doute, Monsieur!"

" — And you kept the keys of the stable?"

"I nebber let him go, at all!"

" — And you bade her call her mistress?"

"She no make answair, de tout."

" — The animals were fed and watered, as I ordered?"

"'Em nebber take he food, better!"

" — You entered the chamber of my niece, yourself, to awake her?"

"Monsieur a raison."

"What the devil has befallen the innocent?"

"He lose he stomach quite, and I t'ink it great time 'fore it ebber come back."

" — Mister Francis, I desire to know the answer of Monsieur Barbérie's daughter."

"Mam'selle no répond, Monsieur; pas un syllabe!"

" — Drenchers and fleams! The beauty should have been drenched and blooded —"

"He'm too late for dat, Masser, on honor."

" — The obstinate hussy! This comes of her Huguenot breed, a race that would quit house and lands rather than change its place of worship!"

"La famille de Barbérie est honorable, Monsieur mais le Grand Monarque fut un pen trop exigeant. Vraiment, la dragonade était mal avisée, pour faire des chrétiens!"

"Apoplexies and hurry! you should have sent for the farrier to administer to the sufferer, thou black hound!"

"'Em go for a butcher, Masser, to save he skin; for he war' too soon dead."

The word dead produced a sudden pause. The preceding dialogue had been so rapid, and question and answer, no less than the ideas of the principal speaker, had got so confused, that, for a moment, he was actually at a loss to understand, whether the last great debt of nature had been paid by la belle Barbérie, or one of the Flemish geldings. Until now, consternation, as well as the confusion of the interview, had constrained the Patroon to be silent, but he profited by the breathing-time to interpose.

"It is evident, Mr. Van Beverout," he said, speaking with a tremor in the voice, which betrayed his own uneasiness, "that some untoward event has occurred. Perhaps the negro and I had better retire, that you may question Francis concerning that which hath befallen Mademoiselle Barbérie, more at your leisure."

The Alderman was recalled from a profound stupor, by this gentlemanlike and considerate proposal. He bowed his acknowledgments, and permitted Mr. Van Staats to quit the room; but when Euclid would have followed, he signed to the negro to remain.

"I may have occasion to question thee farther," he said, in a voice that had lost most of that compass and depth for which it was so remarkable. "Stand there, sirrah, and be in readiness to answer. And now, Mr. Francis, I desire to know why my niece declines taking the breakfast with myself and my guest?"

"Mon Dieu, Monsieur, it is not possible y répondre Les sentiments des demoiselles are nevair décides!"

"Go then, and say to her, that my sentiments are decided to curtail certain bequests and devises, which have consulted her interests more than strict justice to others of my blood — ay, and even of my name, might dictate."

"Monsieur y réfléchira. Mam'selle Alide be so young personne!"

"Old or young, my mind is made up; and so to your Cour des Fées, and tell the lazy minx as much. Thou hast ridden that innocent, thou scowling imp of darkness!"

"Mais, pensez-y, je vous en prie, Monsieur. Mam'selle shall nevair se sauver encore; jamais, je vous en répond."

"What is the fellow jabbering about?" exclaimed the Alderman, whose mouth fell nearly to the degree that rendered the countenance of the valet so singularly expressive of distress. "Where is my niece, Sir? — and what means this allusion to her absence?"

"La fille de Monsieur de Barbérie n'y est pas!" cried François, whose heart was too full to utter more. The aged and affectionate domestic laid his hand on his breast, with an air of acute suffering; and then, remembering the presence of his superior, he turned, bowed with a manner of profound condolence, struggled manfully with his own emotion, and succeeded in getting out of the room with dignity and steadiness.

It is due to the character of Alderman Van Beverout, to say, that the blow occasioned by the sudden death of the Flemish gelding, lost some of its force, in consequence of so unlooked-for a report concerning the inexplicable absence of his niece. Euclid was questioned, menaced, and even anathematized, more than once, during the next ten minutes; but the cunning slave succeeded in confounding himself so effectually with the rest of his connexions of the half-blood, during the search which instantly followed the report of François, that his crime was partially forgotten.

On entering la Cour des Fées, it was, in truth, found to want her whose beauty and grace had lent its chief attraction. The outer rooms, which were small, and ordinarily occupied during the day by François and the negress called Dinah, and in the night by the latter only, were in the state in which they might be expected to be seen. The apartment of the attendant furnished evidence that its occupant had quitted it in haste, though there was every appearance of her having retired to rest at the usual hour. Clothes were scattered carelessly about; and though most of her personal effects had disappeared enough remained to prove that her departure had been hurried and unforeseen.

On the other hand, the little saloon, with the dressing-room and bed-room of la belle Barbérie, were in a state of the most studied arrangement. Not an article of furniture was displaced, a door ajar, or a window open. The pavilion had evidently been quitted by its ordinary passage, and the door had been closed in the customary manner, without using the fastenings. The bed had evidently not been entered, for the linen was smooth and untouched. In short, so complete was the order of the place, that, yielding to a powerful natural feeling, the Alderman called aloud on his truant niece, by name, as if he expected to see her appear from some place, in which she had secreted her person, in idle sport. But this touching expedient was vain. The voice sounded hollow through the deserted rooms; and though all waited long to listen, there came no playful or laughing answer back.

"Alida!" cried the burgher, for the fourth and last time, "come forth, child; I forgive thee thy idle sport, and all I have said of disinheritance was but a jest. Come forth, my sister's daughter, and kiss thy old uncle!"

The Patroon turned aside, as he heard a man so Known for his worldliness yielding to the power of nature; and the lord of a hundred thousand acres forgot his own disappointment, in the force of sympathy.

"Let us retire," he said, gently urging the burgher to quit the place. "A little reflection will enable us to deride what should be done."

The Alderman complied. Before quitting the place, however, its closets and drawers were examined; and the search left no further doubts of the step which the young heiress had taken. Her clothes, books, utensils for drawing, and even the lighter instruments of music, had disappeared.

CHAPTER XIII.

" — Ay, that way goes the game,
Now I perceive that she hath made compare
Between our statures —"
Midsummer-Night's Dream.

THE tide of existence floats downward, and with it go, in their greatest strength, all those affections that unite families and kindred. We learn to know our parents in the fullness of their reason, and commonly in the perfection of their bodily strength. Reverence and respect both mingle with our love; but the affection, with which we watch the helplessness of infancy, the interest with which we see the ingenuous and young profiting by our care, the pride of improvement, and the magic of hope, create an intensity of sympathy in their favor, that almost equals the identity of self-love. There is a mysterious and double existence, in the tie that binds the parent to the child. With a volition and passions of its own, the latter has power to plant a sting in the bosom of the former, that shall wound as acutely as the errors which arise from mistakes, almost from crimes, of its own. But, when the misconduct of the descendant can be traced to neglect, or to a vicious instruction, then, indeed, even the pang of a wounded conscience may be added to the sufferings of those who have gone before. Such, in some measure, was the nature of the pain that Alderman Van Beverout was condemned to feel, when at leisure to reflect on the ill-judged measure that had been taken by la belle Barbérie.

"She was a pleasant and coaxing minx, Patroon," said the burgher, pacing the room they occupied, with a quick and heavy step, and speaking unconsciously of his niece, as of one already beyond the interests of life; "and as wilful and head-strong as an unbroken colt. Thou hard-riding imp! I shall never find a match for the poor disconsolate survivor. But the girl had a thousand agreeable and delightful ways with her, that made her the delight of my old days. She has not done wisely, to desert the friend and guardian of her youth, ay, even of her child-hood, in order to seek protection from strangers. This is an unhappy world, Mr. Van Staats! All our calculations come to nought; and it is in the power of fortune to reverse the most reasonable and wisest of our expectations. A gale of wind drives the richly-freighted ship to the bottom; a sudden fall in the market robs us of our gold, as the November wind strips the oak of its leaves; and bankruptcies and decayed credit often afflict the days of the oldest houses, as disease saps the strength of the body — Alida! Alida! thou hast wounded one that never harmed thee, and rendered my age miserable!"

"It is vain to contend with the inclinations," returned the proprietor of the manor, sighing in a manner that did no discredit to the sincerity of his remark. "I could have been happy to have placed your niece in the situation that my respected mother filled with so much dignity and credit, but it is now too late —"

"We don't know that — we don't know that;" interrupted the Alderman, who still clung to the hope of effecting the first great wish of his heart, with the pertinacity with which he would have clung to the terms of any other fortunate bargain. "We should never despair, Mr. Van Staats, as long as the transaction is left open."

"The manner in which Mademoiselle Barbérie has expressed her preference, is so very decided, that I see no hope of completing the arrangement."

"Mere coquetry, Sir, mere coquetry! The girl has disappeared in order to enhance the value of her future submission. One should never regard a treaty at an end, so long as reasonable hopes remain that it may be productive to the parties."

"I fear, Sir, there is more of the coquette in this step of the young lady, than a gentleman can overlook," returned the Patroon a little dryly, and with far more point than he was accustomed to use. "If the commander of Her Majesty's cruiser be not a happy man, he will not have occasion to reproach his mistress with disdain!"

"I am not certain, Mr. Van Staats, that in the actual situation of our stipulations, I ought to overlook an innuendo that seems to reflect on the discretion of my ward. Captain Ludlow — well, sirrah! what is the meaning of this impertinence?"

"He'm waiting to see Masser," returned the gaping Erasmus, who stood with the door in his hand, admiring the secret intelligence of his master, who had so readily anticipated his errand.

"Who is waiting? — What does the simpleton mean?"

"I mean 'a gentle'um Masser say."

"The fortunate man is here to remind us of his success," haughtily observed Van Staats of Kinderhook. "There can be no necessity of my presence at an interview between Alderman Van Beverout and his nephew."

The justly-mortified Patroon bowed ceremoniously to the equally disappointed burgher, and left the room the moment he had done speaking. The negro took his retreat as a favorable symptom for one who was generally known to be his rival; and he hastened to inform the young captain, that the coast was clear.

The meeting, that instantly succeeded, was sufficiently constrained and awkward. Alderman Van Beverout assumed a manner of offended authority and wounded affection; while the officer of the Queen wore an air of compelled submission to a duty that he found to be disagreeable. The introduction of the discourse was consequently ceremonious, and punctiliously observant of courtesy.

"It has become my office," continued Ludlow, after the preliminaries had been observed, "to express the surprise I feel, that a vessel of the exceedingly equivocal appearance of the brigantine, that is anchored in the Cove, should be found in a situation to create unpleasant suspicions concerning the commercial propriety of a merchant so well known as Mr. Alderman Van Beverout."

"The credit of Myndert Van Beverout is too well established, Captain Cornelius Ludlow, to be affected by the accidental position of ships and bays. I see two vessels anchored near the Lust in Rust, and if called upon to give my testimony before the Queen in Council, I should declare that the one which wears her royal pennant had done more wrong to her subjects than the stranger. But what harm is known of the latter?"

"I shall not conceal any of the facts; for I feel that this is a case, in which a gentleman of your station has the fullest right to the benefit of explanations —"

"Hem —" interrupted the burgher, who disliked the manner in which his companion had opened the interview, and who thought he saw the commencement of a forced compromise in the turn it was taking — "Hem — I commend your moderation, Captain Ludlow. Sir, we are flattered in having a native of the Province in so honorable a command on the coast. Be seated, I pray you, young gentleman, that we may converse more at leisure. The Ludlows are an ancient and well-established family in the colonies; and though they were no friends of King Charles, why — we have others here in the same predicament. There are few crowns in Europe that might not trace some of their discontented subjects to these colonies; and the greater the reason, say I, why we should not be too hasty in giving faith to the wisdom of this European legislation. I do not pretend, Sir, to admire all the commercial regulations which flow from the wisdom of Her Majesty's counsellors. Candor forbids that I should deny this truth: but — what of the brigantine in the Cove?"

"It is not necessary to tell one so familiar with the affairs of commerce, of the character of a vessel called the Water-Witch, nor of that of its lawless commander, the notorious 'Skimmer of the Seas.'"

"Captain Ludlow is not about to accuse Alderman Van Beverout of a connexion with such a man!" exclaimed the burgher, rising as it were involuntarily, and actually recoiling a foot or two, apparently under the force of indignation and surprise.

"Sir, I am not commissioned to accuse any of the Queen's subjects. My duty is to guard her interests on the water, to oppose her open enemies, and to uphold her royal prerogatives."

"An honorable employment, and one I doubt not that is honorably discharged. Resume your seat, Sir; for I foresee that the conference is likely to end as it should, between a son of the late very respectable King's counsellor and his father's friend. You have reason then for thinking that this brigantine, which has so suddenly appeared in the Cove, has some remote connexion with the Skimmer of the Seas?"

"I believe the vessel to be the famous Water-Witch itself, and her commander to be, of course, that well-known adventurer."

"Well, Sir — well, Sir — this may be so. It is impossible for me to deny it — but what should such a reprobate be doing here, under the guns of a Queen's cruiser?"

"Mr. Alderman, my admiration of your niece is not unknown to you."

"I have suspected it, Sir;" returned the burgher, who believed the tenor of the compromise was getting clearer, but who still waited to know the exact value of the concessions the other party would make, before he closed a bargain, in a hurry, of which he might repent at his leisure — "Indeed, it has even been the subject of some discourse between us."

"This admiration induced me to visit your villa, the past night —"

"This is a fact too well established, young gentleman."

"Whence I took away —" Ludlow hesitated, as if anxious to select his words —

"Alida Barbérie."

"Alida Barbérie!"

"Ay, Sir; my niece, or perhaps I should say my heiress, as well as the heiress of old Etienne de Barbérie. The cruise was short, Captain Cornelius Ludlow; but the prize-money will be ample — unless, indeed, a claim to neutral privileges should be established in favor of part of the cargo!"

"Sir, your pleasantry is amusing, but I have little leisure for its enjoyment. That I visited the Cour lies Fées, shall not be denied. I think la belle Barbérie will not be offended, under the circumstances, with this acknowledgment."

"If she is, the jade has a rare squeamishness, after what has passed!"

"I pretend not to judge of more than my duty. The desire to serve my royal mistress had induced me, Mr. Van Beverout, to cause a seaman of odd attire and audacious deportment to enter the Coquette. You will know the man, when I tell you that he was your companion in the island ferry-boat."

"Yes, yes, I confess there was a mariner of the long voyage there, who caused much surprise, and some uneasiness, to myself and niece, as well as to Van Staats of Kinderhook."

Ludlow smiled, like one not to be deceived, as he continued.

"Well, Sir, this man so far succeeded, as to tempt me to suffer him to land, under the obligation of some half-extorted promise — we came into the river together, and entered your grounds in company."

Alderman Van Beverout now began to listen like a man who dreaded, while he desired to catch, each syllable. Observing that Ludlow paused, and watched his countenance with a cool and steady eye, he recovered his self-command, and affected a mere ordinary curiosity, while he signed to him to proceed.

"I am not sure I tell Alderman Van Beverout any thing that is new," resumed the young officer, "when I add, that the fellow suffered me to visit the pavilion, and then contrived to lead me into an ambush of lawless men, having previously succeeded in making captives of my boat's-crew."

"Seizures and warrants!" exclaimed the burgher in his natural strong and hasty manner of speaking.

"This is the first I have heard of the affair. It was ill-judged, to call it by no other term."

Ludlow seemed relieved, when he saw, by the undisguised amazement of his companion, that the latter was, in truth, ignorant of the matter in which lie had been detained.

"It might not have been, Sir, had our watch been as vigilant as their artifice was deep," he continued. "But I was little guarded, and having no means to reach my ship, I —"

"Ay, ay, Captain Ludlow; it is not necessary to be so circumstantial; you proceeded to the wharf, and —"

"Perhaps, Sir, I obeyed my feelings, rather than my duty," observed Ludlow, coloring high, when he perceived that the burgher paused to clear his throat "I returned to the pavilion, where —"

"You persuaded a niece to forget her duty to her uncle and protector."

"This is a harsh and most unjustifiable charge, both as respects the young lady and myself. I can distinguish between a very natural desire to possess articles of commerce that are denied by the laws and a more deliberate and mercenary plot against the revenue of the country. I believe there are few of her years and sex, who would refuse to purchase the articles I saw presented to the eyes of la belle Barbérie, especially when the utmost hazard could be no more than their loss, as they were already introduced into the country."

"A just discrimination, and one likely to render the arrangement of our little affairs less difficult! I was sure that my old friend the counsellor would not have left a son of his ignorant of principles, more especially as he was about to embark in a profession of so much responsibility. And so, my niece had the imprudence to entertain a dealer in contraband?"

"Alderman Van Beverout, there were boats in motion on the water, between this landing and the brigantine in the Cove. A periagua even left the river for the city, at the extraordinary hour of midnight!"

"Sir, boats will move on the water, when the hands of man set them in motion; but what have I to answer for in the matter? If goods have entered the Province, without license, why, they must be found and condemned; and if free-traders are on the coast, they should be caught. Would it not be well to proceed to town, and lay the fact of this strange brigantine's presence before the Governor, withou delay?"

"I have other intentions. If, as you say, goods have gone up the bay, it is too late for me to stop them; but it is not too late to attempt to seize yon brigantine. Now, I would perform this duty in a manner as little likely to offend any of reputable name, as my allegiance will admit."

"Sir, I extol this discretion — not that there is any testimony to implicate more than the crew, but credit is a delicate flower, and it should be handled tenderly. I see an opening for an arrangement — but, we will, as in duty bound, hear your propositions first, since you may be said to speak with the authority of the Queen. I will merely surmise that terms should be moderate, between friends — perhaps I should say, between connexions, Captain Ludlow."

"I am flattered by the word, Sir," returned the young sailor, smiling with an expression of delight. "First suffer me to be admitted to the charming Cour des Fées, but for a moment."

"That is a favor which can hardly be refused you, who may be said to have a right, now, to enter the pavilion at pleasure," returned the Alderman, unhesitatingly leading the way through the long passage to the deserted apartments of his niece, and continuing the blind allusions to the affairs of the preceding night, in the same indirect manner as had distinguished the dialogue during the whole interview. "I shall not be unreasonable, young gentleman, and here is the pavilion of my niece; I wish I could add, and here also is its mistress!"

"And is la belle Barbérie no longer a tenant of la Cour des Fées!" demanded Ludlow, in a surprise too natural to be feigned.

Alderman Van Beverout regarded the young man in wonder; pondered a moment, to consider how far denying a knowledge of the absence of his niece might benefit the officer, in the pending negotiation; and then he dryly observed, "Boats passed on the water, during the night. If the men of Captain Ludlow were at first imprisoned, I presume they were set at liberty at the proper time."

"They are carried I know not whither — the boat itself is gone, and I am here alone."

"Am I to understand, Captain Ludlow, that Alida Barbérie has not fled my house, during the past night, to seek a refuge in your ship?"

"Fled!" echoed the young man, in a voice of horror. "Has Alida de Barbérie fled from the house of her uncle, at all?"

"Captain Ludlow, this is not acting. On the honor of a gentleman, are you ignorant of my niece's absence?"

The young commander did not answer; but, striking his head fiercely, he smothered words that were unintelligible to his companion. When this momentary burst of feeling was past, he sunk into a chair, and gazed about him in stupid amazement. All this pantomime was inexplicable to the Alderman, who, however, began to see that more of the conditions of the arrangement in hand were beyond the control of his companion, than he had at first believed. Still the plot thickened, rather than grew clear; and he was afraid to speak, lest he might utter more than was prudent. The silence, therefore, continued for quite a minute; during which time, the parties sat gazing at each other in dull wonder.

"I shall not deny, Captain Ludlow, that I believed you had prevailed on my niece to fly aboard the Coquette; for, though a man who has always kept his feelings in his own command, as the safest manner of managing particular interests, yet I am not to learn that rash youth is often guilty of folly. I am now equally at a loss with yourself, to know what has become of her, since here she is not."

"Hold!" eagerly interrupted Ludlow. "A boat left your wharf, for the city, in the earlier hours of the morning. Is it not possible that she may have taken a passage in it?"

"It is not possible. I have reasons to know — in short, Sir, she is not there."

"Then is the unfortunate — the lovely — the indiscreet girl for ever lost to herself and us!" exclaimed the young sailor, actually groaning under his mental agony. "Rash, mercenary man! to what an act of madness has this thirst of gold driven one so fair — would I could say, so pure and so innocent!"

But while the distress of the lover was thus violent, and caused him to be so little measured in his terms of reproach, the uncle of the fair offender appeared to be lost in surprise. Though la belle Barbérie had so well preserved the decorum and reserve of her sex, as to leave even her suitors in doubt of the way her inclinations tended, the watchful Alder man had long suspected that the more ardent, open, and manly commander of the Coquette was likely to triumph over one so cold in exterior, and so cautious in his advances, as the Patroon of Kinderhook. When, therefore, it became apparent Alida had disappeared, he quite naturally inferred that she had taken the simplest manner of defeating all his plans for favoring the suit of the latter, by throwing herself, at once, into the arms of the young sailor. The laws of the colonies offered few obstacles to the legality of their union; and when Ludlow appeared that morning, he firmly believed that he beheld one, who, if he were not so already, was inevitably soon to become his nephew. But the suffering of the disappointed youth could not be counterfeited; and, prevented from adhering to his first opinion, the perplexed Alderman seemed utterly at a loss to conjecture what could have become of his niece. Wonder, rather than pain, possessed him; and when he suffered his ample chin to repose on the finger and thumb of one hand, it was with the air of a man that revolved, in his mind, all the plausible points of some knotty question.

"Holes and corners!" he muttered, after a long silence; "the wilful minx cannot be playing at hide-and-seek with her friends! The hussy had ever too much of la famille de Barbérie, and her high Norman blood about her, as that silly old valet has it, to stoop to such childish trifling. Gone she certainly is," he continued, looking, again, into the empty drawers and closets, "and with her the valuables have disappeared. The guitar is missing — the lute I sent across the ocean to purchase, an excellently-toned Dutch lute, that cost every stiver of one hundred guilders, is also wanting, and all the — hem — the recent accessions have disappeared. And there, too, are my sister's jewels, that I persuaded her to bring along, to guard against accidents while our backs are turned, they are not to be seen. François! François I Thou long-tried servitor of Etienne Barbérie, what the devil has become of thy mistress?"

"Mais, Monsieur," returned the disconsolate valet, whose decent features exhibited all the signs of unequivocal suffering, "she no tell le pauvre François! En supposant, que Monsieur ask le capitaine, he shall probablement know."

The burgher cast a quick suspicious glance at Ludlow, and shook his head, to express his belief that the young man was true.

"Go; desire Mr. Van Staats of Kinderhook to favor us with his company."

"Hold," cried Ludlow, motioning to the valet to withdraw. "Mr. Beverout, an uncle should be tender of the errors of one so dear as this cruel, unreflecting girl. You cannot think of abandoning her to so frightful a fortune!"

"I am not addicted to abandoning any thing, Sir to which my title is just and legal. But you speak in enigmas. If you are acquainted with the place where my niece is secreted, avow it frankly, and permit me to take those measures which the case requires."

Ludlow reddened to his forehead, and he struggled powerfully with his pride and his regrets.

"It is useless to attempt concealing the step which Alida Barbérie has been pleased to take," he said, a smile so bitter passing over his features, as to lend them the expression of severe mockery; "she has chosen more worthily than either of us could have believed; she has found a companion more suited to her station, her character, and her sex, than Van Staats of Kinderhook, or a poor commander of a Queen's ship!"

"Cruisers and manors! What in the name of mysteries is thy meaning? The girl is not here; you declare she is not on board of the Coquette, and there remains only —"

"The brigantine!" groaned the young sailor uttering the word by a violent effort of the will.

"The brigantine!" repeated the Alderman, slowly "My niece can have nothing to do aboard a dealer in contraband. That is to say, Alida Barbérie is not a trader."

"Alderman Van Beverout, if we wish to escape the contamination of vice, its society must be avoided. There was one in the pavilion, of a mien and assurance the past night, that might delude an angel. Ah! woman! woman! thy mind is composed of vanities, and thy imagination is thy bitterest foe!"

"Women and vanities!" echoed the amazed burgher. "My niece, the heiress of old Etienne Marie de Barbérie, and the sought of so many of honorable names and respectable professions, to be a refugee with a rover! — always supposing your opinions of the character of the brigantine to be just. This is a conjecture too improbable to be true."

"The eye of a lover, Sir, may be keener than that of a guardian — call it jealousy, if you will — would to Heaven my suspicions were untrue! — but if she be not there, where is she?"

The opinion of the Alderman seemed staggered. If la belle Barbérie had not yielded to the fascinations of that wayward, but seductive, eye and smile, to that singular beauty of face, and to the secret and often irresistible charm that encircles eminent personal attractions, when aided by mystery, to what had she yielded, and whither had she fled?

These were reflections that now began to pass through the thoughts of the Alderman, as they had already planted stings in the bosom of Ludlow. With reflection, conviction began slowly to assert its power. But the truth did not gleam upon the mind of the calculating and wary merchant, with the same instinctive readiness that it had flashed upon the jealous faculties of the lover. He pondered on each circumstance of the interview between the dealer in contraband and his niece; recalled the manner and discourse of the former; drew certain general and vague conjectures concerning the power which novelty, when coupled with circumstances of romance, might exercise over a female fancy; and dwelt long and secretly on some important facts that were alone known to himself — before his judgment finally settled down into the same opinion, as that which his companion had formed, with all the sensitiveness of jealous alarm.

"Women and vagaries!" muttered the burgher, after his study was ended. "Their conceits are as uncertain as the profits of a whaling voyage, or the luck of a sportsman. Captain Ludlow, your assistance will be needed in this affair; and, as it may not be too late, since there are few priests in the brigantine — always supposing her character to be what you affirm — my niece may yet see her error, and be disposed to reward so much assiduity and attachment."

"My services shall always be ready, so long as they can be useful to Alida Barbérie," returned the young officer with haste, and yet a little coldly. "It will be time enough to speak of the reward, when we shall have succeeded."

"The less noise that is made about a little domestic inconvenience like this, the better; and I would therefore suggest the propriety of keeping our suspicions of the character of the vessel a secret, until we shall be better informed."

The captain bowed his assent to the proposal.

"And now that we are of the same mind in the preliminaries, we will seek the Patroon of Kinderhook, who has a claim to participate in our confidence."

Myndert then led the way from the empty and melancholy Cour des Fées, with a step that had regained its busy and firm tread, and a countenance that expressed far more of vexation and weariness, than of real sorrow.

CHAPTER XIV.

" — I'll give thee a wind.
" — Thou art kind.
" — And I another
" — I myself have all the other."

Macbeth.

THE cloud above the mouth of the Raritan had not risen. On the contrary, the breeze still came from off the sea; and the brigantine in the Cove, with the cruiser of the Queen, still lay at their anchors, like two floating habitations that were not intended to be removed. The hour was that at which the character of the day becomes fixed; and there was no longer any expectation that a landwind would enable the vessel of the free-trader to repass the inlet, before the turn of the tide, which was again running swiftly on the flood.

The windows of the Lust in Rust were open, as when its owner was present; and the menials were employed, in and about the villa, in their customary occupations; though it was evident, by the manner in which they stopped to converse, and by the frequent conferences which had place in secret corners, that they wondered none the less at the unaccountable disappearance of their young mistress. In all other respects, the villa and its grounds were, as usual, quiet and seemingly deserted.

But there was a group collected beneath the shade of an oak on the margin of the Cove, and at a point where it was rare for man to be seen. This little party appeared to be in waiting for some expected communication from the brigantine; since they had taken post on the side of the inlet, next the cape, and in a situation so retired, as to be entirely hid from any passing observation of those who might enter or leave the mouth of the Shrewsbury. In short, they were on the long, low, and narrow barrier of sand, that now forms the projection of the Hook, and which, by the temporary breach that the Cove had made between its own waters and that of the ocean, was then an island.

"Snug should be the motto of a merchant," observed one of these individuals, whose opinions will sufficiently announce his name to the reader. "He should be snug in his dealings, and snug in his manner of conducting them; snug in his credits, and, above all, snug in his speculations. There is as little need gentlemen, in calling in the aid of a posse-comitatus for a sensible man to keep his household in order, as that a discreet trader should go whistling through the public markets, with the history of his operations. I gladly court two so worthy assistants, as Captain Cornelius Ludlow and Mr. Oloff Van Staats; for I know there will be no useless gossip concerning the trifling derangement that hath occurred. Ah! the black hath had communications with the free-trader — always supposing the opinion of Mr. Ludlow concerning the character of the vessel to be just — and he is quitting the brigantine."

Neither of the companions of the Alderman made any reply. Each watched the movement of the skiff that contained their messenger, and each seemed to feel an equal interest in the result of his errand. Instead, however, of approaching the spot where his master and his two friends expected him, the negro, though he knew that his boat was necessary to enable the party to recross the inlet, pulled directly for the mouth of the river — a course that was exactly contrary to the one he was expected to take.

"Rank disobedience!" grumbled the incensed master. "The irreverent dog is deserting us, on this neck of barren sand, where we are cut off from all communication with the interior, and are as completely without intelligence of the state of the market, and other necessaries, as men in a desert!"

"Here comes one that seems disposed to bring us to a parley," observed Ludlow, whose practised eye had first detected a boat quitting the side of the brigantine, as well as the direction it was about to steer.

The young commander was not deceived; for a light cutter, that played like a bubble on its element; was soon approaching the shore, where the three expectants were seated. When it was near enough to render sight perfectly distinct, and speech audible without an effort, the crew ceased rowing, and permitted the boat to lie in a state of rest. The mariner of the India-shawl then arose in the stern-sheets, and examined the thicket behind the party, with a curious and suspicious eye. After a sufficient search, he signed to his crew to force the cutter still nigher to the land, and spoke:

"Who has affairs with any of the brigantine?" he coolly demanded, wearing the air of one who had no reason to anticipate the object of their visit. "She has little left that can turn to profit, unless she parts with her beauty."

"Truly, good stranger," returned the Alderman, laying a sufficient emphasis on the latter word, "here are none disposed to a traffic, which might not be pleasing to the authorities of the country, were its nature known. We come with a desire to be admitted to a conference with the commander of the vessel, on a matter of especial but private concern."

"Why send a public officer on the duty? I see one, there, in the livery of

Queen Anne. We are no lovers of Her Majesty's servants, and would not willingly form disagreeable acquaintances."

Ludlow nearly bit-through his lip, in endeavoring to repress his anger, at the cool confidence of one who had already treated him with so little ceremony; and then momentarily forgetting his object, in professional pride, and perhaps we might add in the habits of his rank, he interrupted the dialogue —

"If you see the livery of the royal authority," he said, haughtily, "you must be sensible it is worn by one who is commissioned to cause its rights to be respected. I demand the name and character of yon brigantine?"

"As for character, she is, like any other beauty, something vituperated; nay, some carry their envy so far as to call it cracked! But we are jolly mariners that sail her, and little heed crazy reports at the expense of our mistress. As for a name, we answer any hail that is fairly spoken, and well meant. Call us 'Honesty,' if you will, for want of the register."

"There is much reason to suspect your vessel of illegal practices; and, in the name of the Queen, I demand access to her papers, and the liberty of a free search into her cargo and crew. Else will there be necessity to bring her under the guns of the cruiser, which lies at no great distance, waiting only for orders."

"It takes no scholar to read our documents, Captain Ludlow; for they are written by a light keel on the rolling waters, and he who follows in our wake may guess at their authority. If you wish to overhaul our cargo, you must look sharply into the cuffs and aprons, the negligees and stomachers of the Governor's lady, at the next ball at the fort; or pry into the sail that is set above the farthingales of the wife and daughters of your Admiralty Judge! We are no cheesemongers, to break the shins of a boarding officer among boxes and butter-tubs."

"Your brigantine has a name, sirrah; and, in Her Majesty's authority, I demand to know it."

"Heaven forbid that any here should dispute the Queen's right! You are a seaman, Captain Ludlow, and have an eye for comeliness in a craft, as well as in a woman. Look at those harpings! There is no fall of a shoulder can equal that curve, in grace or richness; this shear surpasses the justness and delicacy of any waist: and there you see the transoms, swelling and rounded like the outlines of a Venus. Ah! she is a bewitching creature; and no wonder that, floating as she does, on the seas, they should have called her —"

"Water-Witch!" said Ludlow, finding that the other paused.

"You deserve to be one of the sisterhood yourself, Captain Ludlow, for this readiness in divination!"

"Amazement and surprise, Patroon!" exclaimed Myndert, with a tremendous hem "Here is a discovery to give a respectable merchant more uneasiness than the undutiful conduct of fifty nieces! This vessel is then the famous brigantine of the notorious 'Skimmer of the Seas!' a man whose misdeeds in commerce are as universally noted, as the stoppage of a general dealer! Pray, Master Mariner, do not distrust our purposes. We do not come, sent by any authority of the country, to pry into your past transactions, of which it is quite unnecessary for you to speak; and far less to indulge in any unlawful thirst of gain, by urging a traffic that is forbidden by the law. We wish solely to confer with the celebrated free-trader and rover, who must, if your account be true, command the vessel, for a few minutes, on an affair of common interest to the three. This officer of the Queen is obliged, by his duty, to make certain demands of you, with which you will comply, or not, at your own good discretion; and since Her Majesty's cruiser is so far beyond reach of bullet, it cannot be expected you will do otherwise; but further than that, he has no present intention to proceed. Parleys and civilities! Captain Ludlow, we must speak the man fair, or he will leave us to get over the inlet and back to the Lust in Rust, as we may; and that, too, as empty-handed as we came. Remember our stipulations, without observing which I shall withdraw from the adventure, altogether."

Ludlow bit his lip, and continued silent. The seaman of the shawl, or Master Tiller, as he has been more than once called, again narrowly examined the background, and caused his boat to approach so near the land, that it was possible to step into it, by the stern.

"Enter," he said to the Captain of the Coquette, who needed no second invitation; "enter, for a valuable hostage is a safe-pledge, in a truce. The Skimmer is no enemy to good company; and I have done justice to the Queen's servitor, by introducing him already, by name and character."

"Fellow, the success of your deception may cause you to triumph for a time; but remember that the Coquette —"

"Is a wholesome boat, whose abilities I have taken, to the admeasurement of her moment-glass;" observed Tiller, very coolly taking the words out of the other's mouth. "But as there is business to be done with the Skimmer, we will speak more of this anon."

The mariner of the shawl, who had maintained his former audacious demeanor, now became grave; and he spoke to his crew with authority, bidding them pull the boat to the side of the brigantine.

The exploits, the mysterious character, and the daring of the Water-Witch, and of him who sailed her, were, in that day, the frequent subjects of anger, admiration, and surprise. Those who found pleasure in the marvellous, listened to the wonders that were recounted of her speed and boldness, with pleasure; they who had been so often foiled in their attempts to arrest the hardy dealers in contraband, reddened at her name; and all wondered at the success and intelligence with which her movements were controlled. It will, therefore, create no astonishment when we say, that Ludlow and the Patroon drew near to the light and graceful fabric with an interest that deepened at each stroke of the oars. So much of a profession which, in that age, was particularly marked and apart from the rest of mankind in habits and opinions, had been interwoven into the character of the former, that he could not see the just proportions, the graceful outlines of the hull, or the exquisite symmetry and neatness of the spars and rigging, without experiencing a feeling somewhat allied to that which undeniable superiority ecites in the heart of even a rival. There was also a taste in the style of the merely ornamental parts of the delicate machine, which caused as much surprise as her model and rig.

Seamen, in all ages, and in every state of their art, have been ambitious of bestowing on their floating habitations, a style of decoration which, while appropriate to their element, should be thought somewhat analogous to the architectural ornaments of the land. Piety, superstition, and national usages, affect these characteristic ornaments, which are still seen, in different quarters of the world, to occasion broad distinctions between the appearances of vessels. In one, the rudder-head is carved with the resemblance of some hideous monster; another shows goggling eyes and lolling tongues from its cat-heads; this has the patron saint, or the ever-kind Marie, embossed upon its mouldings or bows; while that is covered with the allegorical emblems of country and duty. Few of these efforts of nautical art are successful, though a better taste appears to be gradually redeeming even this branch of human industry from the rubbish of barbarism, and to be elevating it to a state which shall do no violence to the more fastidious opinions of the age. But the vessel of which we write, though constructed at so remote a period, would have done credit to the improvements of our own time.

It has been said that the hull of this celebrated smuggler was low, dark, moulded with exquisite art, and so justly balanced as to ride upon its element like a sea-fowl. For a little distance above the water, it showed a blue that vied with the color of the deep ocean, the use of copper being then unknown; while the more superior parts were of a jet black, delicately relieved by two lines, of a straw-color, that were drawn, with mathematical accuracy, parallel to the plane of her upper works, and consequently converging slightly towards the sea, beneath her counter. Glossy hammock-cloths concealed the persons of those who were on the deck, while the close bulwarks gave the brigantine the air of a vessel equipped for war. Still the eye of Ludlow ran curiously along the whole extent of the two straw-colored lines, seeking in vain some evidence of the weight and force of her armament. If she had ports at all, they were so ingeniously concealed as to escape the keenest of his glances. The nature of the rig has been already described. Partaking of the double character of brig and schooner, the sails and spars of the forward-mast being of the former, while those of the after-mast were of the latter construction, seamen have given to this class of shipping the familiar name of Hermaphrodites. But, though there might be fancied, by this term, some want of the proportions that constitute seemliness, it will be remembered that the departure was only from some former rule of art, and that no violence had been done to those universal and permanent laws which constitute the charm of nature. The models of glass, which are seen representing the machinery of a ship, are not more exact or just in their lines than were the cordage and spars of this brigantine. Not a rope varied from its true direction; not a sail, but it resembled the neat folds of some prudent house wife; not a mast or a yard was there, but it rose into the air, or stretched its arms, with the most fastidious attention to symmetry. All was airy, fanciful, and full of grace, seeming to lend to the fabric a character of unreal lightness and speed. As the boat drew near her side, a change of the air caused the buoyant bark to turn, like a vane, in its current; and as the long and pointed proportions of her head-gear came into view, Ludlow saw beneath the bowsprit an image that might be supposed to make, by means of allegory, some obvious allusions to the character of the vessel. A female form, fashioned with the carver's best skill, stood on the projection of the cut-water. The figure rested lightly on the ball of one foot, while the other was suspended in an easy attitude, resembling the airy posture of the famous Mercury of the Bolognese. The drapery was fluttering, scanty, and of a light sea-green tint, as if it had imbibed a hue from the element beneath. The face was of that dark bronzed color which human ingenuity has, from time immemorial, adopted as the best medium to portray a superhuman expression. The locks were dishevelled, wild, and rich; the eye, full of such a meaning as might be fancied to glitter in the organs of a sorceress; while a smile so strangely meaning and malign played about the mouth, that the young sailor started, when it first met his view as if a living thing had returned his look.

"Witchcraft and necromancy!" grumbled the Alderman, as this extraordinary image came suddenly on his vision also. "Here is a brazen-looking hussy and one who might rob the Queen's treasury, itself, without remorse! Your eyes are young, Patroon; what is that the minx holds so impudently above her head?"

"It seems an open book, with letters of red, writ ten on its pages. One need not be a conjurer, to divine it is no extract from the Bible."

"Nor from the statute-books of Queen Anne. I warrant me, 'tis a leger of profit gained in her many wanderings. Goggling and leers! the bold air of the confident creature is enough to put an honest man out of countenance!"

"Will read the motto of the witch?" demanded he of the India-shawl, whose eye had been studying the detail of the brigantine's equipment, rather than attending to the object which so much attracted the looks of his companions. "The night air has taut'ned the cordage of that flying-jib-boom, fellows, until it begins to lift its nose like a squeamish cockney, when he holds it over salt-water! See to it, and bring the spar in line; else shall we have a reproof from the sorceress, who little likes to have any of her limbs deranged. Here, gentlemen, the opinions of the lady may be read, as clearly as woman's mind can ever be fathomed."

While speaking to his crew, Tiller had changed the direction of the boat; and it was soon lying, in obedience to a motion of his hand, directly beneath the wild and significant-looking image, just described. The letters in red were now distinctly visible; and when Alderman Van Beverout had adjusted his spectacles, each of the party read the following sentence —

> "Albeit, I neither lend nor borrow,
> By taking, nor by giving of excess,
> Yet to supply the ripe wants of my friend,
> I'll break a custom."
>
> *Merchant of Venice.*

"The brazen!" exclaimed Myndert, when he had got through this quotation from the immortal bard. "Ripe or green, one could not wish to be the friend of so impudent a thing; and then to impute such sentiments to any respectable commercial man whether of Venice or of Amsterdam! Let us board the brigantine, friend mariner, and end the connexion ere foul mouths begin to traduce our motives for the visit."

"The over-driven ship plows the seas too deep for speed; we shall get into port, in better season without this haste. Wilt take another look into the dark lady's pages? A woman's mind is never known at the first answer!"

The speaker raised the rattan he still carried, and caused a page of painted metal to turn on hinges that were so artfully concealed as not to be visible. A new surface, with another extract, was seen.

"What is it, what is it, Patroon?" demanded the burgher, who appeared greatly to distrust the discretion of the sorceress. "Follies and rhymes! but this is the way of the whole sex; when nature has denied them tongues, they invent other means of speech."

> "Porters of the sea and land,
> Thus do go about, about;
> Thrice to thine, and thrice to thine,
> And thrice again to make up nine."

"Rank nonsense!" continued the burgher! "It is well for those who can, to add thrice and thrice to their stores; but look you, Patroon — it is a thriving trade that can double the value of the adventure, and that with reasonable risks, and months of patient watching."

"We have other pages," resumed Tiller, "but our affairs drag for want of attending to them. One may read much good matter in the book of the sorceress, when there is leisure and opportunity. I often take occasion, in the calms, to look into her volume; and it is rare to find the same moral twice told, as these brave seamen can swear."

The mariners at the oars confirmed this assertion, by their grave and believing faces; while their superior caused the boat to quit the place, and the image of the Water-Witch was left floating in solitude above her proper element.

The arrival of the cutter produced no sensation among those who were found on the deck of the brigantine. The mariner of the shawl welcomed his companions, frankly and heartily; and then he left them for a minute to make their observations, while he discharged some duty in the interior of the vessel. The moments were not lost, as powerful curiosity induced all the visiters to gaze about them, in the manner in which men study the appearance of any celebrated object, that has long been known only by reputation. It was quite apparent that even Alderman Van Beverout had penetrated farther into the mysteries of the beautiful brigantine, than he had ever before been. But it was Ludlow who gathered most from this brief opportunity, and whose understanding glances so rapidly and eagerly ran over all that a seaman could wish to examine.

An admirable neatness reigned in every part. The planks of the deck resembled the work of the cabinetmaker, rather than the coarser labor which is generally seen in such a place; and the same excellence of material, and exactness in the finish, were visible in the ceilings of the light bulwarks, the railings, and all the other objects which necessarily came conspicuously into view, in the construction of such a fabric. Brass was tastefully rather than lavishly used, on many of those parts where metal was necessary; and the paint of the interior was everywhere a light and delicate straw-color. Armament there was none, or at least none visible; nor did the fifteen or twenty grave-looking seamen, who were silently lounging, with folded arms, about the vessel, appear to be those who would find pleasure in scenes of violence. They were, without an exception, men who had reached the middle age, of weather-worn and thoughtful countenances, many of them even showing heads that had begun to be grizzled more by time than even by exposure. Thus much Ludlow had been enabled to ascertain, ere they were rejoined by Tiller. When the latter again came on deck, he showed, however, no desire to conceal any of the perfections of his habitation.

"The wilful sorceress is no niggard in accommodating her followers," said the mariner, observing the manner in which the Queen's officer was employed. "Here, you see, the Skimmer keeps room enough for an admiral, in his cabins; and the fellows are berthed aft, far beyond the fore-mast — wilt step to the hatch, and look below?"

The captain and his companions did as desired, and to the amazement of the former, he perceived that, with the exception of a sort of room fitted with large and water-tight lockers, which were placed in full view, all the rest of the brigantine was occupied by the accommodations of her officers and crew.

"The world gives us the reputation of free-traders," continued Tiller, smiling maliciously; "but if the Admiralty-Court were here, big wigs and high staffs, judge and jury, it would be at a loss to bring us to conviction. There is iron to keep the lady on her feet, and water, with some garnish of Jamaica, and the wines of old Spain and the islands, to cheer the hearts and cool the mouths of my fellows, beneath that deck; and more than that, there is not. We have stores for the table and the breeze, beyond yon bulk-head; and here are lockers beneath you, that are — empty! See, one is open; it is neat as any drawer in a lady's bureau. This is no place for your Dutchman's strong waters, or the coarse skins of your tobacconist. Odd's my life! He who would go on the scent of the Water-Witch's lading, must follow your beauty in her satins, or your parson in his band and gown. There would be much lamentation in the church, and many a heavy-hearted bishop, were it known that the good craft had come to harm!"

"There must be an end to this audacious trifling with the law," said Ludlow; "and the time may be nearer than you suppose."

"I look at the pages of the lady's book, in the pride of each morning; for we have it aboard here, that when she intends to serve us foul, she will at least be honest enough to give a warning. The mottoes often change, but her words are ever true. 'Tis hard to overtake the driving mist, Captain Ludlow, and he must hold good way with the wind itself, who wishes to stay long in our company."

"Many a boastful sailor has been caught. The breeze that is good for the light of draught, and the breeze that is good for the deep keel, are different. You may live to learn what a stout spar, a wide arm, and a steady hull, can do."

"The lady of the wild eye and wicked smile protect me! I have seen the witch buried fathoms deep in brine, and the glittering water falling from her tresses like golden stars; but never have I read an untruth in her pages. There is good intelligence between her and some on board; and, trust me, she knows the paths of the ocean too well, ever to steer a wrong course. But we prate like gossiping rivermen. Wilt see the Skimmer of the Seas?"

"Such is the object of our visit," returned Ludlow, whose heart beat violently at the name of the redoubtable rover. "If you are not he, bring us where he is."

"Speak lower; if the lady under the bowsprit hear such treason against her favorite, I'll not answer for her good-will. If I am not he!" added the hero of the India-shawl, laughing freely. "Well, an ocean is bigger than a sea, and a bay is not a gulf. You shall have an opportunity of judging between us, noble captain, and then I leave opinions to each man's wisdom. Follow."

He quitted the hatchway, and led his companions toward the accommodations in the stern of the vessel.

CHAPTER XV.

"God save you, Sir!"
"And you, Sir; you are welcome.
"Travel you, Sir, or are you at the furthest?"

Taming of the Shrew.

IF the exterior of the brigantine was so graceful in form and so singular in arrangement, the interior was still more worthy of observation. There were two small cabins beneath the main-deck, one on each side of, and immediately adjoining, the limited space that was destined to receive her light but valuable cargoes. It was into one of these that Tiller had descended, like a man who freely entered into his own apartment; but partly above, and nearer to the stern, were a suite of little rooms that were fitted and furnished in a style altogether different. The equipments were those of a yacht, rather than those which might be supposed suited to the pleasures of even the most successful dealer in contraband.

The principal deck had been sunken several feet, commencing at the aftermost bulk-head of the cabins of the subordinate officers, in a manner to give the necessary height, without interfering with the line of the brigantine's shear. The arrangement was consequently not to be seen, by an observer who was not admitted into the vessel itself. A descent of a step or two, however, brought the visiters to the level of the cabin-floor and into an ante-room that was evidently fitted for the convenience of the domestics. A small silver hand-bell lay on a table, and Tiller rung it lightly, like one whose ordinary manner was restrained by respect. It was answered by the appearance of a boy, whose years could not exceed ten, and whose attire was so whimsical as to merit description.

The material of the dress of this young servitor of Neptune, was a light rose-colored silk, cut in a fashion to resemble the habits formerly worn by pages of the great. His body was belted by a band of gold, a collar of fine thread lace floated on his neck and shoulders, and even his feet were clad in a sort of buskins, that were ornamented with fringes of real lace and tassels of bullion. The form and features of the child were delicate, and his air as unlike as possible to the coarse and brusque manner of a vulgar ship-boy.

"Waste and prodigality!" muttered the Alderman, when this extraordinary little usher presented himself, in answer to the summons of Tiller. "This is the very wantonness of cheap goods and an unfettered commerce! There is enough of Mechlin, Patroon, on the shoulders of that urchin, to deck the stomacher of the

Queen. 'Fore George, goods were cheap in the market, when the young scoundrel had his livery!"

The surprise was not confined, however, to the observant and frugal burgher. Ludlow and Van Staats of Kinderhook manifested equal amazement, though their wonder was exhibited in a less characteristic manner. The former turned short to demand the meaning of this masquerade, when he perceived that the hero of the India-shawl had disappeared. They were then alone with the fantastic page, and it became necessary to trust to his intelligence for directions how to proceed.

"Who art thou, child? — and who has sent thee hither?" demanded Ludlow. The boy raised a cap of the same rose-colored silk, and pointed to an image of a female, with a swarthy face and a malign smile, painted, with exceeding art, on its front.

"I serve the sea-green lady, with the others of the brigantine."

"And who is this lady of the color of shallow water, and whence come you, in particular?"

"This is her likeness — if you would speak with her, she stands on the cut-water, and rarely refuses an answer."

"'Tis odd that a form of wood should have the gift of speech!"

"Dost think her then of wood?" returned the child, looking timidly, and yet curiously, up into the face of Ludlow. "Others have said the same; but those who know best, deny it. She does not answer with a tongue, but the book has always something to say."

"Here is a grievous deception practised on the superstition of this boy! I have read the book, and can make but little of its meaning."

"Then read again. 'Tis by many reaches that the leeward vessel gains upon the wind. My master has bid me bring you in —"

"Hold — Thou hast both master and mistress? — You have told us of the latter, but we would know something of the former. Who is thy master?"

The boy smiled and looked aside, as if he hesitated to answer.

"Nay, refuse not to reply. I come with the authority of the Queen."

"He tells us that the sea-green lady is our Queen and that we have no other."

"Rashness and rebellion!" muttered Myndert: "but this foolhardiness will one day bring as pretty a brigantine as ever sailed in the narrow seas, to condemnation; and then will there be rumors abroad, and characters cracked, till every lover of gossip in the Americas shall be tired of defamation."

"It is a bold subject, that dares say this!" rejoined Ludlow, who heeded not the by-play of the Alderman; "Your master has a name?"

"We never hear it. When Neptune boards us, under the tropics, he always hails the 'Skimmer of the Seas,' and then they answer. The old God knows us well, for we pass his latitude oftener than other ships, they say."

"You are then a cruiser of some service, in the brigantine — no doubt you have trod many distant shores, belonging to so swift a craft."

"I! — I never was on the land!" returned the boy, thoughtfully. "It must be droll to be there; they say, one can hardly walk, it is so steady! I put a question to the sea-green lady before we came to this narrow inlet, to know when I was to go ashore."

"And she answered?"

"It was some time, first. Two watches were past before a word was to be seen; but at last I got the lines. I believe she mocked me, though I have never dared show it to my master, that he might say."

"Hast the words, here? — perhaps we might assist thee, as there are some among us who know most of the sea-paths."

The boy looked timidly and suspiciously around, and thrusting a hand hurriedly into a pocket, he drew forth two bits of paper, each of which contained a scrawl, and both of which had evidently been much thumbed and studied.

"Here," he said, in a voice that was suppressed nearly to a whisper. "This was on the first page. I was so frightened, lest the lady should be angry, that I did not look again till the next watch; and then," turning the leaf, "I found this."

Ludlow took the bit of paper first offered, and read, written in a child's hand, the following extract:

> "*I pray thee*
> *Remember, I have done thee worthy service;*
> *Told thee no lies, made no mistakings, serv'd*
> *Without or grudge or grumblings.*"

"I thought that 'twas in mockery," continued the boy, when he saw by the eye of the young captain that he had read the quotation; "for 'twas very like, though more prettily worded, than that which I had said, myself!"

"And that was the second answer?"

"This was found in the first morning-watch," the child returned, reading the second extract himself:

> "*Thou think'st*
> *It much to tread the ooze of the salt deep,*

And run upon the sharp wind of the north!"

"I never dared to ask again. But what matters that? They say, the ground is rough and difficult to walk on; that earthquakes shake it, and make holes to swallow cities; that men slay each other on the highways for money, and that the houses I see on the hills must always remain in the same spot. It must be very melancholy to live always in the same spot; but then it must be odd, never to feel a motion!"

"Except the occasional rocking of an earthquake. Thou art better afloat, child — but thy master, this Skimmer of the Seas —"

" — Hist!" whispered the boy, raising a finger for silence. "He has come up into the great cabin. In a moment, we shall have his signal to enter."

"A few light touches on the strings of a guitar followed, and then a symphony was rapidly and beautifully executed, by one in the adjoining apartment.

"Alida, herself, is not more nimble-fingered," whispered the Alderman; "and I never heard the girl touch the Dutch lute, that cost a hundred Holland guilders, with a livelier movement!"

Ludlow signed for silence. A fine, manly voice, of great richness and depth, was soon heard, singing to an accompaniment on the same instrument. The air was grave, and altogether unusual for the social character of one who dwelt upon the ocean, being chiefly in recitative. The words, as near as might be distinguished, ran as follows:

> *My brigantine!*
> *Just in thy mould, and beauteous in thy form,*
> *Gentle in roll, and buoyant on the surge,*
> *Light as the sea-fowl, rocking in the storm,*
> *In breeze and gale, thy onward course we urge;*
> *My Water-Queen!*
> *Lady of mine!*
> *More light and swift than thou, none thread the sea,*
> *With surer keel, or steadier on its path;*
> *We brave each waste of ocean-mystery,*
> *And laugh to hear the howling tempest's wrath!*
> *For we are thine!*
> *My brigantine!*
> *Trust to the mystic power that points thy way,*
> *Trust to the eye that pierces from afar,*
> *Trust the red meteors that around thee play,*

> And fearless trust the sea-green lady's star;
> Thou bark divine!

"He often sings thus," whispered the boy, when the song was ended; "for they say, the sea-green lady loves music that tells of the ocean, and of her power. Hark! he has bid me enter."

"He did but touch the strings of the guitar, again, boy."

"'Tis his signal, when the weather is fair. When we have the whistling of the wind, and the roar of the water, then he has a louder call."

Ludlow would have gladly listened longer; but the boy opened a door, and, pointing the way to those he conducted, he silently vanished himself, behind a curtain.

The visiters, more particularly the young commander of the Coquette, found new subjects of admiration and wonder, on entering the main cabin of the brigantine. The apartment, considering the size of the vessel, was spacious and high. It received light from a couple of windows in the stern, and it was evident that two smaller rooms, one on each of the quarters, shared with it in this advantage. The space between these state-rooms, as they are called in nautical language, necessarily formed a deep alcove, which might be separated from the outer portion of the cabin, by a curtain of crimson damask, that now hung in festoons from a beam fashioned into a gilded cornice. A luxuriously-looking pile of cushions, covered with red morocco, lay along the transom, in the manner of an eastern divan; and against the bulk-head of each state-room, stood an agrippina of mahogany, that was lined with the same material. Neat and tasteful cases for books were suspended, here and there; and the guitar which had so lately been used, lay on a small table of some precious wood, that occupied the centre of the alcove. There were also other implements, like those which occupy the leisure of a cultivated but perhaps an effeminate rather than a vigorous mind, scattered around, some evidently long neglected, and others appearing to have been more recently in favor.

The outer portion of the cabin was furnished in a similar style, though it contained many more of the articles that ordinarily belong to domestic economy. It had its agrippina, its piles of cushions, its chairs of beautiful wood, its cases for books, and its neglected instruments, intermixed with fixtures of a more solid and permanent appearance, which were arranged to meet the violent motion that was often unavoidable in so small a bark. There was a slight hanging of crimson damask around the whole apartment; and, here and there, a small mirror was let into the bulk-heads and ceilings. All the other parts were of a rich mahogany, relieved by panels of rose-wood, that gave an appearance of exquisite finish to the cabin. The floor was covered with a mat of the finest texture, and of a fragrance that announced both its freshness, and the fact that the grass had been the growth of a warm and luxuriant climate. The place, as was indeed the whole vessel, so far as the keen eye of Ludlow could detect, was entirely destitute of arms, not even a pistol, or a sword, being suspended in those places where weapons of that description are usually seen, in all vessels employed either in war or in a trade that might oblige those who sail them to deal in violence.

In the centre of the alcove stood the youthful-looking and extraordinary person who, in so unceremonious a manner, had visited la Cour des Fées the preceding night. His dress was much the same, in fashion and material, as when last seen; still, it had been changed; for on the breast of the silken frock was painted an image of the sea-green lady, done with exquisite skill, and in a manner to preserve the whole of the wild and unearthly character of the expression. The wearer of this singular ornament leaned lightly against the little table, and as he bowed with entire self-possession to his guests, his face was lighted with a smile, that seemed to betray melancholy, no less than courtesy. At the same time he raised his cap, and stood in the rich jet-black locks with which Nature had so exuberantly shaded his forehead.

The manner of the visiters was less easy. The deep anxiety with which both Ludlow and the Patroon had undertaken to board the notorious smuggler had given place to an amazement and a curiosity that caused them nearly to forget their errand; while Alderman Van Beverout appeared shy and suspicious, manifestly thinking less of his niece, than of the consequences of so remarkable an interview. They all returned the salutation of their host, though each waited for him to speak.

"They tell me I have the pleasure to receive a commander of Queen Anne's service, the wealthy and honorable Patroon of Kinderhook, and a most worthy and respectable member of the city corporation, known as Alderman Van Beverout," commenced the individual who did the honors of the vessel on this occasion. "It is not often that my poor brigantine is thus favored, and, in the name of my mistress, I would express our thanks."

As he ceased speaking, he bowed again with ceremonious gravity, as if all were equally strangers to him; though the young men saw plainly that a smothered smile played about a mouth that even they could not refuse the praise of being of rare and extraordinary attraction.

"As we have but one mistress," said Ludlow, "it is our common duty to wish to do her pleasure."

"I understand you, Sir. It is scarce necessary to say, however, that the wife of George of Denmark has little authority here. Forbear, I pray you," he added quickly, observing that Ludlow was about to answer. "These interviews with the servants of that lady are riot unfrequent; and as I know other matters have sent you hither, we will imagine all said that a vigilant officer and a most loyal subject could utter, to an outlaw and a trifler with the regulations of the customs. That controversy must be settled between us under our canvas, and by virtue of our speed, or other professional qualities, at proper time and in a proper place. We will now touch on different matters."

"I think the gentleman is right, Patroon. When matters are ripe for the Exchequer, there is no use in worrying the lungs with summing up the testimony like a fee'd advocate. Twelve discreet men, who have bowels of compassion for the vicissitudes of trade, and who know how hard it is to earn, and how easy it is to spend, will deal with the subject better than all the idle talkers in the Provinces."

"When confronted to the twelve disinterested Daniels, I shall be fain to submit to their judgment," rejoined the other, still suffering the wilful smile to linger round his lips. "You, Sir, I think, are called Mr. Myndert Van Beverout. To what fall in peltry, or what rise in markets, do I owe the honor of this visit?"

"It is said that some from this vessel were so bold as to land on my grounds, during the past night, without the knowledge and consent of their owner — you will observe the purport of our discourse, Mr. Van Staats, for it may yet come before the authorities — as I said, Sir, without their owner's knowledge, and that there were dealings in articles that are contraband of law, unless they enter the provinces purified and embellished by the air of the Queen's European dominions — God bless Her Majesty!"

"Amen. That which quitteth the Water-Witch commonly comes purified by the air of many different regions. We are no laggards in movement, here; and the winds of Europe scarcely cease to blow upon our sails, before we scent the gales of America. But this is rather Exchequer matter, to be discussed before the twelve merciful burghers than entertainment for such a visit."

"I open with the facts, that there may be no errors. But in addition to so foul an imputation on the credit of a merchant, there has a great calamity befallen me and my household, during the past night. The daughter and heiress of old Etienne de Barbérie has left her abode, and we have reason to think that she has been deluded so far as to come hither. Faith and correspondence! Master Seadrift; but I think this is exceeding the compass of even a trader in contraband! I can make allowances for some errors in an account; but women can be exported and imported without duty, and when and where one pleases, and therefore the less necessity for running them out of their old uncle's habitation, in so secret a manner."

"An undeniable position, and a feeling conclusion! I admit the demand to be made in all form, and I suppose these two gentlemen are to be considered as witnesses of its legality."

"We have come to aid a wronged and distressed relative and guardian, in searching for his misguided ward," Ludlow answered.

The free-trader turned his eyes on the Patroon, who signified his assent by a silent bow.

"'Tis well, gentlemen; I also admit the testimony. But though in common believed so worthy a subject for justice, I have hitherto had but little direct communication with the blind deity. Do the authorities usually give credit to these charges, without some evidence of their truth?"

"Is it denied?"

"You are still in possession of your senses, Captain Ludlow and may freely use them. But this is an artifice to divert pursuit. There are other vessels beside the brigantine, and a capricious fair may have sought a protector, even under a pennant of Queen Anne!"

"This is a truth that has been but too obvious to my mind, Mr. Van Beverout," observed the sententious Patroon. "It would have been well to have ascertained whether she we seek has not taken some less exceptionable course than this, before we hastily believe that your niece would so easily become the wife of a stranger."

"Has Mr. Van Staats any hidden meaning in his words, that he speaks ambiguously?" demanded Ludlow.

"A man, conscious of his good intentions, has little occasion to speak equivocally. I believe, with this reputed smuggler, that la belle Barbérie would be more likely to fly with one she has long known, and whom I fear she has but too well esteemed, than with an utter stranger, over whose life there is cast a shade of so dark mystery."

"If the impression that the lady could yield her esteem with too little discretion, be any excuse for suspicions, then may I advise a search in the manor of Kinderhook!"

"Consent and joy! The girl need not have stolen to church to become the bride of Oloff Van Staats!" interrupted the Alderman. "She should have had my benediction on the match, and a fat gift to give it unction."

"These suspicions are but natural, between men bent on the same object," resumed the free-trader. "The officer of the Queen thinks a glance of the eye, from a wilful fair, means admiration of broad lands and rich meadows; and the lord of the manor distrusts the romance of warlike service, and the power of an imagination which roams the sea. Still may I ask, what is there here, to tempt a proud and courted beauty to forget station, sex, and friends?"

"Caprice and vanity! There is no answering for a woman's mind! Here we bring articles, at great risk and heavy charges, from the farther Indies, to please their fancies, and they change their modes easier than the beaver casts his coat. Their conceits sadly unsettle trade, and I know not why they may not cause a wilful girl to do any other act of folly."

"This reasoning seems conclusive with the uncle. Do the suitors assent to its justice?"

The Patroon of Kinderhook had stood gazing, long and earnestly, at the countenance of the extraordinary being who asked this question. A movement, which bespoke, equally, his conviction and his regret, escaped him, but he continued silent. Not so Ludlow. Of a more ardent temperament, though equally sensible of the temptation which had caused Alida to err, and as keenly alive to all the consequences to herself, as well as to others, there was something of professional rivalry, and of an official right to investigate, which still mingled with his feelings. He had found time to examine more closely the articles that the cabin contained, and when their singular host put his question, he pointed, with an ironical but mournful smile, to a footstool richly wrought in flowers of tints and shades so just as to seem natural.

"This is no work of a sail-maker's needle!" said the captain of the Coquette. "Other beauties have been induced to pass an idle hour in your gay residence, hardy mariner; but, sooner or later, judgment will overtake the light-heeled craft."

"On the wind, or off, she must some day lag, as we seamen have it! Captain Ludlow, I excuse some harshness of construction, that your language might imply; for it becomes a commissioned servant of the crown, to use freedom with one who, like the lawless companion of the princely Hal, is but too apt to propose to 'rob me the King's Exchequer.' But, Sir, this brigantine and her character are little known to you. We have no need of truant damsels, to let us into the mystery of the sex's taste; for a female spirit guides all our humors, and imparts something of her delicacy to all our acts, even though it be the fashion among burghers to call them lawless. See," throwing a curtain carelessly aside, and exhibiting, behind it, various articles of womanly employment, "here are the offspring of both pencil and needle. The sorceress," touching the image on his breast, "will not be entertained, without some deference to her sex."

"This affair must be arranged, I see, by a compromise," observed the Alderman. "By your leave, gentlemen, I will make proposals in private to this bold trader, who perhaps will listen to the offers I have to propose."

"Ah! This savors more of the spirit of trade than of that of the sea-goddess I serve," cried the other, causing his fingers to run lightly over the strings of the guitar. "Compromise and offers are sounds that become a burgher's lips. My tricksy spirit, commit these gentlemen to the care of bold Thomas Tiller, while I confer with the merchant. The character of Mr. Van Beverout, Captain Ludlow, will protect us both from the suspicion of any designs on the revenue!"

Laughing at his own allusion, the free-trader signed to the boy, who had appeared from behind a curtain, to show the disappointed suitors of la belle Barbérie into another part of the vessel.

"Foul tongues and calumnies! Master Seadrift, this unlawful manner of playing round business, after accounts are settled and receipts passed, may lead to other loss besides that of character. The commander of the Coquette is not more than half satisfied of my ignorance of your misdoings in behalf of the customs, already; and these jokes are like so many punches into a smouldering fire, on a dark night. They only give light, and cause people to see the clearer — though, Heaven knows, no man has less reason to dread an inquiry into his affairs than myself! I challenge the best accountant in the colonies to detect a false footing, or a doubtful entry, in any book I have, from the Memorandum to the Leger."

"The Proverbs are not more sententious, nor the Psalms half as poetical, as your library. But why this secret parley? — The brigantine has a swept hold."

"Swept! Brooms and Van Tromp! Thou hast swept the pavilion of my niece of its mistress, no less than my purse of its johannes. This is carrying a little innocent barter into a most forbidden commerce, and I hope the joke is to end, before the affair gets to be sweetening to the tea of the Province gossips. Such a tale would affect the autumn importation of sugars!"

"This is more vivid than clear. You have my laces and velvets; my brocades and satins are already in the hands of the Manhattan dames; and your furs and johannes are safe where no boarding officer from the Coquette —"

"Well, there is no need of speaking-trumpets, to tell a man what he knows already, to his cost! I should expect no less than bankruptcy from two or three such bargains, and you wish to add loss of character to loss of gold. Bulk-heads have ears in a ship, as well as walls in houses. I wish no more said of the trifling traffic that has been between us. If I lose a thousand florins by the operation, I shall know how to be resigned. Patience and afflictions! Have I not buried as full-fed and promising a gelding this morning, as ever paced a pavement, and has any man heard a complaint from my lips? I know how to meet losses, I hope; and so no more of an unlucky purchase."

"Truly, if it be not for trade, there is little in common between the mariners of the brigantine and Alderman Van Beverout."

"The greater the necessity thou shouldst end this silly joke, and restore his niece. I am not sure the affair can be at all settled with either of these hotheaded young men, though I should even offer to throw in a few thousands more, by way of make-weight. When female reputation gets a bad name in the market, 'tis harder to dispose of than falling stock; and your young lords of manors and commanders of cruisers have stomachs like usurers; no per centage will satisfy them; it must be all, or nothing! There was no such foolery in the days of thy worthy father! The honest trafficker brought his cutter into port, with as innocent a look as a mill-boat. We had our discourses on the qualities of his wares, when here was his price, and there was my gold. Odd or even! It was all a chance which had the best of the bargain. I was a thriving man in those days, Master Seadrift; but thy spirit seems the spirit of extortion itself!"

There was momentarily contempt on the lip of the handsome smuggler, but it disappeared in an expression of evident and painful sadness.

"Thou hast softened my heart, ere now, most liberal burgher," he answered, "by these allusions to my parent; and many is the doubloon that I have paid for his eulogies."

"I speak as disinterestedly as a parson preaches! What is a trifle of gold between friends? Yes, there was happiness in trade during the time of thy predecessor. He had a comely and a deceptive craft, that might be likened to an untrimmed racer. There was motion in it, at need, and yet it had the air of a leisurely Amsterdammer. I have known an Exchequer cruiser hail him, and ask the news of the famous free-trader, with as little suspicion as he have in speaking the Lord High Admiral! There were no fooleries in his time; no unseemly hussies stuck under his bowsprit, to put an honest man out of countenance; no high-fliers in sail and paint; no singing and luting — but all was rational and gainful barter. Then, he was a man to ballast his boat with something valuable. I have known him throw in fifty ankers of gin, without a farthing for freight, when a bargain has been struck for the finer articles — ay, and finish by landing them in England for a small premium, when the gift was made!"

"He deserves thy praise, grateful Alderman; but to what conclusion does this opening tend?"

"Well, if more gold must pass between us," continued the reluctant Myndert, "we shall not waste time in counting it; though, Heaven knows, Master Seadrift, thou hast already drained me dry. Losses have fallen heavy on me, of late. There is a gelding, dead, that fifty Holland ducats will not replace on the boom-key of Rotterdam, to say nothing of freight and charges, which come particularly heavy —"

"Speak to thy offer!" interrupted the other, who evidently wished to shorten the interview.

"Restore the girl, and take five-and-twenty thin pieces."

"Half-price for a Flemish gelding! La Belle would blush, with honest pride, did she know her value in the market!"

"Extortion and bowels of compassion! Let it be a hundred, and no further words between us."

"Harkee, Mr. Van Beverout; that I sometimes trespass on the Queen's earnings, is not to be denied and least of all to you; for I like neither this manner of ruling a nation by deputy, nor the principle which says that one bit of earth is to make laws for another. 'Tis not my humor, Sir, to wear an English cotton when my taste is for the Florentine; nor to swallow beer, when I more relish the delicate wines of Gascony Beyond this, thou knowest I do not trifle, even with fancied rights; and had I fifty of thy nieces, sacks of ducats should not purchase one!"

The Alderman stared, in a manner that might have induced a spectator to believe he was listening to an incomprehensible proposition. Still his companion spoke with a warmth that gave him no small reason to believe he uttered no more than he felt, and, inexplicable as it might prove, that he valued treasure less than feeling.

"Obstinacy and extravagance!" muttered Myndert; "what use can a troublesome girl be to one of thy habits? If thou hast deluded —"

"I have deluded none. The brigantine is not an Algerine, to ask and take ransom."

"Then let it submit to what I believe it is yet a stranger. If thou hast not enticed my niece away, by, Heaven knows, a most vain delusion! let the vessel be searched. This will make the minds of the young men tranquil, and keep the treaty open between us, and the value of the article fixed in the market."

"Freely — but mark! If certain bales containing worthless furs of martens and beavers, with other articles of thy colony trade, should discover the character of my correspondents, I stand exonerated of all breach of faith."

"There is prudence in that. Yes, there must be no impertinent eyes peeping into bales and packages. Well, I see, Master Seadrift, the impossibility of immediately coming to an understanding; and therefore I will quit thy vessel, for truly a merchant of reputation should have no unnecessary connexion with one so suspected."

The free-trader smiled, partly in scorn and yet much in sadness, and passed his fingers over the strings of the guitar.

"Show this worthy burgher to his friends, Zephyr," ne said; and, bowing to the Alderman, he dismissed him in a manner that betrayed a singular compound of feeling. One quick to discover the traces of human passion, might have fancied, that regret, and even sorrow, were powerfully blended with the natural or assumed recklessness of the smuggler's air and language.

CHAPTER XVI.

"This will prove a brave kingdom to me;
Where I shall have my music, for nothing."

Tempest.

DURING the time past in the secret conference of the cabin, Ludlow and the Patroon were held in discourse on the quarter-deck, by the hero of the India-shawl. The dialogue was professional, as Van Staats maintained his ancient reputation for taciturnity. The appearance of Myndert, thoughtful, disappointed, and most evidently perplexed, caused the ideas of all to take a new direction. It is probable that the burgher believed he had not yet bid enough to tempt the free-trader to restore his niece; for, by his air, it was apparent his mind was far from being satisfied that she was not in the vessel. Still, when questioned by his companions concerning the result of his interview with the free-trader, for reasons best understood by himself, he was fain to answer evasively.

"Of one thing rest satisfied," he said; "the misconception in this affair will yet be explained, and Alida Barbérie return unfettered, and with a character as free from blemish as the credit of the Van Stoppers of Holland. The fanciful-looking person in the cabin denies that my niece is here, and I am inclined to think the balance of truth is on his side I confess, if one could just look into the cabins, without the trouble of rummaging lockers and cargo, the statement would give more satisfaction; but — hem — gentlemen, we must take the assertion on credit, for want of more sufficient security."

Ludlow looked at the cloud above the mouth of the Raritan, and his lip curled in a haughty smile.

"Let the wind hold here, at east," he said, "and we shall act our pleasure, with both lockers and cabins."

"Hist! the worthy Master Tiller may overhear this threat — and, after all, I do not know whether prudence does not tell us, to let the brigantine depart."

"Mr. Alderman Van Beverout," rejoined the Captain, whose cheek had reddened to a glow, "my duty must not be gauged by your affection for your niece. Though content that Alida Barbérie should quit the country, like an article of vulgar commerce, the commander of this vessel must get a passport of Her Majesty's cruiser, ere she again enter the high sea."

"Wilt say as much to the sea-green lady?" asked the mariner of the shawl, suddenly appearing at his elbow.

The question was so unexpected and so strange, that it caused an involuntary start; but, recovering his recollection on the instant, the young sailor haughtily replied —

"Or to any other monster thou canst conjure!"

"We will take you at the word. There is no more certain method of knowing the past or the future, the quarter of the heavens from which the winds are to come, or the season of the hurricanes, than by putting a question to our mistress. She who knows so much of hidden matters, may tell us what you wish to know. We will have her called, by the usual summons."

Thus saving, the mariner of the shawl gravely quitted his guests, and descended into the inferior cabins of the vessel. It was but a moment, before there arose sounds from some secret though not distant quarter of the brigantine, that caused, in some measure, both surprise and pleasure to Ludlow and the Patroon. Their companion had his motives for being insensible to either of these emotions.

After a short and rapid symphony, a wind-instrument took up a wild strain, while a human voice was again heard chanting to the music, words which were so much involved by the composition of the air, as to render it impossible to trace more than that their burthen was a sort of mysterious incantation of some ocean deity.

"Squeaking and flutes!" grumbled Myndert, ere the last sounds were fairly ended. "This is downright heathenish; and a plain-dealing man, who does business above-board, has good reason to wish himself honestly at church. What have we to do with land-witches, or water-witches, or any other witchcraft, that we stay in the brigantine, now it is known that my niece is not to be found aboard her; and, moreover, even admitting that we were disposed to traffic, the craft has nothing in her that a man of Manhattan should want. The deepest bog of thy manor, Patroon, is safer ground to tread on, than the deck of a vessel that has got a reputation like that of this craft."

The scenes of which he was a witness, had produced a powerful effect on Van Staats of Kinderhook. Of a slow imagination but of a powerful and vast frame, he was not easily excited, either to indulge in fanciful images, or to suffer personal apprehension. Only a few years had passed since men, who in other respects were enlightened, firmly believed in the existence of supernatural agencies in the control of the affairs of this life; and though the New-Netherlanders had escaped the infatuation which prevailed so generally in the religious provinces of New-England, a credulous superstition, of a less active quality, possessed the minds of the most intelligent of the Dutch colonists, and even of their descendants so lately as in our own times. The art of divination was particularly in favor; and it rarely happened, that any inexplicable event affected the fortunes or comforts of the good provincialists, without their having recourse to some one of the more renowned fortunetellers of the country, for an explanation. Men of slow faculties love strong excitement, because they are insensible to less powerful impulses, as men of hard heads find most enjoyment in strong liquors. The Patroon was altogether of the sluggish cast; and to him there was consequently a secret, but deep pleasure, in his present situation.

"What important results may flow from this adventure, we know not, Mr. Alderman Van Beverout," returned Oloff Van Staats; "and I confess a desire to see and hear more, before we land. This 'Skimmer of the Seas' is altogether a different man from what our rumors in the city have reported; and, by remaining, we may set public opinion nearer to the truth. I have heard my late venerable aunt —"

"Chimney-corners and traditions! The good lady was no bad customer of these gentry, Patroon; and it is lucky that they got no more of thy inheritance, in the way of fees. You see the Lust in Rust against the mountain there; well, all that is meant for the public is on the outside, and all that is intended for my own private gratification is kept within-doors. But here is Captain Ludlow, who has matters of the Queen on his hands, and the gentleman will find it disloyal to waste the moments in this juggling."

"I confess the same desire to witness the end," dryly returned the commander of the Coquette. "The state of the wind prevents any immediate change in the positions of the two vessels; and why not get a farther insight into the extraordinary character of those who belong to the brigantine?"

"Ay, there it is!" muttered the Alderman between his teeth. "Your insights and outsights lead to all the troubles of life. One is never snug with these fantastics, which trifle with a secret, like a fly fluttering round a candle, until his wings get burnt."

As his companions seemed resolved to stay, however, there remained no alternative for the burgher, but patience. Although apprehension of some indiscreet exposure was certainly the feeling uppermost in his mind, he was not entirely without some of the weakness which caused Oloff Van Staats to listen and to gaze with so much obvious interest and secret awe. Even Ludlow, himself, felt more affected than he would have willing owned, by the extraordinary situation in which he was placed. No man is entirely insensible to the influence of sympathy, let it exert its power in what manner it will. Of this the young sailor was the more conscious, through the effect that was produced on himself, by the grave exterior and attentive manner of all the mariners of the brigantine. He was a seaman of no mean accomplishments; and, among other attainments that properly distinguish men of his profession, he had learned to know the country of a sailor, by those general and distinctive marks which form the principal difference between men whose common pursuit has in so great a degree created a common character. Intelligence, at that day, was confined to narrow limits among those who dwelt on the ocean. Even the officer was but too apt to be one of rude and boisterous manners, of limited acquirements and of deep and obstinate prejudices. No wonder then, that the common man was, in general, ignorant of most of those opinions which gradually enlighten society. Ludlow had seen, on entering the vessel, that her crew was composed of men of different countries. Age and personal character seemed to have been more consulted, in their selection, than national distinctions. There was a Finlander, with a credulous and oval physiognomy, sturdy but short frame, and a light vacant eye; and a dark-skinned seaman of the Mediterranean, whose classical outline of feature was often disturbed by uneasy and sensitive glances at the horizon. These two men had come and placed themselves near the group on the quarter-deck, when the last music was heard; and Ludlow had ascribed the circumstance to a sensibility to melody, when the child Zephyr stole to their side, in a manner to show that more was meant by the movement than was apparent in the action itself. The appearance of Tiller, who invited the party to re-enter the cabin, explained its meaning, by showing that these men, like themselves, had business with the being, who, it was pretended, had so great an agency in controlling the fortunes of the brigantine.

The party, who now passed into the little ante-room, was governed by very different sensations. The curiosity of Ludlow was lively, fearless, and a little mingled with an interest that might be termed professional; while that of his two companions was not without some inward reverence for the mysterious power of the sorceress. The two seamen manifested dull dependence, while the boy exhibited, in his ingenuous and half-terrified countenance, most unequivocally the influence of childish awe. The mariner of the shawl was grave, silent, and, what was unusual in his deportment, respectful. After a moment's delay, the door of the inner apartment was opened by Seadrift himself, and he signed for the whole to enter.

A material change had been made in the arrangement of the principal cabin. The light was entirely excluded from the stern, and the crimson curtain had been lowered before the alcove. A small window whose effect was to throw a dim obscurity within, had been opened in the side. The objects on which its light fell strongest, received a soft coloring from the hues of the hangings.

The free-trader received his guests with a chastened air, bowing silently, and with less of levity in his mien than in the former interview. Still Ludlow thought there lingered a forced but sad smile about his handsome mouth; and the Patroon gazed at his fine features, with the admiration that one might feel for the most favored of those who were believed to administer at some supernatural shrine. The feelings of the Alderman were exhibited only by some half-suppressed murmurs of discontent, that from time to time escaped him, notwithstanding a certain degree of reverence, that was gradually prevailing over his ill-concealed dissatisfaction.

"They tell me, you would speak with our mistress," said the principal personage of the vessel, in a subdued voice. "There are others, too, it would seem, who wish to seek counsel from her wisdom. It is now many months since we have had direct converse with her, though the book is ever open to all applicants for knowledge. You have nerves for the meeting?"

"Her Majesty's enemies have never reproached me with their want," returned Ludlow, smiling incredulously. "Proceed with your incantations, that we may know."

"We are not necromancers, Sir, but faithful mariners, who do their mistress's pleasure. I know that you are sceptical; but bolder men have confessed their mistakes, with less testimony. Hist! we are not alone. I hear the opening and shutting of the brigantine's transoms."

The speaker then fell back nearly to the line in which the others had arranged themselves, and awaited the result in silence. The curtain rose to a low air on the same wind-instrument; and even Ludlow felt an emotion more powerful than interest, as he gazed on the object that was revealed to view.

A female form, attired, as near as might be, like the figure-head of the vessel, and standing in a similar attitude, occupied the centre of the alcove. As in the image, one hand held a book with its page turned towards the spectators, while a finger of the other pointed ahead, as if giving to the brigantine its course. The sea-green drapery was floating behind, as if it felt the influence of the air; and the face had the same dark and unearthly hue, with its malign and remarkable smile.

When the start and the first gaze of astonishment were over, the Alderman and his companions glanced their eyes at each other, in wonder. The smile on the look of the free-trader became less hidden, and it partook of triumph.

"If any here has aught to say to the lady of our bark, let him now declare it. She has come far, at our call, and will not tarry long."

"I would then know," said Ludlow, drawing a heavy breath, like one recovering from some sudden and powerful sensation, "if she I seek be within the brigantine?"

He who acted the part of mediator in this extraordinary ceremony, bowed and advanced to the book, which, with an air of deep reverence, he consulted, reading, or appearing to read, from its pages.

"You are asked here, in return for that you inquire, if she you seek is sought in sincerity?"

Ludlow reddened; the manliness of the profession to which he belonged, however, overcame the reluctance natural to self-esteem; and he answered, firmly —

"She is."

"But you are a mariner; men of the sea place their affections, often, on the fabric in which they dwell. Is the attachment for her you seek, stronger than love of wandering, of your ship your youthful expectations, and the glory that forms a young soldier's dreams?"

The commander of the Coquette hesitated. After a moment of pause, like that of self-examination, he said —

"As much so, as may become a man."

A cloud crossed the brow of his interrogator, who advanced and again consulted the pages of the book.

"You are required to say, if a recent event has not disturbed your confidence in her you seek?"

"Disturbed — but not destroyed."

The sea-green lady moved, and the pages of the mysterious volume trembled, as if eager to deliver their oracles.

"And could you repress curiosity, pride, and all the other sentiments of your sex, and seek her favor, without asking explanation, as before the occurrence of late events?"

"I would do much to gain a kind look from Alida de Barbérie; but the degraded spirit, of which you speak, would render me unworthy of her esteem. If I found her as I lost her, my life should be devoted to her happiness; and if not, to mourning that one so fair should have fallen!"

"Have you ever felt jealousy?"

"First let me know if I have cause?" cried the young man, advancing a step towards the motionless form, with an evident intent to look closer into its character.

The hand of the mariner of the shawl arrested him, with the strength of a giant.

"None trespass on the respect due our mistress," coolly observed the vigorous seaman, while he motioned to the other to retreat.

A fierce glance shot from his eye; and then the recollection of his present helplessness came, in season, to restrain the resentment of the offended officer.

"Have you ever felt jealousy?" continued his undisturbed interrogator.

"Would any love, that have not?"

A gentle respiration was heard in the cabin, during the short pause that succeeded, though none could tell whence it came. The Alderman turned to regard the Patroon, as if he believed the sigh was his while the startled Ludlow looked curiously around him, at a loss to know who acknowledged, with so much sensibility, the truth of his reply.

"Your answers are well," resumed the free-trader, after a pause longer than usual. Then, turning to Oloff Van Staats, he said, "Whom, or what, do you seek?"

"We come on a common errand."

"And do you seek in all sincerity?"

"I could wish to find."

"You are rich in lands and houses; is she you seek, dear to you as this wealth?"

"I esteem them both, since one could not wish to tie a woman he admired to beggary."

The Alderman hemmed so loud as to fill the cabin, and then, startled at his own interruption, he involuntarily bowed an apology to the motionless form in the alcove, and regained his composure.

"There is more of prudence than of ardor in your answer. Have you ever felt jealousy?"

"That has he!" eagerly exclaimed Myndert "I've known the gentleman raving as a bear that has lost its cub, when my niece has smiled, in church, for instance, though it were only in answer to a nod from an old lady. Philosophy and composure, Patroon! Who the devil knows, but Alida may hear of this questioning? — and then her French blood will boil, to find that your love has always gone as regularly as a town-clock."

"Could you receive her, without inquiring into past events?"

"That would he — that would he!" returned the Alderman. "I answer for it, that Mr. Van Staats complies with all engagements, as punctually as the best house in Amsterdam, itself."

The book again trembled, but it was with a waving and dissatisfied motion.

"What is thy will with our mistress?" demanded the free-trader, of the fair-haired sailor.

"I have bargained with some of the dealers of my country, for a wind to carry the brigantine through the inlet."

"Go. The Water-Witch will sail when there is need — and you?"

"I wish to know whether a few skins I bought last night, for a private venture, will turn to good account?"

"Trust the sea-green lady for your profits. When did she ever let any fail, in a bargain. Child, what has brought thee hither?"

The boy trembled, and a little time elapsed before he found resolution to answer.

"They tell me it is so queer to be upon the land!"

"Sirrah! thou hast been answered. When others go, thou shalt go with them."

"They say 'tis pleasant to taste the fruits from off the very trees —"

"Thou art answered. Gentlemen, our mistress departs. She knows that one among you has threatened her favorite brigantine with the anger of an earthly Queen; but it is beneath her office to reply to threats so idle. Hark! her attendants are in waiting!"

The wind-instrument was once more heard, and the curtain slowly fell to its strains. A sudden and violent noise, resembling the opening and shutting of some massive door, succeeded — and then all was still. When the sorceress had disappeared, the free-trader resumed his former ease of manner, seeming to speak and act more naturally. Alderman Van Beverout drew a long breath, like one relieved; and even the mariner of the gay shawl stood in an easier and more reckless attitude than while in her presence. The two seamen and the child withdrew.

"Few who wear that livery have ever before seen the lady of our brigantine," continued the free-trader, addressing himself to Ludlow; "and it is proof that she has less aversion to your cruiser, than she in common feels to most of the long pennants that are abroad on the water."

"Thy mistress, thy vessel, and thyself, are alike amusing!" returned the young seaman, again smiling incredulously, and with some little official pride. "It will be well, if you maintain this pleasantry much longer, at the expense of Her Majesty's customs."

"We trust to the power of the Water-Witch. She has adopted our brigantine as her abode, given it her name, and guides it with her hand. 'Twould be weak to doubt, when thus protected."

"There may be occasion to try her virtues. Were she a spirit of the deep waters, her robe would be blue. Nothing of a light draught can escape the Coquette!"

"Dost not know that the color of the sea differs in different climes? We fear not, but you would have answers to your questions. Honest Tiller will carry you all to the land, and, in passing, the book may again be consulted. I doubt not she will leave us some further memorial of her visit."

The free-trader then bowed, and retired behind the curtain, with the air of a sovereign dismissing his visiters from an audience; though his eye glanced curiously behind him, as he disappeared, as if to trace the effect which had been produced by the interview. Alderman Van Beverout and his friends were in the boat again, before a syllable was exchanged between them. They had followed the mariner of the shawl, in obedience to his signal; and they quitted the side of the beautiful brigantine, like men who pondered on what they had just witnessed.

Enough has been betrayed, in the course of the narrative, perhaps, to show that Ludlow distrusted, though he could not avoid wondering at, what he had seen. He was not entirely free from the superstition that was then so common among seamen; but his education and native good sense enabled him, in a great measure, to extricate his imagination from that love of the marvellous, which is more or less common to all. He had fifty conjectures concerning the meaning of what had passed, and not one of them was true; though each, at the instant, seemed to appease his curiosity, while it quickened his resolution to pry further into the affair. As for the Patroon of Kinderhook, the present day was one of rare and unequalled pleasure. He had all the gratification which strong excitement can produce in slow natures; and he neither wished a solution of his doubts, nor contemplated any investigation that might destroy so agreeable an illusion. His fancy was full of the dark countenance of the sorceress; and when it did not dwell on a subject so unnatural, it saw the handsome features, ambiguous smile, and attractive air, of her scarcely less admirable minister.

As the boat got to a little distance from the vessel, Tiller stood erect, and ran his eye complacently over the perfection of her hull and rigging.

"Our mistress has equipped and sent upon the wide and unbeaten sea, many a bark," he said; "but never a lovelier than our own! — Captain Ludlow, there has been some double-dealing between us; but that which is to follow, shall depend on our skill, seamanship, and the merits of the two crafts. You serve Queen Anne, and I the sea-green lady. Let each be true to his mistress, and Heaven preserve the deserving! — Wilt see the book, before we make the trial?"

Ludlow intimated his assent, and the boat approached the figure-head. It was impossible to prevent the feeling, which each of our three adventurers, not excepting the Alderman, felt when they came in full view of the motionless image. The mysterious countenance appeared endowed with thought, and the malign smile seemed still more ironical than before.

"The first question was yours, and yours must be the first answer," said Tiller, motioning for Ludlow to consult the page which was open. "Our mistress deals chiefly in verses from the old writer, whose thoughts are almost as common to us all, as to human nature."

"What means this?" said Ludlow, hastily —

> *"She, Claudio, that you wrong'd, look, you restore.*
> *— love her Angelo;*
> *I have confess'd her, and I know her virtue."*

"These are plain words; but I would rather that another priest should shrive her whom I love!"

"Hist! — Young blood is swift and quickly heated. Our lady of the bark will not relish hot speech, over her oracles. Come, Master Patroon, turn the page with the rattan, and see what fortune will give."

Oloff Van Staats raised his powerful arm, with the hesitation, and yet with the curiosity, of a girl. It was easy to read in his eye, the pleasure his heavy nature felt in the excitement; and yet it was easy to detect the misgivings of an erroneous education, by the seriousness of all the other members of his countenance. He read aloud —

> "I have a motion much imports your good;
> Whereto, if you'll a willing ear incline
> What's mine is yours, and what is yours is mine —
> So bring us to our palace, where we'll show,
> What's yet behind, that's meet you all should know."
>
> *Measure For Measure.*

"Fair-dealing, and fairer speech! 'What's yours is mine, and what is mine is yours,' is Measure for Measure, truly, Patroon!" cried the Alderman. "A more equitable bargain cannot be made, when the assets are of equal value. Here is encouragement, in good sooth; and now, Master Mariner, we will land and proceed to the Lust in Rust, which must be the place meant in the verses. 'What's yet behind,' must be Alida, the tormenting baggage! who has been playing hide-and-seek with us, for no other reason than to satisfy her womanish vanity, by showing how uncomfortable she could make three grave and responsible men. Let the boat go, Master Tiller, since that is thy name; and many thanks for thy civilities."

"Twould give grave offence to leave the lady, without knowing all she has to say. The answer now concerns you, worthy Alderman; and the rattan will do its turn, in your hand, as well as in that of another."

"I despise a pitiful curiosity, and content myself with knowing what chance and good luck teach," returned Myndert. "There are men in Manhattan ever prying into their neighbors' credit, like frogs lying with their noses out of water; but it is enough for me to know the state of my books, with some insight into that of the market."

"It will not do. This may appease a quiet conscience, like your own, Sir; but we of the brigantine may not trifle with our mistress. One touch of the rattan will tell you, whether these visits to the Water Witch are likely to prove to your advantage."

Myndert wavered. It has been said, that, like most others of his origin in the colony, he had a secret leaning to the art of divination: and the words of the hero of the shawl contained a flattering allusion to the profits of his secret commerce. He took the offered stick, and, by the time the page was turned, his eyes were ready enough to consult its contents. There was but a line, which was also quoted as coming from the well-known comedy of 'Measure for Measure.'

"Proclaim it, Provost, round about the city."

In his eagerness Myndert read the oracle aloud, and then he sunk into his seat, affecting to laugh at the whole as a childish and vain conceit.

"Proclamation, me, no proclamations! Is it a time of hostilities, or of public danger, that one should go shouting with his tidings through the streets? Measure for Measure, truly! Harkee, Master Tiller, this sea-green trull of thine is no better than she should be; and unless she mends her manner of dealing, no honest man will be found willing to be seen in her company. I am no believer in necro-mancy — though the inlet has certainly opened this year, altogether in an unusual manner — and therefore I put little faith in her words; but as for saying aught of me or mine, in town or country, Holland or America, that can shake my credit, why I defy her! Still, I would not willingly have any idle stories to contradict; and

I shall conclude by saying, you will do well to stop her mouth."

"Stop a hurricane, or a tornado! Truth will come in her book, and he that reads must expect to see it — Captain Ludlow, you are master of your movements, again; for the inlet is no longer between you and your cruiser. Behind yon hillock is the boat and crew you missed. The latter expect you. And now, gentlemen, we leave the rest to the green lady's guidance, our own good skill, and the winds! I salute you."

The moment his companions were on the shore, the hero of the shawl caused his boat to quit it; and in less than five minutes it was seen swinging, by its tackles, at the stern of the brigantine.

CHAPTER XVII.

" — like Arion on the dolphin's back,
I saw him hold acquaintance with the waves,
So long as I could see."

Tempest.

THERE was one curious though half-confounded observer of all that passed in and around the Cove, on the morning in question. This personage was no other than the slave called Bonnie, who was the factotum of his master, over the demesnes of the Lust in Rust, during the time when the presence of the Alderman was required in the city; which was, in truth, at least four-fifths of the year. Responsibility and confidence had produced their effect on this negro, as on more cultivated minds. He had been used to act in situations of care; and practice had produced a habit of vigilance and observation, that was not common in men of his unfortunate condition. There is no moral truth more certain, than that men, when once accustomed to this species of domination, as readily submit their minds, as their bodies, to the control of others. Thus it is, that we see entire nations maintaining so many erroneous maxims, merely because it has suited the interests of those who do the thinking, to give forth these fallacies to their followers. For-tunately, however, for the improvement of the race and the advancement of truth, it is only necessary to give a man an opportunity to exercise his natural faculties, in order to make him a reflecting, and, in some degree, an independent being. Such, though to a very limited extent, certainly, had been the consequence, in the instance of the slave just mentioned.

How far Bonnie had been concerned in the proceedings between his master and the mariners of the brigantine, it is unnecessary to say. Little passed at the villa, of which he was ignorant; and as curiosity, once awakened, increases its own desire for indulgence, could he have had his wish, little would have passed anywhere, near him, without his knowing something of its nature and import. He had seen, while seemingly employed with his hoe in the garden of the Alderman, the trio conveyed by Erasmus across the inlet; had watched the manner in which they fol-lowed its margin to the shade of the oak, and had seen them enter the brigantine, as related. That this extraordinary visit on board a vessel which was in common shrouded by so much mystery, had given rise to much and unusual reflection in the mind of the black, was apparent by the manner in which he so often paused in his labor, and stood leaning on the handle of his hoe, like one who mused. He had never known his master so far overstep his usual caution, as to quit the dwelling, during the occasional visits of the free-trader; and yet he had now gone as it were into the very jaws of the lion, accompanied by the commander of a royal cruiser himself. No wonder, then, that the vigilance of the negro became still more active, and that not even the slightest circumstance was suffered to escape his admiring eye. During the whole time consumed by the visit related in the preceding chapter, not a minute had been suffered to pass, without an inquiring look in the direction, either of the brigantine, or of the adjacent shore.

It is scarcely necessary to say how keen the attention of the slave became, when his master and his companions were seen to return to the land. They imme-diately ascended to the foot of the oak, and then there was a long and apparently a serious conference between them. During this consultation, the negro dropped the end of his hoe, and never suffered his gaze, for an instant, to alter its direction. Indeed he scarcely drew breath, until the whole party quitted the spot together, and buried themselves in the thicket that covered the cape, taking the direction of its outer or northern extremity, instead of retiring by the shore of the Cove, towards the inlet. Then Bonnie respired heavily, and began to look about him at the other objects that properly belonged to the interest of the scene.

The brigantine had run up her boat, and she now lay, as when first seen, a motionless, beautiful, and exquisitely graceful fabric, without the smallest sign about her of an intention to move, or indeed without exhibiting any other proof, except in her admirable order and symmetry, that any of human powers dwelt within her hull. The royal cruiser, though larger and of far less aerial mould and fashion, presented the same picture of repose. The distance between the two was about a league; and Bonnie was sufficiently familiar with the formation of the land and of the position of the vessels, to be quite aware that this inactivity on the part of those whose duty it was to protect the rights of the Queen, proceeded from their utter ignorance of the proximity of their neighbor. The thicket which bounded the Cove and the growth of oaks and pines that stretched along the narrow sandy spit of land quite to its extremity, sufficiently accounted for the fact. The negro, therefore, after gazing for several minutes at the two immovable ves-sels, turned his eye askance on the earth, shook his head, and then burst into a laugh, which was so noisy that it caused his sable partner to thrust her vacant and circular countenance through an open window of the scullery of the villa, to demand the reason of a merriment that to her faithful feelings appeared to be a little unsocial.

"Hey! you alway' keep 'e queer t'ing to heself, Bonnie, but!" cried the vixen.

"I'm werry glad to see old bones like a hoe; an' I wonner dere ar' time to laugh, wid 'e garden full of weed!"

"Grach!" exclaimed the negro, stretching out an arm in a forensic attitude; "what a black woman know of politic! If a hab time to talk, better cook a dinner. Tell one t'ing, Phyllis, and that be dis; vy 'e ship of Captain Ludlow no lif' 'e anchor, an' come take dis rogue in 'e Cove? can a tell dat much, or no? — If no, let a man, who understan' heself, laugh much as he like. A little fun no harm Queen Anne, nor kill 'e Gubbenor!"

"All work and no sleep make old bone ache, Bonnie, but!" returned the consort. "Ten o'clock — twelve o'clock — t'ree o'clock, and no bed; vell I see 'e sun afore a black fool put 'e head on a pillow! An' now a hoe go all 'e same as if he sleep a ten hour. Masser Myn'ert got a heart, and he no wish to kill he people wid work, or old Phyllis war' dead, fifty year, next winter."

"I t'ink a wench's tongue nebber satisfy! What for tell a whole world, when Bonnie go to bed? He sleep for heself, and he no sleep for 'e neighborhood! Dere! A man can't t'ink of ebery t'ing, in a minute. Here a ribbon long enough to hang heself — take him, and den remem'er, Phyllis, dat you be 'e wife of a man who hab care on he shoul'er."

Bonnie then set up another laugh, in which his partner, having quitted her scullery to seize the gift, which in its colors resembled the skin of a garter-snake, did not fail to join, through mere excess of animal delight. The effect of the gift, however, was to leave the negro to make his observations, without any further interruption from one who was a little too apt to disturb his solitude.

A boat was now seen to pull out from among the bushes that lined the shore; and Bonnie was enabled to distinguish, in its stern-sheets, the persons of his master, Ludlow, and the Patroon. He had been acquainted with the seizure of the Coquette's barge, the preceding night, and of the confinement of the crew. Its appearance in that place, therefore, occasioned no new surprise. But the time which past while the men were rowing up to the sloop-of-war, was filled with minutes of increasing interest. The black abandoned his hoe, and took a position on the side of the mountain, that gave him a view of the whole bay. So long as the mysteries of the Lust in Rust had been confined to the ordinary combinations of a secret trade, he had been fully able to comprehend them; but now that there apparently existed an alliance so unnatural as one between his master and the cruiser of the crown, he felt the necessity of double observation and of greater thought.

A far more enlightened mind than that of the slave, might have been excited by the expectation, and the objects which now presented themselves, especially if sufficiently prepared for events, by a knowledge of the two vessels in sight. Though the wind still hung at east, the cloud above the mouth of the Raritan had at length begun to rise. The broad fleeces of white vapor, that had lain the whole morning over the continent, were rapidly uniting; and they formed already a dark and dense mass, that floated in the bottom of the estuary, threatening shortly to roll over the whole of its wide waters. The air was getting lighter, and variable; and while the wash of the surf sounded still more audible, its roll upon the beach was less regular than in the earlier hours of the day. Such was the state of the two elements, when the boat touched the side of the ship. In a minute it was hanging by its tackles, high in the air; and then it disappeared, in the bosom of the dark mass.

It far exceeded the intelligence of Bonnie to detect, now, any further signs of preparation, in either of the two vessels, which absorbed the whole of his attention. They appeared to him to be alike without motion, and equally without people. There were, it is true, a few specks in the rigging of the Coquette, which might be men; but the distance prevented him from being sure of the fact; and, admitting them to be seamen busied aloft, there were no visible consequences of their presence, that his uninstructed eye could trace. In a minute or two, even these scattered specks were seen no longer; though the attentive black thought that the mast-heads and the rigging beneath the tops thickened, as if surrounded by more than their usual mazes of ropes. At that moment of suspense, the cloud over the Raritan emitted a flash, and the sound of distant thunder rolled along the water. This seemed to be a signal for the cruiser; for when the eye of Bonnie, which had been directed to the heavens, returned towards the ship, he saw that she had opened and hoisted her three top-sails, seemingly with as little exertion as an eagle would have spread his wings. The ship now became uneasy; for the wind came in puffs, and the vessel rolled lightly, as if struggling to extricate itself from the hold of its anchor; and then, precisely at the moment when the shift of wind was felt, an the breeze came from the cloud in the west, the cruiser whirled away from its constrained position and appearing, for a short space, restless as a steed that had broken from its fastenings, it came up neatly to the wind, and lay balanced by the action of its sails. There was another minute, or two, of seeming inactivity, after which the broad surfaces of the top-sails were brought in parallel lines. One white sheet was spread after another, upon the fabric; and Bonnie saw that the Coquette, the swiftest cruiser of the crown in those seas, was dashing out from the land, under a cloud of canvas.

All this time, the brigantine, in the Cove, lay quietly at her anchor. When the wind shifted, the light hull swang with its currents, and the image of the sea-green lady was seen offering her dark cheek to be fanned by the breeze. But she alone seemed to watch over the fortunes of her followers; for no other eye could be seen, looking out on the danger that began so seriously to threaten them, both from the heavens, and from a more certain and intelligible, foe.

As the wind was fresh, though unsteady, the Coquette moved through the water with a velocity that did no discredit to her reputation for speed. At first, it seemed to be the intention of the royal cruiser to round the cape, and gain an offing in the open sea; for her head was directed northwardly; but no sooner had she cleared the curve of the little bight which from its shape is known by the name of the Horse-Shoe, than she was seen shooting directly into the eye of the wind, and falling off with the graceful and easy motion of a ship in stays, her head looking towards the Lust in Rust. Her design on the notorious dealer in contraband was now too evident to admit of doubt.

Still, the Water-Witch betrayed no symptoms of alarm. The meaning eye of the image seemed to study the motions of her adversary, with all the understanding of an intelligent being; and occasionally the brigantine turned slightly in the varying currents of the air, as if volition directed the movements of the little fabric. These changes resembled the quick and slight movements of the hound, as he lifts his head in his lair, to listen to some distant sound, or to scent some passing taint in the gale.

In the mean time, the approach of the ship was so swift as to cause the negro to shake his head, with a meaning that exceeded even his usually important look. Every thing was propitious to her progress; and, as the water of the Cove, during the periods that the inlet remained open, was known to be of a sufficient depth to admit of her entrance, the faithful Bonnie began to anticipate a severe blow to the future fortunes of his master. The only hope, that one could perceive, for the escape of the smuggler, was in the changes of the heavens.

Although the threatening cloud had now quitted the mouth of the Raritan, and was rolling eastward with fearful velocity, it had not yet broken. The air had the unnatural and heated appearance which precedes a gust; but, with the exception of a few large drops, that fell seemingly from a clear sky, it was as yet what is called a dry squall. The water of the bay was occasionally dark, angry, and green; and there were moments when it would appear as if heavy currents of air descended to its surface, wantonly to try their power on the sister element. Notwithstanding these sinister omens, the Coquette stood on her course, without lessening the wide surfaces of her canvas, by a single inch. They who governed her movements were no men of the lazy Levant, nor of the mild waters of the Mediterranean, to tear their hair, and call on saints to stand between their helplessness and harm; but mariners trained in a boisterous sea, and accustomed to place their first dependence on their own good manhood, aided by the vigilance and skill of a long and severely-exercised experience. A hundred eyes on board that cruiser watched the advance of the rolling cloud, or looked upon the play of light and shade, that caused the color of the water to vary; but it was steadily, and with an entire dependence on the discretion of the young officer who controlled the movements of the ship.

Ludlow himself paced the deck, with all his usual composure, so far as might be seen by external signs; though, in reality, his mind was agitated by feelings that were foreign to the duties of his station. He too had thrown occasional glances at the approaching squall, but his eye was far oftener riveted on the motionless brigantine, which was now distinctly to be seen from the deck of the Coquette, still riding at her anchor. The cry of 'a stranger in the cove!' which, a few moments before, came out of one of the tops, caused no surprise in the commander; while the crew, wondering but obedient, began, for the first time, to perceive the object of their strange manœuvres. Even the officer, next in authority to the captain, had not presumed to make any inquiry, though, now that the object of their search was so evidently in view, he felt emboldened to presume on his rank, and to venture a remark.

"It is a sweet craft!" said the staid lieutenant, yielding to an admiration natural to his habits, "and one that might serve as a yacht for the Queen! This is some trifler with the revenue, or perhaps a buccaneer from the islands. The fellow shows no ensign!"

"Give him notice, Sir, that he has to do with one who bears the royal commission," returned Ludlow, speaking from habit, and half-unconscious of what he said. "We must teach these rovers to respect a pennant."

The report of the cannon startled the absent man and caused him to remember the order.

"Was that gun shotted?" he asked, in a tone that sounded like rebuke.

"Shotted, but pointed wide, Sir; merely a broad hint. We are no dealers in dumb show, in the Coquette, Captain Ludlow."

"I would not injure the vessel, even should it prove a buccaneer. Be careful, that nothing strikes her, without an order."

"Ay, 'twill be well to take the beauty alive, Sir; so pretty a boat should not be broken up, like an old hulk. Ha! there goes his bunting, at last! He shows a white field — can the fellow be a Frenchman, after all?"

The lieutenant took a glass, and for a moment applied it to his eye, with the usual steadiness. Then he suffered the instrument to fall, and it would seem that he endeavored to recall the different flags that he had seen during the experience of many years.

"This joker should come from some terra incognita;" he said. "Here is a woman in his field, with an ugly countenance, too, unless the glass play me false — as I live, the rogue has her counterpart for a figure-head! — Will you look at the ladies, Sir?"

Ludlow took the glass, and it was not without curiosity that he turned it toward the colors the hardy smuggler dared to exhibit, in presence of a cruiser. The vessels were, by this time, sufficiently near each other, to enable him to distinguish the swarthy features and malign smile of the sea-green lady, whose form was wrought in the field of the ensign, with the same art as that which he had seen so often displayed in other parts of the brigantine. Amazed at the daring of the free-trader, he returned the glass, and continued to pace the deck, in silence. There stood near the two speakers an officer whose head and form began to show the influence of time, and who, from his position, had unavoidably been an auditor of what passed. Though the eye of this person, who was the sailing-master of the sloop, was rarely off the threatening cloud, except to glance along the wide show of canvas that was spread, he found a moment to take a look at the stranger.

"A half-rigged brig, with her fore-top-gallant-mast fidded abaft, a double martingale, and a standing gaft;" observed the methodical and technical mariner, as another would have recounted the peculiarities of complexion, or of feature, in some individual who was the subject of a personal description. "The rogue has no need of showing his brazen-faced trull to be known! I chased him, for six-and-thirty hours, in the chops of St. George's, no later than the last season; and the fellow ran about us, like a dolphin playing under a ship's fore-foot. We had him, now on our weather bow, and now crossing our course, and, once in a while, in our wake, as if he had been a Mother Carey's chicken looking for our crumbs. He seems snug enough in that cove, to be sure, and yet I'll wager the pay of any month in the twelve, that he gives us the slip. Captain Ludlow, the brigantine under our lee, here, in Spermaceti, is the well-known Skimmer of the Seas!"

"The Skimmer of the Seas!" echoed twenty voices, in a manner to show the interest created by the unexpected information.

"I'll swear to his character before any Admiralty Judge in England, or even in France, should there be occasion to go into an outlandish court — but no need of an oath, when here is a written account I took, with my own hands, having the chase in plain view, at noon-day." While speaking, the sailing-master drew a tobacco-box from his pocket, and removing a coil of pig-tail, he came to a deposit of memorandums, that vied with the weed itself in colors. "Now, gentlemen," he continued, "you shall have her build, as justly as if the master-carpenter had laid it down with his rule. 'Remember to bring a muff of marten's fur from America, for Mrs. Trysail — buy it in London, and swear' — this is not the paper — I let your boy, Mr. Luff, stow away the last entry of tobacco for me, and the young dog has disturbed every document I own. This is the way the government accounts get jammed, when Parliament wants to overhaul them. But I suppose young blood will have its run! I let a monkey into a church of a Saturday night myself, when a youngster, and he made such stowage of the prayer-books, that the whole parish was by the ears for six months; and there is one quarrel between two old ladies, that has not been made up to this hour. Ah! here we have it — 'Skimmer of the Seas. Full-rigged forward, with fore-and-aft mainsail, abaft; a gaff-top-sail; taut in his spars, with light top-hamper; neat in his gear, as any beauty — Carries a ring-tail in light weather; main-boom like a frigate's top-sail-yard, with a main-top-mast-stay-sail as big as a jib. Low in the water, with a woman figure-head; carries sail more like a devil than a human being, and lies within five points, when jammed up hard on a wind.' Here are marks by which one of Queen Anne's maids of honor might know the rogue; and there you see them all, as plainly as human nature can show them in a ship!"

"The Skimmer of the Seas!" repeated the young officers, who had crowded round the veteran tar, to hear this characteristic description of the notorious free-trader.

"Skimmer or flyer, we have him now, dead under our lee, with a sandy beach on three of his sides, and the wind in his eye!" cried the first-lieutenant.

"You shall have an opportunity, Master Trysail, of correcting your account, by actual measurement."

The sailing-master shook his head, like one who doubted, and again turned his eye on the approaching cloud.

The Coquette, by this time, had run so far as to have the entrance of the Cove open; and she was separated from her object, only by a distance of a few cables'-length. In obedience to an order given by Ludlow, all the light canvas of the ship was taken in, and the vessel was left under her three top-sails and gib. There remained, however, a question as to the channel; for it was not usual for ships of the Coquette's draught, to be seen in that quarter of the bay, and the threatening state of the weather rendered caution doubly necessary. The pilot shrunk from a responsibility which did not properly belong to his office, since the ordinary navigation had no concern with that secluded place; and even Ludlow, stimulated as he was by so many powerful motives, hesitated to incur a risk which greatly exceeded his duty. There was something so remarkable in the apparent security of the smuggler, that it naturally led to the belief he was certain of being protected by some known obstacle, and it was decided to sound before the ship was hazarded. An offer to carry the free-trader with the boats, though plausible in itself, and perhaps the wisest course of all, was rejected by the commander, on an evasive plea of its being of uncertain issue, though, in truth, because he felt an interest in one whom he believed the brigantine to contain, which entirely forbade the idea of making the vessel the scene of so violent a struggle. A yawl was therefore lowered into the water, the main-top-sail of the ship was thrown to the mast; and Ludlow himself, accompanied by the pilot and the master, proceeded to ascertain the best approach to the smuggler. A flash of lightning, with one of those thunder-claps that are wont to be more terrific on this continent than in the other hemisphere, warned the young mariner of the necessity of haste, if he would regain his ship, before the cloud, which still threatened them, should reach the spot where she lay. The boat pulled briskly into the Cove, both the master and the pilot sounding on each side, as fast as the leads could be cast from their hands and recovered.

"This will do;" said Ludlow, when they had ascertained that they could enter. "I would lay the ship as close as possible to the brigantine, for I distrust her quiet. We will go nearer."

"A brazen witch, and one whose saucy eye and pert figure might lead any honest mariner into contraband, or even into a sea-robbery!" half-whispered Trysail, perhaps afraid to trust his voice within hearing of a creature that seemed almost endowed with the faculties of life. "Ay, this is the hussy! I know her by the book, and her green jacket! But where are her people? The vessel is as quiet as the royal vault on a coronation-day, when the last king, and those who went before him, commonly have the place to themselves. Here would be a pretty occasion to throw a boat's-crew on her decks, and haul down yon impudent ensign, which bears the likeness of this wicked lady, so bravely in the air, if —"

"If what?" asked Ludlow, struck with the plausible character of the proposal.

"Why, if one were sure of the nature of such a minx, Sir; for to own the truth, I would rather deal with a regularly-built Frenchman, who showed his guns honestly, and kept such a jabbering aboard that one might tell his bearings in the dark.

The creature spoke!"

Ludlow did not reply, for a heavy crash of thunder succeeded the vivid glow of a flash of lightning, and glared so suddenly across the swarthy lineaments as to draw the involuntary exclamation from Trysail. The intimation that came from the cloud, was not to be disregarded. The wind, which had so long varied, began to be heard in the rigging of the silent brigantine; and the two elements exhibited unequivocal evidence, in their menacing and fitful colors of the near approach of the gust. The young sailor, with an absorbing interest, turned his eyes on his ship. The yards were on the caps, the bellying canvas was fluttering far to leeward, and twenty or thirty human forms on each spar, showed that the nimble-fingered topmen were gathering in and knotting the sails down to a close reef.

"Give way, men, for your lives!" cried the excited Ludlow.

A single dash of the oars was heard, and the yawl was already twenty feet from the mysterious image. Then followed a desperate struggle to regain the cruiser, ere the gust should strike her. The sullen murmur of the wind, rushing through the rigging of the ship, was audible some time before they reached her side; and the struggles between the fabric and the elements, were at moments so evident, as to cause the young commander to fear he would be too late.

The foot of Ludlow touched the deck of the Coquette, at the instant the weight of the squall fell upon her sails. He no longer thought of any interest but that of the moment; for, with all the feelings of a seaman, his mind was now full of his ship.

"Let run every thing!" shouted the ready officer, in a voice that made itself heard above the roar of the wind. "Clue down, and hand! Away aloft, you topmen! — lay out! — furl away!"

These orders were given in rapid succession, and witout a trumpet, for the young man could, at need, speak loud as the tempest. They were succeeded by one of those exciting and fearful minutes that are so familiar to mariners. Each man was intent on his duty, while the elements worked their will around him, as madly as if the hand by which they are ordinarily restrained was for ever removed. The bay was a sheet of foam, while the rushing of the gust resembled the dull rumbling of a thousand chariots. The ship yielded to the pressure, until the water was seen gushing through her lee-scuppers, and her tall line of masts inclined towards the plane of the bay, as if the ends of the yards were about to dip into the water. But this was no more than the first submission to the shock. The well-moulded fabric recovered its balance, and struggled through its element, as if conscious that there was security only in motion. Ludlow glanced his eye to leeward.

The opening of the Cove was favorably situated, and he caught a glimpse of the spars of the brigantine, rocking violently in the squall. He spoke to demand if the anchors were clear, and then he was heard, shouting again from his station in the weather gangway —

"Hard a-weather! —"

The first efforts of the cruiser to obey her helm, stripped as she was of canvas, were labored and slow. But when her head began to fall off, the driving scud was scarce swifter than her motion. At that moment, the sluices of the cloud opened, and a torrent of rain mingled in the uproar, and added to the confusion. Nothing was now visible but the lines of the falling water, and the sheet of white foam through which the ship was glancing.

"Here is the land, Sir!" bellowed Trysail, from a cat-head, where he stood resembling some venerable sea-god, dripping with his native element. "We are passing it, like a race-horse!"

"See your bowers clear!" shouted back the captain.

"Ready, Sir, ready —"

Ludlow motioned to the men at the wheel, to bring the ship to the wind; and when her way was sufficiently deadened, two ponderous anchors dropped, at another signal, into the water. The vast fabric was not checked without a further and tremendous struggle. When the bows felt the restraint, the ship swung head to wind, and fathom after fathom of the enormous ropes were extracted, by surges so violent as to cause the hull to quiver to its centre. But the first lieutenant and Trysail were no novices in their duty, and, in less than a minute, they had secured the vessel steadily at her anchors. When this important service was per-formed, officers and crew stood looking at each other, like men who had just made a hazardous and fearful experiment. The view again opened, and objects on the land became visible through the still falling rain. The change was like that from night to day. Men who had passed their lives on the sea drew long and relieving breaths, conscious that the danger was happily passed. As the more pressing interest of their own situation abated they remembered the object of their search. All eyes were turned in quest of the smuggler; but, by some inexpli-cable means, he had disappeared.

'The Skimmer of the Seas!' and 'What has become of the brigantine?' were exclamations that the discipline of a royal cruiser could not repress. They were repeated by a hundred mouths, while twice as many eyes sought to find the beau-tiful fabric. All looked in vain. The spot where the Water-Witch had so lately lain, was vacant, and no vestige of her wreck lined the shores of the Cove. During the time the ship was handing her sails, and preparing to enter the Cove, no one had leisure to look for the stranger; and after the vessel had anchored, until that moment, it was not possible to see her length, on any side of them. There was still a dense mass of falling water moving seaward; but the curious and anxious eyes of Ludlow made fruitless efforts to penetrate its secrets. Once indeed, more than an hour after the gust had reached his own ship, and when the ocean in the offing was clear and calm, he thought he could distinguish, far to seaward, the delicate tracery of a vessel's spars, drawn against the horizon, without any canvas set. But a second look did not assure him of the truth of the conjecture.

There were many extraordinary tales related that night, on board Her Britannic Majesty's ship Coquette. The boatswain affirmed that, while piping below in order to overhaul the cables, he had heard a screaming in the air, that sounded as if a hundred devils were mocking him, and which he told the gunner, in confidence, he believed was no more than the winding of a call on board the brigantine, who had taken occasion, when other vessels were glad to anchor, to get under way, in her own fashion. There was also a fore-top-man named Robert Yarn, a fellow whose faculty for story-telling equalled that of Scheherazade, and who not only asserted, but who confirmed the declaration by many strange oaths, that while he lay on the lee-fore-top-sail-yard-arm, stretching forth an arm to grasp the leech of the sail, a dark-looking female fluttered over his head and caused her long hair to whisk into his face, in a manner that compelled him to shut his eyes, which gave occasion to a smart reprimand from the reefer of the top. There was a feeble attempt to explain this assault, by the man who lay next to Yarn, who affected to think the hair was no more than the end of a gasket whipping in the wind; but his shipmate, who had pulled one of the oars of the yawl, soon silenced this explanation, by the virtue of his long-established reputation for veracity. Even Trysail ventured several mysterious conjectures concerning the fate of the brigantine, in the gun-room; but, on returning from the duty of sounding the inlet, whither he had been sent by his captain, he was less communicative and more thoughtful than usual. It appeared, indeed, from the surprise that was manifested by every officer that heard the report of the quarter-master, who had given the casts of the lead on this service, that no one in the ship, with the exception of Alderman Van Beverout, was at all aware that there was rather more than two fathoms of water in that secret passage.

CHAPTER XVIII.

"Sirs, take your places, and be vigilant."

Henry IV.

THE succeeding day was one in which the weather had a fixed character. The wind was east, and, though light, not fluctuating. The air had that thick and hazy appearance, which properly belongs to the Autumn in this climate, but which is sometimes seen at midsummer, when a dry wind blows from the ocean. The roll of the surf, on the shore, was regular and monotonous, and the currents of the air were so steady as to remove every apprehension of a change. The moment to which the action of the tale is transferred, was in the earlier hours of the afternoon.

At that time the Coquette lay again at her anchors, just within the shelter of the cape. There were a few small sails to be seen passing up the bay; but the scene, as was common at that distant day, presented little of the activity of our own times, to the eye. The windows of the Lust in Rust were again open, and the movement of the slaves, in and about the villa, announced the presence of its master.

The Alderman was in truth, at the hour named, passing the little lawn in front of la Cour des Fées, accompanied by Oloff Van Staats and the commander of the cruiser. It was evident, by the frequent glances which the latter threw in the direction of the pavilion, that he still thought of her who was absent; while the faculties of the two others were either in better subjection, or less stimulated by anxiety. One who understood the character of the individual, and who was acquainted with the past, might have suspected, by this indifference on the part of the Patroon, placed as it was in such a singular contrast to a sort of mysterious animation which enlivened a countenance whose ordinary expression was placid content, that the young suitor thought less than formerly of the assets of old Etienne, and more of the secret pleasure he found in the singular incidents of which he had been a witness.

"Propriety and discretion!" observed the burgher, in reply to a remark of one of the young men — "I say again, for the twentieth time, that we shall have Alida Barbérie back among us, as handsome, as innocent, ay, and as rich, as ever! — perhaps I should also say, as wilful. A baggage, to worry her old uncle, and two honorable suitors, in so thoughtless a manner! Circumstances, gentlemen," continued the wary merchant, who saw that the value of the hand of which he had to dispose, was somewhat reduced in the market, "have placed you on a footing, in my esteem. Should my niece, after all, prefer Captain Ludlow for a partner in her worldly affairs, why it should not weaken friendship between the son of old Stephanus Van Staats and Myndert Van Beverout. Our grandmothers were cousins, and there should be charities in the same blood."

"I could not wish to press my suit," returned the Patroon, "when the lady has given so direct a hint that it is disagreeable —"

"Hint me no hints! Do you call this caprice of a moment, this trifling, as the captain here would call it, with the winds and tides, a hint! The girl has Norman blood in her veins, and she wishes to put animation into the courtship. If bargains were to be interrupted by a little cheapening of the buyer, and some affectation of waiting for a better market in the seller, Her Majesty might as well order her custom-houses to be closed at once, and look to other sources for revenue. Let the girl's fancy have its swing, and the profits of a year's peltry against thy rent-roll, we shall see her penitent for her folly, and willing to hear reason. My sister's daughter is no witch, to go journeying for ever about the world, on a broomstick!"

"There is a tradition in our family," said Oloff Van Staats, his eye lighting with a mysterious excitement, while he affected to laugh at the folly he uttered, "that the great Poughkeepsie fortune-teller foretold, in the presence of my grand-mother, that a Patroon of Kinderhook should intermarry with a witch. So, should I see la Belle in the position you name, it would not greatly alarm me."

"The prophecy was fulfilled at the wedding of thy father!" muttered Myndert, who, notwithstanding the outward levity with which he treated the subject, was not entirely free from secret reverence for the provincial soothsayers, some of whom continued in high repute, even to the close of the last century. "His son would not else have been so clever a youth! But here is Captain Ludlow looking at the ocean, as if he expected to see my niece rise out of the water, in the shape of a mermaid."

The commander of the Coquette pointed to the object which attracted his gaze, and which, appearing as it did at that moment, was certainly not of a nature to lessen the faith of either of his companions in supernatural agencies.

It has been said that the wind was dry and the air misty, or rather so pregnant with a thin haze, as to give it the appearance of a dull, smoky light. In such a state of the weather, the eye, more especially of one placed on an elevation, is unable to distinguish what is termed the visible horizon at sea. The two elements become so blended, that our organs cannot tell where the water ends, or where the void of the heavens commences. It is a consequence of this in distinctness, that any object seen beyond the apparent boundary of water, has the appearance of floating in the air. It is rare for the organs of a landsman to penetrate beyond the apparent limits of the sea, when the atmosphere exhibits this peculiarity, though the practised eye of a mariner often detects vessels, which are hid from others, merely because they are not sought in the proper place. The deception may also be aided by a slight degree of refraction.

"Here;" said Ludlow, pointing in a line that would have struck the water some two or three leagues in the offing. "First bring the chimney of yonder low building on the plain, in a range with the dead oak on the shore, and then raise your eyes slowly, till they strike a sail."

"That ship is navigating the heavens!" exclaimed Myndert! "Thy grand-mother was a sensible woman, Patroon; she was a cousin of my pious progenitor, and there is no knowing what two clever old ladies, in their time, may have heard and seen, when such sights as this are beheld in our own!"

"I am as little disposed as another, to put faith in incredible things," gravely returned Oloff Van Staats; "and yet, if required to give my testimony, I should be reluctant to say, that yonder vessel is not floating in the heavens!"

"You might not give it to that effect, in safety;" said Ludlow. "It is no other than a half-rigged brigantine, on a taut bowline, though she bears no great show of canvas. Mr. Van Beverout, Her Majesty's cruiser is about to put to sea."

Myndert heard this declaration in visible dissatisfaction. He spoke of the virtue of patience, and of the comforts of the solid ground; but when he found the intention of the Queen's servant was not to be shaken, he reluctantly professed an intention of repeating the personal experiment of the preceding day. Accordingly, within half an hour, the whole party were on the banks of the Shrewsbury, and about to embark in the barge of the Coquette.

"Adieu, Monsieur François;" said the Alderman nodding his head to the ancient valet, who stood with a disconsolate eye on the shore. "Have a care of the movables in la Cour des Fées; we may have further use for them."

"Mais, Monsieur Beevre, mon devoir, et, ma foi, suppose la mèr was plus agréable, mon désir shall be to suivre Mam'selle Alide. Jamais personne de la famille Barbérie love de sea; mais, Monsieur, comment faire? I shall die sur la mèr de douleur; and I shall die d'ennui, to rester ici, bien sûr!"

"Come then, faithful François," said Ludlow. "You shall follow your young mistress; and perhaps, on further trial, you may be disposed to think the lives of us seamen more tolerable than you had believed."

After an eloquent expression of countenance, in which the secretly-amused though grave-looking boat's-crew thought the old man was about to give a spec-imen of his powers of anticipation, the affectionate domestic entered the barge. Ludlow felt for his distress, and encouraged him by a look of approbation. The language of kindness does not always need a tongue; and the conscience of the valet smote him with the idea that he might have expressed himself too strongly, concerning a profession to which the other had devoted life and hopes.

"La mèr, Monsieur le Capitaine," he said, with an acknowledging reverence, "est un vaste théâtre de la gloire. Voilà Messieurs de Tourville et Dougay Trouin; ce sont des hommes, vraiment remarquables! mais Monsieur, quant à toute la famille de Barbérie, we have toujours un sentiment plus favorable pour la terre."

"I wish your whimsical jade of a mistress, Master François, had found the same sentiment," dryly observed Myndert: "for let me tell you, this cruising about in a suspicious vessel is as little creditable to her judgment as — cheer up, Patroon; the girl is only putting thy mettle to the trial, and the sea air will do no damage to her complexion or her pocket. A little predilection for salt water must raise the girl in your estimation, Captain Ludlow!"

"If the predilection goes no further than to the element, Sir;" was the caustic answer. "But, deluded or not, erring or deceived, Alida Barbérie is not to be deserted, the victim of a villain's arts. I did love your niece, Mr. Van Beverout, and — pull with a will, men; fellows, are you sleeping on the oars?"

The sudden manner in which the young man interrupted himself, and the depth of tone in which he spoke to the boat's crew, put an end to the discourse. It was apparent that he wished to say no more, and that he even regretted the weak-ness which had induced him to say so much. The remainder of the distance, between the shore and the ship, was passed in silence.

When Queen Anne's cruiser was seen doubling Sandy-Hook, past meridian on the 6th June (sea-time) in the year 17 — , the wind, as stated in an ancient journal, which was kept by one of the midshipmen, and is still in existence, was light, steady at south, and by-west-half-west. It appears, by the same document, that the vessel took her departure at seven o'clock, P.M., the point of Sandy-Hook bearing west-half-south, distant three leagues. On the same page which contains these particulars, it is observed, under the head of remarks — "Ship under starboard steering-sails, forward and aft, making six knots. A suspicious half-rigged brigantine lying-to on the eastern board, under her mainsail, with fore-top-sail to the mast; light and lofty sails and jib loose; foresail in the brails. Her starboard steering-sail-booms appear to be rigged out, and the gear rove, ready for a run. This vessel is supposed to be the celebrated hermaphrodite, the

Water-Witch, commanded by the notorious 'Skimmer of the Seas,' and the same fellow who gave us so queer a slip, yesterday. The Lord send us a cap-full of wind, and we'l try his heels, before morning! — Passengers, Alderman Van Beverout, of the second ward of the City of New-York, in Her Majesty's province of the same name; Oloff Van Staats, Esq. commonly called the Patroon of Kinderhook, of the same colony; and a qualmish-looking old chap, in a sort of marine's jacket, who answers when hailed as Francis. A rum set taken altogether, though they seem to suit the Captain's fancy. Mem. Each lipper of a wave works like tartar emetic on the lad in marine gear."

As no description of ours can give a more graphic account of the position of the two vessels in question, at the time named, than that which is contained in the foregoing extract, we shall take up the narrative at that moment, which the reader will see must, in the 43d degree of latitude, and in the month of June have been shortly after the close of the day.

The young votary of Neptune, whose opinions have just been quoted, had indeed presumed on his knowledge of the localities, in affirming the distance and position of the cape, since the low sandy point was no longer visible from the deck. The sun had set, as seen from the vessel, precisely in the mouth of the Raritan; and the shadows from Navesink, or Neversink as the hills are vulgarly called, were thrown far upon the sea. In short, the night was gathering round the mariners, with every appearance of settled and mild weather, but of a darkness deeper than is common on the ocean. Under such circumstances, the great object was to keep on the track of the chase, during the time when she must necessarily be hid from their sight.

Ludlow walked into the lee-gangway of his ship, and, leaning with his elbow on the empty hammock-cloths, he gazed long and in silence at the object of his pursuit. The Water-Witch was lying in the quarter of the horizon most favorable to being seen. The twilight, which still fell out of the heavens, was without glare in that direction; and for the first time that day, he saw her in her true proportions. The admiration of a seaman was blended with the other sensations of the young man. The brigantine lay in the position that exhibited her exquisitely-moulded hull and rakish rig to the most advantage. The head, having come to the wind, was turned towards her pursuer; and as the bows rose on some swell that was heavier than common, Ludlow saw, or fancied he saw, the mysterious image still perched on her cut-water, holding the book to the curious, and ever pointing with its finger across the waste of water. A movement of the hammock-cloths caused the young sailor to bend his head aside, and he then saw that the master had drawn as near to his person as discipline would warrant. Ludlow had a great respect for the professional attainments that his inferior unquestionably possessed; and he was not without some consideration for the chances of a fortune, which had not done much to reward the privations and the services of a seaman old enough to be his father. The recollection of these facts always disposed him to be indulgent to a man who had little, beyond his seaman-like character and long experience, to recommend him.

"We are likely to have a thick night, Master Trysail," said the young captain, without deeming it necessary to change his look, "and we may yet be brought on a bowline, before yonder insolent is overhauled."

The master smiled, like one who knew more, than he expressed, find gravely shook his head.

"We may have many pulls on our bowlines, and some squaring of yards, too, before the Coquette (the figure-head of the sloop-of-war was also a female) gets near enough to the dark-faced woman, under the bowsprit of the brigantine, to whisper her mind. You and I have been nigh enough to see the white of her eyes, and to count the teeth she shows, in that cunning grin of hers — and what good has come of our visit? I am but a subordinate, Captain Ludlow, and I know my duty too well not to be silent in a squall, and I hope too well not to know how to speak when my commander wishes the opinions of his officers at a council; and therefore mine, just now, is perhaps different from that of some others in this ship, that I will not name, who are good men, too, though none of the oldest."

"And what is thy opinion, Trysail? — the ship is doing well, and she carries her canvas bravely."

"The ship behaves like a well-bred young woman in the presence of the Queen; modest, but stately — but, of what use is canvas, in a chase where witchcraft breeds squalls, and shortens sail in one vessel, while it gives flying kites to another! If Her Majesty, God bless her! should be ever persuaded to do so silly a thing as to give old Tom Trysail a ship, and the said ship lay, just here-a-way, where the Coquette is now getting along so cleverly, why then, as in duty bound, I know very well what her commander would do —"

"Which would be — ?"

"To, in all studding-sails, and bring the vessel on the wind."

"That would be to carry you to the southward, while the chase lies here in the eastern board!"

"Who can say, how long she will lie there? They told us, in York, that there was a Frenchman, of our burthen and metal, rummaging about among the fishermen, lower down on the coast. Now, Sir, no man knows that the war is half over better than myself, for not a ha'penny of prize-money has warmed my pocket, these three years; — but, as I was saying, if a Frenchman will come off his ground, and will run his ship into troubled water, why — whose fault is it but his own? A pretty affair might be made out of such a mistake, Captain Ludlow; whereas running after yonder brigantine, is napping out the Queen's canvas for nothing. The vessel's bottom will want new sheathing, in my poor opinion, before you catch him."

"I know not, Trysail," returned his captain, glancing an eye aloft; "every thing draws, and the ship never went along with less trouble to herself. We shall not know which has the longest legs, till the trial is made."

"You may judge of the rogue's speed by his impudence. There he lies, waiting for us, like a line-of-battle ship lying-to for an enemy to come down. Though a man of some experience in my way, I have never seen a lord's son more sure of promotion, than that same brigantine seems to be of his heels! If this old Frenchman goes on with his faces much longer, he will turn himself inside-out, and then we shall get an honest look at him, for these fellows never carry their true characters above-board, like a fair-dealing Englishman. Well, Sir, as I was remarking, yon rover, if rover he be, has more faith in his canvas than in the church. I make no doubt, Captain Ludlow, that the brigantine went through the inlet, while we were handing our top-sails yesterday; for I am none of those who are in a hurry to give credit to any will-o'-the-wisp tale; besides which, I sounded the passage with my own hands, and know the thing to be possible, with the wind blowing heavy over the taffrail; still, Sir, human nature is human nature, and what is the oldest seaman after all, but a man? — And so to conclude, I would rather any day chase a Frenchman, whose disposition is known to me, than have the credit of making traverses, for eight-and-forty hours, in the wake of one of these flyers, with little hope of getting him within hail."

"You forget, Master Trysail, that I have been aboard the chase, and know something of his build and character."

"They say as much aboard, here," returned the old tar, drawing nearer to the person of his captain, under an impulse of strong curiosity; "though crone presume to be acquainted with the particulars. I am not one of those who ask impertinent questions, more especially under Her Majesty's pennant; for the worst enemy I have will not say I am very womanish. One would think, however, that there was neat work on board a craft that is so prettily moulded about her waterlines?"

"She is perfect as to construction, and admirable in gear."

"I thought as much, by instinct! Her commander need not, however, be any the more sure of keeping her off the rocks, on that account. The prettiest young woman in our parish was wrecked, as one might say, on the shoals of her own good looks, having cruised once too often in the company of the squire's son. A comely wench she was, though she luffed athwart all her old companions, when the young lord of the manor fell into her wake. Well, she did bravely enough, Sir, as long as she could carry her flying kites, and make a fair wind of it; but when the squall of which I spoke, overtook her, what could she do but keep away before it? — and as others, who are snugger in their morals hove-to as it were, under the storm-sails of religion and such matters as they had picked up in the catechism, she drifted to leeward of all honest society! A neatly-built and clean-heeled hussy was that girl; and I am not certain, by any means, that Mrs. Trysail would this day call herself the lady of a Queen's officer, had the other known how to carry sail in the company of her betters."

The worthy master drew a long breath, which possibly was a nautical sigh, but which certainly had more of the north wind than of the zephyr in its breathing; and he had recourse to the little box of iron, whence he usually drew consolation.

"I have heard of this accident before;" returned Ludlow, who had sailed as a midshipman in the same vessel with, and indeed as a subordinate to, his present inferior. "But, from all accounts, you have little reason to regret the change, as I hear the best character of your present worthy partner."

"No doubt, Sir, no doubt. I defy any man in the ship to say that I am a back-biter, even against my wife, with whom I have a sort of lawful right to deal candidly. I make no complaints, and am a happy man at sea, and I piously hope Mrs. Trysail knows how to submit to her duty at home. I suppose you see, Sir, that the chase has hauled his yards, and is getting his fore-tack aboard?" Ludlow, whose eye did not often turn from the brigantine, nodded assent; and the master, having satisfied himself, by actual inspection, that every sail in the Coquette did its duty, continued — "The night is coming on thick, and we shall have occasion for all our eyes to keep the rogue in view, when he begins to change his bearings — but, as I was saying, if the commander of yonder half-rig is too vain of her good looks, he may yet wreck her, in his pride! The rogue has a desperate character as a smuggler, though, for my own part, I cannot say that I look on such men with as unfavorable an eye as some others. This business of trade seems to be a sort of chase between one man's wits and another man's wits, and the dullest goer must be content to fall to leeward. When it comes to be a question of revenue, why, he who goes free is lucky, and he who is caught, a prize. I have known a flag-officer look the other way, Captain Ludlow, when his own effects were passing duty-free; and as to your admiral's lady, she is a great patroness of the contraband. I do not deny, Sir, that a smuggler must be caught, and when caught, condemned, after which there must be a fair distribution among the captors; but all that I mean to say is, that there are worse men in the world than your British smuggler — such, for instance, as your Frenchman, your Dutchman, or your Don."

"These are heretodox opinions for a Queen's servant;" said Ludlow, as much inclined to smile as to frown.

"I hope I know my duty too well to preach them to the ship's company, but a man may say that, in a philosophical way, before his captain, that he would not let run into a midshipman's ear. Though no lawyer, I know what is meant by swearing a witness to the truth and nothing but the truth. I wish the Queen got the last, God bless her! several worn-out ships would then be broken up, and better vessels sent to sea in their places. But, Sir, speaking in a religious point of view, what is the difference between passing in a trunk of finery, with a duchess's name on the brass plate, or in passing in gin enough to fill a cutter's hold?"

"One would think a man of your years, Mr. Trysail, would see the difference between robbing the revenue of a guinea, and robbing it of a thousand pounds."

"Which is just the difference between retail and wholesale — and that is no trifle, I admit, Captain Ludlow, in a commercial country, especially in genteel life. Still, Sir, revenue is the country's right and therefore I allow a smuggler to be a bad man only not so bad as those I have just named, particularly your Dutchman! The Queen is right to make those rogues lower their flags to her in the narrow seas, which are her lawful property; because England, being a wealthy island, and Holland no more than a bit of bog turned up to dry, it is reasonable that we should have the command afloat. No, Sir, though none of your outcriers against a man, because he has had bad luck in a chase with a revenue-cutter, I hope I know what the natural rights of an Englishman are. We must be masters, here, Captain Ludlow, will-ye-nill-ye, and look to the main chances of trade and manufactures!"

"I had not thought you so accomplished a statesman, Master Trysail!"

"Though a poor man's son, Captain Ludlow, I am a free-born Briton, and my education has not been entirely overlooked. I hope I know something of the constitution, as well as my betters. Justice and honor being an Englishman's mottoes, we must look manfully to the main chance. We are none of your flighty talkers, but a reasoning people, and there is no want of deep thinkers on the little island; and therefore, Sir, taking all together, why England must stick up for her rights! Here is your Dutchman, for instance, a ravenous cormorant; a fellow with a throat wide enough to swallow all the gold of the Great Mogul, if he could get at it; and yet a vagabond who has not even a fair footing on the earth, if the truth must be spoken! Well, Sir, shall England give up her rights to a nation of such blackguards? No, Sir; our venerable constitution and mother church itself forbid, and therefore I say, dam'me, lay them aboard, if they refuse us any of our natural rights, or show a wish to bring us down to their own dirty level!"

"Reasoned like a countryman of Newton, and an eloquence that would do credit to Cicero! I shall endeavor to digest your ideas at my leisure, since they are much too solid food to be disposed of in a minute. At present we will look to the chase, for I see, by the aid of my glass, that he has set his studding-sails, and is beginning to draw ahead."

This remark closed the dialogue, between the captain and his subordinate. The latter quitted the gangway with that secret and pleasurable sensation which communicates itself to all who have reason to think they have delivered themselves creditably of a train of profound thought.

It was, in truth, time to lend every faculty to the movements of the brigantine; for there was great reason to apprehend, that by changing her direction in the darkness, she might elude them. The night was fast closing on the Coquette, and at each moment the horizon narrowed around her, so that it was only at uncertain intervals the men aloft could distinguish the position of the chase. While the two vessels were thus situated, Ludlow joined his guests on the quarter-deck.

"A wise man will trust to his wits, what cannot be done by force;" said the Alderman. "I do not pretend to be much of a mariner, Captain Ludlow, though I once spent a week in London, and I have crossed the ocean seven times to Rotterdam. We did little in our passages, by striving to force nature. When the nights came in dark, as at present, the honest schippers were content to wait for better times; by which means we were sure not to miss our road, and of finally arriving at the destined port in safety."

"You saw that the brigantine was opening his canvas, when last seen; and he that would move fast, must have recourse to his sails."

"One never knows what may be brewing, up there in the heavens, when the eye cannot see the color of a cloud. I have little knowledge of the character of the 'Skimmer of the Seas,' beyond that which common fame gives him; but, in the poor judgment of a landsman, we should do better by showing lanterns in different parts of the ship, lest some homeward-bound vessel do us an injury, and waiting until the morning, for further movements."

"We are spared the trouble, for look, the insolent has set a light himself, as if to invite us to follow. This temerity exceeds belief! To dare to trifle thus with one of the swiftest cruisers in the English fleet! See that every thing draws, gentlemen, and take a pull at all the sheets. Hail the tops, Sir, and make sure that every thing is home."

The order was succeeded by the voice of the officer of the watch, who inquired, as directed, if each sail was distended to the utmost. Force was applied to some of the ropes, and then a general quiet succeeded to the momentary activity.

The brigantine had indeed showed a light, as if in mockery of the attempt of the royal cruiser. Though secretly stung by this open contempt of their speed, the officers of the Coquette found themselves relieved from a painful and anxious duty. Before this beacon was seen, they were obliged to exert their senses to the utmost, in order to get occasional glimpses of the position of the chase; while they now steered in confidence for the brilliant little spot, that was gently rising and falling with the waves.

"I think we near him," half-whispered the eager captain; "for, see, there is some design visible on the sides of the lantern. Hold! — Ah! 'tis the face of a woman, as I live!"

"The men of the yawl report that the rover shows this symbol in many parts of his vessel, and we know he had the impudence to set it yesterday in our presence, even on his ensign."

"True — true; take you the glass, Mr. Luff, and tell me if there be not a woman's face sketched in front of that light — we certainly near him fast — let there be silence, fore and aft the ship. The rogues mistake our bearings!"

"A saucy-looking jade, as one might wish to see!" returned the lieutenant. "Her impudent laugh is visible to the naked eye."

"See all clear for laying him aboard! Get a party to throw on his decks, Sir! I will lead them myself."

These orders were given in an under tone, and rapidly. They were promptly obeyed. In the mean time, the Coquette continued to glide gently ahead, her sails thickening with the dew, and every breath of the heavy air acting with increased power on their surfaces. The boarders were stationed, orders were given for the most profound silence, and as the ship drew nearer to the light, even the officers were commanded not to stir. Ludlow stationed himself in the mizen channels, to cun the ship; and his directions were repeated to the quarter-master, in a loud whisper.

"The night is so dark, we are certainly unseen!" observed the young man to his second in command; who stood at his elbow. "They have unaccountably mistaken our position. Observe how the face of the painting becomes more distinct — one can see even the curls of the hair. Luff, Sir! luff — we will run him aboard! on his weather-quarter."

"The fool must be lying-to!" returned the lieutenant. "Even your witches fail of common sense; at times! Do you see which way he has his head, Sir?"

"I see nothing but the light. It is so dark that our own sails are scarcely visible — and yet I think here are his yards, a little forward of our lee beam."

"'Tis our own lower boom. I got it out, in readiness for the other tack, in case the knave should ware. Are we not running too full?"

"Luff you may, a little — luff, or we shall crush him!"

As this order was given, Ludlow passed swiftly forward. He found the hoarders ready for a spring, and he rapidly gave his orders. The men were told to carry the brigantine at every hazard, but not to offer violence, unless serious resistance was made. They were thrice enjoined not to enter the cabins, and the young man expressed a generous wish that, in every case, the 'Skimmer of the Seas' might be taken alive. By the time these directions were given, the light was so near that the malign countenance of the sea-green lady was seen in every lineament. Ludlow looked, in vain, for the spars, in order to ascertain in which direction the head of the brigantine lay; but, trusting to luck, he saw that the decisive moment was come.

"Starboard, and run him aboard! — Away there, you boarders, away! Heave with your grapnels; heave, men, with a long swing, heave! Meet her, with the helm — hard down — meet her — steady!" — was shouted in a clear, full, and steady voice, that seemed to deepen at each mandate which issued from the lips of the young captain.

The boarders cheered heartily, and leaped into the rigging. The Coquette readily and rapidly yielded to the power of her rudder. First inclining to the light, and then sweeping up towards the wind again, in another instant she was close upon the chase. The irons were thrown, the men once more shouted, and all on board held their breaths in expectation of the crash of the meeting hulls. At that moment of high excitement, the woman's face rose a short distance in the air, seemed to smile in derision of their attempt, and suddenly disappeared. The ship passed steadily ahead, while no noise but the sullen wash of the waters was audible. The boarding-irons were heard falling heavily into the sea; and the Coquette rapidly overrun the spot where the light had been seen, without sustaining any shock. Though the clouds lifted a little, and the eye might embrace a circuit of a few hundred feet, there certainly was nothing to be seen, within its range, but the unquiet element, and the stately cruiser of Queen Anne floating on its bosom.

Though its effects were different on the differently-constituted minds of those who witnessed the singular incident, the disappointment was general. The common impression was certainly unfavorable to the earthly character of the brigantine; and when opinions of this nature once get possession of the ignorant, they are not easily removed. Even Trysail, though experienced in the arts of those who trifle with the revenue-laws, was much inclined to believe that this was no vulgar case of floating lights or false beacons, but a manifestation that others, besides those who had been regularly trained to the sea, were occasionally to be found on the waters. If Captain Ludlow thought differently, he saw no sufficient reason to enter into an explanation with those who were bound silently to obey. He paced the quarter-deck, for many minutes; and then issued his orders to the equally-disappointed lieutenants. The light canvas of the Coquette was taken in, the studding-sail-gear unrove, and the booms secured. The ship was then brought to the wind, and her courses having been hauled up, the fore-top-sail was thrown to the mast. In this position the cruiser lay, waiting for the morning light, in order to give greater certainty to her movements.

CHAPTER XIX.

"I, John Turner,
Am master and owner
Of a high-deck'd schooner.
That's bound to Carolina —"
etc. etc. etc. etc.
                                Coasting Song.

IT is not necessary to say, with how much interest Alderman Van Beverout, and his friend the Patroon, had witnessed all the proceedings on hoard the Coquette. Something very like an exclamation of pleasure escaped the former, when it was known that the ship had missed the brigantine, and that there was now little probability of overtaking her that night.

"Of what use is it to chase your fire-flies, about the ocean, Patroon?" muttered the Alderman, in the ear of Oloff Van Staats. "I have no further knowledge of this 'Skimmer of the Seas,' than is decent in the principal of a commercial house — but reputation is like a sky-rocket, that may be seen from afar! Her Majesty has no ship that can overtake the free-trader, and why fatigue the innocent vessel for no thing?"

"Captain Ludlow has other desires than the mere capture of the brigantine;" returned the laconic and sententious Patroon. "The opinion that Alida de Barbérie is in her, has great influence with that gentleman."

"This is strange apathy, Mr. Van Staats, in one who is as good as engaged to my niece, if he be not actually married, Alida Barbérie has great influence with that gentleman! And pray, with whom, that knows her, has she not influence?"

"The sentiment in favor of the young lady, in general, is favorable."

"Sentiment and favors! Am I to understand, Sir by this coolness, that our bargain is broken? — that the two fortunes are not to be brought together, and that the lady is not to be your wife?"

"Harkee, Mr. Van Beverout; one who is saving of his income and sparing of his words, can have no pressing necessity for the money of others; and, on occasion, he may afford to speak plainly. Your niece has shown so decided a preference for another, that it has materially lessened the liveliness of my regard."

"It were a pity that so much animation should fail of its object! It would be a sort of stoppage in the affairs of Cupid! Men should deal candidly, in all business transactions, Mr. Van Staats; and you will permit me to ask, as for a final settlement, if your mind is changed in regard to the daughter of old Etienne de Barbérie, or not?"

"Not changed, but quite decided;" returned the young Patroon. "I cannot say that I wish the successor of my mother to have seen so much of the world. We are a family that is content with our situation, and new customs would derange my household."

"I am no wizard, Sir; but for the benefit of a son of my old friend Stephanus Van Staats, I will venture, for once, on a prophecy. You will marry, Mr. Van Staats — yes, marry — and you will wive, Sir, with — prudence prevents me from saying with whom you will wive; but you may account yourself a lucky man, if it be not with one who will cause you to forget house and home, lands and friends, manors and rents, and in short all the solid comforts of life. It would not surprise me to hear that the prediction of the Poughkeepsie fortune-teller should be ful-filled!"

"And what is your real opinion, Alderman Van Beverout, of the different mysterious events we have witnessed?" demanded the Patroon, in a manner to prove that the interest he took in the subject, completely smothered any displea-sure he might otherwise have felt at so harsh a prophecy. "This sea-green lady is no common woman!"

"Sea-green and sky-blue!" interrupted the impatient burgher. "The hussy is but too common, Sir; and there is the calamity. Had she been satisfied with trans-acting her concerns in a snug and reasonable manner, and to have gone upon the high seas again, we should have had none of this foolery, to disturb accounts which ought to have been considered settled. Mr. Van Staats, will you allow me to ask a few direct questions, if you can find leisure for their answer?"

The Patroon nodded his head, in the affirmative.

"What do you suppose, Sir, to have become of my niece?"

"Eloped."

"And with whom?"

Van Staats of Kinderhook stretched an arm towards the open ocean, and again nodded. The Alderman mused a moment; and then he chuckled, as if some amusing idea had at once gotten the better of his ill-humor.

"Come, come, Patroon," he said, in his wonted amicable tone, when addressing the lord of a hundred thousand acres, "this business is like a compli-cated account, a little difficult till one gets acquainted with the books, and then all becomes plain as your hand. There were referees in the settlement of the estate of Kobus Van Klinck, whom I will not name; but what between the handwriting of the old grocer, and some inaccuracy in the figures, they had but a blind time of it until they discovered which way the balance ought to come; and then by working backward and forward, which is the true spirit of your just referee, they got all straight in the end. Kobus was not very lucid in his statements, and he was a little apt to be careless of ink. His leger might be called a book of the black art; for it was little else than fly-tracks and blots, though the last were found of great assistance in rendering the statements satisfactory. By calling three of the biggest of them sugar-hogsheads, a very fair balance was struck between him and a peddling Yankee who was breeding trouble for the estate; and I challenge, even at this distant day, when all near interests in the results may be said to sleep, any responsible man to say that they did not look as much like those articles as any thing else. Something they must have been, and as Kobus dealt largely in sugar, there was also a strong moral probability that they were the said hogsheads. Come, come, Patroon; we shall have the jade back again, in proper time. Thy ardor gets the better of reason; but this is the way with true love, which is none the worse for a little delay Alida is not one to balk thy merriment; these Norman wenches are not heavy of foot at a dance, or apt to go to sleep when the fiddles are stirring!"

With this consolation, Alderman Van Beverout saw fit to close the dialogue, for the moment. How far he succeeded in bringing back the mind of the Patroon to its allegiance, the result must show; though we shall take this occasion to observe again, that the young proprietor found a satisfaction in the excitement of the present scene, that, in the course of a short and little diversified life, he had never before experienced.

While others slept, Ludlow passed most of the night on deck. He laid himself down in the hammock-cloths, for an hour or two, towards morning though the wind did not sigh through the rigging louder than common, without arousing him from his slumbers. At each low call of the officer of the watch to the crew, his head was raised to glance around the narrow horizon; and the ship never rolled heavily without causing him to awake. He believed that the brigantine was near, and, for the first watch, he was not without expectation that the two vessels might unexpectedly meet in the obscurity. When this hope failed, the young seaman had recourse to artifice, in his turn, in order to entrap one who appeared so practised and so expert in the devices of the sea.

About midnight, when the watches were changed, and the whole crew, with the exception of the idlers, were on deck, orders were given to hoist out the boats. This operation, one of exceeding toil and difficulty in lightly-manned ships, was soon performed on board the Queen's cruiser, by the aid of yard and stay-tackles, to which the force of a hundred seamen was applied. When four of these little attendants on the ship were in the water, they were entered by their crews, prepared for serious service. Officers, on whom Ludlow could rely, were put in command of the three smallest, while he took charge of the fourth in person. When all were ready, and each inferior had received his especial instructions, they quitted the side of the vessel, pulling off, in diverging lines, into the gloom of the ocean. The boat of Ludlow had not gone fifty fathoms, before he was perfectly conscious of the inutility of a chase; for the obscurity of the night was so great, as to render the spars of his own ship nearly indistinct, even at that short distance. After pulling by compass some ten or fifteen minutes, in a direction that carried him to windward of the Coquette, the young man commanded the crew to cease rowing, and prepared himself to await, patiently, for the result of his undertaking.

There was nothing to vary the monotony of such a scene, for an hour, but the regular rolling of a sea that was but little agitated, a few occasional strokes of the oars, that were given in order to keep the barge in its place, or the heavy breathing of some smaller fish of the cetaceous kind, as it rose to the surface to inhale the atmosphere. In no quarter of the heavens was any thing visible; not even a star was peeping out, to cheer the solitude and silence of that solitary place. The men were nodding on the thwarts and our young sailor was about to relinquish his design as fruitless, when suddenly a noise was heard, at no great distance from the spot where they lay. It was one of those sounds which would have been inexplicable to any but a seaman, but which conveyed a meaning to the ears of Ludlow, as plain as that which could be imparted by speech to a landsman. A moaning creak was followed by the low rumbling of a rope, as it rubbed on some hard or distended substance; and then succeeded the heavy flap of canvas, that, yielding first to a powerful impulse, was suddenly checked.

"Hear ye that?" exclaimed Ludlow, a little above a whisper. "'Tis the brigantine, gybing his main-boom! Give way, men — see all ready to lay him aboard!"

The crew started from their slumbers; the splash of oars was heard, and, in the succeeding moment, the sails of a vessel, gliding through the obscurity, nearly across their course, were visible.

"Now spring to your oars, men!" continued Ludlow, with the eagerness of one engaged in chase. "We have him to advantage, and he is ours! — a long pull and a strong pull — steadily, boys, and together!"

The practised crew did their duty. It seemed but a moment, before they were close upon the chase.

"Another stroke of the oars, and she is ours!" cried Ludlow. "Grapple! — to your arms! — away, boarders, away!"

These orders came on the ears of the men with the effect of martial blasts. The crew shouted, the clashing of arms was heard, and the tramp of feet on the deck of the vessel announced the success of the enterprise. A minute of extreme activity and of noisy confusion followed. The cheers of the boarders had been heard, at a distance; and rockets shot into the air, from the other boats, whose crews answered the shouts with manful lungs. The whole ocean appeared in a momentary glow, and the roar of a gun from the Coquette added to the fracas. The ship set several lanterns, in order to indicate her position; while blue-lights, and other marine signals were constantly burning in the approaching boats, as if those who guided them were anxious to intimidate the assailed by a show of numbers.

In the midst of this scene of sudden awakening from the most profound quiet, Ludlow began to look about him, in order to secure the principal objects of the capture. He had repeated his orders about entering the cabins, and concerning the person of the 'Skimmer of the Seas,' among the other instructions given to the crews of the different boats; and the instant they found themselves in quiet possession of the prize, the young man dashed into the private recesses of the vessel, with a heart that throbbed even more violently than during the ardor of boarding. To cast open the door of a cabin, beneath the high quarter-deck, and to descend to the level of its floor, were the acts of a moment. But disappointment and mortification succeeded to triumph. A second glance was not necessary to show that the coarse work and foul smells he saw and encountered, did not belong to the commodious and even elegant accommodations of the brigantine.

"Here is no Water-Witch!" he exclaimed aloud under the impulse of sudden surprise.

"God be praised!" returned a voice, which was succeeded by a frightened face from out a state-room. "We were told the rover was in the offing, and thought the yells could come from nothing human!"

The blood, which had been rushing through the arteries and veins of Ludlow so tumultuously now crept into his cheeks, and was felt tingling at his fingers'-ends. He gave a hurried order to his men to re-enter their boat, leaving every thing as they found it. A short conference between the commander of Her Majesty's ship Coquette, and the seaman of the state-room, succeeded; and then the former hastened on deck, whence his passage into the barge occupied but a moment. The boat pulled away from the fancied prize, amid a silence that was uninterrupted by any other sound than that of a song, which, to all appearance, came from one who by this time had placed himself at the vessel's helm. All that can be said of the music is, that it was suited to the words, and all that could be heard of the latter, was a portion of a verse, if verse it might be called, which had exercised the talents of some thoroughly nautical mind. As we depend, for the accuracy of the quotation, altogether on the fidelity of the journal of the midshipman already named, it is possible that some injustice may be done the writer; but, according to that document, he sang a strain of the coasting song, which we have prefixed to this chapter as its motto.

The papers of the coaster did not give a more detailed description of her character and pursuits, than that which is contained in this verse. It is certain that the log-book of the Coquette was far less explicit. The latter merely said, that 'a coaster called the Stately Pine, John Turner, master, bound from New-York to the Province of North Carolina, was boarded at one o'clock, in the morning, all well.' But this description was not of a nature to satisfy the sea men of the cruiser. Those who had been actually engaged in the expedition were much too excited to see things in their true colors; and, coupled with the two previous escapes of the Water-Witch, the event just related had no small share in confirming their former opinions concerning her character. The sailing-master was not now alone, in believing that all pursuit of the brigantine was perfectly useless.

But these were conclusions that the people of the Coquette made at their leisure, rather than those which suggested themselves on the instant. The boats, led by the flashes of light, had joined each other, and were rowing fast towards the ship, before the pulses of the actors beat with sufficient calmness to allow of serious reflection; nor was it until the adventurers were below, and in their hammocks, that they found suitable occasion to relate what had occurred to a wondering auditory. Robert Yarn, the fore-top-man who had felt the locks of the sea-green lady blowing in his face during the squall, took advantage of the circumstance to dilate on his experiences; and, after having advanced certain positions that particularly favored his own theories, he produced one of the crew of the barge, who stood ready to affirm, in any court in Christendom, that he actually saw the process of changing the beautiful and graceful lines that distinguished the hull of the smuggler, into the coarser and more clumsy model of the coaster.

"There are know-nothings," continued Robert, after he had fortified his position by the testimony in question, "who would deny that the water of the ocean is blue, because the stream that turns the parish-mill happens to be muddy. But your real mariner, who has lived much in foreign parts, is a man who understands the philosophy of life, and knows when to believe a truth and when to scorn a lie. As for a vessel changing her character when hard pushed in a chase, there are many instances; though having one so near us, there is less necessity to be roving over distant seas, in search of a case to prove it. My own opinion concerning this here brigantine, is much as follows — that is to say, I do suppose there was once a real living hermaphrodite of her build and rig, and that she might be employed in some such trade as this craft is thought to be in; and that, in some unlucky hour, she and her people met with a mishap, that has condemned her ever since to appear on this coast at stated times. She has, however, a natural dislike to a royal cruiser; and no doubt the thing is now sailed by those who have little need of compass or observation! All this being true, it is not wonderful that when the boat's-crew got on her decks, they found her different from what they had expected. This much is certain, that when I lay within a boat-hook's length of her sprit-sail-yard-arm, she was a half-rig, with a woman figure-head, and as pretty a show of gear aloft, as eye ever looked upon; while every thing below was as snug as a tobacco-box with the lid down — and here you all say that she is a high-decked schooner, with nothing ship-shape about her! What more is wanting to prove the truth of what has been stated? — If any man can gainsay it, let him speak."

As no man did gainsay it, it is presumed that the reasoning of the top-man gained many proselytes. It is scarcely necessary to add, how much of mystery and fearful interest was thrown around the redoubtable 'Skimmer of the Seas,' by the whole transaction.

There was a different feeling on the quarter-deck. The two lieutenants put their heads together, and looked grave; while one or two of the midshipmen, who had been in the boats, were observed to whisper with their messmates, and to indulge in smothered laughter. As the captain, however, maintained his ordinary dignified and authoritative mien, the merriment went no further, and was soon entirely repressed.

While on this subject, it may be proper to add that, in course of time, the Stately Pine reached the capes of North Carolina, in safety; and that, having effected her passage over Edenton bar, without striking, she ascended the river to the point of her destination. Here the crew soon began to throw out hints, relative to an encounter of their schooner with a French cruiser. As the British empire, even in its most remote corners, was at all times alive to its nautical glory, the event soon became the discourse in more distant parts of the colony; and in less than six months, the London journals contained a very glowing account of an engagement, in which the names of the Stately Pine, and of John Turner, made some respectable advances towards immortality.

If Captain Ludlow ever gave any further account of the transaction than what was stated in the log-book of his ship, the bienséance, observed by the Lords of the Admiralty, prevented it from becoming public.

Returning from this digression, which has no other connexion with the immediate thread of the narrative, than that which arises from a reflected interest, we shall revert to the further proceedings on board the cruiser.

When the Coquette had hoisted in her boats, that portion of the crew which did not belong to the watch was dismissed to their hammocks, the lights were lowered, and tranquillity once more reigned in the ship. Ludlow sought his rest, and although there is reason to think that his slumbers were a little disturbed by dreams, he remained tolerably quiet in the hammock-cloths, the place in which it has already been said he saw fit to take his repose, until the morning watch had been called.

Although the utmost vigilance was observed among the officers and look-outs, during the rest of the night, there occurred nothing to arouse the crew from their usual recumbent attitudes between the guns. The wind continued light but steady, the sea smooth, and the heavens clouded, as during the first hours of darkness.

CHAPTER XX.

"The mouse ne'er shunned the cat, as they did budge
From rascals worse than they."

Coriolanus.

DAY dawned on the Atlantic, with its pearly light, succeeded by the usual flushing of the skies, and the stately rising of the sun from out the water. The instant the vigilant officer, who commanded the morning watch, caught the first glimpses of the returning brightness, Ludlow was awakened. A finger laid on his arm, was sufficient to arouse one who slept with the responsibility of his station ever present to his mind. A minute did not pass, before the young man was on the quarter-deck, closely examining the heavens and the horizon. His first question was to ask if nothing had been seen during the watch. The answer was in the negative.

"I like this opening in the north-west," observed the captain, after his eye had thoroughly scanned the whole of the still dusky and limited view. "Wind will come out of it. Give us a cap-full, and we shall try the speed of this boasted Water-Witch! — Do I not see a sail, on our weather-beam? — or is it the crest of a wave?"

"The sea is getting irregular, and I have often been thus deceived, since the light appeared."

"Get more sail on the ship. Here is wind, in-shore of us; we will be ready for it. See every thing clear, to show all our canvas."

The lieutenant received these orders with the customary deference and communicated them to his inferiors again, with the promptitude that distinguishes sea discipline. The Coquette, at the moment, was lying under her three top-sails, one of which was thrown against its mast, in a manner to hold the vessel as nearly stationary as her drift and the wash of the waves would allow. So soon, however, as the officer of the watch summoned the people to exertion, the massive yards were swung; several light sails, that served to balance the fabric as well as to urge it ahead, were hoisted or opened; and the ship immediately began to move through the water. While the men of the watch were thus employed, the flapping of the canvas announced the approach of a new breeze.

The coast of North America is liable to sudden and dangerous transitions, in the currents of the air. It is a circumstance of no unusual occurrence, for a gale to alter its direction with so little warning, as greatly to jeopard the safety of a ship, or even to overwhelm her. It has been often said, that the celebrated Ville de Paris was lost through one of these violent changes, her captain having inadvertently hove-to the vessel under too much after-sail, a mistake by which he lost the command of his ship during the pressing emergency that ensued. Whatever may have been the fact as regards that ill-fated prize, it is certain that Ludlow was perfectly aware of the hazards that sometimes accompany the first blasts of a north-west wind on his native coast, and that he never forgot to be prepared for the danger.

When the wind from the land struck the Coquette, the streak of light, which announced the appearance of the sun, had been visible several minutes. As the broad sheets of vapor, that had veiled the heavens during the prevalence of the south-easterly breeze, were rolled up into dense masses of clouds, like some immense curtain that is withdrawn from before its scene, the water, no less than the sky, became instantly visible, in every quarter. It is scarcely necessary to say, how eagerly the gaze of our young seaman ran over the horizon, in order to observe the objects which might come within its range. At first disappointment was plainly painted in his countenance, and then succeeded the animated eye and flushed cheek of success.

"I had thought her gone!" he said to his immediate subordinate in authority. "But here she is, to leeward, just within the edge of that driving mist, and as dead under our lee as a kind fortune could place her. Keep the ship away, Sir, and cover her with canvas, from her trucks down. Call the people from their hammocks, and show yon insolent what Her Majesty's sloop can do, at need!"

This command was the commencement of a general and hasty movement, in which every seaman in the ship exerted his powers to the utmost. All hands were no sooner called, than the depths of the vessel gave up their tenants, who, joining their force to that of the watch on deck, quickly covered the spars of the Coquette with a snow-white cloud. Not content to catch the breeze on such surfaces as the ordinary yards could distend, long booms were thrust out over the water, and sail was set beyond sail, until the bending masts would bear no more. The low hull, which supported this towering and complicated mass of ropes, spars, and sails, yielded to the powerful impulse, and the fabric, which, in addition to its crowd of human beings, sustained so heavy a load of artillery, with all its burthen of stores and ammunition, began to divide the waves, with the steady and imposing force of a vast momentum. The seas curled and broke against her sides, like water washing the rocks, the steady ship feeling, as yet, no impression from their feeble efforts. As the wind increased, however, and the vessel went further from the land, the surface of the ocean gradually grew more agitated, until the highlands, which lay over the villa of the Lust in Rust, finally sunk into the sea; when the top-gallant-royals of the ship were seen describing wide segments of circles against the heavens, and her dark sides occasionally rose, from a long and deep roll, glittering with the element that sustained her.

When Ludlow first descried the object which he believed to be the chase, it seemed a motionless speck on the margin of the sea. It had now grown into all the magnitude and symmetry of the well-known brigantine. Her slight and attenuated spars were plainly to be seen, rolling, easily but wide, with the constant movement of the hull, and with no sail spread, but that which was necessary to keep the vessel in command on the billows. But when the Coquette was just within the range of a cannon, the canvas began to unfold; and it was soon apparent that the "Skimmer of the Seas" was preparing for flight.

The first manœuvre of the Water-witch was an attempt to gain the wind of her pursuer. A short experiment appeared to satisfy those who governed the brigantine that the effort was vain, while the wind was so fresh and the water so rough. She wore, and crowded sail on the opposite tack, in order to try her speed with the cruiser; nor was it until the result sufficiently showed the danger of permitting the other to get any nigher, that she finally put her helm aweather, and ran off, like a sea-fowl resting on its wing, with the wind over her taffrail.

The two vessels now presented the spectacle of a stern chase. The brigantine also opened the folds of all her sails, and there arose a pyramid of canvas, over the nearly imperceptible hull, that resembled a fantastic cloud driving above the sea, with a velocity that seemed to rival the passage of the vapor that floated in the upper air. As equal skill directed the movements of the two vessels, and the same breeze pressed upon their sails, it was long before there was any perceptible difference in their progress. Hour passed after hour, and were it not for the sheets of white foam that were dashed from the bows of the Coquette, and the manner in which she even out stripped the caps of the combing waves, her commander might have fancied his vessel ever in the same spot. While the ocean presented, on every side, the same monotonous and rolling picture, there lay the chase, seemingly neither a foot nearer, nor a foot farther, than when the trial of speed began. A dark line would rise on the crest of a wave, and then, sinking again, leave, nothing visible, but the yielding and waving cloud of canvas, that danced along the sea.

"I had hoped for better things of the ship, Master Trysail!" said Ludlow, who had long been seated on a night-head, attentively watching the progress of the chase. "We are buried to the bob-stays; and yet, there yon fellow lies, nothing plainer than when he first showed his studding-sails!"

"And there he will lie, Captain Ludlow, while the light lasts. I have chased the rover in the narrow seas, till the cliffs of England melted away like the cap of a wave; and we had raised the sand-banks of Holland high as the sprit-sail-yard, and yet what good came of it? The rogue played with us, as your portsman trifles with the entangled trout; and when we thought we had him, he would shoot without the range of our guns, with as little exertion as a ship slides into the water, after the spur shoars are knocked from under her bows."

"Ay, but the Druid had a little of the rust of antiquity about her. The Coquette has never got a chase under her lee, that she did not speak."

"I disparage no ship, Sir, for character is character, and none should speak lightly of their fellow-creatures, and, least of all, of any thing which follows the sea. I allow the Coquette to be a lively boat on a wind, and a real scudder going large; but one should know the wright that fashioned yonder brigantine, before he ventures to say that any vessel in Her Majesty's fleet can hold way with her, when she is driven hard."

"These opinions, Trysail, are fitter for the tales of a top, than for the mouth of one who walks the quarter-deck."

"I should have lived to little purpose, Captain Ludlow, not to know that what was philosophy in my young days, is not philosophy now. They say the world is round, which is my own opinion — first, because the glorious Sir Francis Drake, and divers other Englishmen, have gone in, as it were, at one end, and out at the other; no less than several seamen of other nations, to say nothing of one Magellan, who pretends to have been the first man to make the passage, which I take to be neither more nor less than a Portuguee lie, it being altogether unreasonable to suppose that a Portuguee should do what an Englishman had not yet thought of doing — secondly, if the world were not round, or some such shape, why should we see the small sails of a ship before her courses, or why should her truck heave up into the horizon before the hull? They say, moreover, that the world turns round, which is no doubt true; and it is just as true that its opinions turn round with it, which brings me to the object of my remark — yon fellow shows more of his broadside, Sir, than common! He is edging in for the land, which must lie, hereaway, on our larboard beam, in order to get into smoother water. This tumbling about is not favorable to your light craft, let who will build them."

"I had hoped to drive him off the coast. Could we get him fairly into the

Gulf Stream, he would be ours, for he is too low in the water to escape us in the short seas. We must force him into blue water, though our upper spars crack in the struggle! Go aft, Mr. Hopper, and tell the officer of the watch to bring the ship's head up, a point and a half, to the northward, and to give a slight pull on the braces."

"What a mainsail the rogue carries! It is as broad as the instructions of a roving commission, with a hoist like the promotion of an admiral's son! How every thing pulls aboard him! A thorough-bred sails that brigantine, let him come whence he may!"

"I think we near him! The rough water is helping us, and we are closing. Steer small, fellow; steer small! You see the color of his mouldings begins to show, when he lifts on the seas."

"The sun touches his side — and yet, Captain Ludlow, you may be right — for here is a man in his fore-top, plainly enough to be seen. A shot, or two, among his spars and sails, might now do service."

Ludlow affected not to hear; but the first-lieutenant having come on the forecastle, seconded this opinion, by remarking that their position would indeed enable them to use the chase-gun, without losing any distance. As Trysail sustained his former assertion by truths that were too obvious to be refuted, the commander of the cruiser reluctantly issued an order to clear away the forward gun, and to shift it into the bridle-port. The interested and attentive seamen were not long in performing this service; and a report was quickly made to the captain, that the piece was ready.

Ludlow then descended from his post on the night-head, and pointed the cannon himself.

"Knock away the quoin, entirely;" he said to the captain of the gun, when he had got the range; "now mind her when she lifts, forward; keep the ship steady, Sir — fire!"

Those gentleman 'who live at home at ease,' are often surprised to read of combats, in which so much powder, and hundreds and even thousands of shot, are expended, with so little loss of human life; while a struggle on the land, of less duration, and seemingly of less obstinacy, shall sweep away a multitude. The secret of the difference lies in the uncertainty of aim, on an element as restless as the sea. The largest ship is rarely quite motionless, when on the open ocean; and it is not necessary to tell the reader, that the smallest variation in the direction of a gun at its muzzle, becomes magnified to many yards at the distance of a few hundred feet. Marine gunnery has no little resemblance to the skill of the fowler; since a calculation for a change in the position of the object must commonly be made in both cases, with the additional embarrassment on the part of the seaman, of an allowance for a complicated movement in the piece itself.

How far the gun of the Coquette was subject to the influence of these causes, or how far the desire of her captain to protect those whom he believed to be on board the brigantine, had an effect on the direction taken by its shot, will probably never be known. It is certain, however, that when the stream of fire, followed by its curling cloud, had gushed out upon the water, fifty eyes sought in vain to trace the course of the iron messenger among the sails and rigging of the Water-Witch. The symmetry of her beautiful rig was undisturbed, and the unconscious fabric still glided over the waves, with its customary ease and velocity. Ludlow had a reputation, among his crew, for some skill in the direction of a gun. The failure, therefore, in no degree aided in changing the opinions of the common men concerning the character of the chase. Many shook their heads, and more than one veteran tar, as he paced his narrow limits with both hands thrust into the bosom of his jacket, was heard to utter his belief of the inefficacy of ordinary shot, in bringing-to that brigantine. It was necessary, however to repeat the experiment, for the sake of appearances. The gun was several times discharged, and always with the same want of success.

"There is little use in wasting our powder, at this distance, and with so heavy a sea," said Ludlow, quitting the cannon, after a fifth and fruitless essay. "I shall fire no more. Look at your sails, gentlemen, and see that every thing draws. We must conquer with our heels, and let the artillery rest. Secure the gun."

"The piece is ready, Sir;" observed its captain, presuming on his known favor with the commander, though he qualified the boldness by taking off his hat, in a sufficiently respectful manner — "'Tis a pity to balk it!"

"Fire it, yourself, then, and return the piece to its port;" carelessly returned the captain, willing to show that others could be as unlucky as himself.

The men quartered at the gun, left alone, busied themselves in executing the order.

"Run in the quoin, and, blast the brig, give her a point-blanker!" said the gruff old seaman, who was intrusted with a local authority over that particular piece. "None of your geometry calculations, for me!"

The crew obeyed, and the match was instantly applied. A rising sea, however, aided the object of the directly-minded old tar, or our narration of the exploits of the piece would end with the discharge, since its shot would otherwise have inevitably plunged into a wave, within a few yards of its muzzle. The bows of the ship rose with the appearance of the smoke, the usual brief expectation followed, and then fragments of wood were seen flying above the top-mast-studding-sail-boom of the brigantine, which, at the same time, flew forward, carrying with it, and entirely deranging, the two important sails that depended on the spar for support.

"So much for plain sailing!" cried the delighted tar, slapping the breach of the gun, affectionately. "Witch or no witch, there go two of her jackets at once; and, by the captain's good-will, we shall shortly take off some more of her clothes! In spunge —"

"The order is to run the gun aft, and secure it;" said a merry midshipman, leaping on the heel of the bowsprit to gaze at the confusion on board the chase. "The rogue is nimble enough, in saving his canvas!"

There was, in truth, necessity for exertion, on the part of those who governed the movements of the brigantine. The two sails that were rendered temporarily useless, were of great importance, with the wind over the taffrail. The distance between the two vessels did not exceed a mile, and the danger of lessening it was now too obvious to admit of delay. The ordinary movements of seamen, in critical moments, are dictated by a quality that resembles instinct, more than thought. The constant hazards of a dangerous and delicate profession, in which delay may prove fatal, and in which life, character, and property are so often dependent on the self-possession and resources of him who commands, beget, in time, so keen a knowledge of the necessary expedients, as to cause it to approach a natural quality.

The studding-sails of the Water-Witch were no sooner fluttering in the air, than the brigantine slightly changed her course, like some bird whose wing has been touched by the fowler; and her head was seen inclining as much to the south, as the moment before it had pointed northward. The variation, trifling as it was, brought the wind on the opposite quarter, and caused the boom that distended her mainsail to gybe. At the same instant, the studding-sails, which had been flapping under the lee of this vast sheet of canvas, swelled to their utmost tension; and the vessel lost little, if any, of the power which urged her through the water. Even while this evolution was so rapidly performed, men were seen aloft, nimbly employed, as it has been already expressed by the observant little midshipman, in securing the crippled sails.

"A rogue has a quick wit," said Trysail, whose critical eye suffered no movement of the chase to escape him; "and he has need of it, sail from what haven he may! Yon brigantine is prettily handled! Little have we gained by our fire, but the gunner's account of ammunition expended; and little has the free-trader lost, but a studding-sail-boom, which will work up very well, yet, into top-gallant-yards, and other light spars, for such a cockle-shell."

"It is something gained, to force him off the land into rougher water;" Ludlow mildly answered. "I think we see his quarter-pieces more plainly, than before the gun was used."

"No doubt, Sir, no doubt. I got a glimpse of his lower dead-eyes, a minute ago; but I have been near enough to see the saucy look of the hussy under his bowsprit; yet there goes the brigantine, at large!"

"I am certain that we are closing;" thoughtfully returned Ludlow. "Hand me a glass, quarter master."

Trysail watched the countenance of his young commander, as he examined the chase with the aid of the instrument; and he thought he read strong discontent in his features, when the other laid it aside.

"Does he show no signs of coming back to his allegiance, Sir? — or does the rogue hold out in obstinacy?"

"The figure on his poop is the bold man who ventured on board the Coquette, and who now seems quite as much at his ease as when he exhibited his effrontery here!"

"There is a look of deep water about that rogue; and I thought Her Majesty had gained a prize, when he first put foot on our decks. You are right enough, Sir, in calling him a bold one! The fellow's impudence would unsettle the discipline of a whole ship's company, though every other man were an officer, and all the rest priests. He took up as much room in walking the quarter-deck, as a ninety in waring; and the truck is not driven on the head of that top-gallant-mast, half as hard as the hat is riveted to his head. The fellow has no reverence for a pennant! I managed, in shifting pennants at sunset, to make the fly of the one that came down flap in his impudent countenance, by way of hint; and he took it as a Dutchman minds a signal — that is, as a question to be answered in the next watch. A little polish got on the quarter-deck of a man-of-war, would make a philosopher of the rogue, and fit him for any company, short of heaven!"

"There goes a new boom, aloft!" cried Ludlow, interrupting the discursive discourse of the master. "He is bent on getting in with the shore."

"If these puffs come much heavier," returned the master, whose opinions of the chase vacillated with his professional feelings, "we shall have him at our own play, and try the qualities of his brigantine! The sea has a green spot to windward, and there are strong symptoms of a squall on the water. One can almost see into the upper world, with an air clear as this. Your northers sweep the mists off

America, and leave both sea and land bright as a school-boy's face, before the tears have dimmed it, after the first flogging. You have sailed in the southern seas, Captain Ludlow, I know; for we were shipmates among the islands, years that are past: but I never heard whether you have run the Gibralter passage, and seen the blue water that lies among the Italy mountains?"

"I made a cruise against the Barbary states, when a lad; and we had business that took us to the northern shore."

"Ay! 'Tis your northern shore, I mean! There is not a foot of it all, from the rock at the entrance to the Fare of Messina, that eye of mine hath not seen. No want of look-outs and land-marks in that quarter! Here we are close aboard of America, which lies some eight or ten leagues there-away to the northward of us, and some forty astern; and yet, if it were not for our departure, with the color of the water, and a knowledge of the soundings, one might believe himself in the middle of the Atlantic. Many a good ship plumps upon America before she knows where she is going; while in yon sea, you may run for a mountain, with its side in full view, four-and-twenty hours on a stretch, before you see the town at its foot."

"Nature has compensated for the difference, in defending the approach to this coast, by the Gulf Stream, with its floating weeds and different temperature; while the lead may feel its way in the darkest night, for no roof of a house is more gradual than the ascent of this shore, from a hundred fathoms to a sandy beach."

"I said many a good ship, Captain Ludlow, and not good navigator. No — no — your thorough-bred knows the difference between green water and blue, as well as between a hand-lead and the deep-sea. But I remember to have missed an observation, once, when running for Genoa, before a mistrail. There was a likelihood of making our land-fall in the night, and the greater the need of knowing the ship's position. I have often thought, Sir, that the ocean was like human life — a blind track for all that is ahead, and none of the clearest as respects that which has been passed over. Many a man runs headlong to his own destruction, and many a ship steers for a reef under a press of canvas. Tomorrow is a fog, into which none of us can see; and even the present time is little better than thick weather, into which we look without getting much information. Well, as I was observing, here lay our course, with the wind as near aft as need be, blowing much as at present; for your French mistrail has a family likeness to the American norther. We had the main-top-gallant-sail set, without studding-sails, for we began to think of the deep bight in which Genoa is stowed, and the sun had dipped more than an hour. As our good fortune would have it, clouds and mistrails do not agree long, and we got a clear horizon. Here lay a mountain of snow, northerly, a little west, and there lay another, southerly with easting. The best ship in Queen Anne's navy could not have fetched either in a day's run, and yet there we saw them, as plainly as if anchored under their lee! A look at the chart soon gave us an insight into our situation. The first were the Alps, as they call them, being as I suppose the French for apes, of which there are no doubt plenty in those regions; and the other were the highlands of Corsica, both being as white, in midsummer, as the hair of a man of fourscore. You see, Sir, we had only to set the two, by compass, to know, within a league or two, where we were. So we ran till midnight, and hove-to; and in the morning we took the light to feel for our haven —"

"The brigantine is gybing, again!" cried Ludlow. "He is determined to shoal his water!"

The master glanced an eye around the horizon and then pointed steadily towards the north. Ludlow observed the gesture, and, turning his head, he was at no loss to read its meaning.

CHAPTER XXI.

" — I am gone, Sir
And, anon, Sir,
I'll be with you again."
                    Clown in *Twelfth Night.*

ALTHOUGH it is contrary to the apparent evidence of our senses, there is no truth more certain than that the course of most gales of wind comes from the leeward. The effects of a tempest shall be felt, for hours, at a point that is seemingly near its termination, before they are witnessed at another, that appears to be nearer its source. Experience has also shown that a storm is more destructive, at or near its place of actual commencement, than at that whence it may seem to come. The easterly gales that so often visit the coasts of the republic, commit their ravages in the bays of Pennsylvania and Virginia, or along the sounds of the Carolinas, hours before their existence is known in the states further east; and the same wind, which is a tempest at Hatteras, becomes softened to a breeze, near the Penobscot. There is, however, little mystery in this apparent phenomenon. The vacuum which has been created in the air, and which is the origin of all winds, must be filled first from the nearest stores of the atmosphere; and as each region contributes to produce the equilibrium, it must, in return, receive other supplies from those which lie beyond. Were a given quantity of water to be suddenly abstracted from the sea, the empty space would be replenished by a torrent from the nearest surrounding fluid, whose level would be restored, in succession, by supplies that were less and less violently contributed. Were the abstraction made on a shoal, or near the land, the flow would be greatest from that quarter where the fluid had the greatest force, and with it would consequently come the current.

But while there is so close an affinity between the two fluids, the workings of the viewless winds are, in their nature, much less subject to the powers of human comprehension than those of the sister element. The latter are frequently subject to the direct and manifest influence of the former, while the effects produced by the ocean on the air are hid from our knowledge by the subtle character of the agency. Vague and erratic currents, it is true, are met in the waters of the ocean; but their origin is easily referred to the action of the winds, while we often remain in uncertainty as to the immediate causes which give birth to the breezes themselves. Thus the mariner, even while the victim of the irresistible waves, studies the heavens as the known source from whence the danger comes; and while he struggles fearfully, amid the strife of the elements, to preserve the balance of the delicate and fearful machine he governs, he well knows that the one which presents the most visible, and to a landsman much the most formidable object of apprehension, is but the instrument of the unseen and powerful agent that heaps the water on his path.

It is in consequence of this difference in power, and of the mystery that envelops the workings of the atmosphere, that, in all ages, seamen have been the subjects of superstition, in respect to the winds. There is always more or less of the dependency of ignorance, in the manner with which they have regarded the changes of that fickle element. Even the mariners of our own times are not exempt from this weakness. The thoughtless ship-boy is reproved if his whistle be heard in the howling of the gale, and the officer sometimes betrays a feeling of uneasiness, if at such a moment he should witness any violation of the received opinions of his profession. He finds himself in the situation of one whose ears have drunk in legends of supernatural appearances, which a better instruction has taught him to condemn, and who when placed in situations to awaken their recollection, finds the necessity of drawing upon his reason to quiet emotions that he might hesitate to acknowledge.

When Trysail directed the attention of his young commander to the heavens, however, it was more with the intelligence of an experienced mariner, than with any of the sensations to which allusion has just been made. A cloud had suddenly appeared on the water, and long ragged portions of the vapor were pointing from it, in a manner to give it what seamen term a windy appearance.

"We shall have more than we want, with this canvas!" said the master, after both he and his commander had studied the appearance of the mist, for a sufficient time. "That fellow is a mortal enemy of lofty sails; he likes to see nothing but naked sticks, up in his neighbourhood!"

"I should think his appearance will force the brigantine to shorten sail;" returned the Captain. "We will hold-on to the last, while he must begin to take in soon, or the squall will come upon him too fast for a light-handed vessel."

"'Tis a cruiser's advantage! And yet the rogue shows no signs of lowering a single cloth!"

"We will look to our own spars;" said Ludlow, turning to the lieutenant of the watch. "Call the people up, Sir, and see all ready, for yonder cloud."

The order was succeeded by the customary hoarse summons of the boatswain, who prefaced the effort of his lungs by a long, shrill winding of his call, above the hatchways of the ship. The cry of "all hands shorten sail, ahoy!" soon brought the crew from the depths of the vessel to her upper deck. Each trained seaman silently took his station; and after the ropes were cleared, and the few necessary preparations made, all stood in attentive silence, awaiting the sounds that might next proceed from the trumpet, which the first-lieutenant had now assumed in person.

The superiority of sailing, which a ship fitted for war possesses over one employed in commerce, proceeds from a variety of causes. The first is in the construction of the hull, which in the one is as justly fitted, as the art of naval architecture will allow, to the double purposes of speed and buoyancy; while in the other, the desire of gain induces great sacrifices of these important objects, in order that the vessel may be burthensome. Next comes the difference in the rig, which is not only more square, but more lofty, in a ship of war than in a trader; because the greater force of the crew of the former enables them to manage both spars and sails that are far heavier than any ever used in the latter. Then comes the greater ability of the cruiser to make and shorten sail, since a ship manned by one or two hundred men may safely profit by the breeze to the last moment, while one manned by a dozen often loses hours of a favorable wind, from the weakness of her crew. This explanation will enable the otherwise uninitiated reader to understand the reason why Ludlow had hoped the coming squall would aid his designs on the chase.

To express ourselves in nautical language, 'the Coquette held on to the last.' Ragged streaks of vapor were whirling about in the air, within a fearful proximity to the lofty and light sails, and the foam on the water had got so near the ship, as already to efface her wake; when Ludlow, who had watched the progress of the cloud with singular coolness, made a sign to his subordinate that the proper instant had arrived.

"In, of all!" shouted through the trumpet, was the only command necessary; for officers and crew were well instructed in their duty.

The words had no sooner quitted the lips of the lieutenant, than the steady roar of the sea was drowned in the flapping of canvas. Tacks, sheets, and halyards, went together; and, in less than a minute, the cruiser showed naked spars and whistling ropes, where so lately had been seen a cloud of snow-white cloth. All her steering-sails came in together, and the lofty canvas was furled to her top-sails. The latter still stood, and the vessel received the weight of the little tempest on their broad surfaces. The gallant ship stood the shock nobly; but, as the wind came over the taffrail, its force had far less influence on the hull, than on the other occasion already described. The danger, now, was only for her spars; and these were saved by the watchful, though bold, vigilance of her captain.

Ludlow was no sooner certain that the cruiser felt the force of the wind, and to gain this assurance needed but a few moments, than he turned his eager look on the brigantine. To the surprise of all who witnessed her temerity, the Water-Witch still showed all her light sails. Swiftly as the ship was now driven through the water, its velocity was greatly outstripped by that of the wind. The signs of the passing squall were already visible on the sea, for half the distance between the two vessels; and still the chase showed no consciousness of its approach. Her commander had evidently studied its effects on the Coquette; and he awaited the shock, with the coolness of one accustomed to depend on his own resources, and able to estimate the force with which he had to contend.

"If he hold-on a minute longer, he will get more than he can bear, and away will go all his kites, like smoke from the muzzle of a gun!" muttered Trysail. "Ah! there come down his studding-sails — ha! settle away the mainsail — in royal, and top-gallant sail, with top-sail on the cap! — The rascals are nimble as pickpockets in a crowd!"

The honest master has sufficiently described the precautions taken on board of the brigantine. Nothing was furled; but as every thing was hauled up, or lowered, the squall had little to waste its fury on. The diminished surfaces of the sails protected the spars, while the canvas was saved by the aid of cordage. After a few moments of pause, half-a-dozen men were seen busied in more effectually securing the few upper and lighter sails.

But though the boldness with which the 'Skimmer of the Seas' carried sail to the last, was justified by the result, still the effects of the increased wind and rising waves on the progress of the two vessels, grew more sensible. While the little and low brigantine began to labor and roll, the Coquette rode the element with buoyancy, and consequently with less resistance from the water. Twenty minutes, during which the force of the wind was but little lessened, brought the cruiser so near the chase, as to enable her crew to distinguish most of the smaller objects that were visible above her ridge-ropes.

"Blow winds, and crack your cheeks!" said Ludlow, in an under tone, the excitement of the chase growing with the hopes of success. "I ask but one half-hour, and then shift at your pleasure!"

"Blow, good devil, and you shall have the cook!" muttered Trysail, quoting a very different author. "Another glass will bring us within hail."

"The squall is leaving us!" interrupted the captain. "Pack on the ship, again, Mr. Luff, from her trucks to her ridge-ropes!"

The whistle of the boatswain was again heard at the hatchways, and the hoarse summons of 'all hands make sail, ahoy!' once more called the people to their stations. The sails were set, with a rapidity which nearly equalled the speed with which they had been taken in; and the violence of the breeze was scarcely off the ship, before its complicated volumes of canvas were spread, to catch what remained. On the other hand, the chase, even more hardy than the cruiser, did not wait for the end of the squall; but, profiting by the notice given by the latter, the 'Skimmer of the Seas' began to sway his yards aloft, while the sea was still white with foam.

"The quick-sighted rogue knows we are done with it," said Trysail; "and he is getting ready for his own turn. We gain but little of him, notwithstanding our muster of hands."

The fact was too true to be denied, for the brigand tine was again under all her canvas, before the ship had sensibly profited by her superior physical force. It was at this moment, when, perhaps, in consequence of the swell on the water, the Coquette might have possessed some small advantage, that the wind suddenly failed. The squall had been its expiring effort; and, within an hour after the two vessels had again made sail, the canvas was flapping against the masts, in a manner to throw back, in eddies, a force as great as that it received. The sea fell fast, and ere the end of the last or forenoon watch, the surface of the ocean was agitated only by those long undulating swells, that seldom leave it entirely without motion. For some little time, there were fickle currents of air playing in various directions about the ship, but always in sufficient force to urge her slowly through the water; and then, when the equilibrium of the element seemed established, there was a total calm. During the half-hour of the baffling winds, the brigantine had been a gainer, though not enough to carry her entirely beyond the reach of the cruiser's guns.

"Haul up the courses!" said Ludlow, when the fast breath of wind had been felt on the ship, and quitting the gun where he had long stood, watching the movements of the chase. "Get the boats into the water, Mr. Luff, and arm their crews."

The young commander issued this order, which needed no interpreter to explain its object, firmly, but in sadness. His face was thoughtful, and his whole air was that of a man who yielded to an imperative but an unpleasant duty. When he had spoken, he signed to the attentive Alderman and his friend to follow, and entered his cabin.

"There is no alternative," continued Ludlow, as he laid the glass, which so often that morning had been at his eye, on the table, and threw himself into a chair. "This rover must be seized at every hazard, and here is a favorable occasion to carry him by boarding. Twenty minutes will bring us to his side, and five more will put us in possession; but —"

"You think the Skimmer is not a man to receive such visiters with an old woman's welcome;" pithily observed Myndert.

"I much mistake the man, if he yield so beautiful a vessel, peacefully. Duty is imperative on a seaman, Alderman Van Beverout; and, much as I lament the circumstance, it must be obeyed."

"I understand you, Sir. Captain Ludlow has two mistresses, Queen Anne and the daughter of old Etienne de Barbérie. He fears both. When the debts exceed the means of payment, it would seem wise to offer to compound; and, in this case, Her Majesty and my niece may be said to stand in the case of creditors."

"You mistake my meaning, Sir;" said Ludlow proudly. "There can be no composition between a faithful officer and his duty, nor do I acknowledge more than one mistress in my ship — but seamen are little to be trusted in the moment of success, and with their passions awakened by resistance. Alderman Van Beverout, will you accompany the party and serve as mediator?"

"Pikes and hand-grenades! Am I a fit subject for mounting the sides of a smuggler, with a broadsword between my teeth! If you will put me into the smallest and most peaceable of your boats, with a crew of two boys, that I can control with the authority of a magistrate, and covenant to remain here with your three top-sails aback, having always a flag of truce at each mast, I will bear the olive-branch to the brigantine, but not a word of menace. If report speaks true, your 'Skimmer of the Seas' is no lover of threats, and Heaven forbid that I should do violence to any man's habits! I will go forth as your turtle-dove, Captain Ludlow; but not one foot will I proceed as your Goliath."

"And you equally refuse endeavoring to avert hostilities?" continued Ludlow, turning his look on the Patroon of Kinderhook.

"I am the Queen's subject, and ready to aid in supporting the laws;" quietly returned Oloff Van Staats.

"Patroon!" exclaimed his watchful friend; "you know not what you say! If there were question of an inroad of Mohawks, or an invasion from the Canadas, the case would differ; but this is only a trifling difference, concerning a small balance in the revenue duties, which had better be left to your tide-waiter, and the other wild-cats of the law. If Parliament will put temptation before our eyes, let the sin light on their own heads. Human nature is weak, and the vanities of our system are so many inducements to overlook unreasonable regulations. I say, therefore, it is better to remain in peace, on board this ship, where our characters will be as safe as our bones, and trust to Providence for what will happen."

"I am the Queen's subject, and ready to uphold her dignity;" repeated Oloff, firmly.

"I will trust you, Sir;" said Ludlow, taking his rival by the arm, and leading him into his own state-room.

The conference was soon ended, and a midshipman shortly after reported that the boats were ready for service. The master was next summoned to the cabin and admitted to the private apartment of his commander. Ludlow then proceeded to the deck, where he made the final dispositions for the attack. The ship was left in charge of Mr. Luff, with an injunction to profit by any breeze that might offer, to draw as near as possible to the chase. Trysail was placed in the launch, at the head of a strong party of boarders. Van Staats of Kinderhook was provided with the yawl, manned only by its customary crew; while Ludlow entered his own barge, which contained its usual complement, though the arms that lay in the stern-sheets sufficiently showed that they were prepared for service.

The launch, being the soonest ready, and of much the heaviest movement, was the first to quit the side of the Coquette. The master steered directly for the becalmed and motionless brigantine. Ludlow took a more circuitous course, apparently with an intention of causing such a diversion as might distract the attention of the crew of the smuggler, and with the view of reaching the point of attack at the same moment with the boat that contained his principal force. The yawl also inclined from the straight line steering as much on one side as the barge diverged on the other. In this manner the men pulled in silence for some twenty minutes — the motion of the larger boat, which was heavily charged, being slow and difficult. At the end of this period, a signal was made from the barge, when all the men ceased rowing and prepared themselves for the struggle. The launch was within pistol-shot of the brigantine, and directly on her beam; the yawl had gained her head where Van Staats of Kinderhook was studying the malign expression of the image, with an interest that seemed to increase as his sluggish nature became excited; and Ludlow, on the quarter opposite to the launch, was examining the condition of the chase by the aid of a glass. Trysail profited by the pause, to address his followers:

"This is an expedition in boats," commenced the accurate and circumstantial master, "made in smooth water, with little, or one may say no wind, in the month of June, and on the coast of North America. You are not such a set of know-nothings, men, as to suppose the launch has been hoisted out, and two of the oldest, not to say best seamen, on the quarter-deck of Her Majesty's ship, have gone in boats, without the intention of doing something more than to ask the name and character of the brig in sight. The smallest of the young gentlemen might have done that duty, as well as the captain, or myself. It is the belief of those who are best informed, that the stranger, who has the impudence to lie quietly within long range of a royal cruiser, without showing his colors, is neither more nor less than the famous 'Skimmer of the Seas;' a man against whose seamanship I will say nothing, but who has none of the best reputation for honesty, as relates to the Queen's revenue. No doubt you have heard many extraordinary accounts of the exploits of this rover, some of which seem to insinuate, that the fellow has a private understanding with those who manage their transactions in a less religious manner than it may be supposed is done by the bench of bishops. But what of that? You are hearty Englishmen, who know what belongs to church and state; and, damn me, you are not the boys to be frightened by a little witchcraft. [a cheer] Ay, that is intelligible and reasonable language, and such as satisfies me you understand the subject. I shall say no more, than just to add, that Captain Ludlow desires there may be no indecent language, nor, for that matter, any rough treatment of the people of the brigantine, over and above the knocking on the head, and cutting of throats, that may be necessary to take her. In this particular, you will take example by me, who, being older, have more experience than most of you, and who, in all reason, should better know when and where to show his manhood. Lay about you like men, so long as the free-traders stand to their quarters — but remember mercy, in the hour of victory! You will on no account enter the cabins; on this head my orders are explicit, and I shall make no more of throwing the man into the sea, who dares to transgress them, than if he were a dead Frenchman; and, as we now clearly understand each other, and know our duty so well, there remains no more than to do it. I have said nothing of the prize-money, [a cheer] seeing you are men that love the Queen and her honor, more than lucre, [a cheer]; but this much I can safely promise, that there will be the usual division, [a cheer] and as there is little doubt but the rogues have driven a profitable trade, why the sum-total is likely to be no trifle." [Three hearty cheers.]

The report of a pistol from the barge, which was immediately followed by a gun from the cruiser, whose shot came whistling between the masts of the Water-Witch, was the signal to resort to the ordinary means of victory. The master cheered, in his turn; and in a full, steady, and deep voice, he gave the order to 'pull away!' At the same instant, the barge and yawl were seen advancing towards the object of their common attack, with a velocity that promised to bring the event to a speedy issue.

Throughout the whole of the preparations in and about the Coquette, since the moment when the breeze failed, nothing had been seen of the crew of the brigantine. The beautiful fabric lay rolling on the heaving and setting waters; but no human form appeared to control her movements, or to make the arrangements that seemed so necessary for her defence. The sails continued hanging as they had been left by the breeze, and the hull was floating at the will of the waves. This deep quiet was undisturbed by the approach of the boats; and if the desperate individual, who was known to command the free-trader, had any intentions of resistance, they had been entirely hid from the long and anxious gaze of Ludlow. Even the shouts, and the dashing of the oars on the water, when the boats commenced their final advance, produced no change on the decks of the chase; though the commander of the Coquette saw her head-yards slowly and steadily changing their direction. Uncertain of the object of this movement, he rose on the seat of his boat, and, waving his hat, cheered the men to greater exertion. The barge had got within a hundred feet of the broadside of the brigantine, when the whole of her wide folds of canvas were seen swelling outwards. The exquisitely-ordered machinery of spars, sails, and rigging, bowed towards the barge, as in the act of a graceful leave-taking, and then the light hull glided ahead, leaving the boat to plow through the empty space which it had just occupied. There needed no second look to assure Ludlow of the inefficacy of further pursuit, since the sea was already ruffled by the breeze which had so opportunely come to aid the smuggler. He signed to Trysail to desist; and both stood looking, with disappointed eyes, at the white and bubbling streak which was left by the wake of the fugitive.

But while the Water-Witch left the boats, commanded by the captain and master of the Queen's cruiser, behind her, she steered directly on the course that was necessary to bring her soonest in contact with the yawl. For a few moments, the crew of the latter believed it was their own advance that brought them so rapidly near their object; and when the midshipman who steered the boat discovered his error, it was only in season to prevent the swift brigantine from passing over his little bark. He gave the yawl a wide sheer, and called to his men to pull for their lives. Oloff Van Staats had placed himself at the head of the boat, armed with a banger, and with every faculty too intent on the expected attack, to heed a danger that was scarcely intelligible to one of his habits. As the brigantine glided past, he saw her low channels bending towards the water, and, with a powerful effort, he leaped into them, shouting a sort of war-cry, in Dutch. At the next instant, he threw his large frame over the bulwarks, and disappeared on the deck of the smuggler.

When Ludlow had caused his boats to assemble on the spot which the chase had so lately occupied, he saw that the fruitless expedition had been attended by no other casualty than the involuntary abduction of the Patroon of Kinderhook.

CHAPTER XXII.

"What country, friends, is this?"
" — Illyria, lady."
What You Will.

MEN are as much indebted to a fortuitous concurrence of circumstances, for the characters they sustain in this world, as to their personal qualities. The same truth is applicable to the reputations of ships. The properties of a vessel, like those of an individual, may have their influence on her good or evil fortune; still, something is due to the accidents of life, in both. Although the breeze, which came so opportunely to the aid of the Water-Witch, soon filled the sails of the Coquette, it caused no change in the opinions of her crew concerning the fortunes of that ship; while it served to heighten the reputation which the 'Skimmer of the Seas' had already obtained, as a mariner who was more than favored by happy chances, in the thousand emergencies of his hazardous profession. Trysail, himself, shook his head, in a manner that expressed volumes, when Ludlow vented his humor on what the young man termed the luck of the smuggler; and the crews of the boats gazed after the retiring brigantine, as the inhabitants of Japan would now most probably regard the passage of some vessel propelled by steam. As Mr. Luff was not neglectful of his duty, it was not long before the Coquette approached her boats. The delay occasioned by hoisting in the latter, enabled the chase to increase the space between the two vessels, to such a distance, as to place her altogether beyond the reach of shot. Ludlow, however, gave his orders to pursue, the moment the ship was ready; and he hastened to conceal his disappointment in his own cabin.

"Luck is a merchant's surplus, while a living profit is the reward of his wits!" observed Alderman Van Beverout, who could scarce conceal the satisfaction he felt, at the unexpected and repeated escapes of the brigantine. "Many a man gains doubloons, when he only looked for dollars; and many a market falls, while the goods are in the course of clearance. There are Frenchmen enough, Captain Ludlow to keep a brave officer in good-humor; and the less reason to fret about a trifling mischance in overhauling a smuggler."

"I know not how highly you may prize your niece, Mr. Van Beverout; but were I the uncle of such a woman, the idea that she had become the infatuated victim of the arts of yon reckless villain, would madden me!"

"Paroxysms and straight-jackets! Happily you are not her uncle, Captain

Ludlow, and therefore the less reason to be uneasy. The girl has a French fancy, and she is rummaging the smuggler's silks and laces; when her choice is made, we shall have her back again, more beautiful than ever, for a little finery."

"Choice! Oh, Alida, Alida! this is not the election that we had reason to expect from thy cultivated mind and proud sentiments!"

"The cultivation is my work, and the pride is an inheritance from old Etienne de Barbérie;" dryly rejoined Myndert. "But complaints never lowered a market, nor raised the funds. Let us send for the Patroon, and take counsel coolly, as to the easiest manner of finding our way back to the Lust in Rust, before Her Majesty's ship gets too far from the coast of America."

"Thy pleasantry is unseasonable, Sir. Your Patroon is gone with your niece, and a pleasant passage they are likely to enjoy, in such company! We lost him, in the expedition with our boats."

The Alderman stood aghast.

"Lost! — Oloff Van Staats lost, in the expedition of the boats! Evil betide the day when that discreet and affluent youth should be lost to the colony! Sir, you know not what you utter when you hazard so rash an opinion. The death of the young Patroon of Kinderhook would render one of the best and most substantial of our families extinct, and leave the third best estate in the Province without a direct heir!"

"The calamity is not so overwhelming;" returned the captain, with bitterness. "The gentleman has boarded the smuggler, and gone with la belle Barbérie to examine his silks and laces!"

Ludlow then explained the manner in which the Patroon had disappeared. When perfectly assured that no bodily harm had befallen his friend, the satisfaction of the Alderman was quite as vivid, as his consternation had been apparent but the moment before.

"Gone with la belle Barbérie, to examine silks and laces!" he repeated, rubbing his hands together, in delight. "Ay, there the blood of my old friend, Stephanus, begins to show itself! Your true Hollander is no mercurial Frenchman, to beat his head and make grimaces at a shift in the wind, or a woman's frown; nor a blustering Englishman (you are of the colony yourself, young gentleman) to swear a big oath and swagger; but, as you see, a quiet, persevering, and, in the main, an active son of old Batavia, who watches his opportunity, and goes into the very presence of —"

"Whom?" — demanded Ludlow, perceiving that the Alderman had paused.

"Of his enemy; seeing that all the enemies of the Queen are necessarily the enemies of every loyal subject. Bravo, young Oloff! thou art a lad after my own heart, and no doubt — no doubt — fortune will favor the brave! Had a Hollander a proper footing on this earth, Captain Cornelius Ludlow, we should hear a different tale concerning the right to the Narrow Seas, and indeed to most other questions of commerce."

Ludlow arose with a bitter smile on his face, though with no ill feeling towards the man whose exultation was so natural.

"Mr. Van Staats may have reason to congratulate himself on his good fortune," he said, "though I much mistake if even his enterprise will succeed, against the wiles of one so artful, and of an appearance so gay, as the man whose guest he has now become. Let the caprice of others be what it may, Alderman Van Beverout, my duty must be done. The smuggler, aided by chance and artifice, has thrice escaped me; the fourth time, it may be our fortune. If this ship possesses the power to destroy the lawless rover, let him look to his fate!"

With this menace on his lips, Ludlow quitted the cabin, to resume his station on the deck, and to renew his unwearied watching of the movements of the chase.

The change in the wind was altogether in favor of the brigantine. It brought her to windward, and was the means of placing the two vessels in positions that enabled the Water-Witch to profit the most by her peculiar construction. Consequently, when Ludlow reached his post, he saw that the swift and light craft had trimmed every thing close upon the wind, and that she was already so far ahead, as to render the chances of bringing her again within range of his guns almost desperate; unless, indeed, some of the many vicissitudes, so common on the ocean, should interfere in his behalf. There remained little else to be done, therefore, but to crowd every sail on the Coquette that the ship would bear, and to endeavor to keep within sight of the chase, during the hours of darkness which must so shortly succeed. But before the sun had fallen to the level of the water, the hull of the Water-Witch had disappeared; and when the day closed, no part of her airy outline was visible, but that which was known to belong to her upper and lighter spars. In a few minutes afterwards, darkness covered the ocean; and the seamen of the royal cruiser were left to pursue their object, at random.

How far the Coquette had run during the night does not appear, but when her commander made his appearance on the following morning, his long and anxious gaze met no other reward than a naked horizon. On every side, the sea presented the same waste of water. No object was visible, but the sea-fowl wheeling on his wide wing, and the summits of the irregular and green billows.

Throughout that and many succeeding days, the cruiser continued to plow the ocean, sometimes running large, with every thing opened to the breeze that the wide booms would spread, and, at others, pitching and laboring with adverse winds, as if bent on prevailing over the obstacles which even nature presented to her progress. The head of the worthy Alderman had got completely turned; and though he patiently awaited the result, before the week was ended, he knew not even the direction in which the ship was steering. At length he had reason to believe that the end of their cruise approached. The efforts of the seamen were observed to relax, and the ship was permitted to pursue her course, under easier sail.

It was past meridian, on one of those days of moderate exertion, that François was seen stealing from below, and staggering from gun to gun, to a place in the centre of the ship, where he habitually took the air, in good weather, and where he might dispose of his person, equally without presuming too far on the good-nature of his superiors, and without courting too much intimacy with the coarser herd who composed the common crew.

"Ah!" exclaimed the valet, addressing his remark to the midshipman who has already been mentioned by the name of Hopper — "Voilà la terre! Quel bonheur! I shall be so happy — le batiment be trop agréable, mais vous savez, Monsieur Aspirant; que je ne suis point marin — What be le nom du pays?"

"They call it, France," returned the boy, who understood enough of the other's language to comprehend his meaning; "and a very good country it is — for those that like it."

"Ma foi, non!" — exclaimed François, recoiling a pace, between amazement and delight.

"Call it Holland, then, if you prefer that country most."

"Dites-moi, Monsieur Hoppair," continued the valet, laying a trembling finger on the arm of the remorseless young rogue; "est-ce la France?"

"One would think a man of your observation could tell that for himself. Do you not see the church-tower, with a chateau in the back-ground, and a village built in a heap, by its side. Now look into yon wood! There is a walk, straight as a ship's wake in smooth water, and one — two — three — ay, eleven statues, with just one nose among them all!"

"Ma foi — dere is not no wood, and no château and no village, and no statue, and no no nose — mais Monsieur, je suis agé — est-ce la France?"

"Oh, you miss nothing by having an indifferent sight, for I shall explain it all, as we go along. You see yonder hill-side, looking like a pattern-card, of green and

yellow stripes, or a signal-book, with the flags of all nations, placed side by side —
well, that is — les champs; and this beautiful wood, with all the branches trimmed
till it looks like so many raw marines at drill, is — la forêt —"

The credulity of the warm-hearted valet could swallow no more; but,
assuming a look of commiseration and dignity, he drew back, and left the young
tyro of the sea to enjoy his joke with a companion who just then joined him.

In the meantime, the Coquette continued to advance. The château, and
churches, and villages, of the midshipman, soon changed into a low sandy beach,
with a back-ground of stunted pines, relieved here and there, by an opening, in
which appeared the comfortable habitation and numerous out-buildings of some
substantial yeoman, or occasionally embellished by the residence of a country
proprietor. Towards noon, the crest of a hill rose from the sea: and, just as the sun
set behind the barrier of mountain, the ship passed the sandy cape, and anchored
at the spot that she had quitted when first joined by her commander after his visit
to the brigantine. The vessel was soon moored, the light yards were struck, and a
boat was lowered into the water. Ludlow and the Alderman then descended the
side, and proceeded towards the mouth of the Shrewsbury. Although it was nearly
dark before they had reached the shore, there remained light enough to enable
the former to discover an object of unusual appearance floating in the bay, and at
no great distance from the direction of his barge. He was led by curiosity to steer
for it.

"Cruisers and Water-Witches!" muttered Myndert, when they were near
enough to perceive the nature of the floating object. "That brazen hussy haunts
us, as if we had robbed her of gold! Let us set foot on land, and nothing short of a
deputation from the City Council shall ever tempt me to wander from my own
abode, again!"

Ludlow shifted the helm of the boat, and resumed his course towards the
river. He required no explanation, to tell him more of the nature of the artifice, by
which he had been duped. The nicely-balanced tub, the upright spar, and the
extinguished lantern, with the features of the female of the malign smile traced on
its horn faces, reminded him, at once, of the false light by which the Coquette had
been lured from her course, on the night she sailed in pursuit of the brigantine.

CHAPTER XXIII.

" — His daughter, and the heir of his kingdom,
— hath referred herself
Unto a poor but worthy gentleman —"
Cymbeline.

WHEN Alderman Van Beverout and Ludlow drew near to the Lust in Rust, it was already dark. Night had overtaken them, at some distance from the place of landing; and the mountain already threw its shadow across the river, the narrow strip of land that separated it from the sea, and far upon the ocean itself. Neither had an opportunity of making his observations on the condition of things in and about the villa, until they had ascended nearly to its level, and had even entered the narrow but fragrant lawn in its front. Just before they arrived at the gate which opened on the latter, the Alderman paused, and addressed his companion, with more of the manner of their ancient confidence, than he had manifested during the few preceding days of their intercourse.

"You must have observed, that the events of this little excursion on the water, have been rather of a domestic than of a public character;" he said. "Thy father was a very ancient and much-esteemed friend of mine, and I am far from certain that there is not some affinity between us, in the way of intermarriages. Thy worthy mother, who is a thrifty woman, and a small talker, had some of the blood of my own stock. It would grieve me to see the good understanding, which these recollections have created, in any manner interrupted. I admit, Sir, that revenue is to the state what the soul is to the body — the moving and governing principle; and that, as the last would be a tenantless house without its inhabitants, so the first would be an exacting and troublesome master without its proper products. But there is no need of pushing a principle to extremities! If this brigantine be, as you appear to suspect, and indeed as we have some reason from various causes to infer, the vessel called the Water-Witch she might have been a legal prize had she fallen into your power; bait now that she has escaped, I cannot say what may be your intentions; but were thy excellent father, the worthy member of the King's Council, living, so discreet a man would think much before he opened his lips, to say more than is discreet, on this or any other subject."

"Whatever course I may believe my duty dictates, you may safely rely on my discretion concerning the — the remarkable — the very decided step which your niece has seen proper to take;" returned the young man, who did not make this

217

allusion to Alida without betraying, by the tremor of his voice, how great was her influence still over him. "I see no necessity of violating the domestic feelings to which you allude, by aiding to feed the ears of the idly curious, with the narrative of her errors."

Ludlow stopped suddenly, leaving the uncle to infer what he would wish to add.

"This is generous, and manly, and like a loyal — lover, Captain Ludlow," returned the Alderman; "though it is not exactly what I intended to suggest. We will not, however, multiply words in the night air — ha! when the cat is asleep, the mice are seen to play! Those night-riding, horse-racing blacks have taken possession of Alida's pavilion; and we may be thankful the poor girl's rooms are not as large as Harlaem Common, or we should hear the feet of some hard-driven beast galloping about in them."

The Alderman, in his turn, cut short his speech, and started as if one of the spukes of the colony had suddenly presented itself to his eyes. His language had drawn the look of his companion towards la Cour des Fées; and Ludlow had, at the same moment as the uncle, caught an unequivocal view of la belle Barbérie, as she moved before the open window of her apartment. The latter was about to rush forward, but the hand of Myndert arrested the impetuous movement.

"Here is more matter for our wits, than our legs;" observed the cool and prudent burgher. "That was the form of my ward and niece, or the daughter of old Etienne Barbérie has a double. Francis! didst thou not see the image of a woman at the window of the pavilion, or are we deceived by our wishes? I have sometimes been deluded in an unaccountable manner, Captain Ludlow, when my mind has been thoroughly set on the bargain, in the quality of the goods; for the most liberal of us all are subject to mental weakness of this nature, when hope is alive!"

"Certainement, oui!" exclaimed the eager valet "Quel malheur to be obligé to go on la mèr, when Mam'selle Alide nevair quit la maison! J'étais sûr, que nous nous trompions, car jamais la famille de Barbérie love to be marins!"

"Enough, good Francis; the family of Barbérie is as earthy as a fox. Go and notify the idle rogues in my kitchen, that their master is at hand; and remember, that there is no necessity for speaking of all the wonders we have seen on the great deep. Captain Ludlow, we will now join my dutiful niece, with as little fracas as possible."

Ludlow eagerly accepted the invitation, and instantly followed the dogmatical and seemingly unmoved Alderman towards the dwelling. As the lawn was crossed, they involuntarily paused, a moment, to look in at the open windows of the pavilion.

La belle Barbérie had ornamented la Cour des Fées, with a portion of that national taste, which she inherited from her father. The heavy magnificence that distinguished the reign of Louis XIV. had scarcely descended to one of the middling rank of Monsieur de Barbérie, who had consequently brought with him to the place of his exile, merely those tasteful usages which appear almost exclusively the property of the people from whom he had sprung, without the encumbrance and cost of the more pretending fashions of the period. These usages had become blended with the more domestic and comfortable habits of English, or what is nearly the same thing, of American life — an union which, when it is found, perhaps produces the most just and happy medium of the useful and the agreeable. Alida was seated by a small table of mahogany, deeply absorbed in the contents of a little volume that lay before her. By her side stood a tea-service, the cups and the vessels of which were of the diminutive size then used, though exquisitely wrought, and of the most beautiful material. Her dress was a negligee suited to her years; and her whole figure breathed that air of comfort, mingled with grace, which seems to be the proper quality of the sex, and which renders the privacy of an elegant woman so attractive and peculiar. Her mind was intent on the book, and the little silver urn hissed at her elbow, apparently unheeded.

"This is the picture I have loved to draw," half-whispered Ludlow, "when gales and storms have kept me on the deck, throughout many a dreary and tempestuous night! When body and mind have been impatient of fatigue, this is the repose I have most coveted, and for which I have even dared to hope!"

"The China trade will come to something, in time and you are an excellent judge of comfort, Master Ludlow;" returned the Alderman. "That girl now has a warm glow on her cheek, which would seem to swear she never faced a breeze in her life; and it is not easy to fancy, that one who looks so comfortable has lately been frolicking among the dolphins. Let us enter."

Alderman Van Beverout was not accustomed to use much ceremony in his visits to his niece. Without appearing to think any announcement necessary, therefore, the dogmatical burgher coolly opened a door, and ushered his companion into the pavilion.

If the meeting between la belle Alida and her guests was distinguished by the affected indifference of the latter, their seeming ease was quite equalled by that of the lady. She laid aside her book, with a calmness that might have been expected had they parted but an hour before, and which sufficiently assured both Ludlow and her uncle that their return was known and their presence expected. She simply arose at their entrance, and with a smile that betokened breeding, rather than feeling, she requested them to be seated. The composure of his niece had the effect to throw the Alderman into a brown study, while the young sailor scarcely knew which to admire the most, the exceeding loveliness of a woman who was always so beautiful, or her admirable self-possession in a scene that most others would have found sufficiently embarrassing. Alida, herself, appeared to feel no necessity for any explanation; for, when her guests were seated, she took occasion to say, while busied in pouring out the tea —

"You find me prepared to offer the refreshment of a cup of delicious bohea. I think, my uncle calls it the tea of the Caernarvon Castle."

"A lucky ship, both in her passages and her wares! Yes, it is the article you name; and I can recommend it to all who wish to purchase. But niece of mine, will you condescend to acquaint this commander in Her Majesty's service, and a poor Alderman of her good city of New-York, how long you may have been expecting our company?"

Alida felt at her girdle, and, drawing out a small and richly-ornamented watch, she coolly examined its hands, as if to learn the hour.

"We are nine. I think it was past the turn of the day, when Dinah first mentioned that this pleasure might be expected. But, I should also tell you, that packages which seem to contain letters have arrived from town."

This was giving a new and sudden direction to the thoughts of the Alderman. He had refrained from entering on those explanations which the circumstances seemed to require, because he well knew that he stood on dangerous ground, and that more might be said than he wished his companion to hear, no less than from amazement at the composure of his ward. He was not sorry, therefore, to have an excuse to delay his inquiries, that appeared so much in character as that of reading the communications of his business correspondents. Swallowing the contents of the tiny cup he held, at a gulp, the eager merchant seized the packet that Alida now offered; and, muttering a few words of apology to Ludlow, he left the pavilion.

Until now, the commander of the Coquette had not spoken. Wonder, mingled with indignation, sealed his mouth, though he had endeavored to penetrate the veil which Alida had drawn around her conduct and motives, by a diligent use of his eyes. During the first few moments of the interview, he thought that he could detect, in the midst of her studied calmness, a melancholy smile struggling around her beautiful mouth; but only once had their looks met, as she turned her full, rich, and dark eyes furtively on his face, as if she were curious to know the effect produced by her manner on the mind of the young sailor.

"Have the enemies of the Queen reason to regret the cruise of the Coquette?" said la Belle, hurriedly, when she found her glance detected; "or have they dreaded to encounter a prowess that has already proved their inferiority?"

"Fear, or prudence, or perhaps I might say conscience, has made them wary;" returned Ludlow, pointedly emphasizing the latter word. "We have run from the Hook to the edge of the Grand Bank, and returned without success."

"'Tis unlucky. But, though the French escaped, have none of the lawless met with punishment? There is a rumor among the slaves, that the brigantine which visited us is an object of suspicion to the Government?"

"Suspicion! — But I may apply to la belle Barbérie, to know whether the character her commander has obtained be merited?"

Alida smiled, and, her admirer thought, sweetly as ever.

"It would be a sign of extraordinary complaisance, were Captain Ludlow to apply to the girls of the colony for instruction in his duty! We may be secret encouragers of the contraband, but surely we are not to be suspected of any greater familiarity with their movements. These hints may compel me to abandon the pleasures of the Lust in Rust, and to seek air and health in some less exposed situation. Happily the banks of the Hudson offer many, that one need be fastidious indeed to reject."

"Among which you count the Manor House of Kinderhook?"

Again Alida smiled, and Ludlow thought it was triumphantly.

"The dwelling of Oloff Van Staats is said to be commodious, and not badly placed. I have seen it —"

"In your images of the future?" said the young man, observing she hesitated.

Alida laughed downright. But, immediately recovering her self-command, she replied —

"Not so fancifully. My knowledge of the beauties of the house of Mr. Van Staats, is confined to very unpoetical glimpses from the river, in passing and repassing. The chimneys are twisted in the most approved style of the Dutch Brabant, and, although wanting the stork's nests on their summits, it seems as if there might be that woman's tempter, comfort, around the hearths beneath. The offices, too, have an enticing air, for a thrifty housewife!"

"Which office, in compliment to the worthy Patroon, you intend shall not long be vacant?"

Alida was playing with a spoon, curiously wrought to represent the stem and leaves of a tea-plant. She started, dropped the implement, and raised her eyes to the face of her companion. The look was steady, and not without an interest in the evident concern betrayed by the young man.

"It will never be filled by me, Ludlow;" was the answer, uttered solemnly, and with a decision that denoted a resolution fixed.

"That declaration removes a mountain! — Oh! Alida, if you could as easily —"

"Hush!" whispered the other, rising and standing for a moment in an attitude of intense expectation. Her eye became brighter, and the bloom on her cheek even deeper than before, while pleasure and hope were both strongly depicted on her beautiful face — "Hush!" she continued, motioning to Ludlow to repress his feelings. "Did you hear nothing?"

The disappointed and yet admiring young man was silent, though he watched her singularly interesting air, and lovely features, with all the intenseness that seemed to characterize her own deportment. As no sound followed that which Alida had heard or fancied she had heard, she resumed her seat, and appeared to lend her attention once more to her companion.

"You were speaking of mountains?" she said, scarce knowing what she uttered. "The passage between the bays of Newburgh and Tappan, has scarce a rival, as I have heard from travelled men."

"I was indeed speaking of a mountain, but it was of one that weighs me to the earth. Your inexplicable conduct and cruel indifference have heaped it on my feelings, Alida. You have said that there is no hope for Oloff Van Staats; and one syllable, spoken with your native ingenuousness and sincerity, has had the effect to blow all my apprehensions from that quarter to the winds. There remains only to account for your absence, to resume the whole of your power over one who is but too readily disposed to confide in all you say or do."

La belle Barbérie seemed touched. Her glance at the young sailor was kinder, and her voice wanted some of its ordinary steadiness, in the reply.

"That power has then been weakened?"

"You will despise me, if I say no — you will distrust me, if I say yes."

"Then silence seems the course best adapted to maintain our present amity. Surely I heard a blow struck, lightly, on the shutter of that window?"

"Hope sometimes deceives us. This repeated belief would seem to say that you expect a visiter?"

A distinct tap on the shutter confirmed the impression of the mistress of the pavilion. Alida looked at her companion, and appeared embarrassed. Her color varied, and she seemed anxious to utter something that either her feelings or her prudence suppressed.

"Captain Ludlow, you have once before been an unexpected witness of an interview in la Cour des Fées, that has, I fear, subjected me to unfavorable surmises. But one manly and generous as yourself can have indulgence for the little vanities of woman. I expect a visit, that perhaps a Queen's officer should not countenance."

"I am no exciseman, to pry into wardrobes and secret repositories, but one whose duty it is to act only on the high seas, and against the more open violators of the law. If you have any without, whose presence you desire, let them enter without dread of my office. When we meet in a more suitable place, I shall know how to take my revenge."

His companion looked grateful, and bowed her acknowledgments. She then made a ringing sound, by using a spoon on the interior of one of the vessels of the tea equipage. The shrubbery, which shaded a window, stirred; and presently, the young stranger, already so well known in the former pages of this work, and in the scenes of the brigantine, appeared in the low balcony. His person was scarcely seen, before a light bale of goods was tossed past him, into the centre of the room.

"I send my certificate of character as an avant-courier;" said the gay dealer in contraband, or Master Seadrift, as he was called by the Alderman, touching his cap, gallantly, to the mistress of la Cour des Fées, and then, somewhat more ceremoniously to her companion; after which he returned the goldbound covering to its seat, on a bed of rich and glossy curls, and sought his package. "Here is one more customer than I bargained for, and I look to more than common gain! We have met before, Captain Ludlow."

"We have, Sir Skimmer of the Seas, and we shall meet again. Winds may change, and fortune yet favor the right!"

"We trust to the sea-green lady's care;" returned the extraordinary smuggler, pointing, with a species of reverence, real or affected, to the image that was beautifully worked, in rich colors, on the velvet of his cap. "What has been will be, and the past gives a hope for the future. We meet, here, on neutral ground, I trust."

"I am the commander of a royal cruiser, Sir:" haughtily returned the other.

"Queen Anne may be proud of her servant! — but we neglect our affairs. A thousand pardons, lovely mistress of la Cour des Fées. This meeting of two rude mariners does a slight to your beauty, and little credit to the fealty due the sex. Having done with all compliments, I have to offer certain articles that never failed to cause the brightest eyes to grow more brilliant, and at which duchesses have gazed with many longings."

"You speak with confidence of your associations, Master Seadrift, and rate noble personages among your customers, as familiarly as if you dealt in offices of state."

"This skilful servitor of the Queen will tell you, lady, that the wind which is a gale on the Atlantic, may scarce cool the burning cheek of a girl on the land, and that the links in life are as curiously interlocked as the ropes of a ship. The Ephesian temple, and the Indian wigwam, rested on the same earth."

"From which you infer that rank does not alter nature. We must admit, Captain Ludlow, that Master Seadrift understands a woman's heart, when he tempts her with stores of tissues gay as these!"

Ludlow had watched the speakers in silence. The manner of Alida was far less embarrassed, than when he had before seen her in the smuggler's company; and his blood fired, when he saw that their eyes met with a secret and friendly intelligence. He had remained, however, with a resolution to be calm, and to know the worst. Conquering the expression of his feelings by a great effort, he answered with an exterior of composure, though not without some of that bitterness in his emphasis, which he felt at his heart.

"If Master Seadrift has this knowledge, he may value himself on his good fortune;" was the reply.

"Much intercourse with the sex, who are my best customers, has something helped me;" returned the cavalier dealer in contraband. "Here is a brocade, whose fellow is worn openly in the presence of our royal mistress, though it came from the forbidden looms of Italy; and the ladies of the court return from patriotically dancing, in the fabrics of home, to please the public eye, once in the year, to wear these more agreeable inventions, all the rest of it, to please themselves. Tell me, why does the Englishman, with his pale sun, spend thousands to force a sickly imitation of the gifts of the tropics, but because he pines for forbidden fruit? or why does your Paris gourmand roll a fig on his tongue, that a Lazzarone of Naples would cast into his bay, but because he wishes to enjoy the bounties of a low latitude, under a watery sky? I have seen an individual feast on the eau sucre of an European pine, that cost a guinea, while his palate would have refused the same fruit, with its delicious compound of acid and sweet, mellowed to ripeness under a burning sun, merely because he could have it for nothing. This is the secret of our patronage; and as the sex are most liable to its influence, we owe them most gratitude."

"You have travelled, Master Seadrift," returned la Belle smiling, while she tossed the rich contents of the bale on the carpet, "and treat of usages as familiarly as you speak of dignities."

"The lady of the sea-green mantle does not permit an idle servant. We follow the direction of her guiding hand; sometimes it points our course among the isles of the Adriatic, and at others on your stormy American coasts. There is little of Europe between Gibraltar and the Cattegat, that I have not visited."

"But Italy has been the favorite, if one may judge by the number of her fabrics that you produce."

"Italy, France, and Flanders, divide my custom; though you are right, in believing the former most in favor. Many years of early life did I pass on the noble coasts of that romantic region. One who protected and guided my infancy and youth, even left me for a time, under instruction, on the little plain of Sorrento."

"And where can this plain be found? — for the residence of so famous a rover may, one day, become the theme of song, and is likely to occupy the leisure of the curious."

"The grace of the speaker may well excuse the irony! Sorrento is a village on the southern shore of the renowned Naples bay. Fire has wrought many changes in that soft but wild country, and if, as religionists believe, the fountains of the great deep were ever broken up, and the earth's crust disturbed, to permit its secret springs to issue on the surface, this may have been one of the spots chosen by him whose touch leaves marks that are indelible, in which to show his power. The bed of the earth, itself, in all that region, appears to have been but the vomitings of volcanoes; and the Sorrentine passes his peaceable life in the bed of an extinguished crater. 'Tis curious to see in what manner the men of the middle ages have built their town, on the margin of the sea, where the element has swallowed one-half the ragged basin, and how they have taken the yawning crevices of the tufo, for ditches to protect their walls! I have visited many lands, and seen nature in nearly every clime; but no spot has yet presented, in a single view, so pleasant a combination of natural objects, mingled with mighty recollections, as that lovely abode on the Sorrentine cliffs!"

"Recount me these pleasures, that in memory seem so agreeable, while I examine further into the contents of the bale."

The gay young free-trader paused, and seemed lost in images of the past. Then, with a melancholy smile, he soon continued. "Though many years are gone," he said, "I can recall the beauties of that scene, as vividly as if they still stood before the eye. Our abode was on the verge of the cliffs. In front lay the deep-blue water, and on its further shore was a line of objects such as accident or design rarely assembles in one view. Fancy thyself, lady, at my side, and follow the curvature of the northern shore, as I trace the outline of that glorious scene! That high, mountainous, and ragged island, on the extreme left, is modern Ischia. Its origin is unknown, though piles of lava lie along its coast, which seems fresh as that thrown from the mountain yesterday. The long, low bit of land, insulated like its neighbor, is called Procida, a scion of ancient Greece. Its people still preserve, in dress and speech, marks of their origin. The narrow strait conducts you to a high and naked bluff! That is the Misenum, of old. Here Eneas came to land, and Rome held her fleets, and thence Pliny took the water, to get a nearer view of the labors of the volcano, after its awakening from centuries of sleep. In the hollow of the ridge, between that naked bluff and the next swell of the mountain, lie the fabulous Styx, the Elysian fields, and the place of the dead, as fixed by the Mantuan. More on the height and nearer to the sea, lie, buried in the earth, the vast vaults of the Piscina Mirabile — and the gloomy caverns of the Hundred Chambers; places that equally denote the luxury and the despotism of Rome. Nearer to the vast pile of castle, that is visible so many leagues, is the graceful and winding Baiæn harbor; and against the side of its sheltering hills, once lay the city of villas. To that sheltered hill, emperors, consuls, poets, and warriors, crowded from the capital, in quest of repose, and to breathe the pure air of a spot in which pestilence has since made its abode. The earth is still covered with the remains of their magnificence, and ruins of temples and baths are scattered freely among the olives and fig-trees of the peasant. A fainter bluff limits the north-eastern boundary of the little bay. On it, once, stood the dwellings of emperors. There Cæsar sought retirement, and the warm springs on its side are yet called the baths of the bloody Nero. That small conical hill, which, as you see, possesses a greener and fresher look than the adjoining land, is a cone ejected by the caldron beneath, but two brief centuries since. It occupies, in part, the site of the ancient Lucrine lake. All that remains of that famous receptacle of the epicure, is the small and shallow sheet at its base, which is separated from the sea by a mere thread of sand. More in the rear, and surrounded by dreary hills, lie the waters of Avernus. On their banks still stand the ruins of a temple, in which rites were celebrated to the infernal deities. The grotto of the Sybil pierces that ridge on the left, and the Cumæan passage is nearly in its rear. The town, which is seen a mile to the right, is Pozzuoli — a port of the ancients, and a spot now visited for its temples of Jupiter and Neptune, its mouldering amphitheatre, and its half-buried tombs. Here Caligula attempted his ambitious bridge; and while crossing thence to Baiæ, the vile Nero had the life of his own mother assailed. It was there, too, that holy Paul came to land, when journeying a prisoner to Rome. The small but high island, nearly in its front, is Nisida, the place to which Marcus Brutus retired after the deed at the foot of Pompey's statue, where he possessed a villa, and whence he and Cassius sailed to meet the shade and the vengeance of the murdered Cæsar, at Philippi. Then comes a crowd of sites more known in the middle ages; though just below that mountain, in the back-ground, is the famous subterranean road of which Strabo and Seneca are said to speak, and through which the peasant still daily drives his ass to the markets of the modern city. At its entrance is the reputed tomb of Virgil, and then commences an amphitheatre of white and terraced dwellings. This is noisy Napoli itself, crowned with its rocky castle of St. Elmo! The vast plain, to the right, is that which held the enervating Capua and so many other cities on its bosom. To this succeeds the insulated mountain of the volcano, with its summit torn in triple tops. 'Tis said that villas and villages, towns and cities, lie buried beneath the vineyards and palaces which crowd its base. The ancient and unhappy city of Pompeii stood on that luckless plain, which, following the shores of the bay, comes next; and then we take up the line of the mountain promontory, which forms the Sorrentine side of the water!"

"One who has had such schooling, should know better how to turn it to a good account;" said Ludlow, sternly, when the excited smuggler ceased to speak.

"In other lands, men derive their learning from books; in Italy, children acquire knowledge by the study of visible things:" was the undisturbed answer

"Some from this country are fond of believing that our own bay, these summer skies, and the climate in general, should have a strict resemblance to those of a region which lies precisely in our own latitude;" observed Alida, so hastily, as to betray a desire to preserve the peace between her guests.

"That your Manhattan and Raritan waters are broad and pleasant, none can deny, and that lovely beings dwell on their banks, lady," returned Seadrift, gallantly lifting his cap, "my own senses have witnessed. But 'twere wiser to select some other point of your excellence, for comparison, than a competition with the glorious waters, the fantastic and mountain isles, and the sunny hill-sides of modern Napoli! 'Tis certain the latitude is even in your favor, and that a beneficent sun does not fail of its office in one region more than in the other. But the forests of America are still too pregnant of vapors and exhalations, not to impair the purity of the native air. If I have seen much of the Mediterranean, neither am I a stranger to these coasts. While there are so many points of resemblance in their climates, there are also many and marked causes of difference."

"Teach us, then, what forms these distinctions, that, in speaking of our bay and skies, we may not be led into error."

"You do me honor, lady; I am of no great schooling, and of humble powers of speech. Still, the little that observation may have taught me, shall not be churlishly withheld. Your Italian atmosphere, taking the humidity of the seas, is sometimes hazy. Still water in large bodies, other than in the two seas, is little known in those distant countries. Few objects in nature are drier than an Italian river, during those months when the sun has most influence. The effect is visible in the air, which is in general elastic, dry, and obedient to the general laws of the climate. There floats less exhalation, in the form of fine and nearly invisible vapor, than in these wooded regions. At least, so he of whom I spoke, as one who guided my youth, was wont to say."

"You hesitate to tell us of our skies, our evening light, and of our bay?"

"It shall be said, and said sincerely — Of the bays, each seems to have been appropriated to that for which nature most intended it. The one is poetic, indolent, and full of graceful but glorious beauty; more pregnant of enjoyment than of usefulness. The other will, one day, be the mart of the world!"

"You still shrink from pronouncing on their beauty;" said Alida, disappointed, in spite of an affected indifference to the subject.

"It is ever the common fault of old communities to overvalue themselves, and to undervalue new actors in the great drama of nations, as men long successful disregard the efforts of new aspirants for favor;" said Seadrift, while he looked with amazement at the pettish eye of the frowning beauty. "In this instance, however, Europe has not so greatly erred. They who see much resemblance between the bay of Naples and this of Manhattan, have fertile brains; since it rests altogether on the circumstance that there is much water in both, and a passage between an island and the main-land, in one, to resemble a passage between two islands in the other. This is an estuary, that a gulf; and while the former has the green and turbid water of a shelving shore and of tributary rivers, the latter has the blue and limpid element of a deep sea. In these distinctions, I take no account of ragged and rocky mountains, with the indescribable play of golden and rosy light upon their broken surfaces, nor of a coast that teems with the recollections of three thousand years!"

"I fear to question more. But surely our skies may be mentioned, even by the side of those you vaunt?"

"Of the skies, truly, you have more reason to be confident. I remember that standing on the Capo di Monte, which overlooks the little, picturesque, and crowded beach of the Marina Grande, and Sorrento, a spot that teems with all that is poetic in the fisher man's life, he of whom I have spoken, once pointed to the transparent vault above, and said, 'There is the moon of America!' The colors of the rocket were not more vivid than the stars that night, for a Tramontana had swept every impurity from the air, far upon the neighboring sea. But nights like that are rare, indeed, in any clime! The inhabitants of low latitudes enjoy them occasionally; those of higher never."

"And then our flattering belief, that these western sunsets rival those of Italy, is delusion?"

"Not so, lady. They rival, without resembling. The color of the étui, on which so fair a hand is resting, is not softer than the hues one sees in the heavens of Italy. But if your evening sky wants the pearly light, the rosy clouds, and the soft tints which, at that hour, melt into each other, across the entire vault of Napoli, it far excels in the vividness of the glow, in the depth of the transitions, and in the richness of colors. Those are only more delicate, while these are more gorgeous! When there shall be less exhalation from your forests, the same causes may produce the same effects. Until then, America must be content to pride herself on an exhibition of nature's beauty, in a new, though scarcely in a less pleasing, form."

"Then they who come among us from Europe, are but half right, when they deride the pretensions of our bay and heavens?"

"Which is much nearer the truth than they are wont to be, on the subject of this continent. Speak of the many rivers, the double outlet, the numberless basins, and the unequalled facilities of your Manhattan harbor; for in time, they will come to render all the beauties of the unrivalled bay of Naples vain: but tempt not the stranger to push the comparison beyond. Be grateful for your skies, lady, for few live under fairer or more beneficent — But I tire you with these opinions, when here are colors that have more charms for a young and lively imagination, than even the tints of nature!"

La belle Barbérie smiled on the dealer in contraband, with an interest that sickened Ludlow; and she was about to reply, in better humor, when the voice of her uncle announced his near approach.

CHAPTER XXIV.

"There shall be, in England, seven half-penny loaves sold for a penny.
The three-hooped pot shall have ten hoops; and I will make it felony, to
drink small beer."

— *Jack Cade.*

HAD Alderman Van Beverout been a party in the preceding dialogue, he could
not have uttered words more apposite, than the exclamation with which he first
saluted the ears of those in the pavilion.

"Gales and climates!" exclaimed the merchant, entering with an open letter
in his hand. "Here are advices received, by way of Curaçoa, and the coast of
Africa, that the good ship Musk-Rat met with foul winds off the Azores, which
lengthened her passage home to seventeen weeks — this is too much precious
time wasted between markets, Captain Cornelius Ludlow, and 'twill do discredit
to the good character of the ship, which has hitherto always maintained a sound
reputation, never needing more than the regular seven months to make the
voyage home and out again. If our vessels fall into this lazy train, we shall never get
a skin to Bristol, till it is past use. What have we here, niece? Merchandise! and of a
suspicious fabric! — who has the invoice of these goods, and in what vessel were
they shipped?"

"These are questions that may be better answered by their owner;" returned
la Belle, pointing gravely, and not without tremor in her voice, towards the dealer
in contraband, who, at the approach of the Alderman, had shrunk back as far as
possible from view.

Myndert cast an uneasy glance at the unmoved countenance of the commander of the royal cruiser, after having bestowed a brief but understanding look
at the contents of the bale. "Captain Ludlow, the chaser is chased!" he said. "After
sailing about the Atlantic, for a week or more, like a Jew broker's clerk running up
and down the Boom Key at Rotterdam, to get off a consignment of damaged tea,
we are fairly caught ourselves! To what fall in prices, or change in the sentiments
of the Board of Trade, am I indebted for the honor of this visit, Master a — a —
a — gay dealer in green ladies and bright tissues?"

The confident and gallant manner of the free-trader had vanished. In its
place, there appeared a hesitating and embarrassed air, that the individual was not
wont to exhibit, blended with some apparent indecision, on the subject of his
reply.

"It is the business of those who hazard much, in order to minister to the wants of life," he said, after a pause that was sufficiently expressive of the entire change in his demeanor, "to seek customers where there is a reputation for liberality. I hope my boldness will be overlooked, on account of its motive, and that you will aid the lady in judging of the value of my articles, and of their reasonableness as to price, with your own superior experience."

Myndert was quite as much astonished, by this language, and the subdued manner of the smuggler, as Ludlow himself. When he expected the heaviest demand on his address, in order to check the usual forward and reckless familiarity of Seadrift, in order that his connexion with the 'Skimmer of the Seas' might be as much as possible involved in ambiguity, to his own amazement, he found his purpose more than aided by the sudden and extraordinary respect with which he was treated. Emboldened, and perhaps a little elevated in his own esteem, by this unexpected deference, which the worthy Alderman, shrewd as he was in common, did not fail, like other men, to impute to some inherent quality of his own, he answered with a greater depth of voice, and a more protecting air, than he might otherwise have deemed it prudent to assume to one who had so frequently given him proofs of his own fearless manner of viewing things.

"This is being more eager as a trader, than prudent as one who should know the value of credit;" he said, making, at the same time, a lofty gesture to betoken indulgence for so venial an error. "We must overlook the mistake, Captain Ludlow; since, as the young man truly observes in his defence, gain acquired in honest traffic is a commendable and wholesome pursuit. One who appears as if he might not be ignorant of the laws, should know that our virtuous Queen and her wise counsellors have decided that Mother England can produce most that a colonist can consume! Ay! and that she can consume, too, most that the colonist can produce!"

"I pretend not to this ignorance, Sir; but, in pursuing my humble barter, I merely follow a principle of nature, by endeavoring to provide for my own interests. We of the contraband do but play at hazard with the authorities. When we pass the gauntlet unharmed, we gain; and when we lose, the servants of the crown find their profit. The stakes are equal, and the game should not be stigmatized as unfair. Would the rulers of the world once remove the unnecessary shackles they impose on commerce, our calling would disappear, and the name of free-trader would then belong to the richest and most esteemed houses."

The Alderman drew a long, low whistle. Motioning to his companions to be seated, he placed his own compact person in a chair, crossed his legs with an air of self-complacency, and resumed the discourse.

"These are very pretty sentiments, Master — a — a — a — , you bear a worthy name, no doubt, my ingenious commentator on commerce?"

"They call me Seadrift, when they spare a harsher term;" returned the other, meekly declining to be seated.

"These are pretty sentiments, Master Seadrift, and they much become a gentleman who lives by practical comments on the revenue-laws. This is a wise world, Captain Cornelius Ludlow, and in it there are many men whose heads are tilled, like bales of goods, with a general assortment of ideas. Hornbooks and primers! Here have Van Bummel, Schoenbroeck, and Van der Donck, just sent me a very neatly-folded pamphlet, written in good Leyden Dutch, to prove that trade is an exchange of what the author calls equivalents, and that nations have nothing to do but to throw open their ports, in order to make a millennium among the merchants!"

"There are many ingenious men who entertain the same opinions;" observed Ludlow, steady in his resolution to be merely a quiet observer of all that passed.

"What cannot a cunning head devise, to spoil paper with! Trade is a racer, gentlemen, and merchants the jockeys who ride. He who carries most weight may lose; but then nature does not give all men the same dimensions, and judges are as necessary to the struggles of the mart as to those of the course. Go, mount your gelding, if you are lucky enough to have one that has not been melted into a weasel by the heartless blacks, and ride out to Harlaem Flats, on a fine October day, and witness the manner in which the trial of speed is made. The rogues of riders cut in here, and over there; now the whip and now the spur; and though they start fair, which is more than can always be said of trade, some one is sure to win. When it is neck and neck, then the neat is to be gone over, until the best bottom gains the prize."

"Why is it then that men of deep reflection so often think that commerce flourishes most when least encumbered?"

"Why is one man born to make laws, and another to break them? — Does not the horse run faster with his four legs free, than when in hopples? But in trade, Master Seadrift, and Captain Cornelius Ludlow, each of us is his own jockey; and putting the aid of custom-house laws out of the question, just as nature has happened to make him. Fat or lean, big bones or fine bones, he must get to the goal as well as he can. Therefore your heavy weights call out for sandbags and belts, to make all even. That the steed may be crushed with his load, is no proof that his chance of winning will not be better by bringing all the riders to the same level."

"But to quit these similies," continued Ludlow, "if trade be but an exchange of equivalents —"

"Beggary and stoppages!" interrupted the Alder man, who was far more dogmatical than courteous in argument. "This is the language of men who have read all sorts of books, but legers. Here have advices from Tongue and Twaddle, of London, which state the nett proceeds of a little adventure, shipped by the brig Moose, that reached the river on the 16th of April, ultimo. The history of the whole transaction can be put in a child's muff — you are a discreet youth, Captain Cornelius; and as to you, Master Seadrift, the affair is altogether out of your line — therefore, as I was observing, here are the items, made out only a fortnight since, in the shape of a memorandum;" while speaking, the Alderman had placed his spectacles and drawn his tablets from a pocket. Adjusting himself to the light, he continued: "Paid bill of Sand, Furnace, and Glass, for beads, L. 3. 2. 6. Package and box, 1. 10½ — Shipping charges, and freight, 11. 4. Insurance, averaged at, 1. 5. Freight, charges, and commission of agent among Mohawks, L. 10. Do. do. do. of shipment and sale of furs, in England, L. 7. 2 Total of costs and charges, L. 20. 18. 8½, all in sterling money. Note, sale of furs, to Frost and Rich, nett avails, L. 196. 11. 3. — Balance, as per contra, L. 175. 12. 5½. — a very satisfactory equivalent this, Master Cornelius, to appear on the books of Tongue and Twaddle, where I stand charged with the original investment of L. 20. 19. 8½! How much the Empress of Germany may pay the firm of Frost and Rich for the articles, does not appear."

"Nor does it appear that more was got for your beads, in the Mohawk country, than they were valued at there, or was paid for the skins than they were worth where they were produced."

"Whe — w — w — w!" whistled the merchant, as he returned the tablets to his pocket.

"One would think that thou hadst been studying the Leyden pamphleteer, son of my old friend! If the savage thinks so little of his skins, and so much of my beads, I shall never take, the pains to set him right; else, always by permission of the Board of Trade, we shall see him, one day, turning his bark canoe into a good ship, and going in quest of his own ornaments. Enterprise and voyages! Who knows but that the rogue would see fit to stop at London, even; in which case the Mother Country might lose the profit of the sale at Vienna, and the Mohawk set up his carriage, on the difference in the value of markets! Thus, you see, in order to run a fair race, the horses must start even, carry equal weights, and, after all, one commonly wins. Your metaphysics are no better than so much philosophical gold leaf, which a cunning reasoner beats out into a sheet as large as the broadest American lake, to make dunces believe the earth can be transmuted into the precious material; while a plain practical man puts the value of the metal into his pocket, in good current coin."

"And yet I hear you complain that Parliament has legislated more than is good for trade, and speak in a manner of the proceedings at home, that, you will excuse me for saying, would better become a Hollander than a subject of the crown."

"Have I not told you, that the horse will run faster without a rider, than with a pack-saddle on his back? Give your own jockey as little, and your adversary's as much weight as you can, if you wish to win. I complain of the borough-men, because they make laws for us, and not for themselves. As I often tell my worthy friend, Alderman Gulp, eating is good for life, but a surfeit makes a will necessary."

"From all which I infer, that the opinions of your Leyden correspondent are not those of Mr. Van Beverout."

The Alderman laid a finger on his nose, and looked at his companions, for a moment, without answering.

"Those Leydeners are a sagacious breed! If the United Provinces had but ground to stand on, they would, like the philosopher who boasted of his lever, move the world! The sly rogues think that the Amsterdammers have naturally an easy seat, and they wish to persuade all others to ride bare-back. I shall send the pamphlet up into the Indian country, and pay some scholar to have it translated into the Mohawk tongue, in order that the famous chief Schendoh, when the missionaries shall have taught him to read, may entertain right views of equivalents! I am not certain that I may not make the worthy divines a present, to help the good fruits to ripen."

The Alderman leered round upon his auditors, and, folding his hands meekly on his breast, he appeared to leave his eloquence to work its own effects.

"These opinions favor but little the occupation of the — the gentleman — who now honors us with his company," said Ludlow, regarding the gay-looking smuggler with an eye that showed how much he was embarrassed to find a suitable appellation for one whose appearance was so much at variance with his pursuits. "If restrictions are necessary to commerce, the lawless trader is surely left without an excuse for his calling."

"I as much admire your discretion in practice, as the justice of your sentiments in theory, Captain Ludlow;" returned the Alderman. "In a rencontre on the high seas, it would be your duty to render captive the brigantine of this person; but, in what may be called the privacy of domestic retirement, you are content to ease your mind in moralities! I feel it my duty, too, to speak on this point, and shall take so favorable an occasion, when all is pacific, to disburthen myself of some sentiments that suggest themselves, very naturally, under the circumstances." Myndert then turned himself towards the dealer in contraband, and continued, much in the manner of a city magistrate, reading a lesson of propriety to some disturber of the peace of society. "You appear here, Master Seadrift," he said, "under what, to borrow a figure from your profession, may be called false colors. You bear the countenance of one who might be a useful subject, and yet are you suspected of being addicted to certain practices which — I will not say they are dishonest, or even discreditable — for on that head the opinions of men are much divided, but which certainly have no tendency to assist Her Majesty, in bringing her wars to a glorious issue, by securing to her European dominions that monopoly of trade, by which it is her greatest desire to ease us of the colonies of looking any further after our particular interests, than beyond the doors of her own custom-houses. This is an indiscretion, to give the act its gentlest appellation; and I regret to add, it is accompanied by certain circumstances which rather heighten than lessen the delinquency." The Alderman paused a moment, to observe the effect of his admonition, and to judge, by the eye of the free-trader, how much farther he might push his artifice; but perceiving, to his own surprise, that the other bent his face to the floor, and stood like one rebuked, he took courage to proceed. "You have introduced into this portion of my dwelling, which is exclusively inhabited by my niece, who is neither of a sex nor of years to be legally arraigned for any oversight of this nature, sundries of which it is the pleasure of the Queen's advisers that her subjects in the colonies should not know the use, since, in the nature of fabrications, they cannot be submitted to the supervising care of the ingenious artisans of the mother island. Woman, Master Seadrift, is a creature liable to the influence of temptation, and in few things is she weaker than in her efforts to resist the allurements of articles which may aid in adorning her person. My niece, the daughter of Etienne Barbérie, may also have an hereditary weakness on this head, since the females of France study these inventions more than those of some other countries. It is not my intention, however, to manifest any unreasonable severity; since, if old Etienne has communicated any hereditary feebleness on the subject of fancy, he has also left his daughter the means of paying for it. Hand in your account, therefore, and the debt shall be discharged, if debt has been incurred. And this brings me to the last and the gravest of your offences.

"Capital is no doubt the foundation on which a merchant builds his edifice of character," continued Myndert, after taking another jealous survey of the countenance of him he addressed; "but credit is the ornament of its front. This is a corner-stone; that the pilasters and carvings, by which the building is rendered pleasant; sometimes, when age has undermined the basement, it is the columns on which the superstructure rests, or even the roof by which the occupant is sheltered. It renders the rich man safe, the dealer of moderate means active and respectable, and it causes even the poor man to hold up his head in hope: though I admit that buyer and seller need both be wary, when it stands unsupported by any substantial base. This being the value of credit, Master Seadrift, none should assail it without sufficient cause, for its quality is of a nature too tender for rude treatment. I learned, when a youth, in my travels in Holland, through which country, by means of the Trekschuyts, I passed with sufficient deliberation to profit by what was seen, the importance of avoiding, on all occasions, bringing credit into disrepute. As one event that occurred offers an apposite parallel to what I have now to advance, I shall make a tender of the facts in the way of illustration. The circumstances show the awful uncertainty of things in this transitory life, Captain Ludlow, and forewarn the most vigorous and youthful, that the strong of arm may be cut down, in his pride, like the tender plant of the fields! The banking-house of Van Gelt and Van Stopper, in Amsterdam, had dealt largely in securities issued by the Emperor for the support of his wars. It happened, at the time, that Fortune had favored the Ottoman, who was then pressing the city of Belgrade, with some prospects of success. Well, Sirs, a headstrong and ill-advised laundress had taken possession of an elevated terrace in the centre of the town, in order to dry her clothes. This woman was in the act of commencing the distribution of her linens and muslins, with the break of day, when the Mussulmans awoke the garrison by a rude assault. Some, who had been posted in a position that permitted of retreat, having seen certain bundles of crimson, and green, and yellow, on an elevated parapet, mistook them for the heads of so many Turks; and they spread the report, far and near, that a countless band of the Infidels, led on by a vast number of sherriffes in green turbans, had gained the heart of the place, before they were induced to retire. The rumor soon took the shape of a circumstantial detail, and, having reached Amsterdam, it caused the funds of the Imperialists to look down. There was much question, on the Exchange, concerning the probable loss of Van Gelt and Van Stopper in consequence. Just as speculation was at its greatest height on this head, the monkey of a Savoyard escaped from its string, and concealed himself in a nut-shop, a few doors distant from the banking-house of the firm, where a crowd of Jew boys collected to witness its antics. Men of reflection, seeing what they mistook for a demonstration on the part of the children of the Israelites, began to feel uneasiness for their own property. Drafts multiplied; and the worthy bankers, in order to prove their solidity, disdained to shut their doors at the usual hour. Money was paid throughout the night; and before noon, on the following day, Van Gelt had cut his throat, in a summer-house that stood on the banks of the Utrecht canal; and Van Stopper was seen smoking a pipe, among strong boxes that were entirely empty. At two o'clock, the post brought the intelligence that the Mussulmans were repulsed, and that the laundress was hanged; though I never knew exactly for what crime, as she certainly was not a debtor of the unhappy firm. These are some of the warning events of life, gentlemen; and as I feel sure of addressing those who are capable of making the application, I shall now conclude by advising all who hear me to great discretion of speech on every matter connected with commercial character."

When Myndert ceased speaking, he threw another glance around him, in order to note the effect his words had produced, and more particularly to ascertain whether he had not drawn a draft on the forbearance of the free-trader, which might still meet with a protest. He was at a loss to account for the marked and unusual deference with which he was treated, by one who, while he was never coarse, seldom exhibited much complaisance for the opinions of a man he was in the habit of meeting so familiarly, on matters of pecuniary interest. During the whole of the foregoing harangue, the young mariner of the brigantine had maintained the same attitude of modest attention; and when his eyes were permitted to rise, it was only to steal uneasy looks at the face of Alida. La belle Barbérie had also listened to her uncle's eloquence, with a more thoughtful air than common. She met the occasional glances of the dealer in contraband, with answering sympathy; and, in short, the most indifferent observer of their deportment might have seen that circumstances had created between them a confidence and intelligence which, if it were not absolutely of the most tender, was unequivocally of the most intimate, character. Ail this Ludlow plainly saw, though the burgher had been too much engrossed with the ideas he had so complacently dealt out, to note the fact.

"Now that my mind is so well stored with maxims on commerce, which I shall esteem as so many commentaries on the instructions of my Lords of the Admiralty," observed the Captain, after a brief interval of silence, "it may be permitted to turn our attention to things less metaphysical. The present occasion is favorable to inquire after the fate of the shipmate we lost in the last cruise; and it ought not to be neglected."

"You speak truth, Mr. Cornelius — The Patroon of Kinderhook is not a man to fall into the sea, like an anker of forbidden liquor, and no questions asked. Leave this matter to my discretion, Sir; and trust me, the tenants of the third best estate in the colony shall not long be without tidings of their landlord. If you will accompany Master Seadrift into the other part of the villa for a reasonable time, I shall possess myself of all the facts that are at all pertinent to the right understanding of the case."

The commander of the royal cruiser, and the young mariner of the brigantine, appeared to think that a compliance with this invitation would bring about a singular association. The hesitation of the latter, however, was far the most visible, since Ludlow had coolly determined to maintain his neutral character, until a proper moment to act, as a faithful servitor of his royal mistress, should arrive. He knew, or firmly believed, that the Water-Witch again lay in the Cove, concealed by the shadows of the surrounding wood; and as he had once before suffered by the superior address of the smugglers, he was now resolved to act with so much caution, as to enable him to return to his ship in time to proceed against her with decision, and, as he hoped, with effect. In addition to this motive for artifice, there was that in the manner and language of the contraband dealer to place him altogether above the ordinary men of his pursuit, and indeed to create in his favor a certain degree of interest, which the officer of the crown was compelled to admit. He therefore bowed with sufficient courtesy, and professed his readiness to follow the suggestions of the Alderman.

"We have met on neutral ground, Master Seadrift," said Ludlow to his gay companion, as they quitted the saloon of la Cour des Fées; "and though bent on different objects, we may discourse amicably of the past. The 'Skimmer of the Seas' has a reputation in his way, that almost raises him to the level of a seaman distinguished in a better service. I will ever testify to his skill and coolness as a mariner, however much I may lament that those fine qualities have received so unhappy a direction."

"This is speaking with a becoming reservation for the rights of the crown, and with meet respect for die Barons of the Exchequer!" retorted Seadrift, whose former, and we may say natural, spirit seemed to return, as he left the presence of the burgher. "We follow the pursuit, Captain Ludlow, in which accident has cast our fortunes. You serve a Queen you never saw, and a nation who will use you in her need and despise you in her prosperity; and I serve myself. Let reason decide between us."

"I admire this frankness, Sir, and have hopes of a better understanding between us, now that you have done with the mystifications of your sea-green woman. The farce has been well enacted; though, with the exception of Oloff Van Staats and those enlightened spirits you lead about the ocean, it has not made many converts to necromancy."

The free-trader permitted his handsome mouth to relax in a smile.

"We have our mistress, too," he said; "but she exacts no tribute. All that is gained goes to enrich her subjects, while all that she knows is cheerfully imparted for their use. If we are obedient, it is because we have experienced her justice and wisdom I hope Queen Anne deals as kindly by those who risk life and limb in her cause?"

"Is it part of the policy of her you follow, to reveal the fate of the Patroon; for though rivals in one dear object — or rather I should say, once rivals in that object — I cannot see a guest quit my ship with so little ceremony, without an interest in his welfare."

"You make a just distinction," returned Seadrift, smiling still more mean-ingly — "Once rivals is indeed the better expression. Mr. Van Staats is a brave man, however ignorant he may be of the seaman's art. One who has showed so much spirit will be certain of protection from personal injury, in the care of the 'Skimmer of the Seas.'"

"I do not constitute myself the keeper of Mr. Van Staats; still, as the com-mander of the ship whence he has been — what shall I term the manner of his abduction? — for I would not willingly use, at this moment, a term that may prove disagreeable —"

"Speak freely, Sir, and fear not to offend. We of the brigantine are accus-tomed to divers epithets that might startle less practised ears. We are not to learn, at this late hour, that, in order to become respectable, roguery must have the sanc-tion of government. You were pleased, Captain Ludlow, to name the mystifica-tions of the Water-Witch; but you seem indifferent to those that are hourly practised near you in the world, and which, without the pleasantry of this of ours, have not half its innocence."

"There is little novelty in the expedient of seeking to justify the delinquency of individuals, by the failings of society."

"I confess it is rather just than original. Triteness and Truth appear to be sis-ters! And yet do we find ourselves driven to this apology, since the refinement of us of the brigantine has not yet attained to the point of understanding all the excellence of novelty in morals."

"I believe there is a mandate of sufficient antiquity, which bids us to render unto Cæsar the things which are Cæsar's."

"A mandate which our modern Cæsars have most liberally construed! I am a poor casuist, Sir; nor do I think the loyal commander of the Coquette would wish to uphold all that sophistry can invent on such a subject. If we begin with potentates, for instance, we shall find the Most Christian King bent on appropriating as many of his neighbors' goods to his own use, as ambition, under the name of glory, can covet; the Most Catholic, covering with the mantle of his Catholicity, a greater multitude of enormities on this very continent, than even charity itself could conceal; and our own gracious Sovereign, whose virtues and whose mildness are celebrated in verse and prose, causing rivers of blood to run, in order that the little island over which she rules may swell out, like the frog in the fable, to dimensions that nature has denied, and which will one day inflict the unfortunate death that befell the ambitious inhabitant of the pool. The gallows awaits the pickpocket; but your robber under a pennant is dubbed a knight! The man who amasses wealth by gainful industry is ashamed of his origin; while he who has stolen from churches, laid villages under contribution, and cut throats by thousands, to divide the spoils of a galleon or a military chest, has gained gold on the highway of glory! Europe has reached an exceeding pass of civilization, it may not be denied; but before society inflicts so severe censure on the acts of individuals, notwithstanding the triteness of the opinion, I must say it is bound to look more closely to the example it sets, in its collective character."

"These are points on which our difference of opinion is likely to be lasting;" said Ludlow, assuming the severe air of one who had the world on his side "We will defer the discussion to a moment of greater leisure, Sir. Am I to learn more of Mr. Van Staats, or is the question of his fate to become the subject of a serious official inquiry?"

"The Patroon of Kinderhook is a bold boarder!" returned the free-trader, laughing. "He has carried the residence of the lady of the brigantine by a coup-de-main; and he reposes on his laurels! We of the contraband are merrier in our privacy than is thought, and those who join our mess seldom wish to quit it."

"There may be occasion to look further into its mysteries — until when, I wish you adieu."

"Hold!" gaily cried the other, observing that Ludlow was about to quit the room — "Let the time of our uncertainty be short, I pray thee. Our mistress is like the insect, which takes the color of the leaf on which it dwells. You have seen her in her sea-green robe, which she never fails to wear when roving over the soundings of your American coast: but in the deep waters, her mantle vies with the blue of the ocean's depths. Symptoms of a change, which always denote an intended excursion far beyond the influence of the land, have been seen!"

"Harkee, Master Seadrift! This foolery may do while you possess the power to maintain it. But remember, that though the law only punishes the illegal trader by confiscation of his goods when taken, it punishes the kidnapper with personal pains, and sometimes with — death! — And, more — remember that the line which divides smuggling from piracy is easily past, while the return becomes impossible."

"For this generous counsel, in my mistress's name I thank thee;" the gay mariner replied, bowing with a gravity that rather heightened than concealed his irony — "Your Coquette is broad in the reach of her booms, and swift on the water, Captain Ludlow, but let her be capricious, wilful, deceitful, nay powerful, as she may, she shall find a woman in the brigantine equal to all her arts, and far superior to all her threats!"

With this prophetic warning on the part of the Queen's officer, and cool reply on that of the dealer in contraband, the two sailors separated. The latter took a book, and threw himself into a chair, with a well-maintained indifference; while the other left the house, in a haste that was not disguised.

In the mean time, the interview between Alderman Van Beverout and his niece still continued. Minute passed after minute, and yet there was no summons to the pavilion. The gay young seaman of the brigantine had continued his studies for some time after the disappearance of Ludlow, and he now evidently awaited an intimation that his presence was required in la Cour des Fées. During these moments of anxiety, the air of the free-trader was sorrowful rather than impatient; and when a footstep was heard at the door of the room, he betrayed symptoms of strong and uncontrollable agitation. It was the female attendant of Alida, who entered, presented a slip of paper, and retired. The eager expectant read the following words, hastily written in pencil —

"I have evaded all his questions, and he is more than half-disposed to believe in necromancy. This is not the moment to confess the truth, for he is not in a condition to hear it, being already much disturbed by the uncertainty of what may follow the appearance of the brigantine on the coast, and so near his own villa. But, be assured, he shall and will acknowledge claims that I know how to support, and which, should I fail of establishing, he would not dare to refuse to the redoubtable 'Skimmer of the Seas.' Come hither, the moment you hear his foot in the passage."

The last injunction was soon obeyed. The Alderman entered by one door, as the active fugitive retreated by another; and where the weary burgher expected to see his guests, he found an empty apartment. This last circumstance, however, gave Myndert Van Beverout but little surprise and no concern, as would appear by the indifference with which he noted the circumstance.

"Vagaries and womanhood!" thought, rather than muttered, the Alderman. "The jade turns like a fox in his tracks, and it would be easier to convict a merchant who values his reputation, of a false invoice, than this minx of nineteen of an indiscretion! There is so much of old Etienne and his Norman blood in her eye, that one does not like to provoke extremities; but here, when I expected Van Staats had profited by his opportunity, the girl looks like a nun, at the mention of his name. The Patroon is no Cupid, we must allow; or, in a week at sea, he would have won the heart of a mermaid! — Ay — and here are more perplexities, by the return of the Skimmer and his brig, and the notions that young Ludlow has of his duty. Life and mortality! One must quit trade, at some time or other, and begin to close the books of life. I must seriously think of striking a final balance. If the sum-total was a little more in my favor it should be gladly done tomorrow!"

CHAPTER XXV.

" — Thou, Julia, thou hast metamorphosed me;
Made me neglect my studies, lose my time,
War with good counsel, set the world at nought."

Two Gentlemen of Verona.

LUDLOW quitting the Lust in Rust with a wavering purpose. Throughout the whole of the preceding interview, he had jealously watched the eye and features of la belle Barbérie; and he had not failed to draw his conclusions from a mien that too plainly expressed a deep interest in the free-trader. For a time, only, had he been induced, by the calmness and self-possession with which she received her uncle and himself, to believe that she had not visited the Water-Witch at all; but when the gay and reckless being who governed the movements of that extraordinary vessel, appeared, he could no longer flatter himself with this hope. He now believed that her choice for life had been made; and while he deplored the infatuation which could induce so gifted a woman to forget her station and character, he was himself too frank not to see that the individual who had in so short a time gained this ascendency over the feelings of Alida, was, in many respects, fitted to exercise a powerful influence over the imagination of a youthful and secluded female.

There was a struggle in the mind of the young commander, between his duty and his feelings. Remembering the artifice by which he had formerly fallen into the power of the smugglers, he had taken his precautions so well in the present visit to the villa, that he firmly believed he had the person of his lawless rival at his mercy. To avail himself of this advantage, or to retire and leave him in possession of his mistress and his liberty, was the point mooted in his thoughts. Though direct and simple in his habits, like most of the seamen of that age, Ludlow had all the loftier sentiments that become a gentleman. He felt keenly for Alida, and he shrunk, with sensitive pride, from incurring the imputation of having acted under the impulses of disappointment. To these motives of forbearance, was also to be added the inherent reluctance which, as an officer of rank, he felt to the degradation of being employed in a duty that more properly belongs to men of less elevated ambition. He looked on himself as a defender of the rights and glory of his sovereign, and not as a mercenary instrument of those who collected her customs; and though he would not have hesitated to incur any rational hazard, in capturing the vessel of the smuggler, or in making captives of all or any of her crew on their proper element, he disliked the appearance of seeking a solitary individual on the land. In addition to this feeling, there was his own pledge that he met the proscribed dealer in contraband on neutral ground. Still the officer of the Queen had his orders, and he could not shut his eyes to the general obligations of duty. The brigantine was known to inflict so much loss on the revenue of the crown, more particularly in the other hemisphere, that an especial order had been issued by the Admiral of the station, for her capture. Here then was an opportunity of depriving the vessel of that master-spirit which, notwithstanding the excellence of its construction, had alone so long enabled it to run the gauntlet of a hundred cruisers with impunity. Agitated by these contending feelings and reflections, the young sailor left the door of the villa, and came upon its little lawn, in order to reflect with less interruption, and, indeed, to breathe more freely.

The night had advanced into the first watch of the seaman. The shadow of the mountain, however, still covered the grounds of the villa, the river, and the shores of the Atlantic, with a darkness that was deeper than the obscurity which dimmed the surface of the rolling ocean beyond. Objects were so indistinct as to require close and steady looks to ascertain their character, while the setting of the scene might be faintly traced by its hazy and indistinct outlines. The curtains of la Cour des Fées had been drawn, and, though the lights were still shining within, the eye could not penetrate the pavilion. Ludlow gazed about him, and then held his way reluctantly towards the water.

In endeavoring to conceal the interior of her apartment from the eyes of those without, Alida had suffered a corner of the drapery to remain open. When Ludlow reached the gate that led to the landing, he turned to take a last look at the villa; and, favored by his new position, he caught a glimpse, through the opening, of the person of her who was still uppermost in his thoughts.

La belle Barbérie was seated at the little table, by whose side she had been found, earlier in the evening. An elbow rested on the precious wood, and one fair hand supported a brow that was thoughtful far beyond the usual character of its expression, if not melancholy. The commander of the Coquette felt the blood rushing to his heart, for he fancied that the beautiful and pensive countenance was that of a penitent. It is probable that the idea quickened his drooping hopes; for Ludlow believed it might not yet be too late to rescue the woman, he so sincerely loved, from the precipice over which she was suspended. The seemingly irretrievable step, already taken, was forgotten; and the generous young sailor was about to rush back to la Cour des Fées, to implore its mistress to be just to herself, when the hand fell from her polished brow, and Alida raised her face, with a look which denoted that she was no longer alone. The captain drew back, to watch the issue.

When Alida lifted her eyes, it was in kindness, and with that frank ingenuousness with which an unperverted female greets the countenance of those who have her confidence. She smiled, though still in sadness rather than in pleasure; and she spoke, but the distance prevented her words from being audible. At the next instant, Seadrift moved into the space visible through the half-drawn drapery, and took her hand. Alida made no effort to withdraw the member; but, on the contrary, she looked up into his face with still less equivocal interest, and appeared to listen to his voice with an absorbed attention. The gate was swung violently open, and Ludlow had reached the margin of the river before he again paused.

The barge of the Coquette was found where her commander had ordered his people to lie concealed, and he was about to enter it, when the noise of the little gate, again shutting with the wind, induced him to cast a look behind. A human form was distinctly to be seen, against the light walls of the villa, descending towards the river. The men were commanded to keep close, and, withdrawing within the shadow of a fence, the captain waited the approach of the new-comer.

As the unknown person passed, Ludlow recognized the agile form of the free-trader. The latter advanced to the margin of the river, and gazed warily about him for several minutes. A low but distinct note, on a common ship's-call, was then heard. The summons was soon succeeded by the appearance of a small skiff, which glided out of the grass on the opposite side of the stream, and approached the spot where Seadrift awaited its arrival. The free-trader sprang lightly into the little boat, which immediately began to glide out of the river. As the skiff passed the spot where he stood, Ludlow saw that it was pulled by a single seaman; and, as his own boat was manned by six lusty rowers, he felt that the person of the man whom he so much envied was at length fairly and honorably in his power. We shall not attempt to analyze the emotion that was ascendant in the mind of the young officer. It is enough for our purpose to add, that he was soon in his boat and in full pursuit.

As the course to be taken by the barge was diagonal rather than direct, a few powerful strokes of the oars brought it so near the skiff, that Ludlow, by placing his hand on the gunwale of the latter, could arrest its progress.

"Though so lightly equipped, fortune favors you less in boats than in larger craft, Master Seadrift;" said Ludlow, when, by virtue of a strong arm, he had drawn his prize so near, as to find himself seated within a few feet of his prisoner. "We meet on our proper element, where there can be no neutrality between one of the contraband and a servant of the Queen."

The start, the half-repressed exclamation, and the momentary silence, showed that the captive had been taken completely by surprise.

"I admit your superior dexterity," he at length said, speaking low and not without agitation. "I am your prisoner, Captain Ludlow; and I would now wish to know your intentions in disposing of my person."

"That is soon answered. You must be content to take the homely accommodations of the Coquette, for the night, instead of the more luxurious cabin of your Water-Witch. What the authorities of the Province may decide, tomorrow, it exceeds the knowledge of a poor commander in the navy to say."

"The lord Cornbury has retired to — ?"

"A gaol," said Ludlow, observing that the other spoke more like one who mused than like one who asked a question. "The kinsman of our gracious Queen speculates on the chances of human fortune, within the walls of a prison. His successor, the brigadier Hunter, is thought to have less sympathy for the moral infirmities of human nature!"

"We deal lightly with dignities!" exclaimed the captive, with all his former gaiety of tone and manner. "You have your revenge for some personal liberties that were certainly taken, not a fortnight since, with this boat and her crew; still, I have much mistaken your character, if unnecessary severity forms one of its features. May I communicate with the brigantine?"

"Freely — when she is once in the care of a Queen's officer."

"Oh, Sir, you disparage the qualities of my mistress, in supposing there exists a parallel with your own! The Water-Witch will go at large, till a far different personage shall become your captive. — May I communicate with the shore?"

"To that there exists no objection — if you will point out the means."

"I have one, here, who will prove a faithful messenger."

"Too faithful to the delusion which governs all your followers! Your man must be your companion in the Coquette, Master Seadrift, though;" and Ludlow spoke in melancholy, "if there be any on the land, who take so near an interest in your welfare as to find more sorrow in uncertainty than in the truth, one of my own crew, in any of whom confidence may be placed, shall do your errand."

"Let it be so;" returned the free-trader, as if satisfied that he could, in reason, expect no more. "Take this ring to the lady of yonder dwelling," he continued, when Ludlow had selected the messenger, "and say that he who sends it is about to visit the cruiser of Queen Anne in company with her commander. Should there be question of the motive, you can speak to the manner of my arrest."

"And, mark me, fellow —" added his captain; "that duty done, look to the idlers on the shore, and see that no boat quits the river, to apprize the smugglers of their loss."

The man, who was armed in the fashion of a seaman on boat duty, received these orders with the customary deference; and the barge having drawn to the shore for that purpose, he landed.

"And now, Master Seadrift, having thus far complied with your wishes, I may expect you will not be deaf to mine. Here is a seat at your service in my barge, and I confess it will please me to see it occupied."

As the captain spoke, he reached forth an arm, partly in natural complaisance, and partly with a carelessness that denoted some consciousness of the difference in their rank, both to aid the other to comply with his request, and, at need, to enforce it. But the free-trader seemed to repel the familiarity; for he drew back, at first, like one who shrunk sensitively from the contact, and then, without touching the arm that was extended with a purpose so equivocal, he passed lightly from the skiff into the barge, declining assistance. The movement was scarcely made, before Ludlow quitted the latter, and occupied the place which Seadrift had just vacated. He commanded one of his men to exchange with the seaman of the brigantine; and, having made these preparations, he again addressed his prisoner.

"I commit you to the care of my cockswain and these worthy tars, Master Seadrift. We shall steer different ways. You will take possession of my cabin, where all will be at your disposal; ere the middle watch is called I shall be there to prevent the pennant from coming down, and your sea-green flag turning the people's heads from their allegiance."

Ludlow then whispered his orders to his cockswain, and they separated. The barge proceeded to the mouth of the river, with the long and stately sweep of the oars, that marks the progress of a man-of-war's boat; while the skiff followed, noiselessly and, aided by its color and dimensions, nearly invisible.

When the two boats entered the waters of the bay, the barge held on its course towards the distant ship; while the skiff inclined to the right, and steered directly for the bottom of the Cove. The precaution of the dealer in contraband had provided his little boat with muffled sculls; and Ludlow, when he was enabled to discover the fine tracery of the lofty and light spars of the Water-Witch, as they rose above the tops of the dwarf trees that lined the shore, had no reason to think

his approach was known. Once assured of the presence and position of the brigantine, he was enabled to make his advances with all the caution that might be
necessary.

Some ten or fifteen minutes were required to bring the skiff beneath the
bowsprit of the beautiful craft, without giving the alarm to those who doubtless
were watching on her decks. The success of our adventurer, however, appeared to
be complete; for he was soon holding by the cable, and not the smallest sound, of
any kind, had been heard in the brigantine. Ludlow now regretted he had not
entered the Cove with his barge; for, so profound and unsuspecting was the quiet
of the vessel, that he doubted not of his ability to have carried her by a coup-de-
main. Vexed by his oversight, and incited by the prospects of success, he began to
devise those expedients which would naturally suggest themselves to a seaman in
his situation.

The wind was southerly, and, though not strong it was charged with the
dampness and heaviness of the night air. As the brigantine lay protected from the
influence of the tides, she obeyed the currents of the other element; and, while
her bows looked outward, her stern pointed towards the bottom of the basin. The
distance from the land was not fifty fathoms, and Ludlow did not fail to perceive
that the vessel rode by a kedge, and that her anchors, of which there was a good
provision, were all snugly stowed. These facts induced the hope that he might
separate the hawser that alone held the brigantine, which, in the event of his succeeding, he had every reason to believe would drift ashore, before the alarm could
be given to her crew, sail set, or an anchor let go. Although neither he nor his
companion possessed any other implement to effect this object, than the large
seaman's knife of the latter, the temptation was too great not to make the trial.
The project was flattering; for, though the vessel in that situation would receive
no serious injury, the unavoidable delay of heaving her off the sands would enable
his boats, and perhaps the ship herself, to reach the place in time to secure their
prize. The bargeman was asked for his knife, and Ludlow himself made the first
cut upon the solid and difficult mass. The steel had no sooner touched the compact yarns, than a dazzling glare of light shot into the face of him who held it.
Recovering from the shock, and rubbing his eyes, our startled adventurer gazed
upwards, with that consciousness of wrong which assails us when detected in any
covert act, however laudable may be its motive — a sort of homage that nature,
under every circumstance, pays to loyal dealings.

Though Ludlow felt, at the instant of this interruption, that he stood in jeopardy of his life, the concern it awakened was momentarily lost in the spectacle

before him. The bronzed and unearthly features of the image were brightly illuminated; and, while her eyes looked on him steadily, as if watching his smallest movement, her malign and speaking smile appeared to turn his futile effort into scorn! There was no need to bid the seaman at the oars to do his duty. No sooner did he catch the expression of that mysterious face, than the skiff whirled away from the spot, like a sea-fowl taking wing under alarm. Though Ludlow, at each moment, expected a shot, even the imminence of the danger did not prevent him from gazing, in absorbed attention, at the image. The light by which it was illumined, though condensed, powerful, and steadily cast, wavered a little, and exhibited her attire. Then the captain saw the truth of what Seadrift had asserted; for, by some process of the machine into which he had not leisure to inquire, the sea-green mantle had been changed for a slighter robe of the azure of the deep waters. As if satisfied with having betrayed the intention of the sorceress to depart, the light immediately vanished.

"This mummery is well maintained!" muttered Ludlow, when the skiff had reached a distance that assured him of safety. "Here is a symptom that the rover means soon to quit the coast. The change of dress is some signal to his superstitious and deluded crew. It is my task to disappoint his mistress, as he terms her, though it must be confessed that she does not sleep at her post."

During the ten succeeding minutes, our foiled adventurer had leisure, no less than motive, to feel how necessary is success to any project whose means admit of dispute. Had the hawser been cut and the brigantine stranded, it is probable that the undertaking of the captain would have been accounted among those happy expedients which, in all pursuits, are thought to distinguish the mental efforts of men particularly gifted by Nature; while, under the actual circumstances, he who would have reaped all the credit of so felicitous an idea, was mentally chafing with the apprehension that his unlucky design might become known. His companion was no other than Robert Yarn, the fore-top-man, who, on a former occasion, had been heard to affirm, that he had already enjoyed so singular a view of the lady of the brigantine, while assisting to furl the fore-top-sail of the Coquette.

"This has been a false board, Master Yarn," observed the captain, when the skiff was past the entrance of the Cove, and some distance down the bay; "for the credit of our cruise, we will not enter the occurrence in the log. You understand me, Sir: I trust a word is sufficient for so shrewd a wit?"

"I hope I know my duty, your Honor, which is to obey orders, though it may break owners," returned the top-man. "Cutting a hawser with a knife is but slow work in the best of times; but though one who has little right to speak in the pres-

ence of a gentleman so well taught, it is my opinion that the steel is not yet sharp-
ened which is to part any rope aboard yon rover, without the consent of the
black-looking woman under her bowsprit."

"And what is the opinion of the berth-deck concerning this strange brigantine, that we have so long been following without success?"

"That we shall follow her till the last biscuit is eaten, and the scuttle-butt shall
be dry, with no better fortune. It is not my business to teach your Honor; but
there is not a man in the ship, who ever expects to be a farthing the better for her
capture. Men are of many minds concerning the 'Skimmer of the Seas;' but all are
agreed that, unless aided by some uncommon luck, which may amount to the
same thing as being helped by him who seldom lends a hand to any honest
undertaking, that he is altogether such a seaman as another like him does not sail
the ocean!"

"I am sorry that my people should have reason to think so meanly of our
own skill. The ship has not yet had a fair chance. Give her an open sea, and a cap-
full of wind, and she'll defy all the black women that the brigantine can stow. As
to your 'Skimmer of the Seas,' man or devil, he is our prisoner."

"And does your Honor believe that the trim-built and light-sailing gentleman we overhauled in this skiff, is in truth that renowned rover?" asked Yarn,
resting on his sculls, in the interest of the moment. "There are some on board the
ship, who maintain that the man in question is taller than the big tide-waiter at
Plymouth, with a pair of shoulders —"

"I have reason to know they are mistaken. If we are more enlightened than
our shipmates, Master Yarn, let us be close-mouthed, that others do not steal our
knowledge — hold, here is a crown with the face of King Louis; he is our bitterest
enemy, and you may swallow him whole, if you please, or take him in morsels, as
shall best suit your humor. But remember that our cruise in the skiff is under
secret orders, and the less we say about the anchor-watch of the brigantine, the
better."

Honest Bob took the piece of silver, with a gusto that no opinions of the
marvellous could diminish; and, touching his hat, he did not fail to make the usual
protestations of discretion. That night the messmates of the fore-top-man
endeavored, in vain, to extract from him the particulars of his excursion with the
captain; though the direct answers to their home questions were only evaded by
allusions so dark and ambiguous, as to give to that superstitious feeling of the crew,
which Ludlow had wished to lull, twice its original force.

Not long after this short dialogue, the skiff reached the side of the Coquette.

Her commander found his prisoner in possession of his own cabin, and, though grave if not sad in demeanor, perfectly self-possessed. His arrival had produced a deep effect on the officers and men, though, like Yarn, most of both classes refused to believe that the handsome and gayly-attired youth they had been summoned to receive, was the notorious dealer in contraband.

Light observers of the forms under which human qualities are exhibited, too often mistake their outward signs. Though it is quite in reason to believe, that he who mingles much in rude and violent scenes should imbibe some of their rough and repelling aspects, still it would seem that, as the stillest waters commonly conceal the deepest currents, so the powers to awaken extraordinary events are not unfrequently cloaked under a chastened, and sometimes under a cold, exterior. It has often happened, that the most desperate and self-willed men are those whose mien and manners would give reason to expect the mildest and most tractable dispositions; while he who has seemed a lion sometimes proves, in his real nature, to be little better than a lamb.

Ludlow had reason to see that the incredulity of his top-man had extended to most on board; and, as he could not conquer his tenderness on the subject of Alida and all that concerned her, while on the other hand there existed no motive for immediately declaring the truth, he rather favored the general impression by his silence. First giving some orders of the last importance at that moment, he passed into the cabin, and sought a private interview with his captive.

"That vacant state-room is at your service, Master Seadrift," he observed, pointing to the little apartment opposite to the one he occupied himself.

"We are likely to be shipmates several days, unless you choose to shorten the time, by entering into a capitulation for the Water-Witch; in which case —"

"You had a proposition to make."

Ludlow hesitated, cast an eye behind him, to be certain they were alone, and drew nearer to his captive.

"Sir, I will deal with you as becomes a seaman. La belle Barbérie is dearer to me than ever woman was before — dearer, I fear, than ever woman will be again. You need not learn that circumstances nave occurred — Do you love the lady?"

"I do."

"And she — fear not to trust the secret to one who will not abuse the trust — returns she your affection?"

The mariner of the brigantine drew back with dignity; and then, instantly recovering his ease, as if fearful he might forget himself, he said with warmth.

"This trifling with woman's weakness is the besetting sin of man! None may speak of her inclinations, Captain Ludlow, but herself. It never shall be said, that any of the sex had aught but fitting reverence for their dependent state, their constant and confiding love, their faithfulness in all the world's trials, and their singleness of heart, from me."

"These sentiments do you honor; and I could wish, for your own sake, as well as that of others, there was less of contrariety in your character. One cannot but grieve —"

"You had a proposition, for the brigantine?"

"I would have said, that were the vessel yielded without further pursuit, means might be found to soften the blow to those who will otherwise be most wounded by her capture."

The face of the dealer in contraband had lost some of its usual brightness and animation; the color of the cheek was not as rich, and the eye was less at ease, than in his former interviews with Ludlow. But a smile of security crossed his fine features, when the other spoke of the fate of the brigantine.

"The keel of the ship that is to capture the Water-Witch is not yet laid," he said, firmly; "nor is the canvas that is to drive her through the water, wove! Our mistress is not so heedless as to sleep, when there is most occasion for her services."

"This mummery of a supernatural aid may be of use in holding the minds of the ignorant beings who follow your fortunes, in subjection, but it is lost when addressed to me. I have ascertained the position of the brigantine — nay, I have been under her very bowsprit, and so near her cut-water, as to have examined her moorings. Measures are now taking to improve my knowledge, and to secure the prize."

The free-trader heard him without exhibiting alarm, though he listened with an attention that rendered his breathing audible.

"You found my people vigilant?" he rather carelessly observed, than asked.

"So much so, that I have said the skiff was pulled beneath her martingale, without a hail! Had there been means, it would not have required many moments to cut the hawser by which she rides, and to have laid your beauteous vessel ashore!"

The gleam of Seadrift's eye was like the glance of an eagle. It seemed to inquire, and to resent, in the same instant. Ludlow shrunk from the piercing look, and reddened to the brow — whether with his recollections, or not, it is unnecessary to explain.

"The worthy device was thought of! — nay, it was attempted!" exclaimed the other, gathering confirmation in the consciousness of his companion. — "You did not — you could not succeed!"

"Our success will be proved in the result."

"The lady of the brigantine forgot not her charge! You saw her bright eye — her dark and meaning face! Light shone on that mysterious countenance — my words are true, Ludlow, thy tongue is silent, but that honest countenance confesses all!"

The gay dealer in contraband turned away, and laughed in his merriest manner.

"I knew it would be so," he continued, "what is the absence of one humble actor from her train. Trust me, you will find her coy as ever, and ill-disposed to hold converse with a cruiser who speaks so rudely through his cannon. Ha! — here are auditors!"

An officer, to announce the near approach of a boat, entered. Both Ludlow and his prisoner started at this intelligence, and it was not difficult to fancy both believed that a message from the Water-Witch might be expected. The former hastened on deck; while the latter, notwithstanding a self-possession that was so much practised, could not remain entirely at his ease. He passed into the state-room, and it is more than probable that he availed himself of the window of its quarter-gallery, to reconnoitre those who were so unexpectedly coming to the ship.

But after the usual hail and reply, Ludlow no longer anticipated any proposal from the brigantine. The answer had been what a seaman would call lubberly; or it wanted that attic purity that men of the profession rarely fail to use on all occasions, and by the means of which they can tell a pretender to their mysteries, with a quickness that is almost instinctive. When the short, quick "boat-ahoy!" of the sentinel on the gangway, was answered by the "what do you want?" of a startled respondent in the boat, it was received among the crew of the Coquette with such a sneer as the tyro, who has taken two steps in any particular branch of knowledge, is apt to bestow on the blunders of him who has taken but one.

A deep silence reigned, while a party consisting of two men and as many females mounted the side of the ship, leaving a sufficient number of forms behind them in the boat to man its oars. Notwithstanding more than one light was held in such a manner as would have discovered the faces of the strangers had they not all been closely muffled, the party passed into the cabin without recognition.

"Master Cornelius Ludlow, one might as well put on the Queen's livery at once, as to be steering in this uncertain manner, between the Coquette and the land, like a protested note sent from endorser to endorser, to be paid," commenced Alderman Van Beverout, uncasing himself in the great cabin with the coolest deliberation, while his niece sunk into a chair unbidden, her two attendants standing near in submissive silence. "Here is Alida, who has insisted on paying so unseasonable a visit, and, what is worse still, on dragging me in her train, though I am past the day of following a woman about, merely because she happens to have a pretty face. The hour is unseasonable, and as to the motive — why, if Master Seadrift has got a little out of his course, no great harm can come of it, while the affair is in the hands of so discreet and amiable an officer as yourself."

The Alderman became suddenly mute; for the door of the state-room opened, and the individual he had named entered in person.

Ludlow needed no other explanation than a knowledge of the persons of his guests, to understand the motive of their visit. Turning to Alderman Van Beverout, he said, with a bitterness he could not repress —

"My presence may be intrusive. Use the cabin as freely as your own house, and rest assured that while it is thus honored, it shall be sacred to its present uses. My duty calls me to the deck."

The young man bowed gravely, and hurried from the place. As he passed Alida, he caught a gleam of her dark and eloquent eye, and he construed the glance into an expression of gratitude.

CHAPTER XXVI.

"If it were done when 'tis done, then 'twere well
It were done quickly —"

Macbeth.

THE words of the immortal poet, with which, in deference to an ancient usage in the literature of the language, we have prefaced the incidents to be related in this chapter, are in perfect conformity with that governing maxim of a vessel, which is commonly found embodied in its standing orders, and which prescribes the necessity of exertion and activity in the least of its operations. A strongly-manned ship, like a strong-armed man, is fond of showing its physical power, for it is one of the principal secrets of its efficiency. In a profession in which there is an unceasing contest with the wild and fickle winds, and in which human efforts are to be manifested in the control of a delicate and fearful machinery on an inconstant element, this governing principle becomes of the last importance. Where 'delay may so easily be death,' it soon gets to be a word that is expunged from the language; and there is perhaps no truth more necessary to be known to all young aspirants for naval success, than that, while nothing should be attempted in a hurry, nothing should be done without the last degree of activity that is compatible with precision.

The commander of the Coquette had early been impressed with the truth of the foregoing rule, and he had not neglected its application in the discipline of his crew. When he reached the deck, therefore, after relinquishing the cabin to his visiters, he found those preparations which he had ordered to be commenced when he first returned to the ship, already far advanced towards their execution. As these movements are closely connected with the future events it is our duty to explain, we shall relate them with some particularity.

Ludlow had no sooner given his orders to the officer in charge of the deck, than the whistle of the boatswain was heard summoning all hands to their duty. When the crew had been collected, tackles were hooked to the large boats stowed in the centre of the ship, and the whole of them were lowered into the water. The descent of those suspended on the quarters, was of course less difficult and much sooner effected. So soon as all the boats, with the exception of one at the stern, were out, the order was given to 'cross top-gallant-yards.' This duty had been commenced while other things were in the course of performance, and a minute had scarcely passed before the upper masts were again in possession of their light sails. Then was heard the usual summons of, 'all hands up anchor, ahoy!' and the rapid orders of the young officers to 'man capstan-bars,' to 'nipper,' and finally to 'heave away.' The business of getting the anchor on board a cruiser and on board a ship engaged in commerce, is of very different degrees of labor, as well as of expedition. In the latter, a dozen men apply their powers to a slow-moving and reluctant windlass, while the untractable cable, as it enters, is broken into coils by the painful efforts of a grumbling cook, thwarted, perhaps, as much as he is aided by the waywardness of some wilful urchin who does the service of the cabin. On the other hand, the upright and constantly-moving capstan knows no delay. The revolving 'messenger' is ever ready to be applied, and skilful petty officers are always in the tiers, to dispose of the massive rope, that it may not encumber the decks.

Ludlow appeared among his people, while they were thus employed. Ere he had made one hasty turn on the quarter-deck, he was met by the busy first-lieutenant.

"We are short, Sir," said that agent of all work.

"Set your top-sails."

The canvas was instantly permitted to fall, and it was no sooner stretched to the yards, than force was applied to the halyards, and the sails were hoisted.

"Which way, Sir, do you wish the ship cast?" demanded the attentive Luff.

"To seaward."

The head-yards were accordingly braced aback in the proper direction, and it was then reported to the captain that all was ready to get the ship under way.

"Trip the anchor at once, Sir; when it is stowed, and the decks are cleared, report to me."

This sententious and characteristic communication between Ludlow and his second in command, was sufficient for all the purposes of that moment. The one was accustomed to issue his orders without explanation, and the other never hesitated to obey, and rarely presumed to inquire into their motive.

"We are aweigh and stowed, Sir; every thing clear," said Mr. Luff, after a few minutes had been allowed to execute the preceding commands.

Ludlow then seemed to arouse himself from a deep reverie. He had hitherto spoken mechanically, rather than as one conscious of what he uttered, or whose feelings had any connexion with his words. But it was now necessary to mingle with his officers and to issue mandates that, as they were less in routine, required both thought and discretion. The crews of the different boats were 'called away,' and arms were placed in their hands. When nearly or quite one-half of the ship's company were in the boats, and the latter were all reported to be ready, officers were assigned to each, and the particular service expected at their hands was distinctly explained.

A master's mate in the captain's barge, with the crew strengthened by half-a-dozen marines, was ordered to pull directly for the Cove, into which he was to enter with muffled oars, and where he was to await a signal from the first-lieutenant, unless he met the brigantine endeavoring to escape, in which case his orders were imperative to board and carry her at every hazard. The high-spirited youth no sooner received this charge, than he quitted the ship and steered to the southward, keeping inside the tongue of land so often named.

Luff was then told to take command of the launch. With this heavy and strongly-manned boat, he was ordered to proceed to the inlet, where he was to give the signal to the barge, and whence he was to go to the assistance of the latter, so soon as he was assured the Water-Witch could not again escape by the secret passage.

The two cutters were intrusted to the command of the second-lieutenant, with orders to pull into the broad passage between the end of the cape, or the 'Hook,' and that long narrow island which stretches from the harbor of New-York for more than forty leagues to the eastward, sheltering the whole coast of Connecticut from the tempests of the ocean. Ludlow knew, though ships of a heavy draught were obliged to pass close to the cape, in order to gain the open sea, that a light brigantine, like the Water-Witch, could find a sufficient depth of water for her purposes further north. The cutters were, therefore, sent in that direction, with orders to cover as much of the channel as possible, and to carry the smuggler should an occasion offer. Finally, the yawl was to occupy the space between the two channels, with orders to repeat signals, and to be vigilant in reconnoitring.

While the different officers intrusted with these duties were receiving their instructions, the ship, under the charge of Trysail, began to move towards the cape. When off the point of the Hook, the two cutters and the yawl 'cast off,' and took to their oars, and when fairly without the buoys, the launch did the same, each boat taking its prescribed direction.

If the reader retains a distinct recollection of the scene described in one of the earlier pages of this work, he will understand the grounds on which Ludlow based his hopes of success. By sending the launch into the inlet, he believed he should inclose the brigantine on every side; since her escape through either of the ordinary channels would become impossible, while he kept the Coquette in the offing. The service he expected from the three boats sent to the northward, was to trace the movement of the smuggler, and, should a suitable opportunity offer, to attempt to carry him by surprise.

When the launch parted from the ship, the Coquette came slowly up to the wind, and with her fore-top-sail thrown to the mast, she lay, waiting to allow her boats the time necessary to reach their several stations. The different expeditions had reduced the force of the crew quite one-half, and as both the lieutenants were otherwise employed, there now remained on board no officer of a rank between those of the captain and Trysail. Some time after the vessel had been stationary, and the men had been ordered to keep close, or, in other words, to dispose of their persons as they pleased, with a view to permit them to catch 'cat's naps,' as some compensation for the loss of their regular sleep, the latter approached his superior, who stood gazing over the hammock-cloths in the direction of the Cove, and spoke.

"A dark night, smooth water, and fresh hands make boating agreeable duty!" he said. "The gentlemen are in fine heart, and full of young men's hopes; but he who lays that brigantine aboard, will, in my poor judgment, have more work to do than merely getting up her side. I was in the foremost boat that boarded a Spaniard in the Mona, last war; and though we went into her with light heels, some of us were brought out with broken heads. — I think the fore-top-gallant-mast has a better set, Captain Ludlow, since we gave the last pull at the rigging?"

"It stands well;" returned his half-attentive commander. "Give it the other drag, if you think best."

"Just as you please, Sir; 'tis all one to me. I care not if the mast is hove all of one side, like the hat on the head of a country buck; but when a thing is as it ought to be, reason would tell us to let it alone. Mr. Luff was of opinion, that by altering the slings of the main-yard, we should give a better set to the top-sail sheets; but it was little that could be done with the stick aloft, and I am ready to pay Her Majesty the difference between the wear of the sheets as they stand now, and as Mr. Luff would have them, out of my own pocket, though it is often as empty as a parish church in which a fox-hunting parson preaches. I was present, once, when a real tally-ho was reading the service, and one of your godless squires got in the wake of a fox, with his hounds, within hail of the church-windows! The cries had some such effect on my roarer, as a puff of wind would have on this ship; that is to say, he sprung his luff, and though he kept on muttering something I never knew what, his eyes were in the fields the whole time the pack was in view. But this wasn't the worst of it; for when he got fairly back to his work again, the wind had been blowing the leaves of his book about, and he plumped us into the middle of the marriage ceremony. I am no great lawyer, but there were those who said it was a god-send that half the young men in the parish weren't married to their own grandmothers!"

"I hope the match was agreeable to the family," said Ludlow, relieving one elbow by resting the weight of his head on the other.

"Why, as to that, I will not take upon me to say since the clerk corrected the parson's reckoning before the mischief was entirely done. There has been a little dispute between me and the first-lieutenant, Captain Ludlow, concerning the trim of the ship. He maintains that we have got too much in forward of what he calls the centre of gravity; and he is of opinion that had we been less by the head, the smuggler would never have had the heels of us, in the chase; whereas I invite any man to lay a craft on her water-line —"

"Show our light!" interrupted Ludlow. "Yonder goes the signal of the launch!"

Trysail ceased speaking, and, stepping on a gun, he also began to gaze in the direction of the Cove. A lantern, or some other bright object, was leisurely raised three times, and as often hid from view. The signal came from under the land, and in a quarter that left no doubt of its object.

"So far, well;" cried the Captain, quitting his stand, and turning, for the first time, with consciousness, to his officer. "'Tis a sign that they are at the inlet, and that the offing is clear. I think, Master Trysail, we are now sure of our prize. Sweep the horizon thoroughly with the night-glass, and then we will close upon this boasted brigantine."

Both took glasses, and devoted several minutes to this duty. A careful examination of the margin of the sea, from the coast of New-Jersey to that of Long-Island, gave them reason to believe that nothing of any size was lying without the cape. The sky was more free from clouds to the eastward than under the land and it was not difficult to make certain of this important fact. It gave them the assurance that the Water-Witch had not escaped by the secret passage, during the time lost in their own preparations.

"This is still well;" continued Ludlow. "Now he cannot avoid us — show the triangle."

Three lights, disposed in the form just named were then hoisted at the gaff-end of the Coquette. It was an order for the boats in the Cove to proceed. The signal was quickly answered from the launch, and then a small rocket was seen sailing over the trees and shrubbery of the shore. All on board the Coquette lis-

tened intently, to catch some sound that should denote the tumult of an assault.
Once Ludlow and Trysail thought the cheers of seamen came on the thick air of
the night; and once, again, either fancy or their senses told them they heard the
menacing hail which commanded the outlaws to submit. Many minutes of
intense anxiety succeeded. The whole of the hammock-cloths on the side of the
ship nearest to the land were lined with curious faces, though respect left Ludlow
to the sole occupation of the short and light deck which covered the accommodations; whither he had ascended, to command a more perfect view of the
horizon.

"'Tis time to hear their musketry, or to see the signal of success!" said the
young man to himself, so intently occupied by his interest in the undertaking, as
to be unconscious of having spoken.

"Have you forgotten to provide a signal for failure?" said one at his elbow.

"Ha! Master Seadrift — I would have spared you this spectacle."

"'Tis one too often witnessed, to be singular. A life passed on the ocean has
not left me ignorant of the effect of night, with a view seaward, a dark coast, and a
back-ground of mountain!"

"You have confidence in him left in charge of your brigantine! I shall have
faith in your sea-green lady, myself, if he escape my boats, this time."

"See! — there is a token of her fortune;" returned the other, pointing
towards three lanterns that were shown at the inlet's mouth, and over which many
lights were burnt in rapid succession.

"'Tis of failure! Let the ship fall-of, and square away the yards! Round in,
men, round in. We will run down to the entrance of the bay, Mr. Trysail. The
knaves have been aided by their lucky star!"

Ludlow spoke with deep vexation in his tones, but always with the authority
of a superior and the promptitude of a seaman. The motionless being, near him,
maintained a profound silence. No exclamation of triumph escaped him, nor did
he open his lips either in pleasure or in surprise. It appeared as if confidence in his
vessel rendered him as much superior to exultation as to apprehension.

"You look upon this exploit of your brigantine, Master Seadrift, as a thing of
course;" Ludlow observed, when his own ship was steering towards the extremity
of the cape, again. "Fortune has not deserted you, yet; but with the land on three
sides, and this ship and her boats on the fourth, I do not despair yet of prevailing
over your bronzed goddess!"

"Our mistress never sleeps;" returned the dealer in contraband, drawing a
long breath, like one who had struggled long to repress his interest.

"Terms are still in your power. I shall not conceal that the Commissioners of Her Majesty's customs set so high a price on the possession of the Water-Witch, as to embolden me to assume a responsibility from which I might, on any other occasion, shrink. Deliver the vessel, and I pledge you the honor of an officer that the crew shall land without question. — Leave her to us, with empty decks and a swept hold, if you will — but, leave the swift boat in our hands."

"The lady of the brigantine thinks otherwise. She wears her mantle of the deep waters, and, trust me, spite of all your nets, she will lead her followers beyond the offices of the lead, and far from soundings — ay! spite of all the navy of Queen Anne!"

"I hope that others may not repent this obstinacy! But this is no time to bandy words; the duty of the ship requires my presence."

Seadrift took the hint, and reluctantly retired to the cabin. As he left the poop, the moon rose above the line of water in the eastern board, and shed its light along the whole horizon. The crew of the Coquette were now enabled to see, with sufficient distinctness, from the sands of the Hook to the distance of many leagues to seaward. There no longer remained a doubt that the brigantine was still within the bay. Encouraged by this certainty, Ludlow endeavored to forget all motives of personal feeling, in the discharge of a duty that was getting to be more and more interesting, as the prospect of its successful accomplishment grew brighter.

It was not long before the Coquette reached the channel which forms the available mouth of the estuary. Here the ship was again brought to the wind, and men were sent upon the yards and all her more lofty spars, in order to overlook, by the dim and deceitful light, as much of the inner water as the eye could reach; while Ludlow, assisted by the master, was engaged in the same employment on the deck. Two or three midshipmen were included, among the common herd, aloft.

"There is nothing visible within," said the captain after a long and anxious search, with a glass. "The shadow of the Jersey mountains prevents the sight in that direction, while the spars of a frigate might be confounded with the trees of Staten Island, here, in the northern board. — Cross-jack-yard, there!"

The shrill voice of a midshipman answered to the hail.

"What do you make within the Hook, Sir?"

"Nothing visible. Our barge is pulling along the land, and the launch appears to be lying off the inlet; ay — here is the yawl, resting on its oars without the Romar; but we can find nothing which looks like the cutter, in the range of Coney."

"Take another sweep of the glass more westward, and look well into the mouth of the Raritan — mark you any thing in that quarter?"

"Ha! — here is a speck on our lee quarter!"

"What do you make of it?"

"Unless sight deceives me greatly, Sir, there is a light boat pulling in for the ship, about three cables' length distant"

Ludlow raised his own glass, and swept the water in the direction named. After one or two unsuccessful trials, his eye caught the object; and as the moon had now some power, he was at no loss to distinguish its character. There was evidently a boat, and one that, by its movements, had a design of holding communication with the cruiser.

The eye of a seaman is acute on his element, and his mind is quick in forming opinions on all things that properly appertain to his profession. Ludlow saw instantly, by the construction, that the boat was not one of those sent from the ship; that it approached in a direction which enabled it to avoid the Coquette, by keeping in a part of the bay where the water was not sufficiently deep to admit of her passage; and that its movements were so guarded as to denote great caution, while there was an evident wish to draw as near to the cruiser as prudence might render advisable. Taking a trumpet, he hailed in the well-known and customary manner.

The answer came up faintly against the air, but it was uttered with much practice in the implement, and with an exceeding compass of voice.

"Ay, ay!" and, "a parley from the brigantine!" were the only words that were distinctly audible.

For a minute or two, the young man paced the deck in silence. Then he suddenly commanded the only boat which the cruiser now possessed, to be lowered and manned.

"Throw an ensign into the stern-sheets," he said when these orders were executed; "and let there be arms beneath it. We will keep faith while faith is observed, but there are reasons for caution in this interview."

Trysail was directed to keep the ship stationary, and after giving to his subordinate private instructions of importance in the event of treachery, Ludlow went into the boat in person. A very few minutes sufficed to bring the jolly-boat and the stranger so near each other, that the means of communication were both easy and sure. The men of the former were then commanded to cease rowing, and, raising his glass, the commander of the cruiser took a more certain and minute survey of those who awaited his coming. The strange boat was dancing on the waves, like a light shell that floated so buoyantly as scarce to touch the element which sustained it, while four athletic seamen leaned on the oars which lay ready to urge it ahead. In the stern-sheets stood a form, whose attitude and mien could not readily be mistaken. In the admirable steadiness of the figure, the folded arms, the fine and manly proportions, and the attire, Ludlow recognized the mariner of the India-shawl. A wave of the hand induced him to venture nearer.

"What is asked of the royal cruiser?" demanded the captain of the vessel named, when the two boats were as near each other as seemed expedient.

"Confidence!" was the calm reply. — "Come nearer Captain Ludlow; I am here with naked hands! Our conference need not be maintained with trumpets."

Ashamed that a boat belonging to a ship of war should betray doubts, the people of the yawl were ordered to go within reach of the oars.

"Well, Sir, you have your wish. I have quitted my ship, and come to the parley, with the smallest of my boats."

"It is unnecessary to say what has been done with the others!" returned Tiller, across the firm muscles of whose face there passed a smile that was scarcely perceptible. "You hunt us hard, Sir, and give but little rest to the brigantine. But again are you foiled!"

"We have a harbinger of better fortune, in a lucky blow that has been struck tonight."

"You are understood, Sir; Master Seadrift has fallen into the hands of the Queen's servants — but take good heed! if injury, in word or deed, befall that youth, there live those who well know how to resent the wrong!"

"These are lofty expressions, to come from a proscribed man; but we will overlook them, in the motive. Your brigantine, Master Tiller, lost its master spirit in the 'Skimmer of the Seas,' and it may be wise to listen to the suggestions of moderation. If you are disposed to treat, I am here with no disposition to extort."

"We meet in a suitable spirit, then; for I come prepared to offer terms of ransom, that Queen Anne, if she love her revenue, need not despise — but, as in duty to Her Majesty, I will first listen to her royal pleasure."

"First, then, as a seaman, and one who is not ignorant of what a vessel can perform, let me direct your attention to the situation of the parties. I am certain that the Water-Witch, though for the moment concealed by the shadows of the hills, or favored perhaps by distance and the feebleness of this light, is in the waters of the bay. A force, against which she has no power of resistance, watches the inlet; you see the cruiser in readiness to meet her off the Hook. My boats are so stationed as to preclude the possibility of escape, without sufficient notice, by the northern channel; and, in short, the outlets are all closed to your passage. With the morning light, we shall know your position, and act accordingly."

"No chart can show the dangers of rocks and shoals more clearly! — and to avoid these dangers — ?"

"Yield the brigantine, and depart. Though outlawed, we shall content ourselves with the possession of the remarkable vessel in which you do your mischief, and hope that, deprived of the means to err, you will return to better courses."

"With the prayers of the church for our amendment! Now listen, Captain Ludlow, to what I offer. You have the person of one much loved by all who follow the lady of the sea-green mantle, in your power; and we have a brigantine that does much injury to Queen Anne's supremacy in the waters of this hemisphere — yield you the captive, and we promise to quit this coast, never to return."

"This were a worthy treaty, truly, for one whose habitation is not a madhouse! Relinquish my right over the principal doer of the evil, and receive the unsupported pledge of a subordinate's word! Your happy fortune, Master Tiller, has troubled your reason. What I offer, was offered because I would not drive an unfortunate and remarkable man, like him we have, to extremities, and — there may be other motives, but do not mistake my lenity. Should force become necessary to put your vessel into our hands, the law may view your offences with a still harsher eye. Deeds which the lenity of our system now considers as venial, may easily turn to crime!"

"I ought not to take your distrust, as other than excusable," returned the smuggler, evidently suppressing a feeling of haughty and wounded pride. "The word of a free-trader should have little weight in the ears of a queen's officer. We have been trained in different schools, and the same objects are seen in different colors. Your proposal has been heard, and, with some thanks for its fair intentions, it is refused without a hope of acceptation. Our brigantine is, as you rightly think, a remarkable vessel! Her equal, Sir, for beauty or speed, floats not the ocean. By heaven! I would sooner slight the smiles of the fairest woman that walks the earth, than entertain a thought which should betray the interest I feel in that jewel of naval skill! You have seen her, at many times, Captain Ludlow — in squalls and calms; with her wings abroad, and her pinions shut; by day and night; near and far; fair and foul — and I ask you, with a seaman's frankness, is she not a toy to fill a seaman's heart?"

"I deny not the vessel's merits, nor her beauty — 'tis a pity she bears no better reputation."

"I knew you could not withhold this praise! But I grow childish when there is question of that brigantine! Well Sir, each has been heard, and now comes the conclusion. I part with the apple of my eye, ere a stick of that lovely fabric is willingly deserted. Shall we make other ransom for the youth? — What think you of a pledge in gold, to be forfeited should we forget our word."

"You ask impossibilities. In treating thus at all, I quit the path of proud authority, because, as has been said, there is that about the 'Skimmer of the Seas' that raises him above the coarse herd who in common traffic against the law. The brigantine, or nothing!"

"My life, before that brigantine! Sir, you forget our fortunes are protected by one who laughs at the efforts of your fleet; You think that we are inclosed and that, when light shall return, there will remain merely the easy task to place your iron-mounted cruiser on our beam, and drive us to seek mercy. Here are honest mariners, who could tell you of the hopelessness of the expedient. The Water-Witch has run the gauntlet of all your navies, and shot has never yet defaced her beauty."

"And yet her limbs have been known to fall before a messenger from my ship!"

"The stick wanted the commission of our mistress," interrupted the other, glancing his eye at the credulous and attentive crew of the boat. "In a thoughtless moment, 'twas taken up at sea, and fashioned to our purpose without counsel from the book. Nothing that touches our decks, under fitting advice, comes to harm. — You look incredulous, and 'tis in character to seem so. If you refuse to listen to the lady of the brigantine, at least lend an ear to your own laws. Of what offence can you charge Master Seadrift, that you hold him captive?"

"His redoubted name of 'Skimmer of the Seas' were warranty to force him from a sanctuary," returned Ludlow, smiling. "Though proof should fail of any immediate crime, there is impunity for the arrest, since the law refuses to protect him."

"This is your boasted justice! Rogues in authority combine to condemn an absent and a silent man. But if you think to do your violence with impunity, know there are those who take deep interest in the welfare of that youth."

"This is foolish bandying of menaces," said the captain, warmly. "If you accept my offers, speak; and if you reject them, abide the consequences."

"I abide the consequences. But since we cannot come to terms, as victor and the submitting party, we may part in amity. Touch my hand, Captain Ludlow, as one brave man should salute another, though the next minute they are to grapple at the throat."

Ludlow hesitated. The proposal was made with so frank and manly a mien, and the air of the free-trader, as he leaned beyond the gunwale of his boat, was so superior to his pursuit, that, unwilling to seem churlish, or to be outdone in courtesy, he reluctantly consented, and laid his palm within that the other offered. The smuggler profited by the junction to draw the boats nearer, and, to the amazement of all who witnessed the action, he stepped boldly into the yawl, and was seated, face to face, with its officer in a moment.

"These are matters that are not fit for every ear," said the decided and confident mariner, in an under tone, when he had made this sudden change in the position of the parties. "Deal with me frankly, Captain Ludlow — is your prisoner left to brood on his melancholy, or does he feel the consolation of knowing that others take an interest in his welfare?"

"He does not want for sympathy, Master Tiller — since he has the pity of the finest woman in America."

"Ha! la belle Barbérie owns her esteem! — is the conjecture right?"

"Unhappily, you are too near the truth. The infatuated girl seems but to live in his presence. She has so far forgotten the opinions of others, as to follow him to my ship!"

Tiller listened intently, and, from that instant, all concern disappeared from his countenance.

"He who is thus favored may, for a moment, even forget the brigantine!" he exclaimed, with all his natural recklessness of air. "And the Alderman — ?"

"Has more discretion than his niece, since he did not permit her to come alone."

"Enough. — Captain Ludlow, let what will follow. We part as friends. Fear not, Sir, to touch the hand of a proscribed man, again; it is honest after its own fashion, and many is the peer and prince who keeps not so clean a palm. Deal tenderly with that gay and rash young sailor; he wants the discretion of an older head, but the heart is kindness itself — I would hazard life, to shelter his — but at every hazard the brigantine must be saved. — Adieu!"

There was strong emotion in the voice of the mariner of the shawl, notwithstanding his high bearing. Squeezing the hand of Ludlow, he passed back into his own barge, with the ease and steadiness of one who made the ocean his home.

"Adieu!" he repeated, signing to his men to pull in the direction of the shoals, where it was certain the ship could not follow. "We may meet again; until then, adieu."

"We are sure to meet, with the return of light."

"Believe it not, brave gentleman. Our lady will thrust the spars under her girdle, and pass a fleet unseen. — A sailor's blessing on you — fair winds and a plenty; a safe landfall, and a cheerful home! Deal kindly by the boy, and, in all but evil wishes to my vessel, success light on your ensign!"

The seamen of both boats dashed their oars into the water at the same instant, and the two parties were quickly without the hearing of the voice.

CHAPTER XXVII.

" — Did I tell this,
Who would believe me?"
Measure for Measure.

THE time of the interview related in the close of the preceding chapter, was in the early watches of the night. It now becomes our duty to transport the reader to another, that had place several hours later, and after day had dawned on the industrious burghers of Manhattan.

There stood, near one of the wooden wharves which lined the arm of the sea on which the city is so happily placed, a dwelling around which there was every sign that its owner was engaged in a retail commerce, that was active and thriving, for that age and country. Notwithstanding the earliness of the hour, the windows of this house were open; and an individual, of a busy-looking face, thrust his head so often from one of the casements, as to show that he already expected the appearance of a second party in the affair that had probably called him from his bed, even sooner than common. A tremendous rap at the door relieved his visible uneasiness; and, hastening to open it, he received his visiter, with much parade of ceremony, and many protestations of respect, in person.

"This is an honor, my lord, that does not often befall men of my humble condition," said the master of the house, in the flippant utterance of a vulgar cockney; "but I thought it would be more agreeable to your lordship, to receive the a — a — here, than in the place where your lordship, just at this moment, resides. Will your lordship please to rest yourself, after your lordship's walk?"

"I thank you, Carnaby," returned the other, taking the offered seat, with an air of easy superiority. "You judge with your usual discretion, as respects the place, though I doubt the prudence of seeing him at all. Has the man come?"

"Doubtless, my lord; he would hardly presume to keep your lordship waiting, and much less would I countenance him in so gross a disrespect. He will be most happy to wait on you, my lord, whenever your lordship shall please."

"Let him wait: there is no necessity for haste. He has probably communicated some of the objects of this extraordinary call on my time, Carnaby; and you can break them, in the intervening moments."

"I am sorry to say, my lord, that the fellow is as obstinate as a mule. I felt the impropriety of introducing him, personally, to your lordship; but as he insisted he had affairs that would deeply interest you, my lord, I could not take upon me to say, what would be agreeable to your lordship, or what not; and so I was bold enough to write the note."

"And a very properly expressed note it was, Master Carnaby. I have not received a better worded communication, since my arrival in this colony."

"I am sure the approbation of your lordship might justly make any man proud! It is the ambition of my life, my lord, to do the duties of my station in a proper manner, and to treat all above me with a suitable respect, my lord, and all below me as in reason bound. If I might presume to think in such a matter, my lord, I should say, that these colonists are no great judges of propriety, in their correspondence, or indeed in any thing else."

The noble visiter shrugged his shoulder, and threw an expression into his look, that encouraged the retailer to proceed.

"It is just what I think myself, my lord," he continued, simpering; "but then," he added, with a condoling and patronizing air, "how should they know any better? England is but an island, after all; and the whole world cannot be born and educated on the same bit of earth."

"'Twould be inconvenient, Carnaby, if it led to no other unpleasant consequence."

"Almost, word for word, what I said to Mrs. Carnaby myself, no later than yesterday, my lord, only vastly better expressed. 'Twould be inconvenient, said I, Mrs. Carnaby, to take in the other lodger, for every body cannot live in the same house; which covers, as it were, the ground taken in your lordship's sentiment. I ought to add, in behalf of the poor woman, that she expressed, on the same occasion, strong regrets that it is reported your lordship will be likely to quit us soon, on your return to old England."

"That is really a subject on which there is more cause to rejoice than to weep. This imprisoning, or placing within limits, so near a relative of the crown, is an affair that must have unpleasant consequences, and which offends sadly against all propriety."

"It is awful, my lord! If it be not sacrilege by the law, the greater the shame of the opposition in Parliament, who defeat so many other wholesome regulations, intended for the good of the subject."

"Faith, I am not sure I may not be driven to join them myself, bad as they are, Carnaby; for this neglect of ministers, not to call it by a worse name, might goad a man to even a more heinous measure.'

"I am sure nobody could blame your lordship, were your lordship to join any body, or any thing but the French! I have often told Mrs. Carnaby as much as that, in our frequent conversations concerning the unpleasant situation in which your lordship is just now placed."

"I had not thought the awkward transaction attracted so much notice," observed the other, evidently wincing under the allusion.

"It attracts it only in a proper and respectful way, my lord. Neither Mrs. Carnaby, nor myself, ever indulges in any of these remarks, but in the most proper and truly English manner."

"The reservation might palliate a greater error. That word proper is a prudent term, and expresses all one could wish. I had not thought you so intelligent and shrewd a man, Master Carnaby: clever in the way of business, I always knew you to be; but so apt in reason, and so matured in principle, is what I will confess I had not expected. Can you form no conjecture of the business of this man?"

"Not in the least, my lord. I pressed the impropriety of a personal interview; for, though he alluded to some business or other, I scarcely know what, with which he appeared to think your lordship had some connexion, I did not understand him, and we had like to have parted without an explanation."

"I will not see the fellow."

"Just as your lordship pleases — I am sure that, after so many little affairs have passed through my hands, I might be safely trusted with this; and I said as much — but as he positively refused to make me an agent, and he insisted that it was so much to your lordship's interests — why, I thought, my lord, that perhaps — just now —"

"Show him in."

Carnaby bowed low and submissively, and after busying himself in placing the chairs aside, and adjusting the table more conveniently for the elbow of his guest, he left the room.

"Where is the man I bid you keep in the shop?" demanded the retailer, in a coarse, authoritative voice, when without; addressing a meek and humble-looking lad, who did the duty of clerk. "I warrant me, he is left in the kitchen, and you have been idling about on the walk! A more heedless and inattentive lad than yourself is not to be found in America, and the sun never rises but I repent having signed your indentures. You shall pay for this, you —"

The appearance of the person he sought, cut short the denunciations of the obsequious grocer and the domestic tyrant. He opened the door, and, having again closed it, left his two visiters together.

Though the degenerate descendant of the great Clarendon had not hesitated

to lend his office to cloak the irregular and unlawful trade that was then so preva-
lent in the American seas, he had paid the sickly but customary deference to
virtue, of refusing on all occasions, to treat personally with its agents. Sheltered
behind his official and personal rank, he had soothed his feelings, by tacitly
believing that cupidity is less venal when its avenues are hidden, and that in protecting his station from an immediate contact with its ministers, he had discharged an important, and, for one in his situation, an imperative, duty. Unequal
to the exercise of virtue itself, he thought he had done enough in preserving some
of its seemliness. Though far from paying even this slight homage to decency, in
his more ordinary habits, his pride of rank had, on the subject of so coarse a
failing, induced him to maintain an appearance which his pride of character
would not have suggested. Carnaby was much the most degraded and the lowest
of those with whom he ever condescended to communicate directly; and even
with him there might have been some scruple, had not his necessities caused him
to stoop so far as to accept pecuniary assistance from one he both despised and
detested.

When the door opened, therefore, the lord Cornbury rose, and, determined
to bring the interview to a speedy issue, he turned to face the individual who
entered, with a mien, into which he threw all the distance and hauteur that he
thought necessary for such an object. But he encountered, in the mariner of the
India-shawl, a very different man from the flattering and obsequious grocer who
had just quitted him. Eye met eye; his gaze of authority receiving a look as steady,
if not as curious, as his own. It was evident, by the composure of the fine manly
frame he saw, that its owner rested his claims on the aristocracy of nature. The
noble forgot his acting under the influence of surprise, and his voice expressed as
much of admiration as command when he said —

"This, then, is the Skimmer of the Seas!"

"Men call me thus: if a life passed on oceans gives a claim to the title, it has
been fairly earned."

"Your character — I may say that some portions of your history, are not
unknown to me. Poor Carnaby, who is a worthy and an industrious man, with a
growing family dependent on his exertions, has entreated me to receive you, or
there might be less apology for this step than I could wish. Men of a certain rank,
Master Skimmer, owe so much to their station, that I rely on your discretion."

"I have stood in nobler presences, my lord, and found so little change by the
honor, that I am not apt to boast of what I see. Some of princely rank have found
their profit in my acquaintance."

"I do not deny your usefulness, Sir; it is only the necessity of prudence, I would urge. There has been, I believe, some sort of implied contract between us — at least, so Carnaby explains the transaction, for I rarely enter into these details, myself — by which you may perhaps feel some right to include me in the list of your customers. Men in high places must respect the laws, and yet it is not always convenient, or even useful, that they should deny themselves every indulgence, which policy would prohibit to the mass. One who has seen as much of life as yourself, needs no explanations on this head; and I cannot doubt, but our present interview will have a satisfactory termination."

The Skimmer scarce deemed it necessary to conceal the contempt that caused his lip to curl, while the other was endeavoring to mystify his cupidity; and when the speaker was done, he merely expressed an assent by a slight inclination of the head. The ex-governor saw that his attempt was fruitless, and, by relinquishing his masquerade, and yielding more to his natural propensities and tastes, he succeeded better.

"Carnaby has been a faithful agent," he continued, "and by his reports, it would seem that our confidence has not been misplaced. If fame speaks true, there is not a more dexterous navigator of the narrow seas than thyself, Master Skimmer. It is to be supposed that your correspondents on this coast, too, are as lucrative as I doubt not they are numerous."

"He who sells cheap can never want a purchaser. I think your lordship has no reason to complain of prices."

"As pointed as his compass! Well, Sir, as I am no longer master here, may I ask the object of this interview?"

"I have come to seek your interest in behalf of one who has fallen into the grasp of the Queen's officers."

"Hum — the amount of which is, that the cruiser in the bay has entrapped some careless smuggler. We are none of us immortal, and an arrest is but a legal death to men of your persuasion in commerce. Interest is a word of many meanings. It is the interest of one man to lend, and of another to borrow; of the creditor to receive, and of the debtor to avoid payment. Then there is interest at court, and interest in court — in short, you must deal more frankly, ere I can decide on the purport of your visit."

"I am not ignorant that the Queen has been pleased to name another governor over this colony, or that your creditors, my lord, have thought it prudent to take a pledge for their dues, in your person. Still, I must think, that one who stands so near the Queen in blood, and who sooner or later must enjoy both rank and fortune in the mother country, will not solicit so slight a boon as that I ask, without success. This is the reason I prefer to treat with you."

"As clear an explanation as the shrewdest casuist could desire! I admire your succinctness, Master Skimmer, and confess you for the pink of etiquette. When your fortune shall be made, I recommend the court circle as your place of retirement. Governors, creditors, Queen, and imprisonment, all as compactly placed, in the same sentence, as if it were the creed written on a thumb-nail! Well, Sir, we will suppose my interest what you wish it. — Who and what is the delinquent?"

"One named Seadrift — a useful and a pleasant youth, who passes much between me and my customers; heedless and merry in his humors, but dear to all in my brigantine, because of tried fidelity and shrewd wit. We could sacrifice the profits of the voyage, that he were free. To me he is a necessary agent, for his skill in the judgment of rich tissues, and other luxuries that compose my traffic, is exceeding; and I am better fitted to guide the vessel to her haven, and to look to her safety amid shoals and in tempests, than to deal in these trifles of female vanity."

"So dexterous a go-between should not have mistaken a tide-waiter for a customer — how befell the accident?"

"He met the barge of the Coquette at an unlucky moment, and as we had so lately been chased off the coast by the cruiser, there was no choice but to arrest him."

"The dilemma is not without embarrassment. When once his mind is settled, it is no trifle that will amuse this Mr. Ludlow. I do not know a more literal construer of his orders in the fleet — a man, Sir, who thinks words have but a single set of meanings, and who knows as little as can be imagined on the difference between a sentiment and a practice."

"He is a seaman, my lord, and he reads his instructions with a seaman's simplicity. I think none the worse of him, that he cannot be tempted from his duty; for, let us understand the right as we will, our service once taken, it becomes us all to do it faithfully."

A small red spot came and went on the cheek of the profligate Cornbury. Ashamed of his weakness, he affected to laugh at what he had heard, and continued the discourse.

"Your forbearance and charity might adorn a churchman, Master Skimmer!" he answered. "Nothing can be more true, for this is an age of moral truths, as witness the Protestant succession. Men are now expected to perform, and not to profess. Is the fellow of such usefulness that he may not be abandoned to his fate?"

"Much as I dote on my brigantine, and few men set their affections on woman with a stronger love, I would see the beauteous craft degenerate to a cutter for the Queen's revenue, before I would entertain the thought! But I will not anticipate a long and painful imprisonment for the youth, since those who are not altogether powerless already take a deep and friendly concern in his safety."

"You have overcome the Brigadier!" cried the other, in a burst of exultation, that conquered the little reserve of manner he had thought it necessary to maintain; "that immaculate and reforming representative of my royal cousin has bitten of the golden bait, and proves a true colony governor after all!"

"Lord Viscount, no. What we have to hope or what we have to fear from your successor, is to me a secret."

"Ply him with promises, Master Skimmer — set golden hopes before his imagination; set gold itself before his eyes, and you will prosper. I will pledge my expected earldom that he yields! Sir, these distant situations are like so many half-authorized mints, in which money is to be coined; and the only counterfeit is your mimic representative of Majesty. Ply him with golden hopes; if mortal, he will yield!"

"And yet, my lord, I have met men who preferred poverty and their opinions, to gold and the wishes of others."

"The dolts were lusus naturæ!" exclaimed the dissolute Cornbury, losing all his reserve in a manner that better suited his known and confirmed character. "You should have caged them, Skimmer, and profited by their dullness, to lay the curious under contribution. Don't mistake me, Sir, if I speak a little in confidence. I hope I know the difference between a gentleman and a leveller, as well as another; but trust me, this Mr. Hunter is human, and he will yield if proper appliances are used — and you expect from me — ?"

"The exercise of that influence which cannot fail of success; since there is a courtesy between men of a certain station, which causes them to overlook rivalry, in the spirit of their caste. The cousin of Queen Anne can yet obtain the liberty of one whose heaviest crime is a free trade, though he may not be able to keep his own seat in the chair of the government."

"Thus far, indeed, my poor influence may yet extend, provided the fellow be not named in any act of outlawry. I would gladly enough Mr. Skimmer end my deeds in this hemisphere, with some act of graceful mercy, if — indeed — I saw — the means —"

"They shall not be wanting. I know the law is like any other article of great price; some think that Justice holds the balance, in order to weigh her fees.

Though the profits of this hazardous and sleepless trade of mine be much over-rated, I would gladly line her scales with two hundred broad pieces, to have that youth again safe in the cabin of the brigantine."

As the 'Skimmer of the Seas' thus spoke, he drew, with the calmness of a man who saw no use in circumlocution, a heavy bag of gold from beneath his frock, and deposited it, without a second look at the treasure, on the table. When this offering was made, he turned aside, less by design than by a careless movement of the body, and, when he faced his companion again, the bag had vanished.

"Your affection for the lad is touching, Master Skimmer," returned the corrupt Cornbury; "it were a pity such friendship should be wasted. Will there be proof to insure his condemnation?"

"It may be doubted. His dealings have only been with the higher class of my customers, and with but few of them. The care I now take is more in tenderness to the youth, than with any great doubts of the result. I shall count you, my lord, among his protectors, in the event that the affair is noised?"

"I owe it to your frankness — but will Mr. Ludlow content himself with the possession of an inferior, when the principal is so near? and shall we not have a confiscation of the brigantine on our hands?"

"I charge myself with the care of all else. There was indeed a lucky escape, only the last night, as we lay at a light kedge, waiting for the return of him who has been arrested. Profiting by the possession of our skiff, the commander of the Coquette, himself, got within the sweep of my hawse — nay, he was in the act of cutting the very fastenings, when the dangerous design was discovered. 'Twould have been a fate unworthy of the Water-Witch, to be cast on shore like a drifting log, and to check her noble career by some such a seizure as that of a stranded waif!"

"You avoided the mischance?"

"My eyes are seldom shut, lord Viscount, when danger is nigh. The skiff was seen in time, and watched; for I knew that one in whom I trusted was abroad. — When the movement grew suspicious, we had our means of frightening this Mr. Ludlow from his enterprise, without recourse to violence."

"I had not thought him one to be scared from following up a business like this."

"You judged him rightly — I may say we judged him rightly. But when his boats sought us at our anchorage, the bird had flown."

"You got the brigantine to sea, in season?" observed Cornbury, not sorry to believe that the vessel was already off the coast.

"I had other business. My agent could not be thus deserted, and there were affairs to finish in the city. Our course lay up the bay."

"Ha! Master Skimmer, 'twas a bold step, and one that says little for your discretion!"

"Lord Viscount, there is safety in courage," calmly and perhaps ironically returned the other. "While the Queen's captain closed all the outlets, my little craft was floating quietly under the hills of Staten. Before the morning watch was set, she passed these wharves; and she now awaits her captain, in the broad basin that lies beyond the bend of yonder head-land."

"This is a hardiness to be condemned! A failure of wind, a change of tide, or any of the mishaps common to the sea, may throw you on the mercy of the law, and will greatly embarrass all who feel an interest in your safety."

"So far as this apprehension is connected with my welfare, I thank you much, my lord; but, trust me, many hazards have left me but little to learn in this particular. We shall run the Hell-Gate, and gain the open sea by the Connecticut Sound."

"Truly, Master Skimmer, one has need of nerves to be your confidant! Faith in a compact constitutes the beauty of social order; without it, there is no security for interests, nor any repose for character. But faith may be implied, as well as expressed; and when men in certain situations place their dependence on others who should have motives for being wary, the first are bound to respect, even to the details of a most scrupulous construction, the conditions of the covenant. Sir, I wash my hands of this transaction, if it be understood that testimony is to be accumulated against us, by thus putting your Water-Witch in danger of trial before the Admiralty."

"I am sorry that this is your decision," returned the Skimmer. "What is done, cannot be recalled, though I still hope it may be remedied. My brigantine now lies within a league of this, and 'twould be treachery to deny it. Since it is your opinion, my lord, that our contract is not valid, there is little use in its seal — the broad pieces may still be serviceable, in shielding that youth from harm."

"You are as literal in constructions, Master Skimmer, as a school-boy's version of his Virgil. There is an idiom in diplomacy, as well as in language, and one who treats so sensibly should not be ignorant of its phrases. Bless me, Sir; an hypothesis is not a conclusion, any more than a promise is a performance. That which is advanced by way of supposition, is but the ornament of reasoning, while your gold has the more solid character of demonstration. Our bargain is made."

The unsophisticated mariner regarded the noble casuist a moment, in doubt whether to acquiesce in this conclusion, or not; but ere he had decided on his course, the windows of the room were shaken violently, and then came the heavy roar of a piece of ordnance.

"The morning gun!" exclaimed Cornbury, who started at the explosion, with the sensitiveness of one unworthily employed. — "No! 'tis an hour past the rising of the sun!"

The Skimmer showed no yielding of the nerves though it was evident, by his attitude of thought and the momentary fixedness of his eye, that he foresaw danger was near. Moving to the window, he looked out on the water, and instantly drew back, like one who wanted no further evidence.

"Our bargain then is made," he said, hastily approaching the Viscount, whose hand he seized and wrung in spite of the other's obvious reluctance to allow the familiarity; "our bargain then is made. Deal fairly by the youth, and the deed will be remembered — deal treacherously, and it shall be revenged!"

For one instant longer, the Skimmer held the member of the effeminate Cornbury imprisoned; and then, raising his cap with a courtesy that appeared more in deference to himself than his companion, he turned on his heel, and with a firm but quick step he left the house.

Carnaby, who entered on the instant, found his guest in a state between resentment, surprise, and alarm. But habitual levity soon conquered other feelings, and, finding himself freed from the presence of a man who had treated him with so little ceremony, the ex-governor shook his head, like one accustomed to submit to evils he could not obviate, and assumed the ease and insolent superiority he was accustomed to maintain in the presence of the obsequious grocer.

"This may be a coral or a pearl, or any other lion — ha! do I not see the masts of a ship, moving above the roofs of yonder line of stores?"

"Well, your lordship has the quickest eye! — and the happiest way of seeing things, of any nobleman in England! Now I should have stared a quarter of an hour, before I thought of looking over the roofs of those stores, at all; and yet your lordship looks there at the very first glance."

"Is it a ship or a brig, Master Carnaby — you have the advantage of position, for I would not willingly be seen — speak quickly, dolt — is it ship, or brig?"

"My lord — 'tis a brig — or a ship — really I must ask your lordship, for I know so little of these things —"

"Nay, complaisant Master Carnaby — have an opinion of your own for one moment, if you please — there is smoke curling upward, behind those masts —"

Another rattling of windows, and a second report, removed all doubts on the subject of the firing. At the next instant, the bows of a vessel of war appeared at the opening of a ship-yard, and then came gun after gun in view, until the whole broadside and frowning battery of the Coquette were visible.

The Viscount sought no further solution of the reason why the Skimmer had left him so hurriedly. Fumbling a moment in a pocket, he drew forth a hand filled with broad pieces of gold. These he appeared about to lay upon the table; but, as it were by forgetfulness, he kept the member closed, and bidding the grocer adieu, he left the house, with as firm a resolution as was ever made by any man, conscious of having done both a weak and a wicked action, of never again putting himself in familial contact with so truckling a miscreant.

CHAPTER XXVIII.

" — What care these roarers for the name of king?"
Tempest.

THE Manhattanese will readily comprehend the situation of the two vessels; but those of our countrymen who live in distant parts of the Union, may be glad to have the localities explained.

Though the vast estuary, which receives the Hudson and so many minor streams, is chiefly made by an indentation of the continent, that portion of it which forms the port of New-York is separated from the ocean by the happy position of its islands. Of the latter, there are two, which give the general character to the basin, and even to a long line of coast; while several, that are smaller, serve as useful and beautiful accessories to the haven and to the landscape. Between the bay of Raritan and that of New-York there are two communications, one between the islands of Staten and Nassau, called the Narrows, which is the ordinary ship-channel of the port, and the other between Staten and the main, which is known by the name of the Kilns. It is by means of the latter, that vessels pass into the neighboring waters of New-Jersey, and have access to so many of the rivers of that state. But while the island of Staten does so much for the security and facilities of the port, that of Nassau produces an effect on a great extent of coast. After sheltering one-half of the harbor from the ocean, the latter approaches so near the continent as to narrow the passage between them to the length of two cables, and then stretching away eastward for the distance of a hundred miles, it forms a wide and beautiful sound. After passing a cluster of islands, at a point which lies forty leagues from the city, by another passage, vessels can gain the open sea.

The seaman will at once understand, that the tide of flood must necessarily flow into these vast estuaries from different directions. The current which enters by Sandy-Hook (the scene of so much of this tale) flows westward into the Jersey rivers, northward into the Hudson, and eastward along the arm of the sea that lies between Nassau and the Main. The current, that comes by the way of Montauk, or the eastern extremity of Nassau, raises the vast basin of the Sound, fills the streams of Connecticut, and meets the western tide at a place called Throg morton, and within twenty miles of the city.

As the size of the estuaries is so great, it is scarcely necessary to explain that the pressure of so wide sheets of water causes the currents, at all the narrow passes, to be exceedingly rapid; since that equal diffusion of the element, which depends on a natural law, must, wherever there is a deficiency of space, be obtained by its velocity. There is, consequently, a quick tide throughout the whole distance between the harbor and Throgmorton; while it is permitted to poetic license to say, that at the narrowest part of the channel, the water darts by the land like an arrow parting from its bow. Owing to a sudden bend in the course of the stream, which makes two right-angles within a short distance, the dangerous position of many rocks that are visible and more that are not, and the confusion produced by currents, counter-currents, and eddies, this critical pass has received the name of "Hell-Gate." It is memorable for causing many a gentle bosom to palpitate with a terror that is a little exaggerated by the boding name, though it is constantly the cause of pecuniary losses, and has in many instances been the source of much personal danger. It was here, that a British frigate was lost, during the war of the Revolution, in consequence of having struck a rock called 'the Pot,' the blow causing the ship to fill and to founder so suddenly, that even some of her people are said to have been drowned. A similar but a greatly lessened effect is produced in the passage among the islands, by which vessels gain the ocean at the eastern extremity of the sound; though the magnitude of the latter sheet of water is so much greater than that of Raritan-bay and the harbor of New-York, that the force of its pressure is diminished by a corresponding width in the outlets. With these explanations, we shall return to the thread of the narrative.

When the person, who has so long been known in our pages by the nom de guerre of Tiller, gained the open street, he had a better opportunity of understanding the nature of the danger which so imminently pressed upon the brigantine. With a single glance at the symmetrical spars and broad yards of the ship that was sweeping past the town, he knew her to be the Coquette. The little flag at her fore-top-gallant mast sufficiently explained the meaning of the gun; for the two, in conjunction with the direction the ship was steering, told him, in language that any seaman could comprehend, that she demanded a Hell-Gate pilot. By the time the Skimmer reached the end of a lone wharf, where a light and swift-rowing boat awaited his return, the second report bespoke the impatience of his pursuers to be furnished with the necessary guide.

Though the navigation in this Republic, coastwise, now employs a tonnage equalling that used in all the commerce of any other nation of Christendom, England alone excepted, it was of no great amount at the commencement of the eighteenth century. A single ship, lying at the wharves, and two or three brigs and schooners at anchor in the rivers, composed the whole show of sea vessels then in port. To these were to be added some twenty smaller coasters and river-craft, most of whom were the shapeless and slow-moving masses which then plied, in voyages of a month's duration, between the two principal towns of the colony. The appeal of the Coquette, therefore, at that hour and in that age, was not likely to be quickly answered.

The ship had got fairly into the arm of the sea which separates the island of Manhattan from that of Nassau, and though it was not then, as now, narrowed by artificial means, its tide was so strong as, aided by the breeze, to float her swiftly onward. A third gun shook the windows of the city, causing many a worthy burgher to thrust his head through his casement; and yet no boat, was seen pulling from the land, nor was there any other visible sign that the signal would be speedily obeyed. Still the royal cruiser stood steadily on, with sail packed above sail, and every sheet of canvas spread, that the direction of a wind, which blew a little forward of the beam, would allow.

"We must pull for our own safety, and that of the brigantine, my men;" said the Skimmer, springing into his boat and seizing the tiller — "A quick stroke, and a strong! — here is no time for holiday feathering, or your man-of-war jerk! Give way, boys; give way, with a will, and together!"

These were sounds that had often saluted the ears of men engaged in the hazardous pursuit of his crew. The oars fell into the water at the same moment, and, quick as thought, the light bark was in the strength of the current.

The short range of wharves was soon passed, and, ere many minutes, the boat was gliding up with the tide, between the bluffs of Long Island and the projection which forms the angle on that part of Manhattan. Here the Skimmer was induced to sheer more into the centre of the passage, in order to avoid the eddies formed by the point, and to preserve the whole benefit of the current. As the boat approached Coerlær's, his eye was seen anxiously examining the wider reach of the water, that began to open above, in quest of his brigantine. Another gun was heard. A moment after the report, there followed the whistling of a shot; and then succeeded the rebound on the water, and the glittering particles of the spray. The ball glanced a few hundred feet further, and, skipping from place to place, it soon sunk into the element.

"This Mr. Ludlow is disposed to kill two birds with the same stone," coolly observed the Skimmer, not even bending his head aside, to note the position of the ship. "He wakes the burghers of the town with his noise, while he menaces our boat with his bullets. We are seen, my friends, and have no dependence but our own manhood, with some assistance from the lady of the sea-green mantle. A quicker stroke, and a strong! You have the Queen's cruiser before you, Master Coil; does she show boats on her quarters, or are the davits empty?"

The seaman addressed pulled the stroke-oar of the boat, and consequently he faced the Coquette. Without in the least relaxing his exertions, he rolled his eyes over the ship, and answered with a steadiness that showed him to be a man accustomed to situations of hazard.

"His boat-falls are as loose as a mermaid's locks, your Honor, and he shows few men in his tops; there are enough of the rogues left, however, to give us another shot."

"Her Majesty's servants are early awake, this morning. Another stroke or two, hearts of oak, and we throw them behind the land!"

A second shot fell into the water, just without the blades of the oars; and then the boat, obedient to its helm, whirled round the point, and the ship was no longer visible. As the cruiser was shut in by the formation of the land, the brigantine came into view on the opposite side of Coerlær's. Notwithstanding the calmness that reigned in the features of the Skimmer, one who studied his countenance closely might have seen an expression of concern shadowing his manly face, as the Water-Witch first met his eye. Still he spoke not, concealing his uneasiness, if in truth he felt any, from those whose exertions were at that moment of the last importance. As the crew of the expecting vessel saw their boat, they altered their course, and the two were soon together.

"Why is that signal still flying?" demanded the Skimmer, the instant his foot touched the deck of his brigantine, and pointing, as he spoke, at the little flag that fluttered at the head of the forward mast.

"We keep it aloft, to hasten off the pilot," was the answer.

"Has not the treacherous knave kept faith?" exclaimed the Skimmer, half recoiling in surprise. "He has my gold, and in return I hold fifty of his worthless promises — ha! — the laggard is in yon skiff; ware the brig round, and meet him, for moments are as precious now as water in a desert."

The helm was a-weather, and the lively brigantine had already turned more than half aside, when another gun drew every eye towards the point. The smoke was seen rising above the bend of the land, and presently the head-sails, followed by all the hull and spars of the Coquette, came into view. At that instant, a voice from forward announced that the pilot had turned, and was rowing with all his powers towards the shore. The imprecations that were heaped on the head of the delinquent were many and deep, but it was no time for indecision. The two vessels were not half a mile apart, and now was the moment to show the qualities of the Water-Witch. Her helm was shifted; and, as if conscious herself of the danger that threatened her liberty, the beautiful fabric came sweeping up to her course, and, inclining to the breeze, with one heavy flap of the canvas, she glided ahead with all her wonted ease. But, the royal cruiser was a ship of ten thousand! For twenty minutes, the nicest eye might have been at a loss to say which lost or which gained, so equally did the pursuer and the pursued hold on their way. As the brigantine was the first, however, to reach the narrow passage formed by Blackwell's, her motion was favored by the increasing power of the stream. It would seem that this change slight as it was, did not escape the vigilance of those in the Coquette; for the gun, which had been silent so long, again sent forth its flame and smoke. Four discharges, in less than so many minutes, threatened a serious disadvantage to the free-traders. Shot after shot passed among their spars, and opened wide rents in the canvas. A few more such assaults would deprive them of their means of motion. Aware of the crisis, the accomplished and prompt seaman who governed her movements needed but an instant to form his decision.

The brigantine was now nearly up with the head of Blackwell's. It was half-flood, on a spring tide. The reef that projects from the western end of the island far into the reach below, was nearly covered; but still enough was visible to show the nature of the barrier it presented to a passage from one shore to the other. There was one rock, near the island itself, which lifted its black head high above the water. Between this dark mass of stone and the land, there was an opening of some twenty fathoms in width. The Skimmer saw, by the even and unbroken waves that rolled through the passage, that the bottom lay less near to the surface of the water, in that opening, than at any other point along the line of reef. He commanded the helm a-weather, once more, and calmly trusted to the issue.

Not a man on board that brigantine was aware that the shot of the royal cruiser was whistling between their masts, and damaging their gear, as the little vessel glided into the narrow opening. A single blow on the rock would have been destruction, and the lesser danger was entirely absorbed in the greater. But when the passage was cleared, and the true stream in the other channel gained, a common shout proclaimed both the weight of their apprehension and their relief. In another minute, the head of Blackwell's protected them from the shot of their pursuers.

The length of the reef prevented the Coquette from changing her direction, and her draught of water closed the passage between the rock and the island. But the deviation from the straight course, and the passage of the eddies, had enabled the ship, which came steadily on, to range up nearly abeam of her chase. Both vessels, though separated by the long narrow island, were now fairly in the force of those currents which glide so swiftly through the confined passages. A sudden thought glanced on the mind of the Skimmer, and he lost no time in attempting to execute its suggestion. Again the helm was put up, and the image of the sea-green lady was seen struggling to stem the rapid waters. Had this effort been crowned with success, the triumph of her followers would have been complete; since the brigantine might have reached some of the eddies of the reach below, and leaving her heavier pursuer to contend with the strength of the tide, she would have gained the open sea, by the route over which she had so lately passed. But a single minute of trial convinced the bold mariner that his decision came too late. The wind was insufficient to pass the gorge, and, environed by the land, with a tide that grew stronger at each moment, he saw that delay would be destruction. Once more the light vessel yielded to the helm, and, with every thing set to the best advantage, she darted along the passage.

In the mean time, the Coquette had not been idle Borne on by the breeze, and floating with the current, she had even gained upon her chase; and as her lofty and light sails drew strongest over the land, there was every prospect of her first reaching the eastern end of Blackwell's. Ludlow saw his advantage, and made his preparations accordingly.

There needs little explanation to render the circumstances which brought the royal cruiser up to town, intelligible to the reader. As the morning approached, she had entered more deeply into the bay: and when the light permitted, those on board her had been able to see that no vessel lay beneath the hills, nor in any of the more retired places of the estuary. A fisherman, however, removed the last of their doubts, by reporting that he had seen a vessel, whose description answered that of the Water-Witch, passing the Narrows in the middle watch. He added that a swiftly-rowing boat was, shortly after, seen pulling in the same direction. This clue had been sufficient. Ludlow made a signal for his own boats to close the passages of the Kilns and the Narrows, and then, as has been seen, he steered directly into the harbor.

When Ludlow found himself in the position just described, he turned all his attention to the double object of preserving his own vessel, and arresting that of the free-trader. Though there was still a possibility of damaging the spars of the brigantine by firing across the land, the feebleness of his own crew, reduced as it was by more than half its numbers, the danger of doing injury to the farm-houses that were here and there placed along the low cliffs, and the necessity of preparation to meet the critical pass ahead, united to prevent the attempt. The ship was no sooner fairly entered into the pass, be tween Blackwell's and Nassau, than he issued an order to secure the guns that had been used, and to clear away the anchors.

"Cock-bill the bowers, Sir," he hastily added, in his orders to Trysail. "We are in no condition to sport with stock-and-fluke; have every thing ready to let go at a word; and see the grapnels ready — we will throw them aboard the smuggler as we close, and take him alive. Once fast to the chain, we are yet strong enough to haul him in under our scuppers, and to capture him with the pumps! Is the signal still abroad, for a pilot?"

"We keep it flying, Sir, but 'twill be a swift boat that overhauls us in this tide's-way. The Gate begins at yonder bend in the land, Captain Ludlow!"

"Keep it abroad; the lazy rogues are sometimes loitering in the cove this side the rocks, and chance may throw one of them aboard us, as we pass. See to the anchors, Sir; the ship is driving through this channel, like a race-horse under the whip!"

The men were hurriedly piped to this duty while their young commander took his station on the poop, now anxiously examining the courses of the tides and the positions of the eddies, and now turning his eyes towards the brigantine, whose upper spars and white sails were to be seen, at the distance of two hundred fathoms, glancing past the trees of the island. But miles and minutes seemed like rods and moments, in that swift current. Trysail had just reported the anchors ready, when the ship swept up abreast of the cove, where vessels often seek an anchorage, to await favorable moments for entering the Gate. Ludlow saw, at a glance, that the place was entirely empty. For an instant he yielded to the heavy responsibility — a responsibility before which a seaman sooner shrinks than before any other — that of charging himself with the duty of the pilot; and he thought of running into the anchorage for shelter. But another glimpse at the spars of the brigantine caused him to waver.

"We are near the Gate, Sir!" cried Trysail, in a voice that was full of warning.

"Yon daring mariner stands on!"

"The rogue sails his vessel without the Queen's permission, Captain Ludlow. They tell me, this is a passage that has been well named!"

"I have been through it, and will vouch for its character — he shows no signs of anchoring!"

"If the woman who points his course can carry him through safely, she deserves her title. We are passing, the Cove, Captain Ludlow!"

"We are past it!" returned Ludlow, breathing heavily. "Let there be no whisper in the ship — pilot or no pilot, we now sink or swim!"

Trysail had ventured to remonstrate, while there was a possibility of avoiding the danger; but, like his commander, he now saw that all depended on their own coolness and care. He passed busily among the crew; saw that each brace and bowline was manned; cautioned the few young officers who continued on board to vigilance, and then awaited the orders of his superior, with the composure that is so necessary to a seaman in the moment of trial. Ludlow himself, while he felt the load of responsibility he had assumed, succeeded equally well in maintaining an outward calm. The ship was irretrievably in the Gate, and no human power could retrace the step. At such moments of intense anxiety, the human mind is wont to seek support in the opinions of others. Notwithstanding the increasing velocity and the critical condition of his own vessel, Ludlow cast a glance, in order to ascertain the determination of the 'Skimmer of the Seas.' Blackwell's was already behind them, and as the two currents were again united, the brigantine had luffed up into the entrance of the dangerous passage, and now followed within two hundred feet of the Coquette, directly in her wake. The bold and manly-looking mariner, who controlled her, stood between the night-heads, just above the image of his pretended mistress, where he examined the foaming reefs, the whirling eddies, and the varying currents, with folded arms and a riveted eye. A glance was exchanged between the two officers, and the free-trader raised his sea-cap. Ludlow was too courteous not to return the salutation, and then all his senses were engrossed by the care of his ship. A rock lay before them, over which the water broke in a loud and unceasing roar. For an instant it seemed that the vessel could not avoid the danger, and then it was already past.

"Brace up!" said Ludlow, in the calm tones that denote a forced tranquillity.

"Luff!" called out the Skimmer, so quickly as to show that he took the move-ments of the cruiser for his guide. The ship came closer to the wind, but the sudden bend in the stream no longer permitted her to steer in a direct line with its course. Though drifting to windward with vast rapidity, her way through the water, which was greatly increased by the contrary actions of the wind and tide, caused the cruiser to shoot across the current; while a reef, over which the water madly tumbled, lay immediately in her course. The danger seemed too imminent for the observances of nautical etiquette, and Trysail railed aloud that the ship must be thrown aback, or she was lost.

"Hard-a-lee!" shouted Ludlow, in the strong voice of authority. — "Up with every thing — tacks and sheets! — main-top-sail haul!"

The ship seemed as conscious of her danger as any on her decks. The bows whirled away from the foaming reef, and as the sails caught the breeze on their opposite surfaces, they aided in bringing her head in the contrary direction. A minute had scarcely passed ere she was aback, and in the next she was about and full again. The intensity of the brief exertion kept Trysail fully employed; but no sooner had he leisure to look ahead, than he again called aloud —

"Here is another roarer under her bows — luff Sir, luff, or we are upon it!"

"Hard down your helm!" once again came in deep tones from Ludlow — "Let fly your sheets — throw all aback, forward and aft — away with the yards, with a will, men!"

There was need for all of these precautions. Though the ship had so happily escaped the dangers of the first reef, a turbulent and roaring caldron in the water, which, as representing the element in ebullition, is called 'the Pot,' lay so directly before her, as to render the danger apparently inevitable. But the power of the canvas was not lost on this trying occasion. The forward motion of the ship diminished, and as the current still swept her swiftly to windward, her bows did not enter the rolling waters until the hidden rocks which caused the commotion had been passed. The yielding vessel rose and fell in the agitated water, as if in homage to the whirlpool; but the deep keel was unharmed.

"If the ship shoot ahead twice her length more, her bows will touch the eddy!" exclaimed the vigilant master.

Ludlow looked around him, for a single moment in indecision. The waters were whirling and roaring on every side, and the sails began to lose their power, as the ship drew near the bluff which forms the second angle in this critical pass. He saw, by objects on the land, that he still approached the shore, and he had recourse to the seaman's last expedient.

"Let go both anchors!" was the final order.

The fall of the massive iron into the water, was succeeded by the rumbling of the cable. The first effort to check the progress of the vessel, appeared to threaten dissolution to the whole fabric, which trembled under the shock from its mast-heads to the keel. But the enormous rope again yielded, and smoke was seen rising round the wood which held it. The ship whirled with the sudden check, and sheered wildly in towards the shore. Met by the helm, and again checked by the efforts of the crew, she threatened to defy restraint. There was an instant when all on board expected to hear the cable snap; but the upper sails filled, and as the wind was now brought over the taffrail, the force of the current was in a great degree met by that of the breeze.

The ship answered her helm and became stationary, while the water foamed against her cut-water, as if she were driven ahead with the power of a brisk breeze.

The time, from the moment when the Coquette entered the Gate, to that when she anchored below 'the Pot,' though the distance was near a mile, seemed but a minute. Certain however that his ship was now checked, the thoughts of Ludlow returned to their other duties with the quickness of lightning.

"Clear away the grapnels!" he eagerly cried — "Stand by to heave, and haul in! — heave!"

But, that the reader may better comprehend the motive of this sudden order, he must consent to return to the entrance of the dangerous passage, and accompany the Water-Witch, also, in her hazardous experiment to get through without a pilot.

The abortive attempt of the brigantine to stem the tide at the western end of Blackwell's, will be remembered. It had no other effect than to place her pursuer more in advance, and to convince her own commander that he had now no other resource than to continue his course; for, had he anchored, boats would have insured his capture. When the two vessels appeared off the eastern end of the island the Coquette was ahead — a fact that the experienced free-trader did not at all regret. He profited by the circumstance to follow her movements, and to make a favorable entrance into the uncertain currents. To him, Hell-Gate was known only by its fearful reputation among mariners; and unless he might avail himself of the presence of the cruiser, he had no other guide than his own general knowledge of the power of the element.

When the Coquette had tacked, the calm and observant Skimmer was satisfied with throwing his head-sails flat to the mast. From that instant, the brigantine lay floating in the current, neither advancing nor receding a foot, and always keeping her position at a safe distance from the ship, that was so adroitly made to answer the purposes of a beacon. The sails were watched with the closest care; and so nicely was the delicate machine tended, that it would have been, at any moment, in her people's power to have lessened her way, by turning to the stream. The Coquette was followed till she anchored, and the call on board the cruiser to heave the grapnels had been given, because the brigantine was apparently floating directly down on her broadside.

When the grapnels were hove from the royal cruiser, the free-trader stood on the low poop of his little vessel, within fifty feet of him who had issued the order. There was a smile of indifference on his firm mouth, while he silently waved a hand to his own crew. The signal was obeyed by bracing round their yards, and suffering all the canvas to fill. The brigantine shot quickly ahead, and the useless irons fell heavily into the water.

"Many thanks for your pilotage, Captain Ludlow!" cried the daring and successful mariner of the shawl, as his vessel, borne on by wind and current, receded rapidly from the cruiser — "You will find the off Montauk; for affairs still keep us on the coast. Our lady has, however, put on the blue mantle; and 'ere many settings of the sun, we shall look for deep water. Take good care of Her Majesty's ship, I pray thee, for she has neither a more beautiful nor a faster!"

One thought succeeded another with the tumult of a torrent, in the mind of Ludlow. As the brigantine lay directly under his broadside, the first impulse was to use his guns; but at the next moment he was conscious, that before they could be cleared, distance would render them useless. His lips had neatly parted with intent to order the cables cut, but he remembered the speed of the brigantine, and hesitated. A sudden freshening of the breeze decided his course. Finding that the ship was enabled to keep her station, he ordered the crew to thrust the whole of the enormous ropes through the hawseholes; and, freed from the restraint, he abandoned the anchors, until an opportunity to reclaim them should offer.

The operation of slipping the cables consumed several minutes; and when the Coquette, with every thing set, was again steering in pursuit, the Water-Witch was already beyond the reach of her guns. Both vessels, however, held on their way, keeping as near as possible to the centre of the stream, and trusting more to fortune, than to any knowledge of the channel, for safety.

When passing the two small islands that lie at no great distance from the Gate, a boat was seen moving towards the royal cruiser. A man in it pointed to the signal, which was still flying, and offered his services.

"Tell me," demanded Ludlow eagerly, "has yonder brigantine taken a pilot?"

"By her movements, I judge not. She brushed the sunken rock, off the mouth of Flushing-bay; and as she passed, I heard the song of the lead. I should have gone on board myself, but the fellow rather flies than sails; and as for signals, he seems to mind none but his own!"

"Bring us up with him, and fifty guineas is thy reward!"

The slow-moving pilot, who in truth had just awoke from a refreshing sleep, opened his eyes, and seemed to gather a new impulse from the promise. When his questions were asked and answered, he began deliberately to count on his fingers all the chances that still existed of a vessel, whose crew was ignorant of the navigation, falling into their hands.

"Admitting that, by keeping mid-channel, she goes clear of White Stone and

Frogs," he said, giving to Throgmorton's its vulgar name, "he must be a wizard, to know that the Stepping-Stones lie directly across his course, and that a vessel must steer away northerly, or bring up on rocks that will as surely hold him as if he were built there. Then he runs his chance for the Executioners, which are as prettily placed as needs be, to make our trade flourish, besides the Middle Ground further east, though I count but little on that, having often tried to find it myself, without success. Courage, noble captain! if the fellow be the man you say, we shall get a nearer look at him before the sun sets; for certainly he who has run the Gate without a pilot in safety, has had as much good luck as can fall to his share in one day."

The opinion of the East River Branch proved erroneous. Notwithstanding the hidden perils by which she was environed, the Water-Witch continued her course, with a speed that increased as the wind rose with the sun, and with an impunity from harm that amazed all who were in the secret of her situation. Off Throgmorton's there was, in truth, a danger that might even have baffled the sagacity of the followers of the mysterious lady, had they not been aided by accident. This is the point where the straitened arm of the sea expands into the basin of the Sound. A broad and inviting passage lies directly before the navigator, while, like the flattering prospects of life, numberless hidden obstacles are in wait to arrest the unheeding and ignorant.

The 'Skimmer of the Seas' was deeply practised in all the intricacies and dangers of the shoals and rocks. Most of his life had been passed in threading the one, or in avoiding the other. So keen and quick had his eye become, in detecting the presence of any of those signs which forewarn the mariner of danger, that a ripple on the surface, or a deeper shade in the color of the water, rarely escaped his vigilance. Seated on the top-sail-yard of his brigantine, he had overlooked the passage from the moment they were through the Gate, and issued his mandates to those below with a precision and promptitude that were not surpassed by the trained conductor of the Coquette himself. But when his sight embraced the wide reach of water that lay in front, as his little vessel swept round the head-land of Throgmorton, he believed there no longer existed a reason for so much care. Still there was a motive for hesitation. A heavily-moulded and dull-sailing coaster was going eastward not a league ahead of the brigantine, while one of the light sloops of those waters was coming westward still further in the distance. Notwithstanding the wind was favorable to each alike, both vessels had deviated from the direct line, and were steering towards a common centre, near an island that was placed more than a mile to the northward of the straight course. A mariner, like him of the India-shawl, could not overlook so obvious an intimation of a change in the channel. The Water-Witch was kept away, and her lighter sails were lowered, in order to allow the royal cruiser, whose lofty canvas was plainly visible above the land, to draw near. When the Coquette was seen also to diverge, there no longer remained a doubt of the direction necessary to be taken; and every thing was quickly set upon the brigantine, even to her studding-sails. Long ere she reached the island, the two coasters had met, and each again changed its course, reversing that on which the other had just been sailing. There was, in these movements, as plain an explanation as a seaman could desire, that the pursued were right On reaching the island, therefore, they again luffed into the wake of the schooner; and having nearly crossed the sheet of water, they passed the coaster, receiving an assurance, in words, that all was now plain sailing, before them.

Such was the famous passage of the 'Skimmer of the Seas' through the multiplied and hidden dangers of the eastern channel. To those who have thus accompanied him, step by step, though its intricacies and alarms, there may seem nothing extraordinary in the event; but, coupled as it was with the character previously earned by that bold mariner, and occurring, as it did, in an age when men were more disposed than at present to put faith in the marvellous, the reader will not be surprised to learn that it greatly increased his reputation for daring, and had no small influence on an opinion, which was by no means uncommon, that the dealers in contraband were singularly favored by a power which greatly exceeded that of Queen Anne and all her servants.

CHAPTER XXIX.

" — Thou shalt see me at Philippi."
Shakspeare.

THE commander of Her Britannic Majesty's ship Coquette slept that night in the hammock-cloths. Before the sun had set, the light and swift brigantine, by following the gradual bend of the land, had disappeared in the eastern board; and it was no longer a question of overtaking her by speed. Still, sail was crowded on the royal cruiser; and, long ere the period when Ludlow threw himself in his clothes between the ridge-ropes of the quarter-deck, the vessel had gained the broadest part of the Sound, and was already approaching the islands that form the 'Race.'

Throughout the whole of that long and anxious day, the young sailor had held no communication with the inmates of the cabin. The servants of the ship had passed to and fro; but, though the door seldom opened that he did not bend his eyes feverishly in its direction, neither the Alderman, his niece, the captive, nor even François or the negress, made their appearance on the deck. If any there felt an interest in the result of the chase, it was concealed in a profound and almost mysterious silence. Determined not to be outdone in indifference, and goaded by feelings which with all his pride he could not overcome, our young seaman took possession of the place of rest we have mentioned, without using any measures to resume the intercourse.

When the first watch of the night was come, sail, was shortened on the ship, and from that moment till the day dawned again, her captain seemed buried in sleep. With the appearance of the sun, however, he arose, and commanded the canvas to be spread, once more, and every exertion made to drive the vessel forward to her object.

The Coquette reached the Race early in the day, and, shooting through the passage on an ebb-tide, she was off Montauk at noon. No sooner had the ship drawn past the cape, and reached a point where she felt the breeze and the waves of the Atlantic, than men were sent aloft, and twenty eyes were curiously employed in examining the offing. Ludlow remembered the promise of the Skimmer to meet him at that spot, and, notwithstanding the motives which the latter might be supposed to have for avoiding the interview, so great was the influence of the free-trader's manner and character, that the young captain entertained secret expectations the promise would be kept.

"The offing is clear!" said the young captain, in a tone of disappointment, when he lowered his glass; "and yet that rover does not seem a man to hide his head in fear —"

"Fear — that is to say, fear of a Frenchman — and a decent respect for Her Majesty's cruisers, are very different sorts of things," returned the master. "I never got a bandanna, or a bottle of your Cogniac ashore, in my life, that I did not think every man that I passed in the street, could see the spots in the one, or scent the flavor of the other; but then I never supposed this shyness amounted to more than a certain suspicion in my own mind, that other people know when a man is running on an illegal course, I suppose that one of your rectors, who is snugly anchored for life in a good warm living, would call this conscience; but, for my own part, Captain Ludlow, though no great logician in matters of this sort, I have always believed that it was natural concern of mind lest the articles should be seized. If this 'Skimmer of the Seas' comes out to give us another chase in rough water, he is by no means as good a judge of the difference between a large and a small vessel as I had thought him — and I confess, Sir, I should have more hopes of taking him, were the woman under his bowsprit fairly burnt."

"The offing is clear!"

"That it is, with a show of the wind holding here at south-half-south. This bit of water that we have passed, between yon island and the main, is lined with bays; and while we are here looking out for them on the high seas, the cunning varlets may be trading in any one of the fifty good basins that lie between the cape and the place where we lost him. For aught we know, he may have run westward again in the night-watches, and be at this moment laughing in his sleeve at the manner in which he dodged a cruiser."

"There is too much truth in what you say, Trysail; for if the Skimmer be now disposed to avoid us, he has certainly the means in his power."

"Sail, ho!" cried the look-out on the main-top-gallant-yard.

"Where-a-way?"

"Broad on the weather-beam, Sir; here, in a range with the light cloud that is just lifting from the water."

"Can you make out the rig?"

"'Fore George, the fellow is right!" interrupted the master. "The cloud caused her to be unseen; but here she is, sure enough — a full-rigged ship, under easy canvas, with her head to the westward!"

The look of Ludlow through the glass was long, attentive, and grave.

"We are weak-handed to deal with a stranger;" he said, when he returned the instrument to Trysail, "You see he has nothing but his top-sails set — a show of canvas that would satisfy no trader, in a breeze like this!"

The master was silent, but his look was even longer and more critical than that of his captain. When it had ended, he cast a cautious glance towards the diminished crew, who were curiously regarding the vessel that had now become sufficiently distinct-by a change in the position of the cloud, and then answered, in an under tone —

"'Tis a Frenchman, or I am a whale' One may see it, by his short yards, and the hoist of his sails; ay, and 'tis a cruiser, too, for no man who had a profit to make on his freight, would be lying there under short canvas, and his port within a day's run."

"Your opinion is my own; would to Heaven our people were all here! This is but a short complement to take into action with a ship whose force seems equal to our own. What number can we count?"

"We are short of seventy — a small muster for four-and-twenty guns, with yards like these to handle."

"And yet the port may not be insulted! We are known to be on this coast —"

"We are seen!" interrupted the master — "The fellow has worn ship, and he is already setting his top-gallant-sails."

There no longer remained any choice between downright flight and preparations for combat. The former would have been easy, for an hour would have taken the ship within the cape; but the latter was far more in consonance with the spirit of the service to which the Coquette belonged. The order was therefore given for "all hands to clear ship for action!" It was in the reckless nature of sailors, to exalt in this summons; for success and audacity go hand in hand, and long familiarity with the first had, even at that early day, given a confidence that often approached temerity to the seamen of Great Britain and her dependencies. The mandate to prepare for battle was received by the feeble crew of the Coquette, as it had often been received before, when her decks were filled with the number necessary to give full efficiency to her armament; though a few of the older and more experienced of the mariners, men in whom confidence had been diminished by time, were seen to shake their heads, as if they doubted the prudence of the intended contest.

Whatever might have been the secret hesitation of Ludlow when the character and force of his enemy were clearly established, he betrayed no signs of irresolution from the moment when his decision appeared to be taken. The necessary orders were issued calmly, and with the clearness and readiness that perhaps con-

stitute the greatest merit of a naval captain. The yards were slung in chains; the
booms were sent down; the lofty sails were furled, and, in short, all the preparations that were then customary were made with the usual promptitude and skill.
Then the drum beat to quarters, and when the people were at their stations, their
young commander had a better opportunity of examining into the true efficiency
of his ship. Calling to the master, he ascended the poop, in order that they might
confer together with less risk of being overheard, and at the same time better
observe the manœuvres of the enemy.

The stranger had, as Trysail perceived, suddenly worn round on his heel, and
laid his head to the northward. The change in the course brought him before the
wind, and, as he immediately spread all the canvas that would draw, he was
approaching fast. During the time occupied in preparation on board the Coquette, his hull had risen as it were from out of the water; and Ludlow and his
companion had not studied his appearance long, from the poop, before the streak
of white paint, dotted with ports which marks a vessel of war, became visible to
the naked eye. As the cruiser of Queen Anne continued also to steer in the direction of the chase, half an hour more brought them sufficiently near to each other,
to remove all doubts of their respective characters and force. The stranger then
came to the wind, and made his preparations for combat.

"The fellow shows a stout heart, and a warm battery," observed the master,
when the broadside of their enemy became visible, by this change in his position.
"Six-and-twenty teeth, by my count! though the eye-teeth must be wanting, or
he would never be so fool-hardy as to brave Queen Anne's Coquette in this
impudent fashion! A prettily turned boat, Captain Ludlow, and one nimble
enough in her movements. But look at his top-sails! Just like his character, Sir, all
hoist; and with little or no head to them. I'll not deny but that the hull is well
enough, for that is no more than carpenter's work; but when it comes to the rig,
or trim, or cut of a sail, how should a l'Orient or a Brest man understand what is
comely? There is no equalling, after all, a good, wholesome, honest English top-
sail; which is neither too narrow in the head, nor too deep in the hoist; with a
bolt-rope of exactly the true size, robands and earings and bowlines that look as if
they grew there, and sheets that neither nature nor art could alter to advantage.
Here are these Americans, now, making innovations in ship-building, and in the
sparring of vessels, as if any thing could be gained by quitting the customs and
opinions of their ancestors! Any man may see that all they have about them, that is
good for any thing, is English; while all their nonsense, and new-fangled changes,
come from their own vanity."

"They get along, Master Trysail, notwithstanding," returned the captain, who, though a sufficiently loyal subject, could not forget his birth-place; "and many is the time this ship, one of the finest models of Plymouth, has been bothered to overhaul the coasters of these seas. Here is the brigantine, that has laughed at us, on our best tack, and with our choice of wind."

"One cannot say where that brigantine was built, Captain Ludlow. It may be here, it may be there; for I look upon her as a nondescript, as old Admiral Top used to call the galliots of the north seas — but, concerning these new American fashions, of what use are they, I would ask, Captain Ludlow? In the first place, they are neither English nor French, which is as much as to confess they are altogether outlandish; in the second place, they disturb the harmony and established usages among wrights and sail-makers, and, though they may get along well enough now, sooner or later, take my word for it, they will come to harm. It is unreasonable to suppose that a new people can discover any thing in the construction of a ship, that has escaped the wisdom of seamen as old — the Frenchman is cluing up his top-gallant-sails, and means to let them hang; which is much the same as condemning them at once — and, therefore, I am of opinion that all these new fashions will come to no good."

"Your reasoning is absolutely conclusive, Master Trysail." returned the captain, whose thoughts were differently employed. "I agree with you, it would be safer for the stranger to send down his yards."

"There is something manly and becoming in seeing a ship strip herself, as she comes into action, Sir! It is like a boxer taking off his jacket, with the intention of making a fair stand-up fight of it. — That fellow is filling away again, and means to manœuvre before he comes up fairly to his work."

The eye of Ludlow had never quitted the stranger. He saw that the moment for serious action was not distant; and, bidding Trysail keep the vessel on her course, he descended to the quarter-deck. For a angle instant, the young commander paused with big hand on the door of the cabin, and then, overcoming his reluctance, he entered the apartment.

The Coquette was built after a fashion much in vogue a century since, and which, by a fickleness that influences marine architecture as well as less important things, is again coming into use, for vessels of her force. The accommodations of the commander were on the same deck with the batteries of the ship, and they were frequently made to contain two or even four guns of the armament. When Ludlow entered his cabin, therefore, he found a crew stationed around the gun which was placed on the side next the enemy, and all the customary arrangements made which precede a combat. The state-rooms abaft, however, as well as the little apartment which lay between them, were closed. Glancing his eye about him, and observing the carpenters in readiness, he made a signal for them to knock away the bulk-heads, and lay the whole of the fighting part of the ship in common. While this duty was going on, he entered the after-cabin.

Alderman Van Beverout and his companions were found together and evidently in expectation of the visit they now received. Passing coolly by the former, Ludlow approached his niece, and, taking her hand, he led her to the quarter-deck, making a sign for her female attendant to follow. Descending into the depths of the ship, the captain conducted his charge into a part of the berth-deck, that was below the water line, and as much removed from danger as she could well be, without encountering a foul air, or sights that might be painful to one of her sex and habits.

"Here is as much safety as a vessel of war affords in a moment like this," he said, when his companion was silently seated on a mess-chest. "On no account quit the spot, till I — or some other, advise you it may be done without hazard."

Alida had submitted to be led thither, without a question. Though her color went and came, she saw the little dispositions that were made for her comfort, and without which, even at that moment, the young sailor could not quit her, in the same silence. But when they were ended, and her conductor was about to retire, his name escaped her lips, by an exclamation that seemed hurried and involuntary.

"Can I do aught else to quiet your apprehensions?" the young man inquired, though he studiously avoided her eye, as he turned to put the question. "I know your strength of mind, and that you have a resolution which exceeds the courage of your sex; else I would not venture so freely to point out the danger which may beset one, even here, without a self-command and discretion that shall restrain all sudden impulses of fear."

"Notwithstanding your generous interpretation of my character, Ludlow, I am but woman after all."

"I did not mistake you for an amazon," returned the young man smiling, perceiving that she checked her words by a sudden effort. "All I expect from you is the triumph of reason over female terror. I shall not conceal that the odds — perhaps I may say that the chances, are against us; and yet the enemy must pay for my ship, ere he has her! She will be none the worse defended, Alida, from the consciousness that thy liberty and comfort depend in some measure on our exertions. — Would you say more?"

La belle Barbérie struggled with herself, and she became calm, at least in exterior.

"There has been a singular misconception between us, and yet is this no moment for explanations! Ludlow, I would not have you part with me, at such a time as this, with that cold and reproachful eye!"

She paused When the young man ventured to raise his look, he saw the beautiful girl standing with a hand extended towards him, as if offering a pledge of amity; while the crimson on her cheek, and her yielding but half-averted eye, spoke with the eloquence of maiden modesty. Seizing the hand, he answered, hastily —

"Time was, when this action would have made me happy —"

The young man paused, for his gaze had unconsciously become riveted on the rings of the hand he held. Alida understood the look, and, drawing one of the jewels, she offered it with a smile that was as attractive as her beauty.

"One of these may be spared," she said. "Take it, Ludlow; and when thy present duty shall be performed, return it, as a gage that I have promised thee that no explanation which you may have a right to ask shall be withheld."

The young man took the ring, and forced it on the smallest of his fingers, in a mechanical manner, and with a bewildered look, that seemed to inquire if some one of those which remained was not the token of a plighted faith. It is probable that he might have continued the discourse, had not a gun been fired from the enemy. It recalled him to the more serious business of the hour. Already more than half disposed to believe all he could wish, he raised the fair hand, which had just bestowed the boon, to his lips, and rushed upon deck.

"The Monsieur is beginning to bluster;" said Trysail, who had witnessed the descent of his commander, at that moment and on such an errand, with great dissatisfaction. "Although his shot fell short, it is too much to let a Frenchman have the credit of first word."

"He has merely given the weather gun, the signal of defiance. Let him come down, and he will not find us in a hurry to leave him!"

"No, no: as for that, we are snug enough!" returned the master, chuckling as he surveyed the half-naked spars, and the light top-hamper, to which he had himself reduced the ship. "If running is to be our play, we have made a false move at the beginning of the game. These top-sails, spanker, and jib, make a show that says more for bottom than for speed. Well, come what will of this affair, it will leave me a master, though it is beyond the power of the best duke in England to rob me of my share of the honor!"

With this consolation for his perfectly hopeless condition as respects promotion, the old seaman walked forward, examining critically into the state of the vessel; while his young commander, having cast a look about him, motioned to his prisoner and the Alderman to follow to the poop.

"I do not pretend to inquire into the nature of the tie which unites you with some in this ship," Ludlow commenced, addressing his words to Seadrift, though he kept his gaze on the recent gift of Alida; "but, that it must be strong, is evident by the interest they have taken in your fate. One who is thus esteemed should set a value on himself. How far you have trifled with the laws, I do not wish to say; but here is an opportunity to redeem some of the public favor. You are a seaman, and need not be told that my ship is not as strongly manned as one could wish her at this moment, and that the services of every Englishman will be welcome. Take charge of these six guns, and depend on my honor that your devotion to the flag shall not go unrequited."

"You much mistake my vocation, noble captain;" returned the dealer in contraband, faintly laughing. "Though one of the seas, I am one more used to the calm latitudes than to these whirlwinds of war. You have visited the brigantine of our mistress, and must have seen that her temple resembles that of Janus more than that of Mars. The deck of the Water-Witch has none of this frowning garniture of artillery."

Ludlow listened in amazement. Surprise, incredulity, and scorn, were each, in turn, expressed in his frowning countenance.

"This is unbecoming language for one of your calling," he said, scarce deeming it necessary to conceal the contempt he felt. "Do you acknowledge fealty to this ensign — are you an Englishman?"

"I am such as Heaven was pleased to make me — fitter for the zephyr, than the gale — the jest, than the war-shout — the merry moment, than the angry mood."

"Is this the man whose name for daring has passed into a proverb? — the dauntless, reckless, skilful 'Skimmer of the Seas!'"

"North is not more removed from south, than I from him in the qualities you seek! It was not my duty to undeceive you as to the value of your captive, while he whose services are beyond price to our mistress was still on the coast. So far from being him you name, brave captain, I claim to be no more than one of his agents, who, having some experience in the caprices of woman, he trusts to recommend his wares to female fancies. Though so useless in inflicting injuries, I may make bold however to rate myself as excellent at consolation. Suffer that I appease the fears of la belle Barbérie during the coming tumult, and you shall own that one more skilful in that merciful office is rare indeed!"

"Comfort whom, where, and what thou wilt, miserable effigy of manhood! — but hold, there is less of terror than of artifice in that lurking smile and treacherous eye!"

"Discredit both, generous captain! On the faith of one who can be sincere at need, a wholesome fear is uppermost, whatever else the disobedient members may betray. I could fain weep rather than be thought valiant, just now!"

Ludlow listened in wonder. He had raised an arm to arrest the retreat of the young mariner, and by a natural movement his hand slid along the limb it had grasped, until it held that of Seadrift. The instant he touched the soft and ungloved palm, an idea, as novel as it was sudden, crossed his brain. Retreating a step or two, he examined the light and agile form of the other, from head to feet. The frown of displeasure, which had clouded his brow, changed to a look of unfeigned surprise; and for the first time, the tones of the voice came over his recollection as being softer and more melodious than is wont in man.

"Truly, thou art not the 'Skimmer of the Seas!'" he exclaimed, when his short examination was ended.

"No truth more certain. I am one of little account in this rude encounter, though, were that gallant seaman here," and the color deepened on the cheeks of Seadrift as he spoke, "his arm and counsel might prove a host! Oh! I have seen him in scenes far more trying than this, when the elements have conspired with other dangers. The example of his steadiness and spirit has given courage even to the feeblest heart in the brigantine! Now, suffer me to offer consolation to the timid Alida."

"I should little merit her gratitude, were the request refused," returned Ludlow. "Go, gay and gallant Master Seadrift! if the enemy fears thy presence on the deck as little as I dread it with la belle Barbérie, thy services here will be useless!"

Seadrift colored to the temples, crossed his arms meekly on his bosom, sunk in an attitude of leave-taking, that was so equivocal as to cause the attentive and critical young captain to smile, and then glided past him and disappeared through a hatchway.

The eye of Ludlow followed the active and graceful form, while it continued in sight; and when it was no longer visible, he faced the Alderman with a look which seemed to inquire how far he might be acquainted with the true character of the individual who had been the cause of so much pain to himself.

"Have I done well, Sir, in permitting a subject of Queen Anne to quit us at this emergency?" he demanded, observing that either the phlegm or the self-command of Myndert rendered him proof to scrutiny.

"The lad may be termed contraband of war," returned the Alderman, without moving a muscle; "an article that will command a better price in a quiet than in a turbulent market. In short, Captain Cornelius Ludlow, this Master Seadrift will not answer thy purpose at all in combat."

"And is this example of heroism to go any farther, or may I count on the assistance of Mr. Alderman Van Beverout? — He has the reputation of a loyal citizen."

"As for loyalty," returned the Alderman, "so far as saying God bless the Queen, at city feasts, will go, none are more so. A wish is not an expensive return for the protection of her fleets and armies, and I wish her and you success against the enemy, with all my heart. But I never admired the manner in which the States General were dispossessed of their territories on this continent, Master Ludlow, and therefore I pay the Stuarts little more than I owe them in law."

"Which is as much as to say, that you will join the gay smuggler, in administering consolation to one whose spirit places her above the need of such succor."

"Not so fast, young gentleman. — We mercantile men like to see offsets in our books, before they are balanced. Whatever may be my opinion of the reigning family, which I only utter to you in confidence, and not as coin that is to pass from one to another, my love for the Grand Monarque is still less. Louis is at loggerheads with the United Provinces, as well as with our gracious Queen; and I see no harm in opposing one of his cruisers, since they certainly annoy trade, and render returns for investments inconveniently uncertain. I have heard artillery in my time, having in my younger days led a band of city volunteers in many a march and countermarch around the Bowling-Green; and for the honor of the second ward of the good town of Manhattan, I am now ready to undertake to show, that all knowledge of the art has not entirely departed from me."

"That is a manly answer, and, provided it be sustained by a corresponding countenance, there shall be no impertinent inquiry into motives. 'Tis the officer that makes the ship victorious; for, when he sets a good example and understands his duty, there is little fear of the men. Choose your position among any of these guns, and we will make an effort to disappoint yon servants of Louis, whether we do it as Englishmen, or only as the allies of the Seven Provinces."

Myndert descended to the quarter-deck, and having deliberately deposited his coat on the capstan, replaced his wig by a handkerchief, and tightened the buckle that did the office of suspenders, he squinted along the guns, with a certain air that served to assure the spectators he had at least no dread of the recoil.

Alderman Van Beverout was a personage far too important, not to be known by most of those who frequented the goodly town of which he was a civic officer. His presence, therefore, among the men, not a few of whom were natives of the colony, had a salutary effect; some yielding to the sympathy which is natural to a hearty and encouraging example, while it is possible there were a few that argued less of the danger, in consequence of the indifference of a man who, being so rich, had so many motives to take good care of his person. Be this as it might, the burgher was received by a cheer which drew a short but pithy address from him, in which he exhorted his companions in arms to do their duty, in a manner which should teach the Frenchmen the wisdom of leaving that coast in future free from annoyance; while he wisely abstained from all the commonplace allusions to king and country — a subject to which he felt his inability to do proper justice.

"Let every man remember that cause for courage, which may be most agreeable to his own habits and opinions," concluded this imitator of the Hannibals and Scipios of old; "for that is the surest and the briefest method of bringing his mind into an obstinate state. In my own case, there is no want of motive; and I dare say each one of you may find some sufficient reason for entering heart and hand into this battle. Protests and credit! what would become of the affairs of the best house in the colonies, were its principal to be led a captive to Brest or l'Orient? It might derange the business of the whole city. I'll not offend your patriotism with such a supposition, but at once believe that your minds are resolved, like my own, to resist to the last; for this is an interest which is general, as all questions of a commercial nature become, through their influence on the happiness and prosperity of society."

Having terminated his address in so apposite and public-spirited a manner, the worthy burgher hemmed loudly, and resumed his accustomed silence, perfectly assured of his own applause. If the matter of Myndert's discourse wears too much the air of an unvided attention to his own interests, the reader will not forget it is by this concentration of individuality that most of the mercantile prosperity of the world is achieved. The seamen listened with admiration, for they understood no part of the appeal; and, next to a statement which shall be so lucid as to induce every hearer to believe it is no more than a happy explanation of his own ideas, that which is unintelligible is apt to unite most suffrages in its favor.

"You see your enemy, and you know your work!" said the clear, deep, manly voice of Ludlow, who, as he passed among the people of the Coquette, spoke to them in that steady unwavering tone which, in moments of danger, goes to the heart. "I shall not pretend that we are as strong as I could wish; but the greater the necessity for a strong pull, the readier a true seaman will be to give it. There are no nails in that ensign. When I am dead, you may pull it down if you please; but, so long as I live, my men, there it shall fly! And now, one cheer to show your humor, and then let the rest of your noise come from the guns."

The crew complied, with a full-mouthed and hearty hurrah! — Trysail assured a young, laughing, careless midshipman, who even at that moment could enjoy an uproar, that he had seldom heard a prettier piece of sea-eloquence than that which had just fallen from the captain; it being both 'neat and gentleman-like.'

CHAPTER XXX.

"Sir, it is
A charge too heavy for my strength; but yet
We'll strive to bear it for your worthy sake,
To the extreme edge of hazard."
All's Well That End's Well.

THE vessel, which appeared so inopportunely for the safety of the ill-manned British cruiser, was, in truth, a ship that had roved from among the islands of the Caribean sea, in quest of some such adventure as that which now presented itself. She was called la belle Fontange, and her commander, a youth of two-and-twenty, was already well known in the salons of the Marais, and behind the walls of the Rue Basse des Remparts, as one of the most gay and amiable of those who frequented the former, and one of the most spirited and skilful among the adventurers who sometimes trusted to their address in the latter. Rank, and influence at Versailles, had procured for the young Chevalier Dumont de la Rocheforte a command to which he could lay no claim either by his experience or his services. His mother, a near relative of one of the beauties of the court, had been commanded to use sea-bathing, as a preventive against the consequences of the bite of a rabid lap-dog. By way of a suitable episode to the long descriptions she was in the daily habit of writing to those whose knowledge of her new element was limited to the constant view of a few ponds and ditches teeming with carp, or an occasional glimpse of some of the turbid reaches of the Seine, she had vowed to devote her youngest child to Neptune! In due time, that is to say, while the poetic sentiment was at the access, the young chevalier was duly enrolled and, in a time that greatly anticipated all regular and judicious preferment, he was placed in command of the corvette in question, and sent to the Indies to gain glory for himself and his country.

The Chevalier Dumont de la Rocheforte was brave, but his courage was not the calm and silent self-possession of a seaman. Like himself, it was lively, buoyant, thoughtless, bustling, and full of animal feeling. He had all the pride of a gentleman, and, unfortunately for the duty which he had now for the first time to perform, one of its dictates caught him to despise that species of mechanical knowledge which it was, just at this moment, so important to the commander of la Fontange to possess. He could dance to admiration, did the honors of his cabin with faultless elegance, and had caused the death of an excellent mariner, who had accidentally fallen overboard, by jumping into the sea to aid him, without knowing how to swim a stroke himself — a rashness that had diverted those exertions which might have saved the unfortunate sailor, from the assistance of the subordinate to the safety of his superior. He wrote sonnets prettily, and had some ideas of the new philosophy which was just beginning to dawn upon the world; but the cordage of his ship, and the lines of a mathematical problem, equally presented labyrinths he had never threaded.

It was perhaps fortunate for the safety of all in her, that la belle Fontange possessed an inferior officer, in the person of a native of Boulogne-sur-Mer, who was quite competent to see that she kept the proper course, and that she displayed none of the top-gallants of her pride, at unpropitious moments. The ship itself was sufficiently and finely moulded of a light and airy rig, and of established reputation or speed. If it was defective in any thing, it had the fault, in common with its commander, of a want of sufficient solidity to resist the vicissitudes and dangers of the turbulent element on which it was destined to act.

The vessels were now within a mile of each other. The breeze was steady, and sufficiently fresh for all the ordinary evolutions of a naval combat; while the water was just quiet enough to permit the ships to be handled with confidence and accuracy. La Fontange was running with her head to the eastward, and, as she had the advantage of the wind, her tall tracery of spars leaned gently in the direction of her adversary. The Coquette was standing on the other tack, and necessarily inclined from her enemy. Both vessels were stripped to their top-sails, spankers, and jibs, though the lofty sails of the Frenchman were fluttering in the breeze, like the graceful folds of some fanciful drapery. No human being was distinctly visible in either fabric, though dark clusters around each mast-head showed that the ready top-men were prepared to discharge their duties, even in the confusion and dangers of the impending contest. Once or twice, la Fontange inclined her head more in the direction of her adversary; and then, sweeping up again to the wind, she stood on in stately beauty The moment was near when the ships were about to cross each other, at a point where a musket would readily send its messenger across the waiter that lay between them. Ludlow, who closely watched each change of position, and every rise and fall of the breeze, went on the poop, and swept the horizon with his glass, for the last time before his ship should be enveloped in smoke. To his surprise, he discovered a pyramid of canvas rising above the sea, in the direction of the wind. The sail was clearly visible to the naked eye, and had only escaped earlier observation in the duties of so urgent a moment. Calling the master to his side, he inquired his opinion concerning the character of the second stranger. But Trysail confessed it exceeded even his long-tried powers of observation to say more than that it was a ship running before the wind, with a cloud of sail spread. After a second and a longer look, however, the experienced master ventured to add that the stranger had the squareness and symmetry of a cruiser, but of what size he would not yet presume to declare.

"It may be a light ship, under her top-gallant and studding-sails, or it may be, that we see only the lofty duck of some heavier vessel, Captain Ludlow — ha! he has caught the eye of the Frenchman, for the corvette has signals abroad!"

"To your glass! — If the stranger answer, we have no choice but our speed."

There was another keen and anxious examination of the upper spars of the distant ship, but the direction of the wind prevented any signs of her communicating with the corvette from being visible. La Fontange appeared equally uncertain of the character of the stranger, and for a moment there was some evidence of an intention to change her course. But the moment for indecision had past. The ships were already sweeping up abreast of each other, under the constant pressure of the breeze.

"Be ready, men!" said Ludlow, in a low but firm voice, retaining his elevated post on the poop, while he motioned to his companion to return to the main-deck. "Fire at his flash!"

Intense expectation succeeded. The two graceful fabrics sailed steadily on, and came within hail. So profound was the stillness in the Coquette, that the rushing sound of the water she heaped under her bows was distinctly audible to all on board, and might be likened to the deep breathing of some vast animal, that was collecting its physical energies for some unusual exertion. On the other hand, tongues were loud and clamorous among the cordage of la Fontange. Just as the ships were fairly abeam, the voice of young Dumont was heard, shouting through a trumpet, for his men to fire. Ludlow smiled, in a seaman's scorn. Raising his own trumpet, with a quiet gesture to his attentive and ready crew, the whole discharge of their artillery broke out of the dark side of the ship, as if it had been by the volition of the fabric. The answering broadside was received almost as soon as their own had been given, and the two vessels passed swiftly without the line of shot.

The wind had sent back their own smoke upon the English, and for a time it floated on their decks, wreathed itself in the eddies of the sails, and passed away to leeward, with the breeze that succeeded to the counter-current of the explosions. The whistling of shot, and the crash of wood, had been heard amid the din of the combat. Giving a glance at his enemy, who still stood on, Ludlow leaned from the poop, and, with all a sailor's anxiety, he endeavored to scan the gear aloft.

"What is gone, Sir?" he asked of Trysail, whose earnest face just then became visible through the drifting smoke. "What sail is so heavily flapping?"

"Little harm done, Sir — little harm — bear a hand with the tackle on that fore-yard-arm, you lubbers! you move like snails in a minuet! The fellow has shot away the lee fore-top-sail-sheet, Sir; but we shall soon get our wings spread again. Lash it down, boys, as if it were butt-bolted — so; steady out your bowline, forward. — Meet her, you can; meet her you may — meet her!"

The smoke had disappeared, and the eye of the captain rapidly scanned the whole of his ship. Three or four top-men had already caught the flapping canvas, and were seated on the extremity of the fore-yard, busied in securing their prize. A hole or two was visible in the other sails, and here and there an unimportant rope was dangling in a manner to show that it had been cut by shot. Further than this, the damage aloft was not of a nature to attract his attention.

There was a different scene on deck. The feeble crew were earnestly occupied in loading the guns, and rammers and spunges were handled, with all the intenseness which men would manifest in a moment so exciting. The Alderman was never more absorbed in his leger than he now appeared in his duty of a cannoneer; and the youths, to whom the command of the batteries had necessarily been confided, diligently aided him with their greater authority and experience. Trysail stood near the capstan, coolly giving the orders which have been related, and gazing upward with an interest so absorbed as to render him unconscious of all that passed around his person. Ludlow saw, with pain, that blood discolored the deck at his feet, and that a seaman lay dead within reach of his arm. The rent plank and shattered ceiling showed the spot where the destructive missile had entered.

Compressing his lips like a man resolved, the commander of the Coquette bent further forward, and glanced at the wheel. The quarter-master, who held the spokes, was erect, steady, and kept his eye on the leech of the head-sail, as unerringly as the needle points to the pole.

These were the observations of a single minute. The different circumstances related had been ascertained with so many rapid glances of the eye, and they had even been noted without losing for a moment the knowledge of the precise situation of la Fontange. The latter was already in stays. It became necessary to meet the evolution by another as prompt.

The order was no sooner given, than the Coquette, as if conscious of the hazard she ran of being raked, whirled away from the wind, and, by the time her adversary was ready to deliver her other broadside she was in a position to receive and to return it. Again the ships approached each other, and once more they exchanged their streams of fire when abeam.

Ludlow now saw, through the smoke, the ponderous yard of la Fontange swinging heavily against the breeze, and the main-top-sail come flapping against her mast. Swinging off from the poop by a backstay that had been shot away a moment before, he alighted on the quarter-deck by the side of the master.

"Touch all the braces!" he said, hastily, but still speaking low and clearly; "give a drag upon the bowlines — luff, Sir, luff; jam the ship up hard against the wind!"

The clear, steady answer of the quarter-master, and the manner in which the Coquette, still vomiting her sheets of flame, inclined towards the breeze, announced the promptitude of the subordinates. In another minute, the vast volumes of smoke which enveloped the two ships joined, and formed one white and troubled cloud, which was rolling swiftly before the explosions, over the surface of the sea, but which, as it rose higher in the air, sailed gracefully to leeward.

Our young commander passed swiftly through the batteries, spoke encouragingly to his people, and resumed his post on the poop. The stationary position of la Fontange, and his own efforts to get to windward, were already proving advantageous to Queen Anne's cruiser. There was some indecision on the part of the other ship, which instantly caught the eye of one whose readiness in his profession so much resembled instinct.

The Chevalier Dumont had amused his leisure by running his eyes over the records of the naval history of his country, where he had found this and that commander applauded for throwing their top-sails to the mast, abreast of their enemies. Ignorant of the difference between a ship in line and one engaged singly, he had determined to prove himself equal to a similar display of spirit. At the moment when Ludlow was standing alone on the poop, watching with vigilant eyes the progress of his own vessel, and the position of his enemy, indicating merely by a look or a gesture to the attentive Trysail beneath, what he wished done, there was actually a wordy discussion on the quarter-deck of the latter, between the mariner of Boulogne-sur-Mer, and the gay favorite of the salons. They debated on the expediency of the step which the latter had taken, to prove the existence of a quality that no one doubted The time lost in this difference of opinion was of the last importance to the British cruiser. Standing gallantly on, she was soon out of the range of her adversary's fire; and, before the Boulognois had succeeded in convincing his superior of his error, their antagonist was on the other tack, and luffing across the wake of la Fontange. The top-sail was then tardily filled, but before the latter ship had recovered her motion, the sails of her enemy overshadowed her deck. There was now every prospect of the Coquette passing to windward. At that critical moment, the fair-setting top-sail of the British cruiser was nearly rent in two by a shot. The ship fell off, the yards interlocked, and the vessels were foul.

The Coquette had all the advantage of position. Perceiving the important fact at a glance, Ludlow made sure of its continuance by throwing his grapnels. When the two ships were thus firmly lashed together, the young Dumont found himself relieved from a mountain of embarrassment. Sufficiently justified by the fact that not a single gun of his own would bear, while a murderous discharge of grape had just swept along his decks, he issued the order to board. But Ludlow, with his weakened crew, had not decided on so hazardous an evolution as that which brought him in absolute contact with his enemy, without foreseeing the means of avoiding all the consequences. The vessels touched each other only at one point, and this spot was protected by a row of muskets. No sooner, therefore, did the impetuous young Frenchman appear on the taffrail of his own ship, supported by a band of followers, than a close and deadly fire swept them away to a man. Young Dumont alone remained. For a single moment, his eye glared wildly; but the active frame, still obedient to the governing impulse of so impetuous a spirit, leaped onward. He fell, without life, on the deck of his enemy.

Ludlow watched every movement, with a calmness that neither personal responsibility, nor the uproar and rapid incidents of the terrible scene, could discompose.

"Now is our time to bring the matter hand to hand!" he cried, making a gesture to Trysail to descend from the ladder, in order that he might pass.

His arm was arrested, and the grave old master pointed to windward.

"There is no mistaking the cut of those sails, or the lofty rise of those spars! The stranger is another Frenchman!"

One glance told Ludlow that his subordinate was right; another sufficed to show what was now necessary.

"Cast loose the forward grapnel — cut it — away with it, clear!" was shouted, through his trumpet, in a voice that rose commanding and clear amid the roar of the combat.

Released forward, the stern of the Coquette yielded to the pressure of her enemy, whose sails were all drawing, and she was soon in a position to enable her head-yards to be braced sharp aback, in a direction opposite to the one in which she had so lately lain. The whole broadside was then delivered into the stern of la Fontange, the last grapnel was released and the ships separated.

The single spirit which presided over the evolutions and exertions of the

Coquette, still governed her movements. The sails were trimmed, the ship was got in command, and, before the vessels had been asunder five minutes, the duty of the vessel was in its ordinary active but noiseless train.

Nimble top-men were on the yards, and broad folds of fresh canvas were flapping in the breeze, as the new sails were bent and set. Ropes were spliced, or supplied by new rigging, the spars examined, and in fine all that watchfulness and sedulous care were observed, which are so necessary to the efficiency and safety of a ship. Every spar was secured, the pumps were sounded, and the vessel held on her way, as steadily as if she had never fired nor received a shot.

On the other hand, la Fontange betrayed the indecision and confusion of a worsted ship. Her torn canvas was blowing about in disorder, many important ropes beat against her masts unheeded, and the vessel itself drove before the breeze in the helplessness of a wreck. For several minutes, there seemed no controlling mind in the fabric; and when, after so much distance was lost as to give her enemy all the advantage of the wind, a tardy attempt was made to bring the ship up again, the tallest and most important of her masts was seen tottering, until it finally fell, with all its hamper, into the sea.

Notwithstanding the absence of so many of his people, success would now have been certain, had not the presence of the stranger compelled Ludlow to abandon his advantage. But the consequences to his own vessel were too sure, to allow of more than a natural and manly regret that so favorable an occasion should escape him. The character of the stranger could no longer be mistaken. The eve of every seaman in the Coquette as well understood the country of the high and narrow-headed sails, the tall taper masts and short yards of the frigate whose hull was now distinctly visible, as a landsman recognizes an individual by the distinguishing marks of his features or attire. Had there been any lingering doubts on the subject, they would have all given place to certainty, when the stranger was seen exchanging signals with the crippled corvette.

It was now time for Ludlow to come to a speedy determination on his future course. The breeze still held to the southward, but it was beginning to lessen, with every appearance that it would fail before nightfall. The land lay a few leagues to the northward, and the whole horizon of the ocean, with the exception of the two French cruisers, was clear. Descending to the quarter-deck, he approached the master, who was seated in a chair, while the surgeon dressed a severe hurt in one of his legs. Shaking the sturdy veteran cordially by the hand, he expressed his acknowledgments for his support in a moment so trying.

"God bless you! God bless you! Captain Ludlow;" returned the old sailor, dashing his hand equivocally across his weatherbeaten brow. "Battle is certainly the place to try both ship and friends, and Heaven be praised! Queen Anne has not failed of either this day. No man has forgotten his duty, so far as my eyes have witnessed; and this is saying no trifle, with half a crew and an equal enemy. As for the ship, she never behaved better! I had my misgivings, when I saw the new main-top-sail go, which it did, as all here know, like a bit of rent muslin between the fingers of a seamstress. Run forward, Mr. Hopper, and tell the men in the fore rigging to take another drag on that swifter, and to be careful and bring the strain equal on all the shrouds. — A lively youth, Captain Ludlow, and one who only wants a little reflection, with some more experience, and a small dash of modesty, together with the seamanship he will naturally get in time, to make a very tolerable officer."

"The boy promises well; but I have come to ask thy advice, my old friend, concerning our next movements. There is no doubt that the fellow who is coming down upon us is both a Frenchman and a frigate."

"A man might as well doubt the nature of a fish-hawk, which is to pick up all the small fry, and to let the big ones go. We might show him our canvas and try the open sea, but I fear that fore-mast is too weak, with three such holes in it, to bear the sail we should need!"

"What think you of the wind?" said Ludlow, affecting an indecision he did not feel, in order to soothe the feelings of his wounded companion. "Should it hold, we might double Montauk, and return for the rest of our people; but should it fail, is there no danger that the frigate should tow within shot! — We have no boats to escape her."

"The soundings on this coast are as regular as the roof of an out-house," said the master, after a moment of thought, "and it is my advice, if it is your pleasure to ask it, Captain Ludlow, that we shoal our water as much as possible, while the wind lasts. Then, I think, we shall be safe from a very near visit from the big one — as for the corvette, I am of opinion, that, like a man who has eaten his dinner, she has no stomach for another slice."

Ludlow applauded the advice of his subordinate, for it was precisely what he had determined on doing; and after again complimenting him on his coolness and skill, he issued the necessary orders. The helm of the Coquette was now placed hard a-weather, the yards were squared, and the ship was put before the wind. After running, in this direction for a few hours, the wind gradually lessening, the lead announced that the keel was quite as near the bottom as the time of the tide, and the dull heaving and setting of the element, rendered at all prudent. The breeze soon after fell, and then our young commander ordered an anchor to be dropped into the sea.

His example, in the latter respect, was imitated by the hostile cruisers. They had soon joined, and boats were seen passing from one to the other, so long as there was light. When the sun fell behind the western margin of the ocean, their dusky outlines, distant about a league, gradually grew less and less distinct, until the darkness of night enveloped sea and land in its gloom.

CHAPTER XXXI.

"Now; the business!"
Othello.

THREE hours later, and every noise was hushed on board the royal cruiser. The toil of repairing damages had ceased, and most of the living, with the dead, lay alike in common silence. The watchfulness necessary to the situation of the fatigued mariners, however, was not forgotten, and though so many slept, a few eyes were still open, and affecting to be alert. Here and there, some drowsy seaman paced the deck, or a solitary young officer endeavored to keep himself awake, by humming a low air, in his narrow bounds. The mass of the crew slept heavily, with pistols in their belts and cutlasses at their sides, between the guns. There was one figure-extended upon the quarter-deck, with the head resting on a shot-box. The deep breathing of this person denoted the unquiet slumbers of a powerful frame, in which weariness contended with suffering. It was the wounded and feverish master, who had placed himself in that position to catch an hour of the repose that was necessary to his situation. Oh an arm-chest, which had been emptied of its contents, lay another but a motionless human form, with the limbs composed in decent order, and with the face turned towards the melancholy stars. This was the body of the young Dumont, which had been kept, with the intention of con-signing it to consecrated earth, when the ship should return to port. Ludlow, with the delicacy of a generous and chivalrous enemy had with his own hands spread the stainless ensign of his country over the remains of the inexperienced but gal-lant young Frenchman.

There was one little group on the raised deck in the stern of the vessel, in which the ordinary interests of life still seemed to exercise their influence. Hither Ludlow had led Alida and her companions, after the duties of the day were over, in order that they might breathe an air fresher than that of the interior of the vessel. The negress nodded near her young mistress; the tired Alderman sate with his back supported against the mizen-mast, giving audible evidence of his situa-tion; and Ludlow stood erect, occasionally throwing an earnest look on the sur-rounding and unruffled waters, and then lending his attention to the discourse of his companions. Alida and Seadrift were seated near each other, on chairs. The conversation was low, while the melancholy and the tremor in the voice of la belle Barbérie denoted how much the events of the day had shaken her usually firm and spirited mind.

"There is a mingling of the terrific and the beautiful, of the grand and the seducing, in this unquiet profession of yours!" observed, or rather continued Alida, replying to a previous remark of the young sailor. "That tranquil sea — the hollow sound of the surf on the shore — and this soft canopy above us form objects on which even a girl might dwell in admiration, were not her ears still ringing with the roar and cries of the combat. Did you say the commander of the Frenchman was but a youth?"

"A mere boy in appearance, and one who doubtless owed his rank to the advantages of birth and family. We know it to be the captain, by his dress, no less than by the desperate effort he made to recover the false step taken in the earlier part of the action."

"Perhaps he has a mother, Ludlow! — a sister — a wife — or —"

Alida paused, for, with maiden diffidence, she hesitated to pronounce the tie which was uppermost in her thoughts.

"He may have had one, or all! Such are the sailor's hazards, and —"

"Such the hazards of those who feel an interest in their safety!" uttered the low but expressive voice of Seadrift.

A deep and eloquent silence succeeded. Then the voice of Myndert was heard muttering indistinctly, "twenty of beaver, and three of marten — as per invoice." The smile which, spite of the train of his thoughts, rose on the lips of Ludlow, had scarcely passed away, when the hoarse tones of Trysail, rendered still hoarser by his sleep, were plainly heard in a stifled cry, saying, "Bear a hand, there, with your stoppers! — the Frenchman is coming round upon us, again."

"That is prophetic!" said one, aloud, behind the listening group. Ludlow turned, quick as the flag fluttering on its vane, and through the darkness he recognized, in the motionless but manly form that stood near him on the poop, the fine person of the 'Skimmer of the Seas.'

"Call away — !"

"Call none!" — interrupted Tiller, stopping the hurried order which involuntarily broke from the lips of Ludlow. "Let thy ship feign the silence of a wreck, but, in truth, let there be watchfulness and preparation even to her store-rooms! You have done well, Captain Ludlow, to be on the alert, though I have known sharper eyes than those of some of your look-outs."

"Whence come you, audacious man, and what mad errand has brought you again on the deck of my ship?"

"I come from my habitation on the sea. My business here is warning!"

"The sea!" echoed Ludlow, gazing about him at the narrow and empty view. "The hour for mockery is past, and you would do well to trifle no more with those who have serious duties to discharge."

"The hour is indeed one for serious duties — duties, more serious than any you apprehend. But before I enter on explanation, there must be conditions between us. You have one of the sea-green lady's servitors, here; I claim his liberty, for my secret."

"The error into which I had fallen exists no longer;" returned Ludlow, looking for an instant towards the shrinking form of Seadrift. "My conquest is worthless, unless you come to supply his place."

"I come for other purposes — here is one who knows I do not trifle when urgent affairs are on hand. Let thy companions retire, that I may speak openly."

Ludlow hesitated, for he had not yet recovered from the surprise of finding the redoubtable free-trader so unexpectedly on the deck of his ship. But Alida and her companion arose, like those who had more confidence in their visiter, and, arousing the negress from her sleep, they descended the ladder and entered the cabin. When Ludlow found himself alone with Tiller, he demanded an explanation.

"It shall not be withheld, for time presses, and that which is to be done must be done with a seaman's care and coolness;" returned the other. "You have had a close brush with one of Louis's rovers, Captain Ludlow, and prettily was the ship of Queen Anne handled! Have your people suffered, and are you still strong enough to make good a defence worthy of your conduct this morning?"

"These are facts you would have me utter to the ear of one who may be false — even a spy!"

"Captain Ludlow — but circumstances warrant thy suspicions!"

"One whose vessel and life I have threatened — an outlaw!"

"This is too true," returned the 'Skimmer of the Seas,' suppressing a sudden impulse of pride and resentment. "I am threatened and pursued — I am a smuggler and an outlaw: still am I human! You see that dusky object, which borders the sea to the northward!"

"It is too plainly land, to be mistaken."

"Land, and the land of my birth! — the earliest, perhaps I may say the happiest of my days, were passed on that long and narrow island."

"Had I known it earlier, there would have been a closer look among its bays and inlets."

"The search might have been rewarded. A cannon would easily throw its shot from this deck to the spot where my brigantine now lies, snug at a single anchor."

"Unless you have swept her near since the setting of the sun, that is impossible! When the night drew on, nothing was in view but the frigate and corvette of the enemy."

"We have not stirred a fathom; and yet, true as the word of a fearless man, there lies the vessel of the sea-green lady. You see the place where the beach falls — here, at the nearest point of the land — the island is nearly severed by the water at that spot, and the Water-Witch is safe in the depths of the bay which enters from the northward. There is not a mile between us. From the eastern hill, I witnessed your spirit this day, Captain Ludlow, and though condemned in person, I felt that the heart could never be outlawed. There is a fealty here, that can survive even the persecutions of the custom-houses!"

"You are happy in your terms, Sir. I will not conceal that I think a seaman, even as skilful as yourself, must allow that the Coquette was kept prettily in command!"

"No pilot-boat could have been more sure, or more lively. I knew your weakness, for the absence of all your boats was no secret to me; and I confess I could have spared some of the profits of the voyage, to have been on your decks this day with a dozen of my truest fellows!"

"A man who can feel this loyalty to the flag, should find a more honorable occupation for his usual life."

"A country that can inspire it, should be cautious not to estrange the affections of its children, by monopolies and injustice. But these are discussions unsuited to the moment. I am doubly your countryman in this strait, and all the past is no more than the rough liberties which friends take with each other. Captain Ludlow, there is danger brooding in that dark void which lies to seaward!"

"On what authority do you speak thus?"

"Sight. I have been among your enemies, and have seen their deadly preparations. I know the caution is given to a brave man, and nothing shall be extenuated. You have need of all your resolution and of every arm — for they will be upon you, in overwhelming numbers!"

"True or false, thy warning shall not be neglected."

"Hold!" said the Skimmer, arresting a forward movement of his companion, with his hand. "Let them sleep to the last moment. You have yet an hour, and rest will renew their strength. You may trust the experience of a seaman who has passed half of the life of man on the ocean, and who has witnessed all its most stirring scenes, from the conflict of the elements to every variety of strife that man has invented to destroy his fellows. For another hour, you will be secure. — After that hour, God protect the unprepared! and God be merciful to him whose minutes are numbered!"

"Thy language and manner are those of one who deals honestly;" returned Ludlow, struck by the apparent sincerity of the free-trader's communication "In every event, we shall be ready, though the manner of your having gained this knowledge is as great a mystery as your appearance on the deck of my ship."

"Both can be explained," returned the Skimmer, motioning to his companion to follow to the tanrail. Here he pointed to a small and nearly imperceptible skiff, which floated at the bottom of a stern-ladder, and continued — "One who so often pays secret visits to the land, can never be in want of the means. This nut-shell was easily transported across the narrow slip of land that separates the bay from the ocean, and though the surf moans so hoarsely, it is easily passed by a steady and dexterous oarsman. I have been under the martingale of the Frenchman, and you see that I am here. If your look-outs are less alert than usual, you will remember that a low gunwale, a dusky side, and a muffled oar, are not readily detected, when the eye is heavy and the body wearied. I must now quit you — unless you think it more prudent to send those who can be of no service, out of the ship, before the trial shall come?"

Ludlow hesitated. A strong desire to put Alida in a place of safety, was met by his distrust of the smuggler's faith. He reflected a moment, ere he answered.

"Your cockle-shell is not sufficiently secure for more than its owner. Go, and as you prove loyal, may you prosper!"

"Abide the blow!" said the Skimmer, grasping his hand. He then stepped carelessly on the dangling ropes, and descended into the boat beneath. Ludlow watched his movements, with an intense and possibly with a distrustful curiosity. When seated at the sculls, the person of the free-trader was nearly indistinct; and as the boat glided noiselessly away, the young commander no longer felt disposed to censure those who had permitted its approach without a warning. In less than a minute, the dusky object was confounded with the surface of the sea.

Left to himself, the young commander of the Coquette seriously reflected on what had passed. The manner of the Skimmer, the voluntary character of his communication, its probability, and the means by which his knowledge had been obtained, united to confirm his truth. Instances of similar attachment to their flag, in seamen whose ordinary pursuits were opposed to its interests, were not uncommon. Their misdeeds resemble the errors of passion, and temptation, while the momentary return to better things is like the inextinguishable impulses of nature.

The admonition of the free-trader, who had enjoined the captain to allow his people to sleep, was remembered. Twenty times, within as many minutes, did our young sailor examine his watch, to note the tardy passage of the time; and as often did he return it to his pocket, with a determination to forbear. At length he descended to the quarter-deck, and drew near the only form that was erect. The watch was commanded by a youth of sixteen, whose regular period of probationary service had not passed, but who, in the absence of his superiors, was intrusted with this delicate and important duty. He stood leaning against the capstan, one hand supporting his cheek, while the elbow rested against the drum, and the body was without motion. Ludlow regarded him a moment, and then lifting a lighted battle-lantern to his face, he saw that he slept. Without disturbing the delinquent, the captain replaced the lantern and passed forward. In the gangway there stood a marine, with his musket shouldered, in an attitude of attention. As Ludlow brushed within a few inches of his eyes, it was easy to be seen that they opened and shut involuntarily, and without consciousness of what lay before them. On the top-gallant-forecastle was a short, square, and well-balanced figure, that stood without support of any kind, with both arms thrust into the bosom of a jacket, and a head that turned slowly to the west and south, as if it were examining the ocean in those directions.

Stepping lightly up the ladder, Ludlow saw that it was the veteran seaman who was rated as the captain of the forecastle.

"I am glad, at last, to find one pair of eyes open, in my ship," said the captain. "Of the whole watch, you alone are alert."

"I have doubled cape fifty, your Honor, and the seaman who has made that voyage, rarely wants the second call of the boatswain. Young heads have young eyes, and sleep is next to food, after a heavy drag at gun-tackles and lanyards."

"And what draws your attention so steadily in that quarter? There is nothing visible but the haze of the sea."

"'Tis the direction of the Frenchmen, Sir — does your Honor hear nothing?"

"Nothing;" said Ludlow, after intently listening for half a minute. "Nothing, unless it be the wash of the surf on the beach."

"It may be only fancy, but there came a sound like the fall of an oar-blade on a thwart, and 'tis but natural, your Honor, to expect the mounsheer will be out, in this smooth water, to see what has become of us. There went the flash of a light, or my name is not Bob Cleet!"

Ludlow was silent. A light was certainly visible in the quarter where the enemy was known to be anchored, and it came and disappeared like a moving lantern. At length it was seen to descend slowly, and vanish as if it were extinguished in the water.

"That lantern went into a boat, Captain Ludlow, though a lubber carried it!" said the positive old forecastle-man, shaking his head and beginning to pace across the deck, with the air of a man who needed no further confirmation of his suspicions.

Ludlow returned towards the quarter-deck, thoughtful but calm. He passed among his sleeping crew, without awaking a man, and even forbearing to touch the still motionless midshipman, he entered his cabin without speaking.

The commander of the Coquette was absent but a few minutes. When he again appeared on deck, there was more of decision and of preparation in his manner.

"'Tis time to call the watch, Mr. Reef," he whispered at the elbow of the drowsy officer of the deck, without betraying his consciousness of the youth's forgetfulness of duty. "The glass is out."

"Ay, ay, Sir. Bear a hand, and turn the glass!" muttered the young man. "A fine night, Sir, and very smooth water. I was just thinking of —"

"Home and thy mother! 'Tis the way with us all in youth. Well, we have now something else to occupy the thoughts. Muster all the gentlemen, here, on the quarter-deck, Sir."

"When the half-sleeping midshipman quitted his captain to obey this order, the latter drew near the spot where Trysail still lay in an unquiet sleep. A light touch of a single finger was sufficient to raise the master on his feet. The first look of the veteran tar was aloft, the second at the heavens, and the last at his captain.

"I fear thy wound stiffens, and that the night air has added to the pain?" observed the latter, speaking in a kind and considerate tone.

"The wounded spar cannot be trusted like a sound stick, Captain Ludlow; but as I am no foot-soldier on a march, the duty of the ship may go on without my calling for a horse."

"I rejoice in thy cheerful spirit, my old friend, for here is serious work likely to fall upon our hands. The Frenchmen are in their boats, and we shall shortly be brought to close quarters, or prognostics are false."

"Boats!" repeated the master. "I had rather it were under our canvas, with a stiff breeze! The play of this ship is a lively foot, and a touching leech but, when, it comes to boats, a marine is nearly as good a man as a quarter-master!"

"We must take fortune as it offers. Here is our council! — It is composed of young heads, but of hearts that might do credit to gray hairs."

Ludlow joined the little group of officers that was by this time assembled near the capstan. Here, in a few words, he explained the reason why he had summoned them from their sleep. When each of the youths understood his orders, and the nature of the new danger that threatened the ship, they separated, and began to enter with activity, but in guarded silence, on the necessary preparations. The sound of footsteps awoke a dozen of the older seamen, who immediately joined their officers.

Half an hour passed like a moment, in such an occupation. At the end of that time, Ludlow deemed his ship ready. The two forward guns had been run in, and the shot having been drawn, their places were supplied with double charges of grape and canister. Several Swivels, a species of armament much used in that age, were loaded to the muzzles, and placed in situations to rake the deck, while the fore-top was plentifully stored with arms and ammunition. The matches were prepared, and then the whole of the crew was mustered, by a particular call of each man. Five minutes sufficed to issue the necessary orders, and to see each post occupied. After this, the low hum ceased in the ship, and the silence again became so deep and general, that the wash of the receding surf was nearly as audible as the plunge of the wave on the sands.

Ludlow stood on the forecastle, accompanied by the master. Here he lent all his senses to the appearance of the elements, and to the signs of the moment. Wind there was none, though occasionally a breath of hot air came from the land, like the first efforts of the night-breeze. The heavens were clouded, though a few thoughtful stars glimmered between the masses of vapor.

"A calmer night never shut in the Americas!" said the veteran Trysail, shaking his head doubtingly and speaking in a suppressed and cautious tone. "I am one of those, Captain Ludlow, who think more than half the virtue is out of a ship when her anchor is down!"

"With a weakened crew, it may be better for us that the people have no yards to handle, nor any bowlines to steady. All our care can be given to defence."

"This is much like telling the hawk he can fight the better with a clipped wing, since he has not the trouble of flying! The nature of a ship is motion, and the merit of a seaman is judicious and lively handling — but of what use is complaining, since it will neither lift an anchor nor fill a sail? What is your opinion, Captain Ludlow, concerning an after life, and of all those matters one occasionally hears of it he happens to drift in the way of a church?"

"The question is broad as the ocean, my good friend, and a fitting answer might lead us into abstrusities deeper than any problem in our trigonometry. Was that the stroke of an oar?"

"'Twas a land noise. Well, I am no great navigator among the crooked channels of religion. Every new argument is a sand-bar, or a shoal, that obliges me to tack and stand off again; else I might have been a bishop, for any thing the world knows to the contrary. 'Tis a gloomy night, Captain Ludlow, and one that is sparing of its stars. I never knew luck come of an expedition on which a natural light did not fall!"

"So much the worse for those who seek to harm us. I surely heard an oar in the row-lock!"

"It came from the shore, and had the sound of the land about it;" quietly returned the master, who still kept his look riveted on the heavens. "This world, in which we live, Captain Ludlow, is one of extraordinary uses; but that, to which we are steering, is still more unaccountable. They say that worlds are sailing above us, like ships in a clear sea; and there are people who believe, that when we take our departure from this planet, we are only bound to another, in which we are to be rated according to our own deeds here; which is much the same as being drafted for a new ship, with a certificate of service in one's pocket."

"The resemblance is perfect;" returned the other leaning far over a timber-head, to catch the smallest sound that might come from the ocean. "That was no more than the blowing of a porpoise!"

"It was strong enough for the puff of a whale. There is no scarcity of big fish on the coast of this island, and bold harpooners are the men who are scattered about on the sandy downs, here-away, to the northward. I once sailed with an officer who knew the name, of every star in the heavens, and often have I passed hours in listening to his history of their magnitude and character, during the middle watches. It was his opinion, that there is but one navigator for all the rovers of the air, whether meteors, comets, or planets."

"No doubt he must be right, having been there."

"No, that is more than I can say for him, though few men have gone deeper into the high latitudes on both sides of our own equator, than he. One surely spoke — here, in a line with yonder low star!"

"Was it not a water-fowl?"

"No gull — ha! here we have the object, just within the starboard jib-boom-guy. There comes the Frenchman in his pride, and 'twill be lucky for him who lives to count the slain, or to boast of his deeds!"

The master descended from the forecastle, and passed among the crew, with every thought recalled from its excursive flight to the duty of the moment. Ludlow continued on the forecastle, alone. There was a low, whispering sound in the ship, like that which is made by the murmuring of a rising breeze — and then all was still as death.

The Coquette lay with her head to seaward, the stern necessarily pointing towards the land. The distance from the latter was less than a mile, and the direction of the ship's hull was caused by the course of the heavy ground-swell, which incessantly rolled the waters on the wide beach of the island. The head-gear lay in the way of the dim *view*, and Ludlow walked out on the bowsprit, in order that nothing should lie between him and the part of the ocean he wished to study. Here he had not stood a minute, when he caught, first a confused and then a more distinct glimpse of a line of dark objects, advancing slowly towards the ship. Assured of the position of his enemy, he returned in-board, and descended among his people. In another moment he was again on the forecastle, across which he paced leisurely, and, to all appearance, with the calmness of one who enjoyed the refreshing coolness of the night.

At the distance of a hundred fathoms, the dusky line of boats paused, and began to change its order. At that instant the first puffs of the land breeze were felt, and the stern of the ship made a gentle inclination seaward.

"Help her with the mizen! Let fall the top-sail!" whispered the young captain to those beneath him. Ere another moment, the flap of the loosened sail was heard. The ship swung still further, and Ludlow stamped on the deck.

A round fiery light shot beyond the martingale, and the smoke rolled along the sea, outstripped by a crowd of missiles that were hissing across the water. A shout, in which command was mingled with shrieks, followed, and then oar-blades were heard dashing the water aside, regardless of concealment. The ocean lighted, and three or four boat-guns returned the fatal discharge from the ship. Ludlow had not spoken. Still alone on his elevated and exposed post, he watched the effects of both fires, with a commander's coolness. The smile that struggled about his compressed mouth, when the momentary confusion among the boats betrayed the success of his own attack, had been wild and exulting; but when he heard the rending of the plank beneath him, the heavy groans that succeeded, and the rattling of lighter objects that were scattered by the shot, as it passed with lessened force along the deck of his ship, it became fierce and resentful.

"Let them have it!" he shouted, in a clear animating voice, that assured the people of his presence and his care. "Show them the humor of an Englishman's sleep, my lads! Speak to them, tops and decks!"

The order was obeyed. The remaining bow-gun was fired, and the discharge of all the Coquette's musketry and blunderbusses followed. A crowd of boats came sweeping under the bowsprit of the ship at the same moment, and then arose the clamor and shouts of the boarders.

The succeeding minutes were full of confusion, and of devoted exertion. Twice were the head and bowsprit of the ship filled with dark groups of men, whose grim visages were only visible by the pistol's flash, and as often were they cleared by the pike and bayonet. A third effort was more successful, and the tread of the assailants was heard on the deck of the forecastle. The struggle was but momentary, though many fell, and the narrow arena was soon slippery with blood. The Boulognese mariner was foremost among his countrymen, and at that desperate emergency Ludlow and Trysail fought in the common herd. Numbers prevailed, and it was fortunate for the commander of the Coquette, that the sudden recoil of a human body that fell upon him, drove him from his footing to the deck beneath.

Recovering from the fall, the young captain cheered his men by his voice, and was answered by the deep-mouthed shouts, which an excited seaman is ever ready to deliver, even to the death.

"Rally in the gangways, and defy them!" was the animated cry — "Rally in the gangways, hearts of oak." was returned by Trysail, in a ready but weakened voice. The men obeyed, and Ludlow saw that he could still muster a force capable of resistance.

Both parties for a moment paused. The fire of the top annoyed the boarders, and the defendants hesitated to advance. But the rush from both was common, and a fierce encounter occurred at the foot of the fore-mast. The crowd thickened in the rear of the French, and one of their number no sooner fell than another filled his place. The English receded, and Ludlow, extricating himself from the mass, retired to the quarter-deck.

"Give way, men!" he again shouted, so clear and steady, as to be heard above the cries and execrations of the fight. "Into the wings; down — between the guns — down — to your covers!"

The English disappeared, as if by magic. Some leaped upon the ridge-ropes, others sought the protection of the guns, and many went through the hatches. At that moment Ludlow made his most desperate effort. Aided by the gunner, he applied matches to the two swivels, which had been placed in readiness for a last resort. The deck was enveloped in smoke, and, when the vapor lifted, the forward part of the ship was as clear as if man had never trod it. All who had not fallen, had vanished.

A shout, and a loud hurrah! brought back the defendants, and Ludlow headed a charge upon the top-gallant-forecastle, again, in person. A few of the assailants showed themselves from behind covers on the deck, and the struggle was renewed. Glaring balls of fire sailed over the heads of the combatants, and fell among the throng in the rear. Ludlow saw the danger, and he endeavored to urge his people on to regain the bow-guns, one of which was known to be loaded. But the explosion of a grenade on deck, and in his rear, was followed by a shock in the hold, that threatened to force the bottom out of the vessel. The alarmed and weakened crew began to waver, and as a fresh attack of grenades was followed by a fierce rally, in which the assailants brought up fifty men in a body from their boats, Ludlow found himself compelled to retire amid the retreating mass of his own crew.

The defence now assumed the character of hopeless but desperate resistance. The cries of the enemy were more and more clamorous; and they succeeded in nearly silencing the top, by a heavy fire of musketry established on the bowsprit and sprit-sail-yard.

Events passed much faster than they can be related. The enemy were in possession of all the forward part of the ship to her fore-hatches, but into these young Hopper had thrown himself, with half-a-dozen men, and, aided by a brother midshipman in the launch, backed by a few followers, they still held the assailants at bay. Ludlow cast an eye behind him, and began to think of selling his life as dearly as possible in the cabins. That glance was arrested by the sight of the malign smile of the sea-green lady, as the gleaming face rose above the taffrail. A dozen dark forms leaped upon the poop, and then arose a voice that sent every tone it uttered to his heart.

"Abide the shock!" was the shout of those who came to the succor; and "abide the shock!" was echoed by the crew. The mysterious image glided along the deck, and Ludlow knew the athletic frame that brushed through the throng at its side.

There was little noise in the onset, save the groans of the sufferers. It endured but a moment, but it was a moment that resembled the passage of a whirlwind. The defendants knew that they were succored, and the assailants recoiled before so unexpected a foe. The few that were caught beneath the forecastle were mercilessly slain, and those above were swept from their post like chaff drifting in a gale.

The living and the dead were heard falling alike into the sea, and in an unconceiv-ably short space of time, the decks of the Coquette were free. A solitary enemy still hesitated on the bowsprit. A powerful and active frame leaped along the spar, and though the blow was not seen, its effects were visible, as the victim tumbled helplessly into the ocean.

The hurried dash of oars followed, and before the defendants had time to assure themselves of the completeness of their success, the gloomy void of the sur-rounding ocean had swallowed up the boats.

CHAPTER XXXII.

"That face of his I do remember well;
Yet, when I saw it last, it was besmear'd
As black as Vulcan, in the smoke of war."

What You Will.

FROM the moment when the Coquette fired her first gun, to the moment when the retiring boats became invisible, was just twenty minutes. Of this time, less than half had been occupied by the incidents related, in the ship. Short as it was in truth, it seemed to all engaged but an instant. The alarm was over, the sound of the oars had ceased, and still the survivors stood at their posts, as if expecting the attack to be renewed. Then came those personal thoughts, which had been suspended in the fearful exigency of such a struggle. The wounded began to feel their pain, and to be sensible of the danger of their injuries; while the few, who had escaped unhurt, turned a friendly care on their shipmates. Ludlow as often happens with the bravest and most exposed, had escaped without a scratch; but he saw by the drooping forms around him, which were no longer sustained by the excitement of battle, that his triumph was dearly purchased.

"Send Mr. Trysail to me;" he said, in a tone that had little of a victor's exultation. "The land breeze has made, and we will endeavor to improve it, and get inside the cape, lest the morning light give us more of these Frenchmen."

The order for 'Mr. Trysail!' 'the captain calls the master!' passed in a low call from mouth to mouth, but it was unanswered. A seaman told the expecting young commander, that the surgeon desired his presence forward. A gleaming of lights and a little group at the foot of the fore-mast, was a beacon not to be mistaken. The weatherbeaten master was in the agony; and his medical attendant had just risen from a fruitless examination of his wounds, as Ludlow approached.

"I hope the hurt is not serious?" hurriedly whispered the alarmed young sailor to the surgeon, who was coolly collecting his implements, in order to administer to some more promising subject. "Neglect nothing that your art can suggest."

"The case is desperate, Captain Ludlow," returned the phlegmatic surgeon; "but if you have a taste for such things, there is as beautiful a case for amputation promised in the fore-topman whom I have had sent below, as offers once in a whole life of active practice!"

"Go, go —" interrupted Ludlow, half pushing the unmoved man of blood

326

away, as he spoke; "go, then, where your services are needed."

The other cast a glance around him, reproved his attendant, in a sharp tone, for unnecessarily exposing the blade of some ferocious-looking instrument to the dew, and departed.

"Would to God, that some portion of these injuries had befallen those who are younger and stronger!" murmured the captain, as he leaned over the dying master. "Can I do aught to relieve thy mind, my old and worthy shipmate?"

"I have had my misgivings, since we have dealt with witchcraft!" returned Trysail, whose voice the rattling of the throat had already nearly silenced "I have had misgivings — but no matter. Take care of the ship — I have been thinking of our people — you'll have to cut — they can never lift the anchor — the wind is here at north."

"All this is ordered. Trouble thyself no further about the vessel; she shall be taken care of, I promise you. Speak of thy wife, and of thy wishes in England."

"God bless Mrs. Trysail! She'll get a pension, and I hope contentment! You must give the reef a good, berth, in rounding Montauk — and you'll naturally wish to find the anchors again, when the coast is clear — if you can find it in your conscience, say a good word of poor old Ben Trysail, in the dispatches —"

The voice of the master sunk to a whisper, and became inaudible. Ludlow thought he strove to speak again, and he bent his ear to his mouth.

"I say — the weather-main-swifter and both backstays are gone; Look to the spars, for — for — there are sometimes — heavy puffs at night — in the Americas!"

The last heavy respiration succeeded, after which came the long silence of death. The body was removed to the poop, and Ludlow, with a saddened heart, turned to duties that this accident rendered still more imperative.

Notwithstanding the heavy loss, and the originally weakened state of her crew, the sails of the Coquette were soon spread, and the ship moved away in silence; as if sorrowing for those who had fallen at her anchorage. When the vessel was fairly in motion, her captain ascended to the poop, in order to command a clearer view of all around him, as well as to profit by the situation to arrange his plans for the future. He found he had been anticipated by the free-trader.

"I owe my ship — I may say my life, since in such a conflict they would have gone together, to thy succor!" said the young commander, as he approached the motionless form of the smuggler. "Without it, Queen Anne would have lost a cruiser, and the flag of England a portion of its well-earned glory."

"May thy royal mistress prove as ready to remember her friends, in emergencies, as mine. In good truth, there was little time to lose, and trust me, we well understood the extremity. If we were tardy, it was because whale-boats were to be brought from a distance; for the land lies between my brigantine and the sea."

"He who came so opportunely, and acted so well, needs no apology."

"Captain Ludlow, are we friends?"

"It cannot be otherwise. All minor considerations must be lost in such a service. If it is your intention to push this illegal trade further, on the coast, I must seek another station."

"Not so. Remain, and do credit to your flag, and the land of your birth. I have long thought that this is the last time the keel of the Water-Witch will ever plow the American seas. Before I quit you, I would have an interview with the merchant. A worse man might have fallen, and just now even a better man might be spared. I hope no harm has come to him?"

"He has shown the steadiness of his Holland lineage, today. During the boarding, he was useful and cool."

"It is well. Let the Alderman be summoned to the deck, for my time is limited, and I have much to say —"

The Skimmer paused, for at that moment a fierce light glared upon the ocean, the ship, and all in it. The two seamen gazed at each other in silence and both recoiled, as men recede before an unexpected and fearful attack. But a bright and wavering light, which rose out of the forward hatch of the vessel explained all. At the same moment, the deep stillness which, since the bustle of making sail had ceased, pervaded the ship, was broken by the appalling cry of "Fire!"

The alarm which brings the blood in the swiftest current to a seaman's heart, was now heard in the depths of the vessel. The smothered sounds below, the advancing uproar, and the rush on deck, with the awful summons in the open air, succeeded each other with the rapidity of lightning. A dozen voices repeated the word 'the grenade!' proclaiming in a breath both the danger and the cause. But an instant before, the swelling canvas, the dusky spars, and the faint lines of the cordage, were only to be traced by the glimmering light of the stars; and now the whole hamper of the ship was the more conspicuous, from the obscure background against which it was drawn in distinct lines. The sight was fearfully beautiful — beautiful, for it showed the symmetry and fine outlines of the vessel's rig, resembling the effect of a group of statuary seen by torch-light — and fearful, since the dark void beyond seemed to declare their isolated and helpless state.

There was one breathless, eloquent moment, in which all were seen gazing at the grand spectacle in mute awe — and then a voice rose, clear, distinct, and commanding, above the sullen sound of the torrent of fire, which was roaring among the avenues of the ship.

"Call all hands to extinguish fire! Gentlemen, to your stations. Be cool, men; and be silent!"

There was a calmness and an authority in the tones of the young commander, that curbed the impetuous feelings of the startled crew. Accustomed to obedience, and trained to order, each man broke out of his trance, and eagerly commenced the discharge of his allotted duty. At that instant, an erect and unmoved form stood on the combings of the main hatch. A hand was raised in the air, and the call, which came from the deep chest, was like that of one used to speak in the tempest.

"Where are my brigantines?" it said — "Come away there, my sea-dogs; wet the light sails, and follow!"

A group of grave and submissive mariners gathered about the 'Skimmer of the Seas,' at the sound of his voice. Glancing an eye over them, as if to scan their quality and number, he smiled, with a look in which high daring and practised self-command was blended with a constitutional gaîté de cœur.

"One deck, or two!" — he added; "what avails a plank, more or less, in an explosion? — Follow!"

The free-trader and his people disappeared in the interior of the ship. An interval of great and resolute exertion succeeded. Blankets, sails, and everything which offered, and which promised to be of use, were wetted and cast upon the flames. The engine was brought to bear, and the ship was deluged with water. But the confined space, with the heat and smoke, rendered it impossible to penetrate to those parts of the vessel where the conflagration raged. The ardor of the men abated as hope lessened, and after half an hour of fruitless exertion, Ludlow saw, with pain, that his assistants began to yield to the inextinguishable principle of nature. The appearance of the Skimmer on deck, followed by all his people, destroyed hope, and every effort ceased as suddenly as it had commenced.

"Think of your wounded;" whispered the free-trader, with a steadiness no danger could disturb. "We stand on a raging volcano!"

"I have ordered the gunner to drown the magazine."

"He was too late. The hold of the ship is a fiery furnace. I heard him fall among the store-rooms, and it surpassed the power of man to give the wretch succor. The grenade has fallen near some combustibles, and, painful as it is to part with a ship so loved Ludlow, thou wilt meet the loss like a man! Think of thy wounded; my boats are still hanging at the stern."

Ludlow reluctantly, but firmly, gave the order to bear the wounded to the boats. This was an arduous and delicate duty. The smallest boy in the ship knew the whole extent of the danger, and that a moment, by the explosion of the powder, might precipitate them all into eternity. The deck forward was getting too hot to be endured, and there were places even in which the beams had given symptoms of yielding.

But the poop, elevated still above the fire, offered a momentary refuge. Thither all retired, while the weak and wounded were lowered, with the caution circumstances would permit, into the whale-boats of the smugglers.

Ludlow stood at one ladder and the free-trader at the other, in order to be certain that none proved recreant in so trying a moment. Near them were Alida, Seadrift, and the Alderman, with the attendants of the former.

It seemed an age, before this humane and tender duty was performed. At length the cry of "all in!" was uttered, in a manner to betray the extent of the self-command that had been necessary to effect it.

"Now, Alida, we may think of thee!" said Ludlow, turning to the spot occupied by the silent heiress.

"And you!" she said, hesitating to move.

"Duty demands that I should be the last —"

A sharp explosion beneath, and fragments of fire flying upwards through a hatch, interrupted his words. Plunges into the sea, and a rush of the people to the boats, followed. All order and authority were completely lost, in the instinct of life. In vain did Ludlow call on his men to be cool, and to wait for those who were still above. His words were lost, in the uproar of clamorous voices. For a moment, it seemed, however, as if the Skimmer of the Seas would overcome the confusion. Throwing himself on a ladder, he glided into the bows of one of the boats, and, holding by the ropes with a vigorous arm, he resisted the efforts of all the oars and boat-hooks, while he denounced destruction on him who dared to quit the ship. Had not the two crews been mingled, the high authority and determined mien of the free-trader would have prevailed; but while some were disposed to obey, others raised the cry of "throw the dealer in witchcraft into the sea!" — Boat-hooks were already pointed at his breast, and the horrors of the fearful moment were about to be increased by the violence of a mutinous contention, when a second explosion nerved the arms of the rowers to madness. With a common and desperate effort, they overcame all resistance. Swinging off upon the ladder, the furious seaman saw the boat glide from his grasp, and depart. The execration that was uttered, beneath the stern of the Coquette, was deep and powerful; but, in another moment, the Skimmer stood on the poop, calm and undejected, in the centre of the deserted group.

"The explosion of a few of the officers' pistols has frightened the miscreants;" he said, cheerfully "But hope is not yet lost! — they linger in the distance, and may return!"

The sight of the helpless party on the poop, and the consciousness of being less exposed themselves, had indeed arrested the progress of the fugitives. Still, selfishness predominated; and while most regretted their danger, none but the young and unheeded midshipmen, who were neither of an age nor of a rank to wield sufficient authority, proposed to return. There was little argument necessary to show that the perils increased at each moment; and, finding that no other expedient remained, the gallant youths encouraged the men to pull towards the land; intending themselves to return instantly to the assistance of their commander and his friends. The oars dashed into the water again, and the retiring boats were soon lost to view in the body of darkness.

While the fire had been raging within, another element, without, had aided to lessen hope for those who were abandoned. The wind from the land had continued to rise, and, during the time lost in useless exertion, the ship had been permitted to run nearly before it. When hope was gone, the helm had been deserted, and as all the lower sails had been hauled up to avoid the flames, the vessel had drifted, many minutes, nearly dead to leeward. The mistaken youths, who had not attended to these circumstances, were already miles from that beach they hoped to reach so soon; and ere the boats had separated from the ship five minutes, they were hopelessly asunder. Ludlow had early thought of the expedient of stranding the vessel, as the means of saving her people; but his better knowledge of their position, soon showed him the utter futility of the attempt.

Of the progress of the flames beneath, the mariners could only judge by circumstances. The Skimmer glanced his eye about him, on regaining the poop, and appeared to scan the amount and quality of the physical force that was still at their disposal. He saw that the Alderman, the faithful François, and two of his own seamen, with four of the petty officers of the ship, remained. The six latter, even in that moment of desperation, had calmly refused to desert their officers.

"The flames are in the state-rooms!" he whispered to Ludlow.

"Not further aft, I think, than the berths of the midshipmen — else we should hear more pistols."

"True — they are fearful signals to let us know the progress of the fire! — our resource is a raft."

Ludlow looked as if he despaired of the means but, concealing the discouraging fear, he answered cheerfully in the affirmative. The orders were instantly given, and all on board gave themselves to the task, heart and hand. The danger was one that admitted of no ordinary or half-conceived expedients; but, in such an emergency, it required all the readiness of their art, and even the greatness of that conception which is the property of genius. All distinctions of rank and authority had ceased, except as deference was paid to natural qualities and the intelligence of experience. Under such circumstances, the 'Skimmer of the Seas' took the lead; and though Ludlow caught his ideas with professional quickness, it was the mind of the free-trader that controlled, throughout, the succeeding exertions of that fearful night.

The cheek of Alida was blanched to a deadly paleness; but there rested about the bright and wild eyes of Seadrift, an expression of supernatural resolution.

When the crew abandoned the hope of extinguishing the flames, they had closed all the hatches, to retard the crisis as much as possible. Here and there, however, little torch-like lights were beginning to show themselves through the planks, and the whole deck, forward of the main-mast, was already in a critical and sinking state. One or two of the beams had failed, but, as yet, the form of the construction was preserved. Still the seamen distrusted the treacherous footing, and, had the heat permitted the experiment, they would have shrunk from a risk which at any unexpected moment might commit them to the fiery furnace beneath.

The smoke ceased, and a clear, powerful light illuminated the ship to her trucks. In consequence of the care and exertions of her people, the sails and masts were yet untouched; and as the graceful canvas swelled with the breeze, it still urged the blazing hull through the water.

The forms of the Skimmer and his assistants were visible, in the midst of the gallant gear, perched on the giddy yards. Seen by that light, with his peculiar attire, his firm and certain step, and his resolute air, the free-trader resembled some fancied sea-god, who, secure in his immortal immunities, had come to act his part in that awful but exciting trial of hardihood and skill. Seconded by the common men, he was employed in cutting the canvas from the yards. Sail after sail fell upon the deck, and, in an incredibly short space of time, the whole of the fore-mast was naked to its spars and rigging.

In the mean time, Ludlow, assisted by the Alderman and François, had not been idle below. Passing forward between the empty ridge-ropes, lanyard after lanyard parted under the blows of their little boarding-axes. The mast now depended on the strength of the wood and the support of a single back-stay.

"Lay down!" shouted Ludlow. "All is gone aft, but this stay!"

The Skimmer leaped upon the firm rope, followed by all aloft, and, gliding downwards, he was instantly in the hammock-cloths. A crash followed their descent, and an explosion, which caused the whole of the burning fabric to tremble to its centre, seemed to announce the end of all. Even the free-trader recoiled before the horrible din; but when he stood near Seadrift and the heiress again, there was cheerfulness in his tones, and a look of high, and even of gay resolution, in his firm countenance.

"The deck has failed forwards," he said, "and our artillery is beginning to utter fearful signal-guns! Be of cheer! — the magazine of a ship-lies deep, and many sheathed bulk-heads still protect us."

Another discharge from a heated gun, however proclaimed the rapid progress of the flames. The fire broke out of the interior anew, and the fore mast kindled.

"There must be an end of this!" said Alida, clasping her hands in a terror that could not be controlled. "Save yourselves, if possible, you who have strength and courage, and leave us to the mercy of him whose eye is over all!"

"Go;" added Seadrift, whose sex could no longer be concealed. "Human courage can do no more: leave us to die!"

The looks, that were returned to these sad requests, were melancholy but unmoved. The Skimmer caught a rope, and still holding it in his hand, he descended to the quarter-deck, on which he at first trusted his weight with jealous caution. Then looking up, he smiled encouragingly, and said — "Where a gun still stands, there is no danger for the weight of a man!"

"It is our only resource;" cried Ludlow, imitating his example. "On, my men, while the beams will still hold us."

In a moment, all were on the quarter-deck, though the excessive heat rendered it impossible to remain stationary an instant. A gun on each side was run in, its tackles loosened, and its muzzle pointed towards the tottering, unsupported, but still upright fore-mast.

"Aim at the cleets!" said Ludlow to the Skimmer who pointed one gun, while he did the same office at the other.

"Hold!" cried the latter "Throw in shot — it is out the chance between a bursting gun and a lighted magazine!"

Additional balls were introduced into each piece; and then, with steady hands, the gallant mariners applied burning brands to the priming. The discharges were simultaneous and, for an instant, volumes of smoke rolled along the deck and seemed to triumph over the conflagration. The rending of wood was audible. It was followed by a sweeping noise in the air, and the fall of the fore-mast, with all its burden of spars, into the sea. The motion of the ship was instantly arrested, and, as the heavy timbers were still attached to the bowsprit by the forward stays, her head came to the wind, when the remaining top-sails flapped, shivered, and took aback.

The vessel was now, for the first time during the fire, stationary. The common mariners profited by the circumstance, and, darting past the mounting flame along the bulwarks, they gained the top-gallant-forecastle, which though heated was yet untouched. The Skimmer glanced an eye about him, and seizing Seadrift by the waist, as if the mimic seaman had been a child, he pushed forward between the ridge-ropes. Ludlow followed with Alida, and the others intimated their example in the best manner they could. All reached the head of the ship in safety; though Ludlow had been driven by the flames into the fore-channels, and thence nearly into the sea.

The petty officers were already on the floating spars, separating them from each other, cutting away the unnecessary weight of rigging, bringing the several parts of the wood in parallel lines, and lashing them anew. Ever and anon, these rapid movements were quickened by one of those fearful signals from the officers' berths, which, by announcing the progress of the flames beneath, betrayed their increasing proximity to the still-slumbering volcano. The boats had been gone an hour, and yet it seemed, to all in the ship, but a minute. The conflagration had, for the last ten minutes, advanced with renewed fury; and the whole of the confined flame, which had been so long pent in the depths of the vessel now glared high in the open air.

"This heat can no longer be borne," said Ludlow; "we must to our raft, for breath."

"To the raft then!" returned the cheerful voice of the free-trader. "Haul in upon your fasts, men, and stand by to receive the precious freight."

The seamen obeyed. Alida and her companions were lowered safely to the place prepared for then reception. The fore-mast had gone over the side, with all its spars aloft; for preparation had been made, before the fire commenced, to carry sail to the utmost, in order to escape the enemy. The skilful and active seamen, directed and aided by Ludlow and the Skimmer, had made a simple but happy disposition of those boy ant materials on which their all now depended. In set-tling in the water, the yards, still crossed, had happily fallen uppermost. The booms and all the light spars had been floated near the top, and laid across, reaching from the lower to the top-sail-yard. A few light spars, stowed outboard, had been cut away and added to the number, and the whole were secured with the readiness and ingenuity of seamen. On the first alarm of fire, some of the crew had seized a few light articles that would float, and rushed to the head, as the place most remote from the magazine, in the blind hope of saving life by swimming. Most of these articles had been deserted, when the people were rallied to exertion by their officers. A couple of empty shot-boxes and a mess-chest were among them, and on the latter were seated the females, while the former served to keep their feet from the water. As the arrangement of the spars forced the principal mast entirely beneath the element, and the ship was so small as to need little artificial work in her masting, the part around the top, which contained the staging, was scarcely submerged. Although a ton in weight was added to the inherent gravity of the wood, still as the latter was of the lightest description, and freed as much as possible of every thing that was unnecessary to the safety of those it supported, the spars floated sufficiently, buoyant for the temporary security of the fugitives.

"Cut the fast!" said Ludlow, involuntarily starting at several explosions in the interior, which followed each other in quick succession, and which were succeeded by one which sent fragments of burning wood into the air. "Cut, and bear the raft off the ship! — God knows, we have need to be further asunder!"

"Cut not!" cried the half-frantic Seadrift — "My brave! — my devoted! —"

"Is safe —" calmly said the Skimmer, appearing in the rattlings of the main-rigging, which was still untouched by the fire — "Cut off all! I stay to brace the mizen-top-sail more firmly aback."

The duty was done, and for a moment the fine figure of the free-trader was seen standing on the edge of the burning ship, looking with regret at the glowing mass.

"'Tis the end of a lovely craft!" he said, loud enough to be heard by those beneath. Then he appeared in the air, and sunk into the sea — "The last signal was from the ward-room," added the dauntless and dexterous mariner, as he rose from the water, and, shaking the brine from his head, he took his place on the stage — "Would to God the wind would blow, for we have need of greater distance!"

The precaution the free-trader had taken, in adjusting the sails, was not without its use. Motion the raft had none, but as the top-sails of the Coquette were still aback, the naming mass, no longer arrested by the clogs in the water, began slowly to separate from the floating spars, though the tottering and half-burnt masts threatened, at each moment, to fall.

Never did moments seem so long, as those which succeeded. Even the Skimmer and Ludlow watched in speechless interest, the tardy movements of the ship. By little and little, she receded; and, after ten minutes of intense expectation, the seamen, whose anxiety had increased as their exertions ended, began to breathe more freely. They were still fearfully near the dangerous fabric, but destruction from the explosion was no longer inevitable. The flames began to glide upwards, and then the heavens appeared on fire, as one heated sail after another kindled and flared wildly in the breeze.

Still the stern of the vessel was entire. The body of the master was seated against the mizen-mast, and even the stern visage of the old seaman was distinctly visible, under the broad light of the conflagration. Ludlow gazed at it in melancholy, and for a time he ceased to think of his ship, while memory dwelt, in sadness, on those scenes of boyish happiness, and of professional pleasures, in which his ancient shipmate had so largely participated. The roar of a gun, whose stream of fire flashed nearly to their faces, and the sullen whistling of its shot, which crossed the raft, failed to awaken him from his trance.

"Stand firm to the mess-chest!" half-whispered the Skimmer, motioning to his companions to place themselves in attitudes to support the weaker of their party, while, with sedulous care, he braced his own athletic person in a manner to throw all of its weight and strength against the seat. "Stand firm, and be ready!"

Ludlow complied, though his eye scarce changed its direction. He saw the bright flame that was rising above the arm-chest, and he fancied that it came from the funeral pile of the young Dumont, whose fate, at that moment, he was almost disposed to envy. Then his look returned to the grim countenance of Trysail. At moments, it seemed as if the dead master spoke; and so strong did the illusion become, that our young sailor more than once bent forward to listen. While under this delusion, the body rose, with the arms stretched upwards. The air was filled with a sheet of streaming fire, while the ocean and the heavens glowed with one glare of intense and fiery red. Notwithstanding the precaution of the 'Skimmer of the Seas,' the chest was driven from its place, and those by whom it was held were nearly precipitated into the water. A deep, heavy detonation proceeded as it were from the bosom of the sea, which, while it wounded the ear less than the sharp explosion that had just before issued from the gun, was audible at the distant capes of the Delaware. The body of Trysail sailed upward for fifty fathoms, in the centre of a flood of flame, and, describing a short curve, it came towards the raft, and cut the water within reach of the captain's arm. A sullen plunge of a gun followed, and proclaimed the tremendous power of the explosion; while a ponderous yard fell athwart a part of the raft, sweeping away the four petty officers of Ludlow, as if they had been dust driving before a gale. To increase the wild and fearful grandeur of the dissolution of the royal cruiser, one of the cannon emitted its fiery contents while sailing in the void.

The burning spars, the falling fragments, the blazing and scattered canvas and cordage, the glowing shot, and all the torn particles of the ship, were seen descending. Then followed the gurgling of water, as the ocean swallowed all that remained of the cruiser which had so long been the pride of the American seas. The fiery glow disappeared, and a gloom like that which succeeds the glare of vivid lightning, fell on the scene.

CHAPTER XXXIII.

" — Please you, read."
Cymbeline.

"It is past!" said the 'Skimmer of the Seas,' raising himself from the attitude of great muscular exertion, which he had assumed in order to support the mess-chest, and walking out along the single mast, towards the spot whence the four seamen of Ludlow had just been swept. "It is past! and those who are called to the last account, have met their fate in such a scene as none but a seaman may witness; while those who are spared, have need of all a seaman's skill and resolution for that which remains! Captain Ludlow, I do not despair; for, see, the lady of the brigantine has still a smile for her servitors!"

Ludlow, who had followed the steady and daring free-trader to the place where the spar had fallen, turned and cast a look in the direction that the other stretched his arm. Within a hundred feet of him, he saw the image of the sea-green lady, rocking in the agitated water, and turned towards the raft, with its usual expression of wild and malicious intelligence. This emblem of their fancied mistress had been borne in front of the smugglers, when they mounted the poop of the Coquette; and the steeled staff on which the lantern was perched, had been struck into a horse-bucket by the standard-bearer of the moment, ere he entered the mêlée of the combat. During the conflagration, this object had more than once met the eye of Ludlow; and now it appeared floating quietly by him, in a manner almost to shake even his contempt for the ordinary superstitions of seamen. While he hesitated in what manner he should reply to his companion's remark, the latter plunged into the sea, and swam towards the light. He was soon by the side of the raft again bearing aloft the symbol of his brigantine. There are none so firm in the dominion of reason, as to be entirely superior to the secret impulses which teach us all to believe in the hidden agency of a good or an evil fortune. The voice of the free-trader was more cheerful, and his step more sure and elastic, as he crossed the stage and struck the armed end of the staff into that part of the top-rim of the Coquette, which floated uppermost.

"Courage!" he gaily cried. "While this light burns, my star is not set! Courage, lady of the land; for here is one of the deep waters, who still looks kindly on her followers! We are at sea, on a frail craft it is certain, but a dull sailer may make a sure passage. Speak, gallant Master Seadrift: thy gaiety and spirit should revive under so goodly an omen!"

But the agent of so many pleasant masquerades, and the instrument of so much of his artifice, had not a fortitude equal to the buoyant temper of the smuggler. The counterfeit bowed his head by the side of the silent Alida, without reply. The 'Skimmer of the Seas' regarded the group, a moment, with manly interest; and then touching the arm of Ludlow, he walked, with a balancing step, along the spars, until they had reached a spot where they might confer without causing unnecessary alarm to their companions.

Although so imminent and so pressing a danger as that of the explosion had passed, the situation of those who had escaped was scarcely better than that of those who had been lost. The heavens showed a few glimmering stars in the openings of the clouds; and now, that the first contrast of the change had lessened, there was just enough light to render all the features of their actual state gloomily imposing.

It has been said, that the fore-mast of the Coquette went by the board, with most of its hamper aloft. The sails, with such portion of the rigging as might help to sustain it, had been hastily cut away as related; and after its fall, until the moment of the explosion, the common men had been engaged, either in securing the staging, or in clearing the wreck of those heavy ropes which, useless as fastenings, only added to the weight of the mass. The whole wreck lay upon the sea, with the yards crossed and in their places, much as the spars had stood. The large booms had been unshipped, and laid in such a manner around the top, with the ends resting on the lower and top-sail yards, as to form the foundation of the staging. The smaller booms, with the mess-chest and shot-boxes, were all that lay between the group in the centre, and the depths of the ocean. The upper part of the top-rim rose a few feet above the water, and formed an important protection against the night-breeze and the constant washing of the waves. In this manner were the females seated, cautioned not to trust their feet on the frail security of the booms, and supported by the unremitting care of the Alderman. François had submitted to be lashed to the top by one of the brigantine's seamen, while the latter, all of the common herd who remained, encouraged by the presence of their standard-light, began to occupy themselves in looking to the fastenings and other securities of the raft.

"We are in no condition for a long or an active cruise, Captain Ludlow," said the Skimmer, when he and his companion were out of hearing. "I have been at sea in all weathers, and in every description of craft; but this is the boldest of my experiments on the water. I hope it may not be the last!"

"We cannot conceal from ourselves the frightful hazards we run," returned Ludlow, "however much we may wish them to be a secret to some among us."

"This is truly a deserted sea, to be abroad in, on a raft! Were we in the narrow passages between the British islands and the Main, or even in the Biscay waters, there would be hope that some trader or roving cruiser might cross our track; but our chance here lies much between the Frenchman and the brigantine."

"The enemy has doubtless seen and heard the explosion, and, as the land is so near, they will infer that the people are saved in the boats. Our chance of seeing more of them is much diminished by the accident of the fire, since there will no longer be a motive for remaining on the coast."

"And will your young officers abandon their captain without a search?"

"Hope of aid from that quarter is faint. The ship ran miles while in flames, and, before the light returns, these spars will have drifted leagues, with the ebbing tide, to seaward."

"Truly, I have sailed with better auguries!" observed the Skimmer — "What are the bearings and distance of the land?"

"It still lies to the north, but we are fast setting east and southerly. Ere morning we shall be abeam of Montauk, or even beyond it; we must already be some leagues in the offing."

"That is worse than I had imagined! — but there is hope on the flood?"

"The flood will bear us northward again — but — what think you of the heavens?"

"Unfavorable, though not desperate. The sea-breeze will return with the sun."

"And with it will return the swell! How long will these ill-secured spars hold together, when agitated by the heave of the water? Or, how long will those with us bear up against the wash of the sea, unsupported by nourishment?"

"You paint in gloomy colors, Captain Ludlow," said the free-trader, drawing a heavy breath, in spite of all his resolution. "My experience tells me you are right, though my wishes would fain contradict you. Still, I think we have the promise of a tranquil night."

"Tranquil for a ship, or even for a boat; but hazardous to a raft like this. You see that this top-mast already works in the cap, at each heave of the water, and as the wood loosens, our security lessens."

"Thy council is not flattering! — Captain Ludlow, you are a seaman and a man, and I shall not attempt to trifle with your knowledge. With you, I think the danger imminent, and almost our only hope dependent on the good fortune of my brigantine."

"Will those in her think it their duty to quit their anchorage, to come in quest of a raft whose existence is unknown to them?"

"There is hope in the vigilance of her of the sea-green mantle! You may deem this fanciful, or even worse, at such a moment; but I, who have run so many gauntlets under her favor, have faith in her fortunes. Surely, you are not a seaman, Captain Ludlow, without a secret dependence on some unseen and potent agency!"

"My dependence is placed in the agency of him who is all-potent, but never visible. If he forget us, we may indeed despair!"

"This is well, but it is not the fortune I would express. Believe me, spite of an education which teaches all you have said, and of a reason that is often too clear for folly, there is a secret reliance on hidden chances, that has been created by a life of activity and hazard, and which, if it should do nothing better, does not abandon me to despair. The omen of the light and the smile of my mistress would cheer me, spite of a thousand philosophers!"

"You are fortunate in purchasing consolation so cheaply;" returned the commander of Queen Anne, who felt a latent hope in his companion's confidence that he would have hesitated to acknowledge. "I see but little that we can do to aid our chances, except it be to clear away all unnecessary weight, and to secure the raft as much as possible by additional lashings."

The 'Skimmer of the Seas' assented to the proposal. Consulting a moment longer, on the details of their expedients, they rejoined the group near the top, in order to see them executed. As the seamen on the raft were reduced to the two people of the brigantine, Ludlow and his companion were obliged to assist in the performance of the duty.

Much useless rigging, that added to the pressure without aiding the buoyancy of the raft, was cut away; and all the boom-irons were knocked off the yards, and suffered to descend to the bottom of the ocean. By these means a great weight was taken from the raft, which in consequence floated with so much additional power to sustain those who depended on it for life. The Skimmer, accompanied by his two silent but obedient seamen, ventured along the attenuated and submerged spars to the extremity of the tapering masts, and after toiling, with the dexterity of men accustomed to deal with the complicated machinery of a ship in the darkest nights, they succeeded in releasing the two smaller masts with their respective yards, and in floating them down to the body of the wreck, or the part around the top. Here the sticks were crossed in a manner to give great additional strength and footing to the stage.

There was an air of hope, and a feeling of increased security, in this employment. Even the Alderman and François aided in the task, to the extent of their knowledge and force. But when these alterations were made, and additional lashings had been applied to keep the top-mast and the larger yards in their places, Ludlow, by joining those who were around the mast-head, tacitly admitted that little more could be done to avert the chances of the elements.

During the few hours occupied in this important duty, Alida and her companion addressed themselves to God, in long and fervent petitions. With woman's faith in that divine being who alone could avail them, and with woman's high mental fortitude in moments of protracted trial, they had both known how to control the exhibition of their terrors, and had sought their support in the same appeal to a power superior to all of earth. Ludlow was therefore more than rewarded by the sound of Alida's voice, speaking to him cheerfully, as she thanked him for what he had done, when he admitted that he could now do no more.

"The rest is with Providence!" added Alida. "All that bold and skilful seamen can do, have ye done; and all that woman in such a situation can do, have we done in your behalf!"

"Thou hast thought of me in thy prayers, Alida! It is an intercession that the stoutest needs, and which none but the fool derides."

"And thou, Eudora! thou hast remembered him who quiets the waters!" said a deep voice, near the bending form of the counterfeit Seadrift.

"I have."

"'Tis well. There are points to which manhood and experience may pass, and there are those where all is left to one mightier than the elements!"

Words like these, coming from the lips of one of the known character of the 'Skimmer of the Seas,' were not given to the winds. Even Ludlow cast an uneasy look at the heavens, when they came upon his ear, as if they conveyed a secret notice of the whole extremity of the danger by which they were environed. None answered; and a long silence succeeded, during which some of the more fatigued slumbered uneasily, spite of their fearful situation.

In this manner did the night pass, in weariness and anxiety. Little was said, and for hours scarce a limb was moved, in the group that clustered around the mess-chest. As the signs of day appeared, however, every faculty was keenly awake, to catch the first signs of what they had to hope, or the first certainty of what they had to fear.

The surface of the ocean was still smooth, though the long swells in which the element was heaving and setting, sufficiently indicated that the raft had floated far from the land. This fact was rendered sure, when the light, which soon appeared along the eastern margin of the narrow view, was shed gradually over the whole horizon. Nothing was at first visible, but one gloomy and vacant waste of water. But a cry of joy from Seadrift, whose senses had long been practised in ocean sights, soon drew all eyes in the direction opposite to that of the rising sun, and it was not long before all on the low raft had a view of the snowy surfaces of a ship's sails, as the glow of morning touched the canvas.

"It is the Frenchman!" said the free-trader. "He is charitably looking for the wreck of his late enemy!"

"It may be so, for our fate can be no secret to him;" was the answer of Ludlow. "Unhappily, we had run some distance from the anchorage, before the flames broke out. Truly, those with whom we so lately struggled for life, are bent on a duty of humanity."

"Ah, yonder is his crippled consort! — to leeward many a league. The gay bird has been too sadly stripped of its plumage, to fly so near the wind! This is man's fortune! He uses his power, at one moment, to destroy the very means that become necessary to his safety, the next."

"And what think you of our hopes?" asked Alida, searching in the countenance of Ludlow a clue to their fate. "Does the stranger move in a direction favorable to our wishes?"

Neither Ludlow nor the Skimmer replied. Both regarded the frigate intently, and then, as objects became more distinct, both answered, by a common impulse, that the ship was steering directly towards them. The declaration excited general hope, and even the negress was no longer restrained by her situation from expressing her joy in vociferous exclamations of delight.

A few minutes of active and ready exertion succeeded. A light boom was unlashed from the raft, and raised on its end, supporting a little signal, made of the handkerchiefs of the party, which fluttered in the light breeze, at the elevation of some twenty feet above the surface of the water. After this precaution was observed, they were obliged to await the result in such patience as they could assume. Minute passed after minute, and, at each moment, the form and proportions of the ship became more distinct, until all the mariners of the party declared they could distinguish men on her yards. A cannon would have readily sent its shot from the ship to the raft, and yet no sign betrayed the consciousness of those in the former of the proximity of the latter.

"I do not like his manner of steering!" observed the Skimmer to the silent and attentive Ludlow. "He yaws broadly, as if disposed to give up the search. God grant him the heart to continue on his course ten minutes longer!"

"Have we no means of making ourselves heard?" demanded the Alderman. "Methinks the voice of a strong man might be sent thus far across the water when life is the stake."

The more experienced shook their heads; but, not discouraged, the burgher raised his voice with a power that was sustained by the imminency of the peril. He was joined by the seamen, and even Ludlow lent his aid, until all were hoarse with the fruitless efforts. Men were evidently aloft, and in some numbers, searching the ocean with their eyes, but still no answering signal came from the vessel.

The ship continued to approach, and the raft was less than half a mile from her bows, when the vast fabric suddenly receded from the breeze, showed the whole of its glittering broadside, and, swinging its yards, betrayed by its new position that the search in that direction was abandoned. The instant Ludlow saw the filling-off of the frigate's bows, he cried —

"Now, raise your voices together — this is the final chance!"

They united in a common shout, with the exception of the 'Skimmer of the Seas.' The latter leaned against the top with folded arms, listening to their impotent efforts with a melancholy smile.

"It is well attempted," said the calm and extraordinary seaman when the clamor had ceased, advancing along the raft and motioning for all to be silent; "but it has failed. The swinging of the yards, and the orders given in waring ship, would prevent a stronger sound from being audible to men so actively employed. I flatter none with hope, but this is truly the moment for a final effort."

He placed his hands to his mouth, and, disregarding words, he raised a cry so clear, so powerful, and yet so full, that it seemed impossible those in the vessel should not hear. Thrice did he repeat the experiment, though it was evident that each successive exertion was feebler than the last.

"They hear!" cried Alida. "There is a movement in the sails!"

"'Tis the beeeze freshening;" answered Ludlow in sadness, at her side. "Each moment takes them away!"

The melancholy truth was too apparent for denial, and for half an hour the retiring ship was watched in the bitterness of disappointment. At the end of that time, she fired a gun, spread additional canvas on her wide booms, and stood away before the wind, to join her consort, whose upper sails were already dipping to the surface of the sea, in the southern board. With this change in her movements, vanished all expectation of succor from the cruiser of the enemy.

Perhaps, in every situation of life, it is necessary that hope should be first lessened by disappointment, before the buoyancy of the human mind will permit it to descend to the level of an evil fortune. Until a frustrated effort teaches him the difficulty of the attempt, he who has fallen may hope to rise again; and it is only when an exertion has been made with lessened means, that we learn the value of advantages, which have perhaps been long enjoyed, with a very undue estimate of their importance. Until the stern of the French frigate was seen retiring from the raft, those who were on it had not been fully sensible of the extreme danger of their situation. Hope had been strongly excited by the return of dawn; for while the shadows of night lay on the ocean, their situation resembled that of one who strove to pierce the obscurity of the future, in order to obtain a presage of better fortunes. With the light had come the distant sail. As the day advanced, the ship had approached, relinquished her search, and disappeared, without a prospect of her return.

The stoutest heart among the group on the raft began to sink at the gloomy fate which now seemed inevitable.

"Here is an evil omen!" whispered Ludlow, directing his companion's eyes to the dark and pointed fins of three or four sharks, that were gliding above the surface of the water, and in so fearful a proximity to their persons, as to render their situation on the low spars, over which the water was washing and retiring at each rise and fall of the waves, doubly dangerous. "The creature's instinct speaks ill for our hopes!"

"There is a belief among seamen, that these animals feel a secret impulse, which directs them to their prey;" returned the Skimmer. "But fortune may yet balk them. Rogerson!" calling to one of his followers — "thy pockets are rarely wanting in a fisherman's tackle. Hast thou, haply, line and hook, for these hungry miscreants? The question is getting narrowed to one, in which the simplest philosophy is the wisest. When eat or to be eaten, is the mooted point, most men will decide for the former."

A hook of sufficient size was soon produced, and a line was quietly provided from some of the small cordage that still remained about the masts. A piece of leather, torn from a spar, answered for the bait; and the lure was thrown. Extreme hunger seemed to engross the voracious animals, who darted at the imaginary prey with the rapidity of lightning. The shock was so sudden and violent, that the hapless mariner was drawn from his slippery and precarious footing, into the sea. The whole passed with a frightful and alarming rapidity. A common cry of horror was heard, and the last despairing glance of the fallen man was witnessed. The mutilated body floated for an instant in its blood, with the look of agony and terror still imprinted on the conscious countenance. At the next moment, it had become food for the monsters of the sea.

All had passed away, but the deep dye on the surface of the ocean. The gorged fish disappeared; but the dark spot remained near the immovable raft, as if placed there to warn the survivors of their fate.

"This is horrible!" said Ludlow.

"A sail!" shouted the Skimmer, whose voice and tone, breaking in on that moment of intense horror and apprehension, sounded like a cry from the heavens. "My gallant brigantine!"

"God grant she come with better fortune than those who have so lately left us!"

"God grant it, truly! If this hope fail, there is none left. Few pass here, and we have had sufficient proof that our top-gallants are not so lofty as to catch every eye."

All attention was now bestowed on the white speck which was visible on the margin of the ocean, and which the 'Skimmer of the Seas' confidently pronounced to be the Water-Witch. None but a seaman could have felt this certainty; for, seen from the low raft, there was little else to be distinguished but the heads of the upper sails. The direction too was unfavorable, as it was to leeward; but both Ludlow and the free-trader assured their companions, that the vessel was endeavoring to beat in with the land.

The two hours that succeeded lingered like days of misery. So much depended on a variety of events, that every circumstance was noted by the seamen of the party, with an interest bordering on agony. A failure of the wind might compel the vessel to remain stationary, and then both brigantine and raft would be at the mercy of the uncertain currents of the ocean; a change of wind might cause a change of course, and render a meeting impossible; an increase of the breeze might cause destruction, even before the succor could come. In addition to these obvious hazards, there were all the chances which were dependent on the fact that the people of the brigantine had every reason to believe the fate of the party was already sealed.

Still, fortune seemed propitious; for the breeze, though steady, was light, the intention of the vessel was evidently to pass somewhere near them, and the hope that their object was search, so strong and plausible, as to exhilarate every bosom.

At the expiration of the time named, the brigantine passed the raft to leeward, and so near as to render the smaller objects in her rigging distinctly visible.

"The faithful fellows are looking for us!" exclaimed the free-trader, with strong emotion in his voice. "They are men to scour the coast, ere they abandon us!"

"They pass us — wave the signal — it may catch their eyes!"

The little flag was unheeded, and, after so long and so intense expectation, the party on the raft had the pain to see the swift-moving vessel glide past them, and drawing so far ahead as to leave little hope of her return. The heart of even the 'Skimmer of the Seas' appeared to sink within him, at the disappointment.

"For myself, I care not;" said the stout mariner mournfully. "Of what consequence is it, in what sea, or on what voyage, a seaman goes into his watery tomb? — but for thee, my hapless and playful Eudora, I could wish another fate — ha! — she tacks! — the sea-green lady has an instinct for her children, after all!"

The brigantine was in stays. In ten or fifteen minutes more, the vessel was again abeam of the raft, and to windward.

"If she pass us now, our chance is gone, without a shadow of hope;" said the Skimmer, motioning solemnly for silence. Then, applying his hands to his mouth, he shouted, as if despair lent a giant's volume to his lungs —

"Ho! The Water-Witch! — ahoy!"

The last word issued from his lips with the clear, audible cry, that the peculiar sound is intended to produce. It appeared as if the conscious little bark knew its commander's voice; for its course changed slightly, as if the fabric were possessed of the consciousness and faculties of life.

"Ho! The Water-Witch! — ahoy!" shouted the Skimmer, with a still mightier effort.

" — Hilloa!" came down faintly on the breeze, and the direction of the brigantine again altered.

"The Water-Witch! — the Water-Witch! — ahoy!" broke out of the lips of the mariner of the shawl, with a supernatural force — the last cry being drawn out, till he who uttered it sunk back exhausted with the effort.

The words were still ringing in the ears of the breathless party on the raft, when a heavy shout swept across the water. At the next moment the boom of the brigantine swung off, and her narrow bows were seen pointing towards the little beacon of white that played above the sea. It was but a moment, but it was a moment pregnant with a thousand hopes and fears, before the beautiful craft was gliding within fifty feet of the top. In less than five minutes, the spars of the Coquette were floating on the wide ocean, unpeopled and abandoned.

The first sensation of the 'Skimmer of the Seas,' when his foot touched the deck of his brigantine might have been one of deep and intense gratitude. He was silent, and seemingly oppressed at the throat. Stepping along the planks, he cast an eye aloft, and struck his hand powerfully on the capstan, in a manner that was divided between convulsion and affection. Then he smiled grimly on his attentive and obedient crew, speaking with all his wonted cheerfulness and authority.

"Fill away the top-sail — brace up and haul aft! Trim every thing flat as boards, boys — jam the hussy in with the coast!"

CHAPTER XXXIV.

"Beseech you, Sir, were you present at this relation?"

Winter's Tale.

ON the following morning, the windows of the Lust in Rust denoted the presence of its owner. There was an air of melancholy, and yet of happiness, in the
faces of many who were seen about the buildings and the grounds, as if a great
good had been accompanied by some grave and qualifying circumstances of
sorrow. The negroes wore an air of that love of the extraordinary which is the
concomitant of ignorance, while those of the more fortunate class resembled men
who retained a recollection of serious evils that were past.

In the private apartment of the burgher, however, an interview took place
which was characterized by an air of deep concern. The parties were only the
free-trader and the Alderman. But it was apparent, in the look of each, that they
met like men who had interesting and serious matters to discuss. Still, one accustomed to the expressions of the human countenance might have seen, that while
the former was about to introduce topics in which his feelings were powerfully
enlisted, the other looked only to the grosser interests of his commerce.

"My minutes are counted;" said the mariner, stepping into the centre of the
room, and facing his companion. "That which is to be said, must be said briefly.
The inlet can only be passed on the rising water, and it will ill consult your opinions of prudence, were I to tarry, till the hue and cry, that will follow the intelligence of that which has lately happened in the offing, shall be heard in the
Province."

"Spoken with a rover's discretion! This reserve will perpetuate friendship,
which is nought weakened by your activity in our late uncomfortable voyage on
the yards and masts of Queen Anne's late cruiser. Well! I wish no ill-luck to any
loyal gentleman in Her Majesty's service; but it is a thousand pities that thou wert
not ready, now the coast is clear, with a good heavy inward cargo! The last was
altogether an affair of secret drawers, and rich laces; valuable in itself, and profitable in the exchange: but the colony is sadly in want of certain articles that can
only be landed at leisure."

"I come on other matters. There have been transactions between us,
Alderman Van Beverout, that you little understand."

"You speak of a small mistake in the last invoice? — 'Tis all explained, Master

Skimmer, on a second examination; and thy accuracy is as well established as that of the bank of England."

"Established or not, let him who doubts cease to deal. I have no other motto than 'confidence,' nor any other rule but 'justice.'"

"You overrun my meaning, friend of mine. I intimate no suspicions; but accuracy is the soul of commerce, as profit is its object. Clear accounts, with reasonable balances, are the surest cements of business intimacies. A little frankness operates, in a secret trade, like equity in the courts; which reestablishes the justice that the law has destroyed. What is thy purpose?"

"It is now many years, Alderman Van Beverout, since this secret trade was commenced between you and my predecessor — he, whom you have thought my father, but who only claimed that revered appellation by protecting the helplessness and infancy of the orphan child of a friend."

"The latter circumstance is new to me;" returned the burgher, slowly bowing his head. "It may explain certain levities which have not been without their embarrassment. 'Tis five-and-twenty years, come August, Master Skimmer, and twelve of them have been under thy auspices. I will not say that the adventures might not have been better managed; as it is, they are tolerable. I am getting old, and think of closing the risks and hazards of life — two or three, or, at the most, four or five, lucky voyages, must, I think, bring a final settlement between us."

"'Twill be made sooner. I believe the history of my predecessor was no secret to you. The manner in which he was driven from the marine of the Stuarts, on account of his opposition to tyranny; his refuge with an only daughter, in the colonies; and his final recourse to the free-trade for a livelihood, have often been alluded to between us."

"Hum — I have a good memory for business, Master Skimmer, but I am as forgetful as a new-made lord of his pedigree, on all matters that should be overlooked. I dare say, however, it was as you have stated."

"You know, that when my protector and predecessor abandoned the land, he took his all with him upon the water."

"He took a wholesome and good-going schooner, Master Skimmer, with an assorted freight of chosen tobacco, well ballasted with stones from off the seashore. He was no foolish admirer of sea-green women, and flaunting brigantines. Often did the royal cruisers mistake the worthy dealer for an industrious fisherman!"

"He had his humors, and I have mine. But you forget a part of the freight he carried — a part that was not the least valuable."

"There might have been a bale of marten's furs — for the trade was just getting brisk in that article."

"There was a beautiful, an innocent, and an affectionate girl —"

The Alderman made an involuntary movement which nearly hid his countenance from his companion.

"There was, indeed, a beautiful, and, as you say, a most warm-hearted girl, in the concern!" he uttered, in a voice that was subdued and hoarse. "She died, as I have heard from thyself, Master Skimmer, in the Italian seas. I never saw the father, after the last visit of his child to this coast."

"She did die, among the islands of the Mediterranean. But the void she left in the hearts of all who knew her, was filled, in time, by her — daughter."

The Alderman started from his chair, and, looking the free-trader intently and anxiously in the face, he slowly repeated the word —

"Daughter!"

"I have said it. Eudora is the daughter of that injured woman — need I say, who is the father?"

The burgher groaned, and, covering his face with his hands, he sunk back into his chair, shivering convulsively.

"What evidence have I of this?" he at length muttered — "Eudora is thy sister!"

The answer of the free-trader was accompanied by a melancholy smile.

"You have been deceived. Save the brigantine my being is attached to nothing. When my own brave father fell by the side of him who protected my youth, none of my blood were left. I loved him as a father, and he called me son, while Eudora was passed upon you as the child of a second marriage But here is sufficient evidence of her birth."

The Alderman took a paper, which his companion put gravely into his hand, and his eyes ran eagerly over its contents. It was a letter to himself from the mother of Eudora, written after the birth of the latter, and with the endearing affection of a woman. The love between the young merchant and the fair daughter of his secret correspondent had been less criminal on his part than most similar connexions. Nothing but the peculiarity of their situation, and the real embarrassment of introducing to the world one whose existence was unknown to his friends, and their mutual awe of the unfortunate but still proud parent, had prevented a legal marriage. The simple forms of the colony were easily satisfied, and there was even some reason to raise a question whether they had not been sufficiently consulted to render the offspring legitimate. As Myndert Van Beverout, therefore, read the epistle of her whom he had once so truly loved, and whose loss had, in more senses than one, been to him an irreparable misfortune, since his character might have yielded to her gentle and healthful influence, his limbs trembled, and his whole frame betrayed the violence of extreme agitation. The language of the dying woman was kind and free from reproach, but it was solemn and admonitory. She communicated the birth of their child; but she left it to the disposition of her own father, while she apprized the author of its being of its existence; and, in the event of its ever being consigned to his care, she earnestly recommended it to his love. The close was a leave-taking, in which the lingering affections of this life were placed in mournful contrast to the hopes of the future.

"Why has this so long been hidden from me?" demanded the agitated merchant — "Why, oh reckless and fearless man! have I been permitted to expose the frailties of nature to my own child?"

The smile of the free-trader was bitter, and proud.

"Mr. Van Beverout, we are no dealers of the short voyage. Our trade is the concern of life — our world, the Water-Witch. As we have so little of the interests of the land, our philosophy is above its weaknesses. The birth of Eudora was concealed from you, at the will of her grandfather. It might have been resentment — it might have been pride. Had it been affection, the girl has that to justify the fraud."

"And Eudora, herself? — Does she — or has she long known the truth?"

"But lately. Since the death of our common friend, the girl has been solely dependent on me for counsel and protection. It is now a year since she first learned she was not my sister. Until then, like you, she supposed us equally derived from one who was the parent of neither. Necessity has compelled me, of late, to keep her much in the brigantine."

"The retribution is righteous!" groaned the Alderman, "I am punished for my pusillanimity, in the degradation of my own child!"

The step of the free-trader, as he advanced nearer to his companion, was full of dignity; and his keen eye glowed with the resentment of an offended man.

"Alderman Van Beverout," he said, with stern rebuke in his voice, "you receive your daughter, stainless as was her unfortunate mother, when necessity compelled him whose being was wrapped up in hers, to trust her beneath your roof. We of the contraband have our own opinions, of right and wrong, and my gratitude, no less than my principles, teaches me that the descendant of my benefactor is to be protected, not injured. Had I, in truth, been the brother of Eudora, language and conduct more innocent could not have been shown her, than that she has both heard and witnessed while guarded by my care."

"From my soul, I thank thee!" burst from the lips the Alderman. "The girl shall be acknowledged; and with such a dowry as I can give, she may yet hope for a suitable and honorable marriage."

"Thou may'st bestow her on thy favorite Patroon;" returned the Skimmer, with a calm but sad eye. "She is more than worthy of all he can return. The man is willing to take her, for he is not ignorant of her sex and history. That much I thought due to Eudora herself, when fortune placed the young man in my power."

"Thou art only too honest for this wicked world, Master Skimmer! Let me see the loving pair, and bestow my blessing, on the instant!"

The free-trader turned slowly away, and, opening a door, he motioned for those within to enter. Alida instantly appeared, leading the counterfeit Seadrift, clad in the proper attire of her sex. Although the burgher had often seen the supposed sister of the Skimmer in her female habiliments, she never before had struck him as a being of so rare beauty as at that moment. The silken whiskers had been removed, and in their places were burning cheeks, that were rather enriched than discolored by the warm touches of the sun. The dark glossy ringlets, that were no longer artfully converted to the purposes of the masquerade, fell naturally in curls about the temples and brows, shading a countenance which in general was playfully arch, though at that moment it was shadowed by reflection and feeling. It is seldom that two such beings are seen together, as those who now knelt at the feet of the merchant. In the breast of the latter, the accustomed and lasting love of the uncle and protector appeared, for an instant, to struggle with the new-born affection of a parent. Nature was too strong for even his blunted and perverted sentiments; and, calling his child aloud by name, the selfish and calculating Alderman sunk upon the neck of Eudora, and wept. It would have been difficult to trace the emotions of the stern but observant free-trader, as he watched the progress of this scene. Distrust, uneasiness, and finally melancholy, were in his eye. With the latter expression predominant, he quitted the room, like one who felt a stranger had no right to witness emotions so sacred.

Two hours later, and the principal personages of the narrative were assembled on the margin of the Cove, beneath the shade of an oak that seemed coeval with the continent. The brigantine was aweigh; and, under a light show of canvas, she was making easy stretches in the little basin, resembling, by the ease and grace of her movements, some beautiful swan sailing up and down in the enjoyment of its instinct. A boat had just touched the shore, and the 'Skimmer of the Seas' stood near, stretching out a hand to aid the boy Zephyr to land.

"We subjects of the elements are slaves to superstition;" he said, when the light foot of the child touched the ground. "It is the consequence of lives which ceaselessly present dangers superior to our powers. For many years have I believed that some great good, or some greater evil, would accompany the first visit of this boy to the land. For the first time, his foot now stands on solid earth. I await the fulfilment of the augury!"

"It will be happy;" returned Ludlow — "Alida and Eudora will instruct him in the opinions of this simple and fortunate country, and he seemeth one likely to do early credit to his schooling."

"I fear the boy will regret the lessons of the sea-green lady! — Captain Ludlow, there is yet a duty to perform, which, as a man of more feeling than you may be disposed to acknowledge, I cannot neglect. I have understood that you are accepted by la belle Barbérie?"

"Such is my happiness."

"Sir, in dispensing with explanation of the past you have shown a noble confidence, that merits a return. When I came upon this coast, it was with a determination of establishing the claims of Eudora to the protection and fortune of her father. If i distrusted the influence and hostility of one so placed, and so gifted to persuade, as this lady, you will remember it was before acquaintance had enabled me to estimate more than her beauty. She was seized in her pavilion by my agency, and transported as a captive to the brigantine."

"I had believed her acquainted with the history of her cousin, and willing to aid in some fantasy which was to lead to the present happy restoration of the latter to her natural friends."

"You did her disinterestedness no more than justice. As some atonement for the personal wrong, and as the speediest and surest means of appeasing her alarm, I made my captive acquainted with the facts. Eudora then heard, also for the first time, the history of her origin. The evidence was irresistible, and we found a generous and devoted friend where we had expected a rival."

"I knew that Alida could not prove less generous!" cried the admiring Ludlow, raising the hand of the blushing girl to his lips. "The loss of fortune is a gain, by showing her true character!"

"Hist — hist —" interrupted the Alderman — "there is little need to proclaim a loss of any kind. What must be done in the way of natural justice, will doubtless be submitted to; but why let all in the colony know how much, or how little, is given with a bride?"

"The loss of fortune will be amply met;" returned the free-trader. "These bags contain gold. The dowry of my charge is ready at a moment's warning, whenever she shall make known her choice."

"Success and prudence!" exclaimed the burgher. "There is no less than a most commendable forethought in thy provision, Master Skimmer; and whatever may be the opinion of the Exchequer Judges of thy punctuality and credit, it is mine that there are less responsible men about the bank of England itself! — This money is, no doubt, that which the girl can lawfully claim in right of her late grand father!"

"It is."

"I take this to be a favorable moment to speak plainly on a subject which is very near my heart, and which may as well be broached under such favorable auspices as under any other. I understand, Mr. Van Staats, that, on a further examination of your sentiments towards an old friend, you are of opinion that a closer alliance than the one we had contemplated will most conduce to your happiness?"

"I will acknowledge that the coldness of la belle Barbérie has damped my own warmth;" returned the Patroon of Kinderhook, who rarely delivered himself of more, at a time, than the occasion required.

"And, furthermore, I have been told, Sir, that an intimacy of a fortnight has given you reason to fix your affections on my daughter, whose beauty is hereditary, and whose fortune is not likely to be diminished by this act of justice on the part of that upright and gallant mariner."

"To be received into the favor of your family, Mr. Van Beverout, would leave me little to desire in this life."

"And as for the other world, I never heard of a Patroon of Kinderhook who did not leave us with comfortable hopes for the future; as in reason they should, since few families in the colony have done more for the support of religion than they. They gave largely to the Dutch churches in Manhattan; have actually built, with their own means, three very pretty brick edifices on the Manor, each having its Flemish steeple and suitable weather-cocks besides having done something handsome towards the venerable structure in Albany. Eudora, my child, this gentleman is a particular friend, and as such I can presume to recommend him to thy favor. You are not absolutely strangers; but, in order that you may have every occasion to decide impartially, you will remain here together for a month longer, which will enable you to choose without distraction and confusion. More than this, for the present, it is unnecessary to say; for it is my practice to leave all matters of this magnitude entirely to Providence."

The daughter, on whose speaking face the color went and came like lights changing in an Italian sky, continued silent.

"You have happily put aside the curtain which concealed a mystery that no longer gave me uneasiness;" interrupted Ludlow, addressing the free-trader. "Can you do more, and say whence came this letter?"

The dark eye of Eudora instantly lighted. She looked at the 'Skimmer of the Seas,' and laughed.

"'Twas another of those womanly artifices which have been practised in my brigantine. It was thought that a young commander of a royal cruiser would be less apt to watch our movements, were his mind bent on the discovery of such a correspondent."

"And the trick has been practised before?"

"I confess it. But I can linger no longer. In a few minutes, the tide will turn, and the inlet become impassable. Eudora, we must decide on the fortunes of this child. Shall he to the ocean again? — or shall he remain, to vary his life with a landsman's chances?"

"Who and what is the boy?" gravely demanded the Alderman.

"One dear to both," rejoined the free-trader "His father was my nearest friend, and his mother long watched the youth of Eudora. Until this moment, he has, been our mutual care — he must now choose between us."

"He will not quit me!" hastily interrupted the alarmed Eudora — "Thou art my adopted son, and none can guide thy young mind like me. Thou hast need of woman's tenderness, Zephyr, and wilt not quit me?"

"Let the child be the arbiter of his own fate. I am credulous on the point of fortune, which is, at least, a happy belief for the contraband."

"Then let him speak. Wilt remain here, amid these smiling fields, to ramble among yonder gay and sweetly-scented flowers? — or wilt thou back to the water, where all is vacant and without change?"

The boy looked wistfully into her anxious eye, and then he bent his own hesitating glance on the calm features of the free-trader.

"We can put to sea," he said; "and when we make the homeward passage again, there will be many curious things for thee, Eudora!"

"But this may be the last opportunity to know the land of thy ancestors. Remember how terrible is the ocean in its anger, and how often the brigantine has been in danger of shipwreck!"

"Nay, that is womanish! — I have been on the royal-yard in the squalls, and it never seemed to me that there was danger."

"Thou hast the unconsciousness and reliance of a ship-boy! But those who are older, know that the life of a sailor is one of constant and imminent hazard. Thou hast been among the islands in the hurricane, and hast seen the power of the elements!"

"I was in the hurricane, and so was the brigantine; and there you see how taut and neat she is aloft, as if nothing had happened!"

"And you saw us yesterday floating on the open sea, while a few ill-fastened spars kept us from going into its depths!"

"The spars floated, and you were not drowned; else, I should have wept bitterly, Eudora."

"But thou wilt go deeper into the country, and see more of its beauties — its rivers, and its mountains — its caverns, and its woods. Here all is change, while the water is ever the same."

"Surely, Eudora, you forget strangely! — Here it is all America. This mountain is America; yonder land across the bay is America, and the anchorage of yesterday was America. When we shall run off the coast, the next land-fall will be England, or Holland, or Africa; and with a good wind, we may run down the shores of two or three countries in a day."

"And on them, too, thoughtless boy! If you lose this occasion, thy life will be wedded to hazard!"

"Farewell, Eudora!" said the urchin, raising his mouth to give and receive the parting kiss.

"Eudora, adieu!" added a deep and melancholy voice, at her elbow. "I can delay no longer, for my people show symptoms of impatience. Should this be the last of my voyages to the coast, thou wilt not forget those with whom thou hast so long shared good and evil!"

"Not yet — not yet — you will not quit us yet! Leave me the boy — leave me some other memorial of the past, besides this pain!"

"My hour has come. The wind is freshening, and I trifle with its favor. 'Twill be better for thy happiness that none know the history of the brigantine; and a few hours will draw a hundred curious eyes, from the town, upon us."

"What care I for their opinions? — thou wilt not — cannot — leave me, yet!"

"Gladly would I stay, Eudora, but a seaman's home is his ship. Too much precious time is already wasted. Once more, adieu!"

The dark eye of the girl glanced wildly about her. It seemed, as if in that one quick and hurried look, it drank in all that belonged to the land and its enjoyments.

"Whither go you?" she asked, scarce suffering her voice to rise above a whisper. "Whither do you sail, and when do you return?"

"I follow fortune. My return may be distant — never! — Adieu then, Eudora — be happy with the friends that Providence hath given thee!"

The wandering eyes of the girl of the sea became still more unsettled. She grasped the offered hand of the free-trader in both her own, and wrung it in an impassioned and unconscious manner. Then releasing her hold, she opened wide her arms, and cast them convulsively about his unmoved and unyielding form.

"We will go together! — I am thine, and thine only!"

"Thou knowest not what thou sayest, Eudora!" gasped the Skimmer — "Thou hast a father — friend — husband —"

"Away, away!" cried the frantic girl, waving her hand wildly towards Alida and the Patroon, who advanced as if hurrying to rescue her from a precipice — "Thine, and thine only!"

The smuggler released himself from her frenzied grasp, and, with the strength of a giant, he held the struggling girl at the length of his arm, while he endeavored to control the tempest of passion that struggled within him.

"Think, for one moment, think!" he said. "Thou wouldst follow an outcast — an outlaw — one hunted and condemned of men!"

"Thine, and thine only!"

"With a ship for a dwelling — the tempestuous ocean for a world! —"

"Thy world is my world! — thy home, my home! — thy danger, mine!"

The shout which burst out of the chest of the 'Skimmer of the Seas' was one of uncontrollable exultation.

"Thou art mine!" he cried. "Before a tie like this, the claim of such a father is forgotten! Burgher, adieu! — I will deal by thy daughter more honestly than thou didst deal by my benefactor's child!"

Eudora was lifted from the ground as if her weight had been that of a feather; and, spite of a sudden and impetuous movement of Ludlow and the Patroon, she was borne to the boat. In a moment, the bark was afloat, with the gallant boy tossing his sea-cap upward in triumph. The brigantine, as if conscious of what had passed, wore round like a whirling chariot; and, ere the spectators had recovered from their confusion and wonder, the boat was hanging at the tackles. The free-trader was seen on the poop, with an arm cast about the form of Eudora, waving a hand to the motionless group on the shore, while the still half-unconscious girl of the ocean signed her faint adieus to Alida and her father. The vessel glided through the inlet, and was immediately rocking on the billows of the surf. Then, taking the full weight of the southern breeze, the fine and attenuated spars bent to its force, and the progress of the swift-moving craft was apparent by the bubbling line of its wake.

The day had begun to decline, before Alida and Ludlow quitted the lawn of the Lust in Rust. For the first hour, the dark hull of the brigantine was seen supporting the moving cloud of canvas. Then the low structure vanished, and sail after sail settled into the water, until nothing was visible but a speck of glittering white. It lingered for a minute, and was swallowed in the void.

The nuptials of Ludlow and Alida were touched with a shade of melancholy. Natural affection in one, and professional sympathy in the other, had given them a deep and lasting interest in the fate of the adventurers.

Years passed away, and months were spent at the villa, in which a thousand anxious looks were cast upon the ocean. Each morning, during the early months of summer, did Alida hasten to the windows of her pavilion, in the hope of seeing the vessel of the contraband anchored in the Cove — but always without success. It never returned — and though the rebuked and disappointed Alderman caused many secret inquiries to be made along the whole extent of the American coast, he never again heard of the renowned 'Skimmer of the Seas' or of his matchless Water-Witch.

THE END

Made in United States
Cleveland, OH
04 January 2025

12954067R10208